VOIDRIFTER III

J.N. CHANEY
JASON ANSPACH

VARIANT
PUBLICATIONS

LAS VEGAS, NV

CONNECT WITH J.N. CHANEY

Don't miss out on these exclusive perks:

- Instant access to free short stories from series like *The Messenger*, *Starcaster*, and more.
- Receive email updates for new releases and other news.
- Get notified when we run special deals on books and audiobooks.

So, what are you waiting for? Enter your email address at the link below to stay in the loop.

https://www.jnchaney.com/void-drifter-subscribe-

CONNECT WITH JASON ANSPACH

Check out his website
https://jasonanspach.com

Connect on Facebook
https://www.facebook.com/authorjasonanspach

Follow him on Amazon
https://www.amazon.com/stores/author/B012DQ3BCM

JOIN THE CONVERSATION

Join the conversation and get updates on new and upcoming releases in the awesomely active **Facebook group**, "JN Chaney's Renegade Readers."

This is a hotspot where readers come together and share their lives and interests, discuss the series, and speak directly to J.N. Chaney and his co-authors.

facebook.com/groups/jnchaneyreaders

CONTENTS

INTRODUCTION

My name is Will Kaufman. Usually, I would tell you that I'm an archaeologist, pursuing my PhD. But lately my role has been more like a… space explorer?

It all started on a dig that went wrong. There was a plane crash, exposure to the elements, and ultimately… a dormant spaceship. Well, technically a Voidship. Somehow, I activated the thing and awoke its AI—a bit of a jerk named Quin who used to be the captain of the ship, *Phaelon*.

Turns out that *Phaelon* was a bounty ship, hauling the galaxy's most wanted criminals before it crashed on earth some 4,000 years ago. When I stumbled on board, one of the prisoners, a war-obsessed Vorvak named Sert, got loose. And promptly jettisoned the escape pod while leaving us stuck on a trajectory toward certain death.

That's how I discovered I had a secret skill. A gift, if you will. I could hear the song of the Void and navigate my way through the mysterious reality that allowed impossibly fast travel between stars. Of all the human-like species in the galaxy, I am the only one who seems capable of Navigating the Void.

Soon the rest of the crew woke up, including a beautiful Astradian co-pilot with blue skin and a tough-as-nails demeanor named Fera. We found that the galaxy was under the brutal rule of a galaxy-spanning empire called the Imperium.

That seriously put a damper on my efforts to get back to Earth.

Somehow, I got myself mixed up in multiple battles against armored soldiers, a rebellion in hiding, and a space battle that would have wiped out any home of freedom in the galaxy had I not been able to execute a Void jump at the last second, bringing *Phaelon* and her allies back to safety orbiting Earth.

Now all we have to worry about is how long we have left until the Imperium hunt us down. My planet isn't exactly ready for a galactic civil war. But then again, we humans might be closer to advanced civilizations than I once believed…

1

"You would think wasting a planet and decimating an entire wing of their fleet *with their own weapon* would have been enough to send the Imperium running with shreds of their dignity balled up to cover their exposed backsides."

Coalition pilot Di's characteristic snark made me laugh at what otherwise was a valid observation undertaken in a critical time. The flight leader was hailing us from aboard *Earthborn,* the flagship of Marcus Eddison's contribution to the United Coalition Fleet.

The Imperium lost nearly a third of their fleet when we detonated their own planet killer prototype weapon over Kastar. The planet itself, along with nearly a hundred Imperium warships and who knows how many crew, had ceased to exist in one supermassive explosion. So you can see how her comment—battle harried complaint, really—made sense.

Outside the bridge, a battle raged with what was left of the

Imperium. Prefect Tror refused to surrender or even so much as acknowledge a setback. He was the sort who never acknowledged a defeat, even slightly. He saw everything as a necessary step in his plans for domination. So far, he'd been correct.

The Imperium was still very much a dangerous force in this galaxy.

I looked at General Mira'dna on my right and Fleet Admiral Tanoka on my left. The general gave a slight smirk at Di's comment, but her statuesque features were etched with concern over the battle. Tanoka, in all his splendor as a United Coalition commander, stood ramrod straight, his eyes sweeping the tactical screens and holographic displays before us.

The tactical map stretched over a circular pool in the center of the bridge, displaying a hologram of the local starfield in startling clarity. Stars hung like diamonds in the distant backdrop of the dark ocean of space, glistening in their majestic beauty. Closer than those distant motes of light, an ice-covered rock that bore the name Delluvia Astra was the primary site of the battle.

"Amber Lead," a comms tech said in reply from his station, ignoring Di's comment to feed some critical info, "you have two squadrons of Imperium fighters banking around the orbital station and vectoring in on you. Watch the crossfire with Green Lead. He's just cleaned up the fighters from that first deployment of lightning rods and is now bearing on your location from sector Two Seven."

I balled my hands into a fist, then released. Watching a battle on a ship the size of *Earthborn* was a different experience for me. I was used to flying in the *Phaelon*, where there was always something to do.

But... my purpose in the cause was changing. Had changed.

I was now the galaxy's first Earthborn human ambassador. That was strange enough. Odder still, at least to me, was that Earth had no say in the matter; I was appointed to the position by General Mira'dna on recommendation from Marcus Eddison. Then again, the vast majority of Earth's population had no idea what was happening in the galaxy. It hadn't been that long since I counted myself among them.

A part of me hoped that my home planet—my root world—could continue on like it was. Free of the chaos of a galaxy now steeped in conflict through a war that had gone from a fledgling rebellion to a full-on series of intergalactic skirmishes as the United Coalition of Free Worlds launched offensive after offensive, slowly purging the Imperium from one star system to the next.

We were steadily driving them to the periphery, inching the enemy back to the galactic border, but it had been touch and go for the past few months.

Of course, I wasn't there on an ambassador's mission. It was my growing skills as a Void Navigator that put me here. A Void Drift—without Quin's help, I might add—got us close enough to put us into orbit over the planet before the Imperium could react. Orbital drops from the *Earthborn* put United Coalition—UC—troops on the ground in a hurry.

We were fighting the sort of offensive the Imperium hadn't seen in a long time.

The ground assault was well underway, leaving the Coalition fleet to defend the atmosphere and surrounding starfield. I wouldn't be needed again until the drop zone was secure and the Imperium outpost was neutralized… unless disaster necessitated another Void Drift.

Assuming that didn't happen, I would switch hats from Void Navigator to Ambassador. I was supposed to go down to the surface to be a part of the team that greeted the surviving members of the Delluvian Parliament, to formally give them back control of their world.

Marcus Eddison's personal militia, plucked from the likes of tier-1 operators—Earth's finest—was part of the drop force that now waged open warfare on the surface against embedded Imperium positions. It was brutal fighting amid rows of snowbanks against embedded rotary pulse cannon positions, hardened bunkers, and legions of Imperium riflemen. This sort of combat was not for the faint of heart. It was bloody and brutal, and many who went to the frontlines did not return. Those that did came back bearing more than physical scars.

In spite of all that, we were winning the war.

The Imperium now had to fight an enemy who didn't cow from their superior numbers. An enemy who, despite being outmanned and outgunned, could *outfight* the galactic rulers so viciously that every defeat couldn't help but demoralize them. Never mind what Tror said.

I recalled a mission brief where Colonel Stallings said, "Common convention is seven to one to pull off a successful assault… but with the caliber of warfighters we have at our disposal, three to one is more than enough."

A haunting smile tugged at the corner of my lips. I remembered thinking his assessment was bravado and wishful thinking, right up until our first engagement.

The United Coalition's ground game was just as deadly as its space game, and that was saying something. The Imperium paid for every tactical error they made, and things seemed almost one-sided, unless Prefect Tror was on site and directly in command. He had an uncanny ability to adapt to our tactics and spin out new tactics of his own.

The war wasn't exactly a rout—not yet—but engagement after engagement, we systematically stacked up a net positive in terms of enemies vanquished and friendlies lost.

Eventually, though... something had to give. The Imperium was at its breaking point. The decisive victory may not be here at Delluvia Astra, but it would be somewhere, and soon.

It was just a matter of time.

For now, the goal of taking this system and turning it back into the hands of the Delluvians who once called it home was our sole objective. The result would be an Imperium-free system, and a new ally added to the roster of the United Coalition. Unfettered access to the advanced synthetics and the snub fighters the Delluvians made was a bonus.

All in all, it would put us one step closer to a better galaxy.

A free one.

The planet itself rotated in the center of the hologram, the starfield slowly spinning around it, showing several Imperium destroyers and light cruisers intermixed with the United Coalition ships. Eddison's cruisers proved to be deadly warships, especially when matched up one on one with their Imperium counterparts— even the destroyers. It was only when Eddison's cruisers were outnumbered two or three to one that they were whipped, though their triple plasma cannons could usually destroy at least one of the Imperium ships before being taken out by the larger number of enemy vessels.

I watched the battle in space and on the ground play out much the way we hoped it would. My feelings of uselessness only increased as the time ticked on.

Finally, I blurted out, "I think I should go down now."

The bridge of *Earthborn* seemed to fall dead quiet.

Genera Mira'dna picked up her cup of *moora*, think a hot tea that carried floral notes of cinnamon spice—the only aroma that seemed capable of making a dent in the *Earthborn's* overpowering new ship smell—freshly fabricated synthetics, clean parchment from the filters in the environmental system's scrubbers operating at peak efficiency to keep the circulated oxygen clean and clear.

"Will," she said. "The drop zone is hardly secure…"

"It's secure enough," I said. "I've been in hotter situations than that with the *Phaelon.*"

Visions of raids on lunar mining camps, planet-wide metropolises, Imperium ships, and a half-dozen other places that should have gotten me killed flashed before my eyes. I could handle this.

"It's important to show the Delluvians not just that we have the will and resources to overthrow the Imperium, but that our leadership isn't afraid to be near the fight personally."

The general gave me a slight smile. "Are you suggesting the entire command staff come down as well?"

I straightened. "Oh. No, General. That… I don't think that's a good idea. The Coalition needs you a lot more than it needs me."

She gave a wry grin. "Of that, I am not so sure, Will."

I paused. "Ma'am?"

Mira'dna grew sober-faced once again. "I trust your judgment on this, Will. It's taken you this far, and we're better for it. I'm not one to play favorites, but when the Universal Balance presents a sliver of light in a galaxy of darkness, you take it and you run with it."

Universal Balance. I had heard the term before, but not from her. I didn't know much about Mira'dna or her dying species except that they were revered by many other species in the galaxy. I was surprised to hear her espouse the same religious beliefs as Fera.

Fera. There had been precious little time to pursue her lately. There was, after all, an intergalactic war going on. All the more reason to win it.

"Okay, let's do it," I announced. "I'll drop now."

The comm chirped with a new report from Di. "Bogeys inbound nine degrees above the ecliptic."

Fleet Admiral Tanoka looked up from his displays to address me. "What does the Hero of the Rebellion say now?"

"First, don't call me that. Everyone on the *Phaelon* is more deserving of that title than me. And second..."

I studied the starfield, the formations of ships as they danced to the beating of the war drums that existed only in my mind—and in the song of the Void that I found increasingly harder to ignore the more I Navigated it. The mysterious dimension of subspace was increasingly taking up more of my thoughts, but I knew better than to dwell on it.

That way lies madness.

"...Our fighters have the situation in control up here. Colonel Stallings has the assault under way. I'll take my ship down to the surface and provide oversight on the assault."

General Mira'dna held up a marble-white finger. "You will take the bot with you, of course."

I frowned. She said it in a way that left no room for argument. "Of course...."

A ROBOT best described as a cross between Benegal's spherical star map and Dumpy's head unit floated next to me as I strapped into my very expensive personal transport. It was a military-grade combat camera drone stuffed with a dumb AI. There was enough memory storage to record fourteen cycles—or two days—worth of ultra-high definition audio and video, plus a host of other sensor data. A black stripe printed on the equator of the bot sat just beneath its optical sensor. When I first saw the stripe, it reminded me of a mustache.

So I named it Earl. It just sort of popped into my head. Don't ask me why.

Using an eye trace over the holographic prompts, courtesy of my fiber-link implant, I sealed the cockpit of my personal AX-71 dual-role fighter. Oxygen misted up from the environmental system vents, dosing me with a small bit of euphoria as I ran through the preflight checks.

"All systems normal," I said under my breath, wishing I was next to Fera and hearing her give the confirmation readouts.

Earl chirp-chirped in response, keeping its lens focused on my face. I slid my helmet on and linked my suit to the ship's onboard oxygen supply. Internal scrubbers set a puff of aluminum-tinged air over me, signaling a solid connection.

"Starting launch sequence."

The MFDs shifted to the appropriate presets I'd programmed

into the main mission computer—telemetry data on the left-side screen, weapons and armor readouts on the right, vector path and targeting reticle overlaid on the center primary display. Once the hull of the ship went translucent, permitting me an unfiltered view of the docking bay, I started to relax.

That might have said something about me; just a few short months ago, the idea of combat would have had me nervous and battling a fresh wave of fatalism. Now, it was my job.

I'd changed. Leaving Earth had changed me. Becoming a part of the *Phaelon*'s crew had changed me. But perhaps most noticeably, war had changed me.

I didn't shrink away from it. I didn't relish it.

But I did focus on it. War was the only way to keep my root world safe.

Diplomacy would come after the Imperium was defeated.

"*Earthborn Actual*, you are clear for launch."

Using my fiber-link to toggle the switches, I deactivated the magnetic clamp that held the ship to the deck, activated the inertial compensator, and flipped the comm channel to open.

"*Earthborn Actual* launching."

Left hand on the throttle, right hand on the sidestick, a knot of adrenaline in my gut, I felt the ship around me like an extra layer of protection beyond my actual Drayth armor and custom helmet Fera helped me make in the *Phaelon* workshop. If I tried hard enough, I could conjure up her cherry blossom scent, just for a moment.

It always took a little bit of the edge off.

I'll see you soon, Fera, I thought for the millionth time since she'd left with the *Phaelon* to work on our Fleuridian problem.

Off-white bulkheads trimmed with non-reflective anodized

beryllium braces fell away as I guided my ship out of the belly of the *Earthborn*. The starfield surrounding the capital ship was congested with fighters deep in the throes of spiraling dogfights, exchanging pulse rounds and zippering between the larger ships for cover when they could.

Off the starboard bow, an Imperium fighter caught a burst of pulse rounds and atomized. A flash of light dissipated into a spreading cloud of shrapnel and gas particles that zipped out of my line of sight as I pushed the throttle to eighty percent thrust. Opposing formations of AX-71s and the Imperium's *Dagger*-class fighters gave chase to one another in a spiraling funnel in open space between the *Earthborn* and a rapidly approaching Imperium destroyer designated the *Six Oh Six*.

Cutting a path straight through the maelstrom, I adjusted my angle of attack to align with the flight plan that would put me down at the landing zone Colonel Stallings's ground forces had cleared only hours ago. It would put me at a little less than a hundred thousand klicks from the destroyer—in targeting range of the fighters, but I'd be moving too fast for the Imperium bruiser to get a lock on me, or to even lay down point defense fire on me with any hope of accuracy.

"Coming around for escort," Di said.

A pair of Imperium fighters broke off from a nearby delta formation, angling right for me—an easy target, all by myself. The enemy fighters were a good distance away, but that didn't stop them from painting me with an active sensor sweep, trying desperately to get a lock on me.

Earl tweedled ominously. I ignored him.

"Two tangos moving to pursue," I announced, appending their coordinates to my transmission.

"I see them," Di said, her voice tight as she bumped her throttle up to max.

On the scopes, Di's ship was tagged AMBER LEAD, and she brought two of her wingmen with her. I banked negative of the ecliptic—space didn't have cardinal directions, so everything was based off an arbitrary equator established by the galaxy-wide Spatial Positioning System—and spun my paper-thin deflector shield to cover my rear.

Eddison wasn't much for shields. He built the AX-71 conceptually off the SR-71 Blackbird, which meant they could go really fast in straight lines. Unlike the spy plane that inspired them, these ships were made to deliver ordnance and execute a quick bank around to escape any return fire.

It worked well, but it put us at a disadvantage in ship-to-ship combat. The Imperium's Daggers were far more maneuverable, and even though their pulse cannons weren't anything special, they didn't have to be when our ships didn't have much for shields.

TARGET LOCK flashed on my HUD and dissolved when I ignored it in favor of keying up the pulse cannons on my fires page. The high-powered lasers fired by fighter ships and point defense cannons on the larger vessels were invisible to the naked eye. Even the most advanced main mission computers could only track and visually render about every fourth or fifth pulse round.

That became relevant when two additional Imperium fighter wings slipped out from under the *Six Oh Six* like bees swarming from their hive. All at once, they began spitting volleys of fire in my direction. The rendered pulses were thick scatters of red dashes—a rainstorm of deadly energy burning right for me.

"*Earthborn Actual*, take evasive action," Di said, urgency in her voice.

"On it," I replied, cutting the throttle to fifty percent and snapping the sidestick to the left.

Earl let out a single, sliding note, like a passenger caught off guard when a driver makes an unannounced sharp turn. Its stabilizers kept it anchored in place, totally immune to any sort of inertia the ship could manage.

G forces pinned me, however, to the sidewall of the cockpit as I rode the maneuver for a few seconds, then snapped the stick back and bumped the throttle up to max. The ship shuddered under the strain, but the reactor obliged, dumping a healthy dose of power to the propulsion section and launching me like a missile toward the surface of the planet.

"Target lock," Di announced. "Firing."

Two Imperium fighters disappeared from my scopes. I breathed a sigh of relief, feeling a bit of the heat dissipating from the back of my neck. My field of view was almost completely atmospheric and snow-covered mountains. The starfield shrank back to my rearview feed where scintillating flashes of pulse rounds zippered through the vacuum, narrowly missing my portside hull.

"Cut that one close, Will," Di said, a smile in her voice.

"You're telling me," I said. "Thanks for breaking off to assist. I'm fond of my ass and prefer it not get shot off."

"You know, I don't do that for just anyone," she said with an air of mischief.

I laughed. "Once again, thanks for the cover, Di. You're one of the good ones."

"Sounds like the first round of drinks is on the Hero of the Rebellion," she said.

Before I could correct her, Amber Two's transponder flashed. "I hear that!"

"Yeah, yeah. See you on the dock," I said, using an eye wave to toggle the frequency from space comm to ground comm.

A grizzled voice was mid-transmission when the frequency dialed in to receive. Colonel Stallings.

"—covering fire on that peak, now! Advance is halted until that arty is taken out of commission!"

"Colonel, this is *Earthborn Actual*, coming in."

"Would have preferred you wait a while longer," the colonel responded. "Enemy presence is significantly higher than we anticipated, but we're making it work. Epsilon and Theta squads have taken down the AA emplacements."

He meant the anti-air missile launchers, which was good for me.

"But they're pinned down in the southern steppes, right on the doorstep of Imperium HQ," the colonel continued. "I've got Gamma squad set to rush and breach the doors, but I'm not giving the order until we stop those plasma launchers raining hellfire and damnation from on high."

Why hadn't any of that made it up to the command center on the *Earthborn*? The way I was viewing it, everything looked like it was going according to plan. I wondered if there was something wrong with the communications equipment down on the ground, or if Colonel Stallings was hip-pocketing the details and only sending the big rocks of data up top.

"Sounds like you could use some close air support," I said, frowning.

"Looks that way," said the colonel.

A second after that, I entered the planet's atmosphere.

Reentry obscured my view with flickering tongues of flame, enhanced by the fact that the hull of the ship was translucent. It felt like riding a fireball into the atmosphere. Even though I knew the ship was there around me because I could feel it, not being able to see it while I flew had taken a while for me to get comfortable with.

The inertial compensator gave way to the true gravitational force of Delluvia Astra as I pierced the mesosphere and continued descending. Turbulence rattled the hull. I tightened my grip on the sidestick, keeping the ship on course with subtle adjustments.

The now *Lieutenant* Fel's familiar voice came on a direct line over my comm. When I'd first met him, he was a Sergeant with Mira'd-na's small rebel army. The larger war effort required officers, and Fel was an obvious choice. His transmission was thick with small arms exchanging fire, but he was calm in the face of the storm. My respect for him only increased as he relayed information in a steady, deliberate tone.

"*Earthborn Actual*, I have a SLAM team being escorted to the escarpment along the western ridge to get you those coordinates. Time hack is four minutes. Out."

SLAM teams were Space Lane Attack Managers, a sort of space-faring equivalent of Joint Terminal Attack Controllers from the United States Military. I thanked the fiber-link for that info dump, then refocused on the flight.

Flipping the frequency back to space comms, I opened a private channel to Di.

"Ground team is stonewalled at the gate. Four minutes until the SLAM team is in position to put in coordinates for fires. Any of your fighters still have payloads they can deliver?"

"Between the three of us, we have enough capacitance left for four plasma rounds. Where do you need us?"

I held my transmission back, focusing on cutting through a patch of cirrus cloud cover, and broke through the other side. Moisture fizzled against the friction-heated nose of my ship. By the time I was through, the SLAM team had sent me a coordinate pin—two minutes ahead of schedule.

Those guys didn't play down there.

I slid the coordinate pin into the comm window and sent it up to Di. "Here. I'll take lead since I'm already in position. You follow up and see if you can't put down any stragglers."

The target rested on a ridge along the face of a mountain at the edge of the city. Two wide-bore plasma cannons jutted out of the entrance to the cave. The image was of such high quality I could make out the white panels of Imperium armor as two troops were caught in the act of firing one of the cannons. A second pair was removing a melted down capacitor from the base of their cannon, while two additional troops were carrying a fresh capacitor to replace it.

"On it," Di said.

If she had any reservations about me hopping from ambassador to combat pilot, she didn't share them. And, knowing Di's propensity to say whatever was on her mind, that meant she probably had no reservations whatsoever.

Di and her two wingmen peeled out of the fight above and descended into the atmosphere. In moments, they were twelve seconds of flight time behind me. I cut the throttle and popped the air brake, decreasing my speed down to a comfortable 220 knots.

The terrain was a black and white marble smear, growing sharper with detail as I increased my rate of descent, dropping into the attack envelope of ten thousand feet. This close to the ground, buildings sprouted up out of the snowdrifts between mountains. I recognized warehouses and staging areas where Imperium soldiers were trying to pack up the last shipments of Delluvian manufacturing before they made a hasty run for the atmosphere.

The major part of the ground conflict was thirty klicks north of this industrial boomtown. I zipped through the clear skies, admiring the smoking rubble that had once been several anti-air cannons planted at the edges of the town.

The mountain range wrapped around the north side of the city up ahead. I established visual on the target, which was highlighted in my HUD thanks to coordinates sent up from the SLAM team.

Muscle memory installed by neural lace training programs guided my fingers over the fires page. I selected the plasma cannons —all three of them—and routed power from the primary capacitor to the coils to charge them up.

Turbulence rumbled through the hull of the ship. Sweat formed at my brow, but it wasn't the insistent kind that smelled of panic and stress. It was focus. Intense, driven focus as I took in all the data, worked it into a firing solution on the mountain peak, and locked it into the main mission computer.

"Target lock," I said. "Fel, is your team clear?"

Lieutenant Fel responded immediately. "SLAM team is covered. Fire away, sir."

"Firing." I depressed the red button on the sidestick.

The ship shook. Metal groaned with the strain of deploying high-powered gouts of roiling plasma and spat them out at relativistic speed.

Three miniature suns leaped from the wide-bore cannons of my AX-71 and raced across the sky like a trio of comets. Two full seconds passed, ending in a triple explosion as the plasma defaced the mountainside in a towering inferno of rock, metal, and mayhem.

"Target serviced," I said into the comm.

"Amber Wing deploying plasma drop," Di followed up.

I watched through the translucent side of the ship. Bolts of energized fire lambasted the mountain, starting low and walking up the snow-covered crags. Each impact was a geyser of water vapor and churned earth. Somewhere in the aftermath of the last explosion, wrecked bits of metal and tiny pieces of Imperium armor cascaded down the mountainside.

When the smoke cleared, the face of the mountain had been glassed into glimmering fractals.

I let out a breath, shook my head, and cleared my throat, a big smile on my face.

"Colonel, *Earthborn Actual*, plasma launchers are neutralized."

The comm traffic became a flurry of calls stacking one on top of the other.

Colonel Stallings echoed my report over the frequency. Lieutenant Fel gave Gamma squad the go-ahead to breach. Someone from Epsilon squad called out with a casualty report.

A quick look over the battlefield below told me the thickest fighting was over. The breaching team would have their hands full clearing out the Imperium HQ, but once that was secured, the

Imperium ships in orbit would have no reason to stay. They could fight down to the last ship, or they could Void Drift out of the battle to serve Prefect Tror another day.

And I needed to land.

"Amber Lead, *Earthborn Actual*, I'm going in to visit. See you topside."

"Topside, and you're buying," Di said with an audible smile. "Don't forget, hero."

2

I PUT the ship down as the primary star began its descent over the horizon, spilling vibrant reds and purples across the sky in shifting hues over the drifts and snowpack that clung to the mountains and the city alike. The initial landing zone of the orbital drop teams was little more than a stretch of snow and ice at the southern tip of the city, and there were still dead bodies freezing where they fell.

The first boots on the ground had only landed eleven hours ago, but already temporary fortifications had been set up to utilize the austere area as a de facto staging base for further assaults. Colonel Stallings's reasoning for setting up in the middle of a snowfield, rather than seizing the spaceport or dropping right into the heart of the city, was to minimize collateral damage.

It seemed to be working. Dark streaks of rent earth crisscrossed the surrounding area, evidence of Imperium artillery strikes—mostly plasma cannons and a few High Explosive, or H-E rounds. Further toward the city, dotted marks of blackened soil filled with melted and refrozen snow showed the Imperium's strafing runs had been quelled by the United Coalition fleet before they could do any serious damage.

My canopy opened, introducing me to the cold air outside. I could smell trace amounts of ozone and fresh air that wafted down from the mountain range to the north, even through my helmet filters.

Colonel Stallings, two junior officers, and a detachment of rebels that served as a personal guard for the colonel abandoned the tactical operations center and headed over to my ship as I performed the down cycle sequences from within the cockpit.

Another man moved quickly to reach the colonel just before he could address me. "Perimeter secure, Colonel!"

I recognized Master Sergeant Arvin by his curled mustache visible through the visor of his helmet.

Colonel Stallings accepted the proclamation with a curt nod. "Good work, Master Sergeant. Let's make sure it stays that way."

There was no saluting in a combat environment. Sergeant Arvin gave the colonel a nod and barked out a promise to do just that before turning back to the business of making sure orders were being executed. "Where's the AG for the RPC? I want four links IA and one bucket of H-E stacked behind the heavy squad at the north defense point. Yesterday!"

My fiber-link continued to pay dividends, translating all of that military jargon into something I could understand. After the past five months of fighting the Imperium across different planets, it wasn't that I didn't pay attention or take the time to learn all of the acronyms; there were just so many of them, it was hard to keep up. And of course, none of it was in English. Everyone spoke in their own language and relied on a brain reconfiguration I received on day one, courtesy of Quin, that made you understand whatever was being said as if it were your native tongue.

But if you paid attention, you saw that the lips never matched the words. I likened it to watching a dubbed movie in real time. It was odd at first, but I was used to it now.

A translation of what the Master Sergeant said could be summed up as, "Where's the assistant gunner for the rotary pulse cannon? I want four crates of belt-linked, ionized ammunition, and one crate of high explosive rounds stacked behind the heavy weapons squad at the north defense point, and quickly!"

Men responded to his commands immediately, hustling back and forth between the four dropships at the rear of the landing zone, carrying ammunition crates. Rifles and armor, grit and determination abounded. This army was a dream of many rebel cells that had become a reality.

Morale was high. We were winning the day, winning the war. Everyone knew it, General Mira'dna all the way down to the AG running ammo up to the RPC.

Someone needed to get that message through Prefect Tror's Foris skull, and then the war would *really* be over.

Colonel Stallings and his entourage arrived at my ship. The grizzled old Anunnaki turned to look up at the cockpit of my AX-71, a worn smile deepening the lines on his face. "Ambassador, welcome to the real fight. Be sure to duck."

I grabbed the KR-44 rifle from the weapons rack behind the seat, attached it to my armor with a single point sling, and slid down the boarding ladder, keeping a hand on the rail pistol in my belt to prevent it knocking against the hull of the ship. Sealed up tight in my Drayth armor, I was spared the wind chill that my HUD told me was four below zero.

"Hell of a job your men have done here, Colonel."

We shook hands.

The camera drone circled overhead, clicking obnoxiously as it captured footage of Colonel Stallings and me discussing the state of the battle. The colonel's chiseled face bore fatigue lines around his eyes, but he was in good spirits despite the stiff resistance his forces had encountered so far, and that told me the tide had turned on the ground. The engagement in the starfield was still in full swing, but even that was tipping in our favor.

"You certainly aren't a liar, Will." He gave me a devilish grin. "That CAS was right on time. Imperium HQ has been breached. I have two teams clearing house right now. Active patrols on the streets are underway to purge any remaining Imperium presence embedded there. My reserve element broke off to conduct an assault on the spaceport fifteen klicks to the west. That should halt the Imperium evacuation and gain us four Imperium transports to add to our own fleet."

An explosion sounded in the distance. We both paused our conversation to search the snow drifts and ice-covered buildings for a debris trail, but none materialized. Small-arms fire echoed from further in the city, the pauses between barrages steadily growing longer as the battle winded down to a close.

Colonel Stallings sniffed, tired eyes roaming the cityscape for a moment longer. "All in all, it's played out more or less how we expected."

"Any contact with the Delluvian Parliament?" I asked.

"They're secure," he said. "Know you're coming."

"Where should I meet them?"

The colonel opened his mouth to reply, when a secondary explosion rocked the cityscape behind him.

Like an ice shelf breaking off and crashing down into the ocean, a four-story building tilted and slammed onto the street, sending a rolling tide of snow and ice and metal careening into nearby buildings.

Stallings frowned and held up a finger. "Wait one, Will. Theta squad, sitrep."

There was no response.

I double-checked my comm was still set to ground transmissions, and noticed I had an incoming request from the *Earthborn*. I accepted the connection with an eye toggle. General Mira'dna's face filled a window in the corner of my HUD.

"Will, is everything all right down there?" She had been watching courtesy of Earl.

I frowned and turned my head to look beyond the secure perimeter of the landing zone. The city looked like a futuristic postcard of an Alaskan village in the heart of winter. Snow drifts covered the slanted rooftops of the buildings. Foot trails were carved deep into the snow, tracing the paths the troops had taken while they spread throughout the gridlock, taking the Imperium resistance down in the streets, which was stained with blood—much of it red, but other colors as well, depending on whose was spilled.

Carnage was everywhere, primarily small fires near vehicles, or the bodies of the dead.

The industrial district where the manufacturing depots and warehouses were situated looked worse. Several Imperium airstrikes had leveled nearly half of the infrastructure in that area. This was a common tactic by the enemy. If they couldn't have something, no one would.

Fortunately, Eddison's superior ships had barreled onto the scene quickly enough to save some of the Delluvian factories from destruction, along with over ninety percent of the city itself. I tried to separate the big picture of the battle, and the war at large, from my immediate surroundings to best provide General Mira'dna with an answer to her question.

"Things seem to be heating up in the city right now, but the LZ looks clear for the moment. I'm about to link up with the Delluvian parliament."

She breathed a sigh of relief. "I was starting to worry that this was the time when following your instincts might prove a problem."

"I'm all right, General, thank you. The colonel has informed me that we're ready to set up the negotiations."

"I don't believe much negotiating will be required, now that the heel of the Imperium boot has been removed from their necks. Remember, speak primarily to Szilka Zin. He'll be the most level-headed among the Delluvian Parliament, and his status as oldest member of the House of Zin will go far in convincing any holdouts still too loyal or afraid of the Imperium."

"Understood," I said. "I'll let you know how it goes."

I ended the transmission and saw the colonel giving me a hard stare.

"Something wrong?" I asked.

The muscle along the colonel's jawline flexed. "The Imperium have retreated into an underground bunker built beneath the city. The locals don't know anything about it except that it's there. We're going in after them, but I wonder if it will do any good for me to ask you to stay put so we can see about a remote meeting with the Delluvian parliament?"

"No, Colonel, it won't," I said. "Delluvian psychology will react strongest to bold, decisive action. Now is our best shot to do that; we can't wait until everything is safe to take it."

I was speaking courtesy of a mix of my fiber-link, personal studies, and what felt like an endless series of briefings on how to best bring the newly liberated species and planets to our side. You'd think it would be a natural progression: kick out the bad guys, get a new ally from it.

But aliens are weird.

There's a method to these things, and I see now why galactic harmony has been so difficult to achieve, aside from what the Federation, and then Imperium, accomplished.

"That's the answer I expected," the colonel said with a nod. "But that doesn't mean you get to go without an escort."

He glanced over at the soldiers moving around his encampment, and then to the captain standing at his side. "Get me a fire team."

The captain nodded and made some quick communications over the comm, then a short while later Sergeant Arvin and six Coalition troops reported in. The Sergeant was all business during introductions and as eager to get going I was.

"Follow me, Ambassador," Arvin said.

I pulled my KR-44 rifle off the back of my armor and pull-checked the chamber. A single flechette at the top of the stack in the magazine was poised and ready to fire.

"Lead the way. Let's go, Earl."

My traveling companion flew just behind my shoulder as I moved to the frontline on the heels of Sergeant Arvin, capturing the footage for the command staff still on *Earthborn*. I noted that of the six battle-hardened warriors who were a part of my escort, nameless and faceless—their identities hidden behind their armor—two had an American flag painted on their shoulder pauldron.

I had considered myself more of the "citizen of the world" type back when I was an archaeologist. But now... for some reason it almost brought tears to my eyes.

Maybe that was just because these were fellow humans. My contact with members of my own species had been almost nil since my journey across the stars began a few months ago. Seeing these operators plucked from Earth's finest fighting forces at my side saddled me with a sense of just how alone I'd been, so far from home.

"Four klicks to the rendezvous point," Sergeant Arvin said as he brought the unit to a halt. "I have things to do. You're in good hands with Sergeant Berrios now. He'll get you there."

Berrios nodded at me and then inclined his head toward the five soldiers in black and green armor kneeling or crouching around him. "We're ready when you are, Ambassador."

I looked at the men, an imposing force equipped for combat courtesy of Eddison. Two carried massive MD-300s, the spiritual successor to the M249B, or Squad Automatic Weapon, which fired 10mm tungsten flechettes with blunted tips, designed for stopping power more so than penetration. Rounds of that size traveled at the high speeds generated from the cycling magnets in the circular focusing chamber of the weapon, so they could punch clean through thinner armor variants like graphene plates regardless. Another trooper carried what looked like a simple ATM-G rocket launcher over his back. The soldier standing next to him acted as his mule, carrying his own weapons kit plus a bandolier with three extra H-E rounds secured to it.

MD-300 gunners like Berrios aside, the rest carried the United Coalition MD-14 rifle, a versatile weapon that could put flechettes out to a distance of just shy of a kilometer with precision accuracy. Rail pistol sidearms were tucked in chest rigs or battle belts.

The ragtag rebels I'd first encountered on Jyraxis were a far cry from this.

"You lead, I'll follow, Sergeant."

Sergeant Berrios easily hefted his MD-300, courtesy of his light, powered armor and turned toward the city. "Let's move."

3

No matter how much time I had with the VR sims in the neural lace, or how much one-on-one training I got from Sert, my Vorvak warrior friend, every combat action I participated in against the Imperium was a learning opportunity. My movement with Berrios and his team wasn't supposed to be anything but a safe escort to a diplomatic necessity, but there was still plenty to learn as I moved through the terrain and examined what I could of the attack.

For example...

The Imperium opting to go underground rather than try to flee to the spaceport and break atmo... that was new. And the intel we were getting from the locals—assuming we could trust it—was that the Imperium started their underground work not long after we obliterated a third of their fleet. It didn't take a tactical genius to understand the kind of problems this could present.

Were they to dig in and stall while Prefect Tror readied a combined fleet attack, seeking to have a final confrontation here of all places? That seemed crazy to me; a big showdown like that would play to our technological and numerical advantage. Did they have another superweapon? Something that Atron didn't know about?

My mind raced over the implications as I followed Staff Sergeant Berrios and his team through the streets of the city.

Snow drifts were broken by patches of black ice where explosions, fire, and pulse rounds had left their mark. Kicking up snow powder and stepping carefully over the ice, I stopped counting the bodies of the Imperium KIA once I got to thirty. Thankfully, our teams had already retrieved the wounded from the streets—a necessity in this cold and something that separated the United Coalition from the Imperium—I'd seen Imperium troops left to die from survivable wounds simply because the man next to the wounded soldier didn't feel like carrying his comrade in arms.

I kept my eyes moving, scanning for any Imperium that may have dodged the earlier patrols. I wasn't a soldier, even though I'd fought in combat multiple times and lived to talk about it, and I had no illusions about living up to the "Hero" moniker I'd been dubbed with as a means of solidifying our growing and united coalition. That said, I wanted to be whatever was the next level higher than useless if something went down.

And... maybe... if I was being honest with myself... I wanted to impress the warfighters at my side. Show them I wasn't a chump from Indiana.

Stupid, I know. But that's how I felt. Like I needed to prove I belonged there.

We crossed an intersection, leaving behind the business district and entering the industrial side of town. Here, staccato bursts of small-arms fire—the supersonic snaps of flechettes—echoed between the buildings, punctuated by long pauses of eerie silence. Colonel Stallings still had several patrols roaming the streets, clearing out stragglers.

"Gonna get lots of quality footage of you on patrol," one of the soldiers said to me as we paused to verify an open street was all clear.

It was the first time anyone but Berrios had spoken to me.

"Make sure to stay out of my light," I joked, drawing a few quiet laughs from the others.

The guys were professionals. Killers. But they were human. I appreciated that more than they knew.

Earl the drone circled overhead, servos clicking as it adjusted its position and kept its lens fixated on me. The thing never left my side unless I was in my personal quarters on the *Earthborn*. I wondered if the bot had already edited that little glimpse behind the curtains from the record.

Sergeant Berrios had been working the comms. He turned to face me. "Gotta find another way. Imperium came up through the tunnels and have control of three avenues we need to cross. For now."

I didn't like the sound of that. I wasn't afraid, not any more than usual, that is, but the clock was ticking on making contact with the Delluvian Parliament.

"Do we have another way?" I asked.

"Not at this time, sir," Berrios replied. "Lieutenant Fel and his team are posted up at the entrance to a warehouse nearby. They're working the tunnels to see about pushing the Peers out; pretty sure that's how they took those streets."

There was something in the sergeant's voice that told me he'd rather be working with Fel to clear those tunnels himself. I took a gamble.

"And what are the odds we could take those tunnels ourselves to bypass the blocked streets?"

There was a pause.

"Not sure that's the safest—"

I cut Berrios off. "My mission is to get to that parliament. If it were to be safe, I'd have stayed up on one of the big ships in orbit."

Another pause, then a slow nod.

"Okay. Let's see what we can do."

WE FOUND Lieutenant Fel and his team posted up at the entrance to a warehouse in the heart of the industrial district. He wore his ramshackle camo patterned fatigues over his armor, and it had seen better days. He had a full-face helmet on, but it had been modified to accept the visor he never took off. Given the deep freeze of the weather, I thought that was a wise choice.

"Will"—he waved at me—"are you sure you're up for this? It's going to be tight quarters. CQB the whole way. No telling what we might still find down there."

Left unsaid was, "I can't guarantee your safety."

This was a newly discovered tunnel entrance. And while there were other tunnels that had already been breached and taken, it was my desire—maybe foolish desire—to keep moving toward my final destination: The Delluvian Parliament.

I didn't want to turn around.

"Sergeant," I said, "the Delluvians have a social structure that abhors a power vacuum. They need to see Coalition leadership in their midst in order to have the kind of binding alliance General Mira'dna is looking for. The sooner the better. Let's go."

Lieutenant Fel led us into the warehouse. Huge machines lay dormant inside. They were like giant harps with strings pulled taut between them, frozen in the act of weaving the smart fibers into tightly wound cords that were used in everything from crash couches on starships to insulating layers in EVA suits and several other applications. As vital as weapons and armor were to the war effort, a spacefaring economy relied on Delluvian manufacturing for a great many things.

"Corporal Styson, you're clear to breach," Lieutenant Fel said over the comm. "Stack up, file inside in pairs. Clear your sectors and stay tight on the corners. We don't want a repeat of Elbun Gal."

I remembered Elbun Gal. That was the closest we'd come to a straight-up defeat since the war started. Clearing the Imperium out of that rock had been intense CQB—close quarters battle—in the hollowed-out mountains of a planetoid in the Perseus Arm. The United Coalition's highest casualty rate came out of that conflict— forty percent of the men that went in did not come back out.

One of the soldiers, presumably Corporal Styson, moved to the heavy door at the back of the warehouse. After taking a knee, he popped the cap on a cylindrical container affixed to the back of his belt and withdrew a shaped charge from inside. Using a mound of synthetic adhesive, he stuck the explosive to the center of the door and made minor adjustments to its placement until he had it just the way he wanted.

Soldiers materialized from around the heavy equipment like

shifting shadows as they stacked up on either side of the door. I had expected them to find a hidden trap door in the floor itself, but instead it looked like some sort of encased chamber that existed inside the warehouse—like a black vault just sitting there. Waiting.

The comm flurried with one-word reports as each man announced he had found his position in the lineup.

"Shaped charge in place," Styson said.

"Clear!" another soldier barked.

Over the span of the next few heartbeats, no one moved. Lieutenant Fel looked up and down the line of his men, then crouched behind the frame of the closest machine and waved for me to take cover beside him.

"Cook it!" he said.

Negative pressure squeezed at my chest. A muffled *crump* sounded from the door, accompanied by a flash of light. Smoke coiled away from the detonation site.

The stack flowed into the room as Lieutenant Fel barked for them to, "Move! Move! Move!"

Boots thundered across the stone foundations of the warehouse, sound profile decreasing as the soldiers disappeared through the hole they'd made in the door. Lieutenant Fel followed in time, his KR-44 rifle up. I mirrored his movements, squeezing through the glowing edges of warped metal left behind by the shaped charge.

The inner vault was devoid of Imperium… and hardly a tunnel entrance. That didn't mean it wasn't important.

Terminals, workstations, and benches covered in bits of scrap metal and nanocircuitry. Embedded inside the manufacturing depot was a research laboratory. Holographic screens were all switched off, save one at the back of the room.

An odd sense of déjà vu, likely from the letdown of there being nothing here, came over me.

"What do we have here," Berrios said, examining the screen.

I moved around Fel to get a look. The shock to my heart was palpable. A cold sweat came over me.

In granular detail, the breakdown of a planet-killer warhead slowly rotated in the projection. Lines of text hung in the air next to it. I didn't need to read all of it to realize they were notes jotted down by engineers. It was the greatest weapon of mass destruction the galaxy had ever seen.

Atron had told me that the only blueprints were his. I'd destroyed them.

But here, on Delluvia Astra, the Imperium was making a second attempt at building it.

4

I STOOD IN DISBELIEF, staring at the weapons diagram, when Lieutenant Fel joined me at the screen.

The sergeant blew out an exasperated breath. "There's a level below this. Two lift banks and a stairwell on the east wing. No Imperium to be found. And given this"—he gestured at the screen —"we have reason to fear this is bait. A trap designed to draw us in and blow us up."

That made sense. But this could be a game changer. Getting to the Delluvian Parliament was one thing, tracking down whoever had been working here before the trail went cold was of a whole other level of vital importance.

It wasn't my call how to commit coalition troops, however.

"Do you think it's a trap?" I asked Fel.

He shrugged. "I think we need to take a look. Colonel Stallings agreed. Now, about getting you to that parliament…"

"Given what we see here," I said, "parliament can wait. I'm going down with you."

"Will—" the comm transmission came from *Earthborn*, rather than Lieutenant Fel.

"General Mira'dna," I said before she could go any farther, "you're seeing exactly what I'm seeing. And unless Atron decided to stop by and pay a visit, I'd count myself as the most qualified person to deal with this weapon."

Okay, that was a stretch. All I'd done was help to steal the prototype after destroying what I thought was the only blueprint available for it. But still. No one else on this planet had done that.

"Just think of the footage Earl will get," I said, hoping that my devotion to the cause of War PR would carry the day.

There was a pause on our line. Meanwhile Lieutenant Fel was busy giving orders to have terminals secured and tagged. Two of his men got busy after pulling out a Tab and interfacing it with the terminal.

No one was waiting to see what the Ambassador—hero of the United Coalition or not—planned to do next.

Staff Sergeant Berrios motioned to the doors on the east side of the room. "We're taking the fight underground. Let's move, people!"

"I'm going with them, General," I said. "Gut instinct."

Another pause and then…

"That will only take you so far, Will," Mira'dna said. "If we decide you need to pull out—you'll do it."

"Of course," I said, not sure that I meant it.

Mira'dna must have guessed the same. "And Will, remember that the men around you *do* follow orders when given. If we call upon you to withdraw, and you refuse, they will have no qualms about bringing you back by force."

I smiled at the absurdity of that thought, me getting dragged out kicking and screaming from an underground tunnel complex by space warriors. "Wouldn't have it any other way. Out."

We moved down a level and then stacked up on the door that led to the stairwell, not wanting to take one of the lifts. My fiber-link showed a golden circle of light over the door, but it was one of Berrios's men who visually traced and opened it.

We filed inside, me last of all, everyone keeping three meters of distance between each man.

The lights were out completely in the stairwell. My fiber-link, interfaced with my Drayth armor, automatically adjusted my view to Color Night Vision. A strip of emergency lighting appeared in a dull zigzag along the outer wall of the stairwell. Not for the first time, I had to acknowledge that Lockett and Quin had been right about the fiber-link; the functionality of the Drayth armor was much improved thanks to the interface with my cybernetic implant.

Still, they were both jerks for how that little event went down.

Everything stayed quiet until we reached the third sublevel, which opened into a tram station of sorts. I wasn't sure if this was how all the underground tunnels we'd discovered were, or just this one. It was a far cry from the carved-out rat holes I'd pictured on first hearing of their existence, though.

What we walked into was a sort of public street dropped under the city. Two aisles lined with wide pillars were split down the middle with a one-meter drop and a mag rail that ran between them.

"Contact right!" one of my escorts shouted.

J.N. CHANEY & JASON ANSPACH

I'd barely made it to the floor when hostile fire zipped overhead. Earl avoided fire and dropped low to hover just above my shoulder, beeping something that I understood to mean, "Look at the camera."

Always the director.

Only… I didn't have the time to give the camera drone special attention. We were in the thick of it now.

The audio pickups in my helmet popped with staccato snaps, the ping of metal ricochets as armor panels attempted to shrug off the incoming fire, the crack of flechettes embedding in the foundations of the floor and the walls.

My escorts were up and returning fire. I didn't hesitate to do the same.

With the stock of my rifle in my shoulder, my fiber-link haloed my right eye with a targeting reticle. The implant painted a laser-like line that tracked with the barrel of my weapon. I brought it into alignment with the first Imperium soldier I could see—hiding in the recess track for the trams—and pulled the trigger.

The snap-pull of the rail-gun technology was familiar to me now. There was no kickback or the bark of chemical propellant sending a bullet through a rifled barrel like the weapons of Earth. It was quiet to the point of feeling like I was using a toy; only the supersonic *snap* of the flechette breaking the sound barrier made any noise.

That, and whatever was on the receiving end of the shot getting hit.

My trigger pull sent a flechette to bounce off the crown of the enemy's helmet. The second trigger pull walked down as I better aligned my sights, pulverizing the visor in a cascade of crystalline and a thin jet of blood from a headshot.

The soldier dropped to his back. Two more soldiers peered around a pillar behind the track to add their own fire to the fresh battle. Their DK-5's needled the air with flechettes headed right for my team.

I rotated my shoulders, moved my feet, and slipped through the fire to find cover behind a nearby pillar on my side of the tracks. The Drayth armor caught three or four flechettes in the process, but nothing got through. Just more bruises.

More flechettes whistled by, crackling against the wall and chewing at the pillar behind me.

"Covering!" I barked into the comm and then spun around to the opposite side of my pillar to put more fire on the Imperium and give the others on my team the chance to move.

The threat detection suite built into the systems of my armor painted a dozen Imperium soldiers holed up behind pillars at a distance of about thirty meters. The red silhouettes flashed as they lit us up with their DK-5 submachine guns, spraying flechettes everywhere.

Earl caught up with me and floated just above my head, periodically peaking around the pillar to see the Imperium threat and then looking back at me. Further in the underground tram station, Coalition soldiers moved under fire, armor sparking with glancing hits. Some went down, but the rest didn't stop or slow. Heedless of the threat, they spread across the length of the nearside platform, intent on destroying the Imperium defenders.

Beside me, one of the ATM-Gs belched a streak of fire and sparks that left the wall coated in soot and glowing embers. The H-

E round lanced into the opposing wall, unleashing a cascade of flame and broken concrete. Concussive force rattled in my chest like a bass drop. The blast lifted two Imperium soldiers off their feet and tossed them down onto the mag rail, trailing flickers of flame.

The ground shook under my boots.

The battle intensified. DK-5s sprayed bursts of automatic fire with the equally the thick, single-shot return fire of the Coalition.

Sergeant Berrios directed his teams to alternate fire between points of cover. I fell into the cadence of combat alongside them, putting down Imperium soldiers every time they broke cover of their own in an attempt to lay down blankets of flechettes on our position.

Two Coalition soldiers beside me were braced against one of the structural pillars, MD-14s knocking the air with resounding booms of steady fire. A hailstorm of flechettes raked over their position from opposing angles—the Imperium overlapping their fire lanes, concentrating on one position.

The soldier closest to me caught a stitching of flechettes to the neck piece of his armor. Metal pinged against his chest plates, ending in a squelching smack. The soldier dropped immediately in a spray of blood, his rifle clattering to the ground at his feet.

"Medic!" I shouted. "Man down!"

A soldier with a red stripe on his left arm broke off from the gunfight and rushed to the side of the fallen. He stowed his rifle on the back of his armor and fumbled with a medical kit attached to his battle belt.

A nasty burst of fire chipped away at my cover and chased me from my firing position. I wound up with a flechette stuck in the shoulder. I grit my teeth. The Drayth armor held, but I'd never seen anything get lodged into it before. And that shot was dangerously close to my helmet visor.

Things were getting heated.

Berrios recognized this as well. "We gotta make a move here," he told the team and then went into the comm to Lieutenant Fel. "Flank right, and we'll cover you."

"Suppress the right flank!" I called, repeating a directive that was being passed among our team. I stepped out of cover and put down a copious amount of fire ahead of the point where Lieutenant Fel would advance.

Moving as the tip of the spear on his fire team, Lieutenant Fel hopped down onto the mag rail. The two soldiers behind him stepped out from behind their pillar, MD-14s knocking the air like jackhammers as they saturated the opposing Imperium positions with steady fire. Sparks and spall radiated from the Imperium's cover. Chips of printed concrete flaked away under the onslaught as we sent enough rounds into the Imperium position to keep their heads down.

Fel's fire team eliminated any Imperium still using the recessed track path and then climbed back out on the far side of the station platform. They continued their movement and swung around to hit the Imperium soldiers on their right flank.

Two Imperium soldiers fell dead and into the open. They were getting hit from two directions now as Lieutenant Fel's fire team worked their rifles, peppering the exposed flanks of the enemy from behind their own cover. The Imperium began to break, which only allowed us to hit men running from Fel and into our sights.

The red silhouettes dropped from ten to five in seconds as Imperium soldiers fell to the onslaught. Opposite the enemy, Lieutenant Fel and his team were highlighted in green overlays. One of them collapsed to the ground, his silhouette fading from view.

"Man down!" someone called out.

My gut clenched.

"Grab him!" Lieutenant Fel's silhouette continued to pulse as he worked his MD-14. A member of his fire team rushed into the maelstrom, grabbed his fallen comrade by the neckpiece of his armor, and dragged him to the relative safety of the sunken tramline.

"Sergeant," I called to Berrios, "I'm going to swing around to their left flank."

"Stay here and keep up suppressive fire," Berrios countered, leaving no room for argument... or the kind of heroics that Earl was likely hoping for.

He selected two of his men and shouted, "Flanking left!"

"Covering!" I shouted, adding my voice to the chorus of troopers doing the same.

Berrios's team ran wide and then hopped down onto the tram's mag rail, crossed over to the other side, and clambered up onto the enemy platform in time to catch the Imperium seeking to flee from Fel's troops. They were careful to keep themselves positioned behind a pillar to avoid any friendly fire.

It all happened so quick and smooth, I was nearly in disbelief.

Beside me, the corpsman patted the wounded soldier and stuffed his medical supplies back into his kit. He had the kit stowed and his rifle drawn a beat later while the wounded's buddy dragged him back to a casualty collection point away from the fighting.

I noted that down by the mag rail, one of Fel's men was motioning for the medic to visit there next. The doc let his weapon hang on its sling and ran toward the wounded. I'm not sure he'd even fired a round.

White light suddenly washed over the left side of the railway, cutting uncomfortably into my color night vision.

"Tram! Tram! Tram!" the medic shouted and then jumped down into the pit to help get the wounded up.

Another tram was coming in, and it was moving fast.

"Clear the rail!" I shouted, already running over to help do just that.

With the tram racing toward us at frightening speed, I helped pull the wounded up and onto our side of the platform while flechettes snapped in all directions. That done, I reached down and gave a hand to the medic and Fel's troop with scant seconds to spare before the tram rushed into the station.

The magnetically propelled tram stopped on a dime. One second it was a blur of motion, and the next it was perfectly still, effectively dividing the two platforms between its three compartments. Its windows shattered from flechette fire, and its accordion-style seals of vulcanized rubber, or some other synthetic material, between cars quickly became holed—and for good reason: the tram was filled with Imperium.

Barrels of Imperium DK-5s were pushed through the broken windows to spout unaimed, but still lethal return fire. We had started shooting at the tram the moment it arrived. That put the Imperium inside on the defensive from the start.

I, along with the medic, pulled the wounded back behind cover as crystalline shattered and sprayed over both walkways. My helmet cut the ambient sound by fifty percent as flechettes chewed at the concrete wall by my head, chipping deep into the structure for a hellacious three seconds.

The sonic storm of magnetic snapping was lost to the sound of rending metal. Pinholes rippled across the formed metal of the tram, trapping sparks and tiny wisps of flame inside.

And then, seemingly all at once, it was over. Ambient audio washed through the inside of my helmet, sounding loud in the absence of constant rifle fire. Calls to cease fire echoed across the comm.

Had we gotten them all?

I looked down to verify that the wounded hadn't been hit again, then took a breath before stepping out from cover. Dozens of small columns of smoke wafted up from the tram, collecting into clouds that slowly rose toward the ceiling. I could smell the burning of synthetic fibers through my helmet filters.

Corporal Styson kicked a shot-to-hell tram door inward and stepped cautiously inside, fellow soldiers covering windows and other exits as they surrounded the wrecked transport.

I watched and waited, looking for the Imperium to hit us again from a different direction as more Coalition troops entered to clear each of the three cars.

It wasn't long before Sergeant Berrios approached me. "You did all right, Ambassador."

I nodded. "Thanks. So… we ready?"

"Ready. You've got some options, though. We can follow the tunnel to our destination"—Berrios inclined his head toward the shot-up tram—"or we can try and use that."

"It still works?" I asked in disbelief.

"Looks like it. Lieutenant Fel wants to send a team. Said we can hitch a ride. Beats walking, sir."

"Let's do it."

Berrios gave a quick nod. "Was hoping you'd say that."

He rounded up his men, and soon we were on board, standing amid the bloody corpses of the last riders. I tried not to take that as a bad omen.

Corporal Styson was in the driver's cockpit; no one wanted to rely on the automated settings. If we needed to stop in the face of heavy resistance, we wanted someone ready to hit the brakes or push straight through depending on the situation.

The tram's comm sounded a chime, then Styson said, "Hang onto your butts, everyone."

Something heavy and mechanical snapped under the tram. The car I stood in shuddered and lurched forward.

We didn't know what we were going to encounter. Come to think of it, I'm surprised that Mira'dna and the others didn't recall me after the firefight. But we were off and moving. Too late to turn around.

Lieutenant Fel moved through the car, making sure the Coalition troops were reloaded and ready to fight. Clicks and clacks played through the compartment as soldiers double-checked their weapons. Several spent magazines dropped to the floor, and new ones were locked into place.

"This weapon in the plans," Sergeant Berrios said beside me, "What does it do, exactly?"

It was a bit of a revelation to me how little what happened to the Imperium fleet was public knowledge, even among the Coalition. I guess that made a certain amount of sense. Parts of Atron's network may still be embedded inside the Imperium. The less we talked, the harder it might be to sort things out. You never knew what little innocent comment might turn out to be the key piece in an investigative trail you knew nothing about.

"Ever heard of Kastar?" I asked Berrios.

He shook his helmet.

"That's where we hit the fleet. With this weapon. It used to be a staging area for the Imperium fleet. Now it's a planet-sized gas cloud."

"Damn," Berrios said.

"Yeah," I said. "That prototype was supposed to be it—all that remained of the project. The initial plans were destroyed, along with every scientist who had a hand in developing them. But if the Imperium has partial plans here, that means someone on the development team survived."

I still didn't like thinking about the measures Atron had taken to make sure the weapon couldn't be mass-produced. These were real people with real lives. At the same time, the feeling of dread I felt over the possibility that what happened on Kastar could happen again elsewhere—like Earth—had me wishing Atron had done the job completely.

What was becoming of me?

I felt as though I were closer in thought to a Vorvak than to the guy who'd first stumbled into a cave... and maybe I was.

There'd be time for reflection later.

"Obstruction ahead," Corporal Styson announced over the comm.

Lieutenant Fel ordered a full stop.

The troopers readied themselves. I moved toward the front

section to see if I could get a good view from the cockpit. As our tram came to a shaky stop—much different from how it reacted before visiting a war zone—I got a good look at the obstruction.

It was another tram, buckled and snaking as far as the mag rail would let it tilt. The windows were shattered, crystalline fragments glinting along the track. Smoke coiled up from somewhere up front. Bodies were splayed over the track. Some were Imperium soldiers, but others were dressed in civilian attire, as best I could see from the tram's forward running lights.

I frowned at the sight of the carnage. What had happened here?

"Kill the lights," Fel ordered.

The dim running lights inside and outside our tram went black. My helmet's night vision went online.

Every trooper watched, expecting an ambush to kick off. But none came.

"Clear out of the cars," Lieutenant Fel said, his voice calm but quiet over the comm. "Clear this section of trail. Look for survivors. Some of these appear to be civilians."

Staff Sergeant Berrios popped open the side door and started issuing orders to his men. I hopped down from the tram and scanned the wreckage for any Imperium or other signs of life amongst the bodies and the sheared metal panels.

We found two living among what had been packed cars. One Imperium soldier, who was quickly flex cuffed and taken into custody by Lieutenant Fel's fire team. The other was an Anunnaki man in a lab coat. He had a bleeding gash on his forehead and a broken arm. He'd been barely conscious when one of Berrios's men found him moaning as though he were having a bad dream.

Being close by, I went over and brushed debris off his chest after he'd been searched for weapons. Unless he was capable of Sert-levels of concealed carry, the man was clean.

"What happened here?" I asked him.

He sucked in a breath and talked in a pinched voice, clearly in pain.

"I… I'm not with them," he muttered, shaking his head. "I work for Marcus Eddison."

Lieutenant Fel had joined us, and I could feel his eyes on me. That was the last thing we expected.

My blood ran cold. "What do you mean?"

"Embedded—" He paused to cough gust and spit blood. "I was… embedded with the research team. I'm a… a spy."

Lieutenant Fel pushed the barrel of his rifle against the man's head. In the darkness, that was likely the only way for the scientist to know what he was up against. "Spies tell us about this kind of mess *before* we invade."

The scientist quickly got the message. He held up a data card—the same style of data storage device that Atron had once offered me.

"No! It's true!" he pleaded.

I took the data card from his hands. "That's an assertion. Eddison said nothing about having spies among the population here. We need proof."

He sucked in another short, stiff breath. "I need your thickest Irish cream."

Lieutenant Fel looked at me. "Is that supposed to mean something?"

"Yeah," I said as I stood up. "Put your rifle away."

5

MY TRIP to the Delluvian Parliament was uneventful after that. They were a squat species. About as wide as a Vorvak but nowhere near as tall. Some were fat. I wouldn't call any of them thin. They had tough, gray skin that brought to mind an elephant because of the fleshy trunks in the middle of their face, but they looked far more human than elephants. The ears were small and proportioned under course black hair about where a human's would be. The eyes were large, but again positioned like my own.

They were duly impressed by my arrival in the midst of battle, boldly negotiating their place in the United Coalition even as the Imperium fought and died around them. The images Earl had provided of me working to reach them only increased their esteem for me.

The mission was a success, and I felt good about that much upon escorting a small delegation up to the *Earthborn*—them in a courier shuttle and me in my personal craft. The official entrance of the Delluvians into the United Council of Planets would take place at Earth in a formal meeting.

That was for the official brass of the UC to handle.

As for me, I was exhausted. My eyelids were heavy, and my body felt like I'd run a marathon by the time I docked my ship on the *Earthborn* and returned to the helm. Earl floated over to his nook beside my terminal, lens clicking as it adjusted to a close-up angle.

It took a bit of effort on my part to ignore the camera drone. I hoped this Hero of the Rebellion nonsense would end with the war. I valued my privacy too much to be "on" all the time.

"Void Drift suite is up and running for you." Fleet Admiral Tanoka greeted me with business. "The fleet is tethered and ready for departure."

"Thank you, Admiral." I took my seat in the Navigator's chair at the apex of the bridge and heaved a sigh.

Somewhere in the back of my head, Quin's warnings about a Navigator needing to be well-rested hung heavy in my mind. If that was true, I was experiencing the limits of just how much rest was truly required. I felt like I could sleep for three days. I needed to eat, and the ripe smell leaking out of my armor insisted that I shower, but I wanted to get back home.

Not back to Earth. Back to the *Phaelon*. Back to my crew.

My friends.

General Mira'dna took a seat in the command chair next to me, her living-stone hair bouncing lightly around her shoulder. She looked me over and said, "I have heard, throughout my long life, that Navigators require rest before testing themselves against the Void. And you, Will, appear exhausted."

I gave a weak smile. "I'm tired, but I'm ready. Eager for what comes next. Adding the Delluvians to the council is going to do a lot for this war."

The second part didn't need to be said, but I said it for the benefit of the camera.

"Their manufacturing and exports are most welcome and need-ed," she said in a small voice, a whimsical smile adding a bit of color to her pale marble cheeks. "And, I suppose, I am not as familiar with humans as I might otherwise be. So if you are ready…"

"I'm ready." I worked the MFD at my terminal to bring the Void engine online.

My thoughts were split between the task at hand and what the general said about Delluvian manufacturing. Mira'dna wasn't exactly conniving, but she didn't shy away from the fiscal realities of running the war effort and the economic considerations of starting up a new form of government. She didn't intend for the United Council to be the final framework for interstellar governance. If she had her way, the Council would be like the senate, and the Federa-tion would rise again to take its place as the Executive branch.

Not everyone was keen on a New Federation, though.

However this ended, it would require convincing on all sides. That much was obvious way back before we'd dealt that blow to the Imperium on Kastar.

Maybe I was just drinking the Kool-Aid that first Quin and Fera, and then Eddison and Mira'dna served me, but I felt as though I really was uniquely qualified to make sure a peaceful aftermath to this war was achieved.

I certainly didn't agree to become Earth's Ambassador for the 401k benefits.

My terminal beeped. The tether was in place, and systems

appeared green across the board. All that remained was for this one last piece of the mission.

The return.

"Void engine online. Setting drift," I announced.

"All readings normal," Peleus, *Earthborn*'s artificial intelligence, informed me in his detached, tinny voice.

It was becoming routine. Void Drifting would never be something I could do in my sleep, but the muscle memory was developing, and Quin trusted me enough to Navigate without his oversight, so that was something.

I gave the countdown and hit the switch.

The starfield inverted, basking me in the song of the Void.

THE MAIN BRIDGE display shifted to a whiteout, thoroughly pinpricked with teeming black dots. The rising swell of music that was not music sent tingles up and down my spine, submerging me in a sonic soundscape that was simultaneously beautiful and terrifying.

It was as impossible as breathing underwater, but I hadn't drowned yet.

Like its own gravitational force, the tug at the corners of my awareness intensified. The whiteout washed over my mental landscape, saturating me in the otherworldly tendrils of the Void.

Sensational tingles crawled along my skin like tiny spider legs. Latent vibrations collected at the small bones in my ear. A shrill ringing sounded just outside my range of hearing, like a dog whistle. Percussive beats ran in a drumline somewhere in the background, spoiling the delicate fanfare with something more malevolent.

Black lightning streaked across the display. A bolt of inverted energy raced from the upper edge to the bottom, jagged lines forking and branching off like pixelated snakes, each of them tens of thousands of kilometers long. Several more Drift Lanes appeared like rifts in the whiteout, like the canopy of the Void was cracking with the beginning stages of just crumbling away into complete and utter darkness.

The Drift Lanes weren't stagnant. They didn't stay in view.

Seconds after they dragged themselves through the unending light of subspace, they began to shift into gradients, slowly fading from black as midnight to a dull gray. Eventually, they completely dissolved.

Each Lane presented with its own signature melody.

Insistent, piercing, moaning.

Begging to be chosen. Demanding to be explored.

But only one of them was safe. By means of quantum interpolation or spiritual alignment, or something else… I might never know the answer, but whatever rules guided the reality of this sub-reality continued to elude me.

Their fluid nature did not make them any less real.

The consequences of failure were dire.

"Void transition complete," Peleus said. "STEM core readings are synchronized with the control terminal. No significant lag detected. Tether integrity has been maintained through the transitory period. The convoy is following at standard interval. You are free to Navigate, Ambassador."

I nodded, not wanting to break my concentration. It was different, doing this without Quin sniping at me, or Fera carefully watching my every move. It probably should have made me feel more like an adult instead of some fifteen-year-old with a bumper sticker slapped on the back of his spaceship: STUDENT DRIFTER.

There was no feeling in control, moisturized, and in my own lane; I felt like no one knew or appreciated what I was doing. I wasn't looking for a pat on the back, but it seemed like the raw magic of Navigating was taken for granted by people when they didn't understand the first thing about it.

Part of me could empathize with how Quin reacted to my early approach to Drifting. Mostly he was still a jerk, though.

Earl whirred and clicked next to me as the bot adjusted its lenses. That was getting on my nerves, too.

Then, a flickering shadow drew my undivided attention.

Somewhere out there in the Void, a darkness teemed. Unnatural, pervasive, and… aware? It was, in some way, a draw for the Drift Lanes. The chain lightning scattering over the display seemed to collect at a point light-years away, forming into something resembling a black hole, vaguely taking on the shape of a dark circle, darkest at the border. A cold shiver ran through me; it was like looking into the eye of some maleficent deity, something not unlike the pictographs of ancient Egypt that depicted the Eye of Ra.

The Universal Eye.

I blinked to reset my vision. It was no eye. Just a void within the Void.

Still, the fact that I could see it from this distance gave me pause. Whatever the anomaly was… it was massive.

I let those thoughts dissolve.

I focused. Controlled.

Quin's logs always came to mind at this stage of the Navigation.

Focus to discern. Control to act.

I let instinct guide me.

Mechanical feedback rattled the sidestick in my grip. It felt like a stream of fast-moving water rippling against my palm. The rise in temperature told me my palms were sweating, but that was internal to the gloves of my suit.

There was no turbulence, no interference from the Void at all in the controls. It was entirely mental, as if the journey of the ship existed only in my mind, like I was dreaming but aware of my body at the same time.

As though it were a sonar beacon, I heard it. The sound that was more a sensation than actual sound raised the hairs on the back of my neck with static cling. It felt like the last piece of a puzzle snapping into place, or the alignment of two opposing magnets drawing together with a *click*.

My left hand shot out to the MFD's touchscreen and dropped a coordinate pin. I pulled the control stick down and to the right, adjusting the heading eleven degrees. I drew my hand back from the MFD and placed it on the throttle and guided it up to ninety percent thrust.

The *Earthborn*'s reactor responded immediately to the surge of power transfer from the reactor. In a way, I could feel the pulse through the ship, though that was owed to my fiber-link's knowledge base and the piloting experience I'd picked up over the last few months. On the scopes, the convoy of Coalition ships fell in line at a tight interval.

Teeming shadows confined to the shape of distant, unfamiliar stars slid across the main bridge display, slowly coasting to their fixed positions as the *Earthborn*'s new heading locked into place. I watched and waited, my breath caught in my throat, slowly slipping through my clenched teeth.

This is it. I'm sure of it.

I rode that wave of confidence, ignoring the spike of doubt that tried to make me second-guess myself.

Two errant Drift Lanes spiked through our travel path. I froze, momentarily transfixed by the anomaly. I let the fear flow through me without taking root. A passing cloud containing an unpleasant smell, or the buzzing of an insect as it zipped close by my ear. The sensation came and went. I adjusted the heading to Navigate around the obstacles, my brow furrowing.

"What're those?" someone asked from the bridge below.

"Let him concentrate," Admiral Tanoka hissed in a hushed tone.

This was the most critical phase of the Drift.

No pressure, I told myself.

Instant, multidimensional atomization if I failed, but hey... no pressure.

The secondary void, the black hole in the distance, shifted. Tension tied my gut into a knot.

There was movement. Detectable movement. The darkness was beginning to spin. To rotate like a planet.

It shouldn't be doing that.

I bumped the throttle up to max and gave the control stick a slight pull. The *Earthborn* slipped around the two Drift Lanes that tried to block our path and came within a few thousand klicks out from the way marker I'd placed.

Something new happened.

It was like a stereo suddenly kicking on at full volume. Pain spiked into the side of my head. I twitched but held the controls firmly in place.

I had too much riding on this Navigation to lose concentration. Too many lives at stake. Nothing short of a flechette to the head would have made me lose focus. I kept firm hold of my controls.

The insistent stab of discomfort somewhere between my skull and my brain didn't let up. I ground my teeth, watching the distance to target parameter ticking down.

A new Drift Lane sprang forth from the Void. The fresh trail of jagged darkness bisected my coordinate pin, carrying the remainder of the signature notes that had signaled our entry into the Void. It was the calling card of safety, a life preserver tossed overboard to save a potential drowning victim.

I latched onto it and adjusted the *Earthborn*'s heading half a degree. The convoy followed suit.

"Cutting Void engine in three, two...."

The tip of the *Earthborn*'s bow crossed the threshold of the black lightning. A surge of adrenaline coursed through me. One by one, the remaining ships in the convoy slipped into the Lane like links in a chain.

"One." I deactivated the Void engine.

A surge of static skittered across my awareness. We rode the shadow bolt like a raft pulled along a fast-moving river, skirting the edges of reality until, seemingly against the will of the laws of physics, the Void began to cede its dominion to the cold darkness of normal space-time.

Darkness laid itself bare before us. The white shrank away to the smallest motes of light far in the distance. Blips appeared on the scope as additional ships from the convoy appeared behind us.

The starfield resolved into the familiar pattern of the Sol system. All traces of the song, the bliss, and the suffering, fell away.

I let out an exasperated breath. Sweat ran in a thin rivulet down the back of my neck.

"Transition completed," I rasped and then collapsed against the seat, drawing ragged breaths.

Tired. I'd been too tired.

Don't make that mistake again, Will.

Earl gave me a congratulatory beep. General Mira'dna put a hand on my shoulder, her concern evident.

"Your value to our cause is great, Will Kaufman."

"We all do our part," I said, conscious of Earl's lens zooming in on my face, somewhat amazed about, despite the mental strain I was under, how easily the lines came out.

In truth, it felt good to be good at something. To be useful and needed.

That feeling, though, paled in comparison to the faint echo of the Void. I tried to put the strange sensations out of my mind, but the desire to transition back, to bask in the Void Song, was nearly overwhelming.

I knew better, but that didn't lessen the impulse.

Fleet Admiral Tanoka broadcasted a transmission to the convoy. "United Coalition battle group Alpha, sitrep."

Calls of "all clear" cascaded over the frequency. I unstrapped myself from the Navigator's chair, smiling in spite of myself. "If you need me, I'll be in my quarters, General."

Earl detached from his base station and floated up over my shoulder.

The general watched me, still studying, appraising behind her stony eyes. "Of course. Catch a few rest cycles. You've more than earned it."

There was an understatement. I knew what was waiting for me on the other side of that rest. There would be a formal debriefing and several meetings, then the planning phase for the next operation would begin.

This war couldn't be over soon enough.

And then there was the question of that spy. Was Marcus Eddison still trying to get his hands on a planet-killer weapon?

It was bad enough that the Imperium was as far along as they were. I reached for the data crystal in my armor's pocket. That would need to be checked and then dealt with the same way I'd dealt with Atron's data card. After that, we would need to get some kind of interstellar accord in place where all factions decided against developing the dangerous technology. There was galactic precedent of such things happening in the past—AI was limited due to prior agreements that not even the Imperium had violated.

So far, anyway.

My fiber-link displayed a message request in my field of view.

I waited until I was halfway across the bridge, out of earshot of most of the crew, before accepting it. Di's smiling face appeared in a translucent window, floating above the deck. "Hi, Di."

She'd already changed out of her flight suit and was leaning over a table in the galley. I could see several pilots, maintenance techs, and soldiers milling about in the background, drinks in hands. "Hey there, Hero of the Rebellion! You coming down to make good on that first round?"

When she smiled, dimples formed in her cheeks. There was a mischievous light in her eyes. She was the embodiment of the *work hard, play hard* maxim. I'd dabbled in alien alcohol over the last few months, but it wasn't my preferred means of relaxing, especially after a Void Drift.

"Put it on my tab," I said. "I've got to get some rack time."

She made an exaggerated pouty face. "I'm saving a seat for you in case you change your mind."

"No danger of that, but thanks, Di. I'll catch up with you before the debrief."

She waved her fingers and cut the connection.

6

Sleep came and went too quickly.

I woke with swollen eyes, feeling slightly dehydrated and like I'd been punched in the head. My equilibrium shifted as I put my bare feet on the cold deck of the ship and took a sharp breath.

My first thought was *shower*.

My second, more dominant thought was about Fera. I missed her and worried that our relationship might become a casualty of too little time, which grew shorter in supply as the war tempo increased. Fera and I stole moments away when we could. At the outset, there was a week or more of downtime to plan new operations. Now, it seemed like the turn time was barely a day or two before the next Void Drift.

My fiber-link displayed the time in my field of view, along with my message logs. One message from Marcus Eddison. A dozen or so from the various delegates on the Council.

I skimmed over the official business, stopping only when I saw the message from Quin.

With an eye wave, I opened it up. The holographic Foris appeared in my HUD and spoke.

"Will Kaufman, my favorite mouth-breathing primitive, how are you?" Though it was a prerecorded message, he paused for a beat before continuing. "Anyway, if you have time between hunting and gathering or whatever you're up to, I felt it necessary to inform you that things are developing along the lines we speculated before our departure."

I began to get ready for the shower while watching the rest of the message. My quarters were little more than a studio apartment —spacious for a ship—and came with a private personal refreshment station. Being made into a PR war hero had at least *some* benefits, I supposed. I stripped out of my underclothes, set the sonic stream to one step below scalding, and basked in the glorious, cleansing heat.

The showers used miniscule amounts of recycled water that pulsated over your body via sonic jets. It was really puffs of steam and air that *felt* like an Earth shower and managed to get you just as clean. The gentle pulses felt heavenly across my skin.

Quin, in his usual style, rattled on about several details that didn't matter before getting to the meat of things: the return of the *Phaelon* to the Sol system.

"...and so, I expect we'll be returning about a day and half after you've received this message." He ended the message with a formal nod and then seemed to think better of signing off that way. "Oh. And if that derelict brain of yours has any trouble keeping up with what I just said, you can replay—and more importantly *slow down*—the message by—"

I closed the recording before Quin could finish insulting me.

"Just couldn't help yourself, could you?" I mumbled.

I left the shower and stepped, fully dry thanks to the closing flourish of warm-air blasts, out of the enclosure. The atmosphere beyond the shower was chilly. I felt goosebumps crawl on my skin as I opened up Marcus Eddison's message. It was text only, asking me if there had been any significant findings during the mission.

"Damn right there were," I said, continuing to speak to my empty room. "You and I are gonna have a talk about them, too."

Of course, my actual reply was more formal. I told him we'd discuss the details during the official debrief.

First, I wanted to run everything by Atron. I sent him a message next, informing him of what I'd found on Delluvia Astra and asking if his fleet had encountered anything in their corner of the fight.

I slipped on my underclothes and stepped into my Drayth armor. After pulling out my holster and rail pistol, I cinched the belt over my waist and checked the itinerary in my fiber-link's HUD. General Mira'dna had last made updates a few hours ago. I didn't think her species slept at all.

The first order of business was the formal debrief on the liberation of Delluvia Astra, immediately followed by a session with the United Council of Planets. Several more meetings were listed after, but I didn't bother reading that far.

One problem at a time.

The thought came in Fera's voice.

I left my quarters, unfortunately with Earl in tow, and met up with Di in the galley. She was talking with a few of her fellow pilots.

The conversation must not have been very important because her eyes lit up when she saw me, and she popped up to her feet, that infectious smile of hers on full display.

"Will! Back from the dead, I see. How was your rest?"

I shrugged indifferently, not to play it cool but because I was getting the sense that she was being a little more than friendly in her attitude toward me. "Sufficient. Debrief's in an hour. You going?"

She gave me a look that said *duh*. "You need a lift?"

"Back down to the surface?" I asked. "Sure. Not every day you get an ace fighter pilot as chauffeur."

She laughed. "Get some breakfast, but not too much. Wouldn't want you to lose it on the trip down to Earth."

THE ROOM at Base X was packed with people from all over the galaxy, segregated by faction. As I'd observed time and again between species, the United Coalition was much less cohesive than their name implied. Right now, it looked like the only commonality was a mutual disdain of the Imperium.

I sat next to Di and Staff Sergeant Berrios in the center section of the room, just below the dais where leaders like Mira'dna, Eddison, and Atron would speak. To the left and right of us, the alien representatives filled out the rest of the seats, reacting to the proceedings with nonverbal cues that I would not have been able to interpret without the help of my fiber-link.

It felt to me like this was a disaster waiting to happen. The fight after the Imperium was defeated would probably be just as big and potentially just as bloody.

Di elbowed me. "Don't look so glum. You're the Hero of the Rebellion, remember?"

"Why does everyone look like they hate each other?" I whispered back.

"Because they do."

The Delluvian delegation sat across from the representatives of the Drayth collective. The leaders of the United Coalition sat at a long white table at the head of the room on a raised dais. All of them had expressions ranging from tired to exasperated as they watched their fledgling alliance crumbling before their eyes.

Marcus Eddison had a smug look on his face. He sat at the end of the table, two of his aides seated behind him. I didn't know what he was so excited about, unless it was the performance of his ships. They were the primary reason the Coalition was doing so well. A close second was my ability to Navigate the Void, which provided a logistical and tactical advantage the rebels could only have dreamed of a few short months ago.

The meeting was rife with political posturing. If it didn't have serious implications for the safety of Earth, I would have found it difficult to pay attention. As such, I listened as Prax, the Drayth representative, continued his filibuster on how important his people were to the cause and why they needed the majority of the defense budget.

"Parts and new ships are being built every day," the Drayth said. It sounded similar to Lockett. A bit of a deeper register, but otherwise the same. I wondered if that had something to do with the species' *upgrades*. "No longer Imperium, but Coalition assets. Production costs are high. Drayth Collective requires remuneration for services rendered if Coalition wishes to continue amicable relations."

Call me a cynic, but it sounded a lot like Lockett's attempts at extortion once we'd pulled him off the ice. I didn't want to typecast the entire Drayth Collective based on the one representative I knew best, but when the opening twenty minutes of the meeting involved a single Drayth grandstanding about how they needed more money, I found it hard to separate Lockett's materialistic demands from those of the rest of his people.

"You have sufficient payment!" Norla Greed, the Delluvian representative, shot up to his feet, his small facial trunk coiled like a viper about to strike. He emphasized his words by pounding his thick, crag-lined fists together.

Not for the first time, I wondered how a species with such brutish physical bodies as the bipedal Delluvians could manufacture such elegant, precision smart fibers. Obviously with machines, but there was a finesse to their products, even their famous snub fighter ships that didn't match their squat, utilitarian physicality.

"Delluvians manufacture smart fibers, space-grade thread-work for ships," the Drayth countered. "No smart fibers, no ship-grade equipment. Budget should flow to us!"

The shouting started up again at that point. Representatives and delegates hopped to their feet, hurling insults at each other at peak volume.

From the center of the table, General Mira'dna sent what looked to me like pleading eyes. It was hard to tell, given her features, but I was already tired of listening to the fighting and didn't want to be stuck waiting for another tirade to unwind.

I took a breath, stood, and yelled, "Enough!"

All eyes turned to me. Earl floated over my head, circling the table, lens clicking as it adjusted for a wide-angle shot to catch the startled reaction of the delegates as the shouting died down.

"The hero of the rebellion wishes to speak," Mira'dna said, much to my chagrin.

There was no sarcasm in her words. Nor in the way those assembled waited to hear me. They really did value my perspective and leadership. Eddison and Mira'dna's PR campaign had been a good one. It was never more obvious to me than right then.

I just had to figure out what to say next.

"This is beneath all of us," I said, trying to sound like a statesman. "We're fighting a war. People are dying. A lot of people, and not just Imperium soldiers."

I paused for a beat to look the representatives in the eyes, willing them to feel the weight of their respective losses… and hoping it wasn't some unknown insult to make eye contact in such a way. Oh well, they all knew I was human and wouldn't know any better.

"Everyone here has lost something at the hands of the Imperium. If we let these political squabbles undermine our war effort, every fallen Drayth, Delluvian, Foris, Astradian, Krayvox, Vorvak, Anunnaki, human… every species, every victim of this war… will have died in vain."

I frowned. "They deserve a greater honor than that. This is a Coalition. An alliance. The consequences of failure are the same for all of us."

The chamber erupted. Some were upset at my including the Vorvak. Others fought about different items altogether. None of them seemed to care much what I'd said.

Norla's voice rose above the others as he yelled toward the dais. "You offer not enough for Delluvia."

"And ask too much of Drayth Collective!" Prax insisted, fiddling with the convoluted tubing that dangled from his iron lung. The lights in his cybernetic eyes dimmed. "Cannot sustain demand without reciprocation on the part of the Coalition. Collective will sell to the highest bidder if terms are not met to our satisfaction."

General Mira'dna held up a hand. Her voice amplified above the shouting. "Prax, that is unreasonable. Will you not consider—"

"No considering! Deal on the table. Take it or leave it."

Sensing that his opponent was getting the upper hand, Norla bristled as if he'd been slapped. "Delluvia moves to withdraw from the Coalition! We will make our own defense."

Like the slow churn of a train chugging its way into motion, small conversations started up in a flurry, moving up in volume, threatening to devolve into open shouting once again.

I cut through it with a knife hand gesture at Norla. "You were just liberated from the fruits of your own self-defense, Delluvian! It was me who reached your parliament under war, not you who came here first!"

To my surprise, he cowed instantly. I gambled a bit on what I knew about their psychology. I had shown great fighting and higher bravery, and as such Norla had no choice but to defer to me.

The Drayth… wouldn't be so easy.

"And you," I said, pivoting my hand toward Prax. "You may wish to sell to the highest bidder. For how long until, in your isolation, the Imperium again subjugates you and fixes your rates?

"You all come here and focus on your own worlds, your own

species. But *all* of us, combining our strengths into one unified front… together, we can win. Only together."

I paused for a beat to let that sink in.

General Mira'dna stood, ready to take up my points while Earl recorded on, no doubt to try and make me seem wiser, shrewder, braver, and otherwise better than I truly was. And then tell the galaxy.

The Imperium was going to put a hefty bounty on my head. If they hadn't already.

"A glaring fact that seems to be missed by the esteemed delegates," Mira'dna began, "is how we got to where we are now. No one here would be in their position were it not for the sacrifices made by Coalition soldiers, pilots, and support personnel. Your seats at the table on this council were bought with blood. Remember that."

I took in a deep breath and slowly let it out. When I thought about the casualties we'd taken up to this point, it became hard for me to keep the frustration bottled up. I hated politics on general principle, but double that for politicians trying to dictate the background of a war effort.

Resetting my expression to be as neutral as I could manage, I tried to remind everyone that more aid, both in money and manpower, was available if only we continued to fight alongside one another instead of with each other. "There are more systems still under the boot of the Imperium. Astrada, Epsilon Eridani, Maynard's Star, Erdon and the Ross system, to name a few. There is still much to do. We can't be going to pieces just yet. We need to finish what we started."

I sat back down and held my breath. Adrenaline coursed

through me, making me lightheaded, but I still held the attention of the room for the moment. I didn't want them to see that I felt nervous.

Di punched me in the shoulder. "I think they got the message."

Norla remained deflated like a stuck balloon, bowing his head slightly. Across from him, Prax was suddenly very interested in fiddling with his iron lung. The tension in the room dissolved.

I watched the two delegates with curiosity. What would they do now that I'd laid the cost of the war on their heads? They had to reach a compromise of some kind, or risk seeming callous and ungrateful.

Prax realized it first. He turned to the panel of leaders and inclined his head in a polite bow. "The Drayth Collective will accept liberation as earnest deposit on manufacturing. Further production will be provided at significant discount... until the war is ended."

The rest of the Drayth in his section of the room grumbled to each other, their iron lungs popping and hissing, but they made no attempt to argue.

Norla straightened out his trunk, oddly reminding me of an elderly man stroking his beard. The stout alien raised its shoulders in a shrug of acceptance. "Delluvians are privileged to be a part of the United Coalition. We accept our seat on the council and wish to provide supplies for the war effort." He tilted his head to the side, as if an idea had just occurred to him. "An opportunity exists for us on Delluvia Astra to retrofit some of our older manufacturing facilities to accommodate weapons proliferation, as well. If the Krayvox can be persuaded to provide shipments of fuel and the Anunnaki their refined oxidizing compounds, it is conceivable that we could contribute missiles at an increased rate of production."

Marcus Eddison's smirk became a full-faced grin. He leaned over his elbows on the table and cleared his throat. "Yes, that is... that would be advantageous to all fleets. The plasma cannons on my cruisers are their most deadly weapon system, but their shortcoming —one of their shortcomings, the biggest disadvantage, you could say—is that they rely largely on pure energy discharged from the advanced capacitors my team has designed. The power draw is massive, often leaving only a handful of firing cycles before significant recharge is required."

Fleet Admiral Tanoka made eye contact with Eddison and shared a nod. "That recharge cycle can take longer than is feasible in a combat environment. We have made do with ship-to-ship missiles thus far, but that has left our inventory dangerously depleted. The current complement of ship-to-ship missiles we have in our inventory is sufficient for defensive measures, but it will need to be replenished and restored to levels that will sustain our next offensive."

Norla was encouraged by the exchange. "A steady production line of additional missiles can be established in two weeks' time, if we secure the materials."

Sinegar, the Krayvox delegate, stood and made a fist. It was a bit melodramatic, but he was a politician, and that came with the territory. "Now that United Coalition has liberated Lilandia, Krayvox have unimpeded access to methane harvesters on all three gas giants in our system. We will provide refined methane to Delluvia Astra."

I noted that Atron, from his place at the table, eyed his fellow Krayvox warily. Perhaps there was an issue among the two dens. Maybe he just didn't trust politicians.

General Mira'dna beamed. "This is all well and good. Primus

Heptali, can the Free Anunnaki agree to supply the Delluvians with shipments of oxidizer?"

Anunnaki were a populous species, with colonies all throughout the galaxy. You could say they were Imperium since the Imperium controlled their home worlds. But that wouldn't be a fair assessment. The Free Anunnaki, having no centralized capital planet like the Delluvians or Astradians, were essentially an association based on their species, agreeing to work together. An Anunnaki may just as likely be loyal to a colony world controlled by Foris, though.

It was all rather complicated.

Speaking on behalf of the Free Anunnaki was Primus Heptali, a tall, bronze-skinned, blonde-haired woman, rail-thin, with ice-blue eyes and a soft air about her that did not match the stern set of her face. She stood to acknowledge the question, clasping her hands in front of her.

"Between Serapis Major and Minor, we have four water-rich worlds, primarily Anunnaki, and in full cooperation. Emphasizing the earlier points made by my colleague in the Delluvian delegation, the war effort requires a steady production line of ship-to-ship missiles. We will continue to manufacture the missiles and provide them under the provisions of our proliferation agreement with the United Coalition. I will designate a representative to form a new operation dedicated to providing oxidizer from our offshore refineries."

She looked directly at Norla and smiled. "Your request will be met with zeal, Representative."

The rest of the meeting took a turn after that. It was hardly a love fest, but neither was it a dysfunctional family Thanksgiving dinner. No, it was something in between. Which meant progress was being made.

Somehow, the throughline of cooperation percolated in between fits and starts of disagreements, but the line held. The notion that if one of these links fell through the whole movement would collapse hung over the proceedings and served as a guide that kept everyone on track.

Di tousled her shoulder-length hair and rubbed her elbow against mine. "Would you look at this? You have a way with words, Will. I think you managed to put the fear of the divine into these people."

I shook my head. "Hardly. I just made it clear that if they don't play nice with each other, we're all going to die, and it's going to be their fault."

Di laughed. "You're going to join us for drinks once this is over, right? Because you still owe us a round. That 'put it on my tab' crap doesn't work with us."

I thought about it, feeling wary of her inviting smile. But… I'd made a promise, and they had gotten me out of a tight spot. "I guess, if we're going to have a few weeks before the next surge. One night won't hurt anything."

She put her hand on top of mine and squeezed it. "I'll hold you to it."

<h1 style="text-align:center">7</h1>

MARCUS EDDISON STOPPED me before I could file out of the meeting.

"Will, do you have a moment for our little chat?"

There was no avoiding it, and I wanted to have a discussion about superweapons anyway. "Sure."

Eddison turned to his entourage. "Dontae, wait here. I'd like this to be a private meeting."

"Of course, sir," Dontae replied, leaning his back against the wall and drawing his tablet from a pocket on his lab coat.

Eddison led me to a smaller room along the hall. It looked like an office, but with little furniture and just a small table and four chairs. I was amazed at how huge his installation was, as it appeared to have endless rooms, with underground hangars that spanned several kilometers in width and depth. All under the Sahara Desert.

He sealed the door shut and took a seat, gesturing for me to do the same. So far, he hadn't said anything. He clasped his hands together and worked his jaw, eyes roaming the room like he was seeing it for the first time. I gave him a moment to collect his thoughts, bracing myself for an interrogation while simultaneously preparing to rip into him for having a spy on the Imperium's research and development team without informing the Coalition of that fact.

"Will, it's good to see you back."

"I'm glad for the respite," I said, trying and failing to gauge his intentions.

He made a face like he was considering whether he wanted to say what was on his mind or change the subject. I realized he was uncomfortable and began to wonder why. If anything, Eddison had always seemed oozing with confidence to the point of being *over*confident.

Earl had come into the room behind me and now settled on the table, lens switching between views of Eddison and me every few seconds. Eddison glanced at the drone, a curious grin forming on the edge of his mouth.

"How goes the documentary, Hero of the Rebellion?" The smile faded as if it had never been.

"About that." I waved a hand at Earl. "Are we sure this is really necessary?"

"It is. I witnessed your actions back there. General Mira'dna did, too. Cameras guarantee the rest of the United Coalition will see it, and that will boost your influence among the soldiers. It conveys a message of power, and steadiness, and joint collaboration among the groups that form the government. Your role in all this is more important than you realize, Will."

"All I did was point out how stupid it is to argue when there's a war going on. We have to finish the fight before we can go back to the good old days of hating each other."

"Don't sell yourself short. You cut right through longstanding grievances in a way that many have tried, and few have succeeded. Your ignorance of the galaxy prevents you from realizing what you're asking of these races. I wonder if you knew what you were up against, whether you'd be so willing to tread in the manner you have. Best not to do the research, Will, because what you're doing— it's working."

It felt like flattery. Like he was putting me on, or building me up. For what, I wasn't sure. All I knew was that now it made me uncomfortable.

I shrugged. "I'm just doing what I think is right. What'll help Earth keep from becoming like the Vorvak root world."

The easy smile returned to Eddison's face. "That's it. That's *exactly* it. You have risen to the forefront of this movement as a sort of moral compass. You are a symbol as much as you are a Navigator and a soldier."

I smiled with self-deprecation. "Well, I'm not much of those, either. I've only been Navigating for a few months, and I wouldn't call myself a soldier. If not for the neural lace…"

"A neural lace can't take up arms against the Imperium, nor can it pull the trigger. You have been a part of every major battle of this war in one way or another. That is an achievement worth recognizing. It is—in fact—the reason why I came up with the PR campaign to get your name and face in front of every member of the United Coalition. What we're building here is more than a military force. It's also more than just reviving the old carcass of the Galactic Federation."

I wondered if this, ultimately, was what Eddison meant to get at. "What do you mean?"

"This is an opportunity to change things. One that may not come again. Now, to an extent, we're already doing that. Just getting all these groups together and willing to call themselves a United Coalition is an achievement. If we can make this a group of sovereign nation states with a coequal arbiter that manages disputes, rather than a centralized governing body that dictates policy, then—"

I frowned and held up my hands. "Slow down there, George Lucas. This is way too much politics for me. I'll leave all that to the Council to decide on. My focus is on the war. I want the Imperium gone, and I want the whole of Earth left out of it so I can get back to living my life."

"Alright, Will," Eddison said. "I won't bore you any further. But please know that I only bring the matter up because I value your opinion. You're more than just a figurehead. Now. Let's get to how you handled my infiltration agent."

I was taken aback by the blunt way Eddison changed subjects.

"He was treated very unfairly by your forces on the ground, I understand."

I couldn't hold my neutral expression. I felt the anger rise up and did my best to keep it in check. "Your *spy* was working to rebuild a weapon that ought not exist. We destroyed the planet-killer weapon on Kastar for a reason, Marcus. That technology needs to disappear and never resurface. It's immoral to possess that kind of power."

He blinked but said nothing.

"When were you going to inform us that you had inserted a spy into the Imperium's development team?" I waited a beat. "Or *were* you going to inform us?"

He let out an awkward laugh. It was the sound of someone getting caught with their hand in the cookie jar and trying to shrug it off with humor.

I didn't laugh with him. If he was feeling tension or pressure, all the better. My face was granite as I waited for him to explain himself.

"Will, if I may be straight with you, this is an area where you could use some refinement. You don't understand the reality of intergalactic warfare. The snippets of exposure and the stories told of the Imperium's rise to power do not provide you with the sorts of insight you seem to think you have."

"I know what that weapon can do. Saw it in action myself. I don't need any other exposure or stories beyond that."

"Granted," he said with a nod. "But do you honestly believe that the Imperium isn't trying to rebuild the technology? Have you somehow convinced yourself that my agent *brought* them the schematics you found? Gave them a lifeline? Will, they already had it, and we wouldn't have had the slightest idea were it not for him."

"So his plan, then, was to sabotage the weapon? Find and destroy all traces of it?"

I could tell from the look on Eddison's face that wasn't it.

He knew that I knew and didn't try to hide it. "The Imperium had a breakthrough. You destroyed the prototype. Despite whatever Atron told you, that wasn't the end of it. You can see that now, I hope. They will work, with or without my agents, to do it again. For as long as they need to. They won't hesitate to use the weapon when they have it." His expression darkened. "We require the ability to respond in kind. That's the only way to prevent such a weapon's use."

I held up a hand. "I understand the concept of mutually assured destruction, believe me. I get why it's necessary, but I'm not convinced it needs to be necessary in this case. We've already pushed the enemy back. The only thing left to do is to put them down for good. We don't need to destroy whole planets to make that happen."

Eddison took in a breath. "That's wishful thinking, Will. Not a strategy for winning this war."

I shook my head. This wasn't my decision alone, and it wasn't his either. I was sure General Mira'dna, Atron, and the other leaders of the coalition would all get their say.

I knew where I stood, though.

"Marcus, how many spies do you have running in Imperium circles? What information are they providing you? Are they working on these elsewhere? Because we should prioritize the worlds that have similar labs if so. Don't keep this information to yourself."

Eddison nodded. "I currently have a network of fourteen spies in various positions and levels of the Imperium. They funnel their informational reports to me, and I direct them. So far, the planet killer work was limited to the one location, which is why I pushed so hard for this campaign."

"It's a wonder the Imperium didn't try harder to defend control of the world in that case," I said.

He shrugged. "Maybe that's all they had. Maybe you're right about how close they are to collapse. My informants don't paint a pretty picture inside the Imperium. Tror is isolated, and the planets from which the Imperium derive their power are incredibly far away, even considering a Void Drift. We're talking *years* in the Void, Will. There's a reason the Federation built its hegemony unchallenged by the Imperium for so long."

That was interesting to me. Most of the research I had time for was all about the "local" planets and species we were looking to free from Imperium rule. The former members of the Federation. What was known about the Imperium itself was scant.

The planets were believed to be Anunnaki home worlds, and the first Anunnaki had made their way to this portion of the galaxy long before there was an Imperium. That species seems capable of thriving just about anywhere, which is why there are so many of them compared to say, Vorvaks.

When the Imperium raiders first showed up, they were deemed a nuisance. Some people, like Benegal, had a love-hate relationship with them. They saw the desire for conquest but also saw a potential tool in their war against the Federation.

Galactic politics was complicated, but what I did know was that the Imperium we were fighting was effectively an occupying force meant to be self-sufficient. Far away from the ruling structure and resources of the Imperium proper.

Eddison stood, signaling that our meeting was now over. "I will have Dontae send you and General Mira'dna a detailed report of my undercover operatives. Perhaps that will disabuse you of the notion that I am working at cross-purposes with the Coalition."

"Thank you," I said, because I didn't know what else to say. I had a lot to think about.

I wished I could talk this stuff over with Fera and Quin. Actually, I'd like to be in the crew room of *Phaelon* to talk it over with everyone.

Eddison smiled. He tilted his head and scratched at his business-perfect hair, eyes roaming the room in his awkward manner for a few moments. I felt a pregnant pause develop and stretch. I stood to leave when he stopped fidgeting. "You know, the rebellion could not have gotten to where it is now without your contribution. I mean that, Will."

"I think you overestimate my value to this whole thing."

He shook his head, the smile still on his face. "No. I have contributed to the fight in my own way, but you have, as well. It's been truly remarkable to see you take to the role of ambassador with such aplomb. You have your own style, and it's infectious. It's the glue holding these very different groups together."

A tickle of pride ran through my chest, but I stowed it. I wasn't looking for compliments. I just wanted to win the war and keep Earth safe. Eddison was a big part of why we had a fighting chance. I didn't like how indebted that made me feel to him, and I could see it on his face that he knew I felt that way.

"You know"—he stretched the words out, steepling his fingers—"now that we've held you up in a very public way in the Coalition media channels, there's been a lot of cross-talk amongst the factions. Astrada is the largest remaining stronghold of Imperium control, but one of my agents has informed me of the situation there."

Astrada. Fera's root world.

It was a significant source of non-Anunnaki Imperium officers. If the people of that world were hesitant to remain aligned with the Imperium, it spoke volumes about the effectiveness of our war effort. I didn't relish the idea of engaging the Imperium there, the same as I wouldn't look forward to fighting them on Earth. Fera had told me a little about her people, and despite their prominence in positions of power and influence, they seemed to live simple lives on their home world. I imagined the villages, filled with the young and the old, trying to raise a defense against white-armored, SMG-toting Imperium soldiers.

"So what's the situation?" I asked.

Eddison inclined his head. "Tenuous, to say the least. The Imperium, rather than strong-arming their largest supporter, is now courting them. This is a significant change in tactics."

"Courting them? Prefect Tror's trying to make a deal or something? That doesn't sound like the Foris I keep hearing about."

"Prefect Tror is no fool. You need to keep that at the forefront of your mind, because by now, he knows your name and he recognizes that it's no coincidence the tide has turned since you got involved. Aside from the chatter amongst the factions concerning your burgeoning celebrity status, the Imperium recognizes your ability to unite various species as their greatest challenge. So far, the plans you have a hand in developing, they have a hard time counteracting."

"And now they're trying to replicate that? Make the Imperium one big happy family?"

"Maybe. But there is something else you're not considering, Will. You have the most to lose here. You are unique amongst the members of the United Coalition. Your world was never conquered. What do you think Tror intends to do about that?"

That threw me. I didn't know how to respond to it. He was right, after all. Earth had been deemed too out of the way, too underdeveloped to be of any use to the Imperium. That had changed since I'd entered the scene. At the first sign of danger, I'd dropped a planet killer that had annihilated a third of Tror's fleet.

No one had seen that coming, least of all, Tror himself.

"So you're telling me that Tror wants to hit Earth to prove a point? Shake up what we're accomplishing? How?"

Ever since we'd gone on the offensive, Tror had been reacting. Adjusting. Trying to tighten his grip on the territory he still controls. He hasn't had the means or the opportunity for a counterattack.

"Astrada," Eddison said in a soft voice. "I don't know everything, Will, but I know a great deal. My agents are telling me Astrada is important."

"To the Coalition, or to the Imperium?"

"To the war. If Astrada can be liberated... the remaining systems will fall in line. If Tror has his way, he may solidify a force capable of punching at Earth. Now, we can stop that, of course. But... if we maneuver our fleets to protect Earth..."

I frowned. "What would the other worlds in the Coalition think about that?"

Eddison gave a curt, single nod. "Now you're thinking like Tror. He's preparing a no-lose situation for himself. If he hits Earth, that shakes the faith of our alliance. If we stop him, he will water any seeds of doubt that you, Will, put your home world ahead of theirs. You see why this is a problem."

I did. I just wasn't sure what to do about it.

Eddison had already considered the matter, and now he was laying it out for me. "I think it would serve us best to get you on the ground, there at Astrada. They are not an Imperium stronghold. They will receive you. The Astradians will feel honored to have the opportunity to speak with the Earthborn ambassador."

I blew out a breath. "Then I guess we should give them that opportunity."

Earl chittered at my ear and slowly orbited my shoulders.

"Don't worry," Eddison said. "He can't record these private conversations."

"Would be nice if there was an off switch to him sometimes," I admitted.

Eddison looked at me compassionately. "I know. This isn't easy for you. But it's good for a shared future."

I nodded and then headed toward the exit, Earl in tow.

"Will," Eddison called out after me. "Would you like me to tell you how to turn your camera drone off?"

I turned and looked at him over my shoulder. "Sure."

He smiled. "Win this war."

I smiled back. "Let's do it."

8

IT HAD BEEN five months of constant action since we'd hit the Imperium fleet on Kastar. I could complain that I was going nonstop, but so had a lot of people. That's not what had me on edge as I killed time sitting at the bar in the officer's mess on the *Earthborn*. No, I was feeling on edge because *Phaelon* was supposed to have arrived yesterday but hadn't shown up in Earth orbit.

No messages from Quin or Fera, either.

They had missions of their own, with timetables matching timetables. Quin had said the expected rendezvous was looking good, but I knew at the time I received that pre-recorded message that it wasn't a sure thing. Knowing that didn't prevent me from worrying.

The shipboard cycle was late—a little after 2200. I should have been catching up on rest. Instead, I was nursing my frayed nerves with a beer.

Di took the seat next to me. She flashed a dimple-ridden smile and ordered a pair of drinks. "Looks like you've been up a while, Will."

"Probably too long," I said and then rolled the bottom of the beer bottle in circles on the bar top. I didn't look up to meet her gaze.

Usually, Di brought a smile to my face. She was a good friend, with an infectious positivity. She's also pulled me out of enough close calls from the seat of her starfighter for me to consider her my guardian angel.

"What's eating you?" she asked.

I shrugged and then figured I may as well confide in her. "*Phaelon.* They were supposed to be back by now."

"Ah," she said, sounding as though it wasn't a topic she was excited to discuss. "You really wear your heart on your sleeve, Will. Don't worry about things you can't control. They'll be back."

The bartender dropped two glasses onto the bar. "Order up."

The liquid that sloshed inside the tumblers was a reddish gold, and it smelled faintly of hickory and spice. Di hefted one of them and drained it in a single gulp. She inverted the glass, set it back on the counter, and pushed it back toward the bartender with a satisfied sigh.

"You trying to catch up?" I asked with a crooked smile, hefting the dregs of my beer bottle.

"Oh, please," she said and then playfully patted my cheek. "I could drink you under the table, human."

I laughed. "I don't doubt that."

"People aren't big drinkers on your root world, huh?" she asked. "Where I grew up, on Trasp, it's a way of life. If you're tall enough to reach the bar, you're old enough to drink."

The sudden memory of her home world—a world ruined by the Imperium—caused her to purse her lips. I wasn't the only one who could wear their heart on their sleeve.

"Sounds like a great way to guarantee everyone's an alcoholic by the time they turn eighteen."

"That some kind of special age for humans?" she asked.

"I suppose so," I said, remembering too late that despite how similarly Anunnaki and humans looked, we were different species. In fact, there was so much cultural difference between the Anunnaki, that they felt sort of like a macrocosm of humanity—diverse cultures spread throughout the galaxy, just like humans were spread across Earth in their own varied cultures.

She lifted her second glass, swirled it, and paused to savor the aroma. "It takes away the mystery of it. Nobody needs to prove how good we are at drinking because we all do and have done it for years."

"That's one way of looking at it, I guess. What're you drinking?"

She said something that translated to bourbon in my ears.

"You game to give it a try?" she asked, shaking the glass in front of me.

I caught a stiff inhale of the stuff. It smelled strong. "I'm not much of a drinker, and what I have historically been able to keep down has been beer. So I'll pass."

She laughed. "Spoken like a true lightweight."

I finished my bottle. "That sounds suspiciously like a challenge, Di."

"Will, stop," she said with a grin. "You're going to bite off more than you can chew."

She downed her second glass and set it upside down next to the first. The bartender came by, swiped up the glasses, and swept a rag beneath them in one smooth motion. He was back a moment later with a third tumbler of the stuff.

"So what brings you out drinking tonight?" Di asked. "If you're feeling blue for your friends, alcohol probably isn't going to be the best help."

I nodded glumly. "Yeah. I know. It's less that and more… it takes the edge off, you know?"

Di nodded. "I know. We're all feeling it. The war's going well, but it's still no picnic. Especially after Elbun Gal."

"Not a picnic for the Imperium, either," I said. "Not when they've got to go up against you and your squad."

She punched my shoulder playfully. "Let's not forget our Hero of the Rebellion."

I shrugged her off. "I hate that, honestly. I'm the same as everyone else."

Di frowned. "No, you're not. You're a Navigator. You're from Earth. Every major move we've made against the Imperium, you've been a part of it. You may not like the title, but you've earned it."

"I'm learning," I allowed, "but I'm not a great soldier, like Sert. Or a great pilot, like Fera. Or even a great Navigator—"

"Like Quin," Di interrupted. "Boo hoo."

I smiled and shrugged. "I get by is what I'm saying. But not enough to get put on a pedestal the way I have been."

"From what I've seen, you've been in the thick of it and you're still kicking," Di said. "How much more do you reckon you'll have to do in order to earn greatness?"

A pause formed, and I let it spread into the next few seconds.

Di's expression grew serious. Some people, they look their best when their eyes are glowing and they have a smile on their face; when you can feel the joy just beaming off of them. Di, she was pretty, but when she got solemn, it was like her features sharpened. Her beauty resolved with a clarity that was diminished when she was being her over-the-top self.

"You okay?" she asked.

I shook my head and smiled. "I'm okay. You're right. They're going to be okay."

She slapped her hand on the bar. "One more!"

The bartender produced another glass and filled it.

"Sure you don't want to slow down?" I asked. "You're about to have more in five minutes than I've had in an hour."

"This one isn't for me. It's for you," she said, offering me the glass. "Drink it. I'm tired of seeing you mopey. It's not very heroic."

I made a face. "Earl is in maintenance. I'm allowed to let the mask fall off when there are no cameras around."

"I've watched you long enough tonight, Will. Trust me, you need this. It'll take your mind off of things. That's why you came here, isn't it?"

I gave the glass a sniff. It made my eyes water.

Sensing my hesitation, Di placed her hand over mine and gently pushed it toward my face.

"You put the glass against your lips, open your mouth, and tilt your head back," she said in a slow, mocking tone.

"I know how to drink from a glass, Di," I said.

"Then do it, hero!"

I took it in one gulp, the same way I saw her. The liquor scorched its way down my throat and distorted my expression. Di clapped me on the back.

"Shake it off, hero."

"Yeah, yeah. I'm good." I cleared my throat, surprised at how much the alcohol burned going down. My eyes watered.

"You know, Will, when I first met you, I never thought things would turn out this way."

I blinked away the welling tears and managed to control the rasp in my voice when I said, "What do you mean?"

She shrugged. "I mean, I didn't think we'd stand a chance against the Imperium. I grew up under their thumb. On Trasp, before… it wasn't an easy life. I'm not crying about how tough it was, I'm just saying… even though we're in the middle of a war and that's its own nightmare…" she trailed off, her mind going to its own troubles.

"It's something," I said.

A wistful cloud came over her eyes. "Yeah. It is."

"Now imagine how surprised the Imperium must be."

That got her smiling again.

We made small talk for a few minutes, razzing each other about flying habits and a dozen little things. The liquor settled into my chest with a warmth like sitting beside a fire in the heart of winter. I felt a little lightheadedness coming on, and a tickle in my gut.

"You know, that stuff wasn't half bad," I said.

Her grin was infectious. "Sometimes, the exotic things are worth trying. At least once."

I blinked. I wasn't sure if it was the alcohol or if the Hero of the Rebellion stuff was inflating my ego, but it sounded like there was some innuendo packed into her remark.

She placed her hand on my shoulder. Nope, not the alcohol or my ego, then.

"Will… are you and Fera a thing?"

I sputtered. "What? What makes you say that?"

Hardly the correct answer to give, but it's what came out.

She pulled on my arm. "I've seen the way you look at each other. The intense eye contact. It's hard not to notice, but I wasn't sure if that meant…"

Di let things trail off, leaving it for me to pick up from there.

Her comment threw me a little bit. Fera and I weren't exactly keeping our relationship a secret, but I thought we'd been more discreet about it in public. "Yeah, we're, uh… we're seeing where it goes."

Di studied me for a moment. "That explains why you're so preoccupied with the ship returning, I suppose. You're protective of her."

I chucked. "Fera doesn't need protecting."

Di patted my cheek. "Oh, don't get me wrong. It's cute."

I leaned away, feeling that I needed to make up for being coy with my earlier response. "Anyway, that's part of it, yeah. But I don't just worry about her. I think about the rest of the crew, too. I want her—and them—to survive the war. But really, that goes for everyone."

A mischievous look crossed Di's face. "Including me?"

I narrowed my brow. "Of course."

She patted my hand with hers, lingering a little longer than the gesture called for, her golden amber eyes locking with mine. "Fera's a lucky one."

I had thought of Di as a friend ever since we'd escaped Jyraxis. I'd noticed her being a little flirty, but she had that sort of fun-loving personality that made me not want to read too much into it. She was great, though. And beautiful.

The booze was driving that aspect home with aplomb.

But I was with Fera, and I was happy about that. I couldn't tell you the ins and outs of Astradian courtship, but I know how it works for humans. Di wasn't an option.

Plus, Fera seemed like she'd literally kill me if I cheated on her.

I drained the last of my beer and stood up, using the bar to steady myself. "I appreciate your friendship, Di."

"Easy there," she said, holding out a hand as if to help steady me. "You gonna be okay finding your quarters?"

Through the alcohol, I still detected the barest hint of hope lifting her tone half an octave.

"I'll manage, thanks."

"Get some rest, hero. Who knows the next time you'll get the chance."

"Ain't that the truth," I said and then did my best not to stagger away from the bar.

"If you need anything, Will," she called after me, a smile returning the dimples to her face, "you know where to find me."

"Likewise," I said without thinking. Then, realizing the kind of trouble a promise like that could get me into, I got out of there.

I AWOKE in my quarters and alone a few cycles later, feeling rested and a little hungover. Despite so many years in college, I was hardly a seasoned drinker. The times I had gone overboard, however, led me to recognize that a workout was a painful but effective remedy for a night of too much drinking.

Thankfully, the *Earthborn* was a capital ship, and as such was basically its own small town. It wasn't all combat stations and sleeping quarters. Anything a warfighting force might need was on board. Including a gym.

The workout didn't suck as bad as I expected it would. After a shower and a trip to the mess hall, I was feeling pretty good. I was just finishing up my meal when I got the message from Sert that he and Benegal had returned from an out-and-back to Farakar.

"I thought you guys were with Fera and *Phaelon*," I said.

Sert, in his blunt way, told me otherwise. "An alternate plan was decided."

Evidently Sert went to recruit a few Vorvak tribes to the United Coalition cause. It was a good idea, the fulfillment of a promise he'd made when last leaving his root world. Despite my disappointment that seeing him wouldn't come with the opportunity to also see Fera —still no word from *Phaelon*—I was eager to hear how the recruitment went.

A brisk ten-minute walk led me to the armory and range. Because where else would a Vorvak be waiting?

The smell of pneumatic grease, oil-based lubricants, and ozone percolated on the air. I strode past a dozen occupied shooting lanes, ignoring the throbbing magnetic pulses of weapons discharges as I made my way to the far side of the room.

Benegal was cycling through several weapons, inspecting the different rifles. Thanks to a transparent safety window, I could see Staff Sergeant Berrios and his team training.

Sert stood at a counter, his shotgun broken down and spread

before him. A pile of soiled rags rested next to the parts. The Vorvak was so large and imposing, he looked like a giant huddled over a garage workbench. It was always surprising to see how dexterous his claws could be when it came to weapons.

His nictitating membranes clicked in their sideways blink over his large, orange eyes as I approached. "Will Kaufman. It has been too long."

"Only a couple of weeks," I said, turning to watch Benegal move into the range with a few rifles he wished to use. "Good to have you back, though. We do our best work together."

Benegal wasted no time selecting a free lane and firing two shots, pinholing dead center on the digital target. Broken pixels floated to the floor, leaving red circles where his rounds had landed. They blinked for a few seconds, then returned to their unaltered state.

These pixelated targets were pretty cool. They could resize by command, allowing you to effectively fire from any range without needing the wide open space that was so often a premium aboard a ship.

The Krayvox's cranial spines flared with a blue hue as he dropped the magazine out of the rifle and inspected the chamber. He set the weapon on the shooting table before him and turned to give me a curt nod through the glass.

"Our mission was semi-successful," he said, communicating over comm, direct to my fiber-link.

"Oh yeah?" I asked, looking to Sert for confirmation.

The big Vorvak grumbled but didn't answer. Evidently, Benegal was doing the talking for them both.

"The Banner of the War Torch flies above Farakar once again," Benegal said.

I thought I detected a bit of sarcasm in his reply.

Sert rolled his eyes. "The lizard is right. My people are so eager for war, they do not wait for the Imperium to attack."

"So… they're launching a preemptive strike? How are they getting off world?"

"The fight was with one another," Benegal hissed.

My eyes went wide. "Another civil war? What would that be, like the fiftieth?"

"Thirty-third," Sert said matter-of-factly. "But I have ended it. Tentatively."

I nodded my approval. "You brought them around. Good, good. So the Vorvak will fight against the Imperium now?"

Sert gave a noncommittal grunt. I looked through the glass at Benegal, who only shook his head.

"The difficulty," Sert began, "is the Vorvak's current state. They see that a war against the Imperium will lift them from their primitive squalor. And so they fight to see which tribe will be the ones to board the Coalition ships once they arrive."

"Kinda hoping to throw all the tribes at the Imperium," I said.

Benegal sighed. "The Imperium's destruction of Farakar was complete. It has set the Vorvak back several millennia, and with no means of sustaining their population. I mean no insult to Sert when I say that the Vorvak cannot see the value in setting aside their differences."

"Not all of my people are worthy to lead. None, in fact, left on Farakar seem to be."

"There's got to be a way to fix that, though," I said. "Maybe we can put together some aid drops? It would have to be subtle, so the

Imperium didn't get wind of what we were trying and hit Farakar again."

Sert stared at me for a moment. "If you need to hydrate, you do not fill your canteen with rocks."

I looked confusedly at my friend. "Is that an analogy, or…?"

"There is no Throne of Stone. Mine is a people who have lost their way. They will commit to no one and nothing." Sert shook his head in disgust. "They will die out as a bitter memory of what they once were."

"That doesn't seem very… I don't know, *Vorvak*, to me. They aren't willing to fight the enemy that did this to them?"

Benegal drew his lips into a thin line. He looked like he wanted to say more but maybe didn't feel like it was his place to do so. Finally, he introduced an alternate problem. "You will find strong opposition in the United Coalition. They will not freely give their resources to the Vorvak."

Sert shrugged like this was a given. "Aid will not fix what ails my people. Factions and tribes make war against each other."

"Well, hey, you gave it a shot," I said. "Benegal said this was semi-successful. What's the good news?"

"I have brought with me the remnant of the Old Guard. A mere four thousand of my brethren."

"You have *thousands* of Vorvak with you?" I said. If a drink had been in my hand, I'd have performed a spit take. "Sert, if they fight half as good as you, that's like having an entire additional army."

"Thousands more remain on Farakar," Sert said somewhat hotly, before he became morose. "Where they will kill each other until the name of Vorvak is erased from galactic history. These refused—*refused*—the call to arms. They are a disgrace to our people."

The big guy stayed quiet for a moment as he pieced together his shotgun. After securing the receiver to the grip, he locked the pins into place and racked back the pump action.

"So these Vorvak," I said. "I'm assuming they fight for you, and not the Coalition."

Sert gave a slight nod. "I am their Warrior General."

"This is great," I said, feeling a surge of adrenaline in my chest. "That's a significant force. Larger than the militia Eddison managed to build up."

Benegal gave me a warning look. "Not all will be as pleased with this development as you, Will. The Vorvak are not held in high esteem by any world."

"Come on," I balked. "We're at war. And if Sert is their Warrior General, there's a track record the United Coalition can grasp onto if it helps them sleep better at night. You've more than proven yourself against the Imperium, big guy."

A wicked grin stretched across Sert's face. At first, I thought he was happy about the compliment, but I soon realized he was reliving a happy memory. "I conquered them. My guard will fight the Imperium until the Day of Reckoning comes for each of us."

"The Coalition is worried about what comes after." I said it for Benegal's benefit, not wanting him to think that I didn't comprehend what he was warning about.

Benegal took another shot with his rifle, a bullseye. He set the weapon down and rejoined the conversation. "Rightly so. The galaxy has seen such things before."

I frowned. "What comes after isn't going to be easy. Everyone seems to have something they're hoping for, and often, those things are mutually exclusive."

Benegal nodded. "There is an expectation that the Federation will be revived from the ashes. Many wish for this. I do not."

He stared at me with his hollow, dark eyes. The lizard-like features of his face still provoked a certain discomfort in me. It was an instinctual thing, something that no matter what I did, I couldn't *not* feel it.

"You will not stand for a New Federation, will you?" I asked. "Even one that is built from the ground up to handle the grievances you fought against?"

Benegal snorted. "I will not. One man's Federation is another man's Imperium."

I crossed my arms. "What's your solution, then?"

Benegal spread his hands. "What we have now is working. It should stay that way. A united coalition. No central governing body to dictate what is acceptable for the whole. We do not need puffed-up dignitaries drawing the boundary lines of our territory, or dictating what we may and may not do on any given day. We need to be left to our own devices."

"I can get behind that," I said, knowing even as I said it that Quin and Fera and several others on the Council would have different ideals. "We'll just have to wait and see where things go once the Imperium are dealt with."

"It is not the way of the Krayvox to kowtow to the will of outsiders."

"I take it that's why you started working with the Imperium, way back in the beginning," I guessed.

Benegal nodded. "They promised us our freedom back. It was a lie. We traded one shackle for another. We will not make the same mistake again."

"Does Atron feel this way, too?"

Benegal stiffened. "Is he not Krayvox?"

I sucked in an exasperated breath and blew it out. "This is going to get messy."

It was something we needed to have ironed out before the war's end; otherwise, we might just roll from one conflict into another. The end of World War II came to mind, and all the atrocities of the Soviet Union and other communist dictatorships. The subsequent Cold War that followed.

"Blood," Sert said, stowing his shotgun into his shell armor. "The Vorvak will be ready."

"The Krayvox, as well," Benegal added.

I put a hand on each of their shoulders. "We'll keep working on it. The Imperium hasn't bowed out yet. One problem at a time, right?"

Both aliens gave me sidelong glances. They were already looking ahead.

The tenuous agreements between factions would start to fray under the strain of our success. It was ironic. The war effort was the only commonality between them. But the likelier victory looked, the easier it was to abandon that commonality and focus on unsettled issues that would soon need a reckoning.

I was starting to feel like we were standing on quicksand, just waiting for the sinkholes to start opening up.

My fiber-link pinged with an alert. I gave a sigh of relief when I read it.

A smile was plastered on my face as I relayed the news.

"They're back."

9

THE *PHAELON* PULLED into the docking bay, atmospheric thrusters unleashing gouts of air as it settled into place. I crossed the threshold of the entrance doors, marveling at the sight of the Voidship against the backdrop of open space. The forcefield that kept the vacuum at bay was undetectable by the human eye, but a highlight in my fiber-link's HUD told me it was in place.

That, and the technicians scrambling around to hook up the refuel line and to secure the struts in place with magnetic clamps were moving about freely in artificial gravity. I remembered when Lockett had opened up the forcefield on the *Seventy*—an Imperium ship we assaulted at the beginning of my starfaring adventures— with disastrous results for the enemy caught in the wave of decompression.

The ramp hit the deck, and Fera came striding down in her armor, her deep blue hair catching the light, accenting the blue hue of her skin.

"You're late," I said.

She put her hands on her hips and gave me a smile that was all mischief. "Don't start with me, Will Kaufman. I've got a lot to talk to you about."

I joined her on the ramp and followed her inside the ship. We weren't two steps in before I saw Lockett bumbling through the hold, buried in spools of nanowire. Dumpy rolled along behind him, flex probes carrying some of the loose wires like the train of a wedding dress. The bot swiveled its head unit toward me and twittered a light greeting.

"Still chasing the power flux issue?" I asked.

Lockett gurgled a curse at me, not even breaking stride as he bobbed like a penguin. The wire bundles swayed over his shoulders as he walked down the ramp.

Fera shrugged. "I've had to keep a tight leash on our Drayth friend. He's been threatening to ditch us again."

"He's had plenty of opportunities. I think he just says that for attention."

Quin's voice floated down from the ceiling. "I never thought I'd be thrilled at the sight of a knuckle-dragging ape like yourself, Will, but after two weeks of trying to swing the Astradians around to our cause, I'd take even the Vorvak's company."

I looked to Fera for confirmation. "Was it that bad?"

She snorted. "It was probably worse, actually."

I gave a teeth-baring grin. "Any good news? *Did* you get the contamination problem sorted out?"

"The Drayth and I are still working on that," Quin groused. "I can't do everything at once, you know, Will. I'm a Foris, not a miracle-worker."

"You're an AI," I said.

"A *Foris* AI. There is some good news, though. How to explain it so a primitive can understand?" Quin paused as if thinking it over. "The power draw on the systems is manageable for the time being. I've worked up an anti-intrusion subroutine, but it's taking up more and more of my processing power. We've rewired about forty percent of the *Phaelon*'s circuitry and need to do more."

"Still a work in progress," Fera concluded as she led me to her quarters. She stopped at the door. "Quin, why don't you dedicate a cycle to attacking that problem while I debrief Will on the mission?"

"Oh, sure. Work, work, work, work, work, work, *work*. Just because I'm an AI, that means I'm not worthy of downtime? Is that it? You know, my systems benefit from a little freedom. Even talking with the human and *especially* after the Drayth has been getting a little too touchy feely with my circuits."

"Glad to know I'm useful to you, Quin," I said. "That's… nice, actually."

"Well, explaining basic math keeps my algorithms sharp."

"…aaaand there it is."

"He missed you," Fera said to me under her breath. "Really."

But I was more interested in whatever lay behind the door to Fera's quarters. The promised debrief.

"Quin," I said, "we've got maybe ten days before we need to be back out there. This is the final push. This next campaign could decide the war. We need the *Phaelon* at full operating capacity. Please listen to Fera and take the time to see what you can do about the Fleuridian. I promise I'll come and hear all about angles and triangles from you in a little while."

"Very well. But don't think I don't know what's really going on in there. I wasn't born an AI, you know."

The speaker clicked, a respectful way the AI let us know that he had switched into an isolated state. Otherwise, you're constantly guessing and asking the ceiling, "Are you still there?"

"So what is 'really going on in there?'" I asked.

Fera threw her arms around me and pressed her lips against mine. The smell of cherry blossoms filled my next breath, sending static down the back of my neck. I wrapped my arms around her, my Drayth armor scraping up against hers.

I broke off the kiss and pressed my cheek against hers, fingers already working at her armor. She did the same, unlatching my shoulder panels. I slapped the switch for the door, sealing us inside her room. We stumbled, armor panels hitting the deck as we careened toward her bunk.

"How'd it go on Delluvia Astra?" she asked me between kisses.

"What's that?" I asked, scooping her up off the ground.

She let out a playful shriek and stopped asking questions.

In love and war, anything could happen.

———

FERA ADJUSTED her head on my chest. I held her against me, savoring the moment.

"You really did miss me, didn't you?" she asked.

"Yeah," I said. "Especially when I hadn't heard from you in a bit. I was worried."

"Worried?"

"A little," I admitted. "Things have been heating up with the

Imperium. The closer we are to winning this war, the harder they seem to fight."

She patted my chest, her blue-skinned fingers seeming almost purple in the faint overhead light. I ran my fingers through her hair, my eyes examining every inch of her. Of the many things I'd never expected when I left Earth, this was right up there at the top of the list. A romantic relationship with one magnetically attractive alien.

"I'll have to write a book about this one day," I said with a satisfied sigh.

She slapped my arm. "You better leave out parts like this."

"Pretty sure those are the parts that sell."

"You're gonna have to pick love or money, Will." She grabbed my chin and kissed me.

I smiled. "Easiest choice ever. I pick the money."

She leveled another slap and then mounted me as if about to deliver a UFC beatdown.

I held up my arms in surrender. "I pick love! I pick love!"

"I thought so," she said drily, rolling off me. She dropped from the bunk. "We'd better get dressed before Quin decides he's respected our privacy for too long."

"He seemed... surprisingly okay with us, didn't he? Did you guys work that out?"

"There's nothing to work out, Will. I never felt this way about him and told him the moment he revealed his... feelings for me." She said it with a shiver, like the thought was repulsive to her. "He's Foris. Or *was* a Foris."

I felt a pang of remorse for Quin's sake. He was a jerk, and he could be downright infuriating when he wanted to be, but he made the ultimate sacrifice to save Fera's life. That was worth a lot, and not just to me. It made him a moral, selfless person.

Or did he just do it because he cared for her and was hoping she'd be a bit more receptive after he saved her life?

No, it had to have come from a good place. He was an AI—knew he would be an AI when the *Phaelon* was finally recharged. They could never have a real relationship after that. At least, not a physical one.

Fera was watching me. "I can see that this is bothering you. More of that human empathy, I suppose? Quin is a good person. A great friend. Now get dressed."

I helped her into her armor, and she returned the favor.

"I really do want to know how it went on Delluvia Astra?" she said.

I gave her the quick version.

She nodded approvingly. "So the Delluvians are officially on the Council now. Sounds like you handled that pretty well. They can be tough to deal with."

"You can say that about every species, I think. Wait until you hear about Sert's mission with the Vorvak. But anyway, yeah, it went well. It would have been smoother with you there, I think. I'm still learning the social politics of the galaxy, but... yeah, I put each of them in their place, and they fell in line eventually."

"So tell me about the Vorvak, then?"

"Most were too busy fighting each other to join. Sert has about four thousand warriors under his command now. So that's terrifying."

She laughed.

I smiled briefly and then grew serious again. "The Vorvak situation does bring up another problem, though."

"What's that?"

"Whatever follows the fall of the Imperium. I get the sense that parts of this Coalition—Vorvak included—aren't on board with the idea of a new Federation."

Fera leaned against a bulkhead. "Well, they're going to have to get on board with it, anyway. A lot of what I talked with my people about was the idea of a New Federation. They didn't want any part of the United Coalition, but a reformed version of the Federation has wings."

"I talked with Eddison. He says the Imperium is trying to play nice with Astrada. You see anything like that?"

"They have a presence there, but no real power." Fera shrugged. "I'm no fan of the Imperium, but they got a few things right in their rise to power. Unfortunately, one of those things was providing the Astradians with an even larger footprint on the intergalactic stage than we had with the Federation."

"So how does that work exactly?" I asked. "Because every time you talk about your home world, you make it sound like a rural farming collective. Those types don't feel like galaxy-conquerors."

Fera gave a conciliatory nod. "Many of us were simple farmers and terrain scouts. Once we joined the Federation, they opened up a whole new outlook on things for us. Gave us the means to seek out opportunities as pilots, politicians, warriors, and the like. It was a good thing for us, and we did well. Progress, conquest, fighting—all of that was away from Astrada. Our world remained at peace. We kept a certain home world serenity while being the muscle for the Federation. That's why I was such a zealous agent. We were protecting our home world. Our way of life. But when the Imperium knocked down the Federation, it created a sort of power vacuum, and rather than fall into decline, my people sided with the new powerhouse."

"So did practically everyone else, so you can't blame them for that. The Imperium would have turned Astrada into another Farakar if they didn't fold."

"I know," she said with a shake of her head, "but I don't see why they wouldn't want to switch sides now. Even for the same reasons, at least. The Imperium is getting its face smashed in, but the Elders are not seeing it. They think the United Coalition is asking for their help because we're in dire straits."

"Wait, like they actually refused to join the Council?"

"Oh, no, they want seats on the Council. They'll straddle both sides of the fence without worry. They know how important they are to all parties."

"So what's the problem?" I asked.

Fera smirked, but it wasn't a real smile. It bordered on disgust. "They've made certain demands that we can't honor."

If the Astradians were being unreasonable, maybe that was why Eddison told me he wanted me to go visit that planet.

"How so?" I asked.

"They want guarantees the war won't come to Astrada airspace. That no soldiers will set foot on the planet, and"—she snapped her fingers as if she'd just thought of it—"they want the confinement and isolation of the Vorvak remnant to continue on after the Imperium, too."

I whistled. "We kind of already broke that Vorvak promise. Where did this all come from?"

"Prefect Tror."

I felt an internal oil slick shoot through my stomach. "You sure?"

"Absolutely. Astrada wants from the Coalition what you've secured for Earth. A promise to be spared the horrors of war."

"That's a side effect of Eddison's work and our good favor. It's not a condition—"

Fera held up her hands. "You don't have to convince me, Will. I already know this. How to convince my people that Tror is wrong... that's the real question."

I shook my head. "I don't know how the Federation pulled off any sort of unity beyond ruling with an iron fist like the Imperium. Everyone is so different, it feels impossible sometimes. Even just among our crew."

My words seem to take some of the spirit out of her. She looked glum, and I wondered if it was because of what I'd said. Were the various species that comprised the Coalition—even down to someone like Fera—*really* counting on me to somehow make this all work?

That seemed crazy.

It would have been crazier to just let her linger there in worry and doubt.

"Hey," I said, brushing a lock of hair out of her face, "we'll work it out. Things like this... politics... it takes time and effort. There's a solution out there, we just have to find it, polish it, and sell it."

She brushed her cheek against my hand. Her smile didn't fully diminish the sadness in her, but she took comfort in what I was saying, and it felt good. "You have a way with words, Will. Even when you're full of it."

I made a mock scowl. "If Earl heard you say that, he'd be very upset."

"If Earl were here you'd be a lot less happy about your life than you are right now," she noted.

The speaker in the ceiling clicked. "Is it safe?"

"I'm glad you're back, Quin," I said in the off chance that the AI really *did* like me.

"Good, you're clothed. I appreciate that. You know, interspecies fluid exchange is—"

Fera held up her hand. "Quin. Remember our deal."

I looked at her, not sure what she meant. She winked.

Quin was silent for a few moments. When he came back, he sounded chastened. "Very well. You are correct, after all. I've just… it's not easy for me, Fera."

"I know," she said in a soft, easy tone that surprised me, "but life is like that sometimes."

"Yes, well—I… I'm trying, Fera. It's—you can't expect me to… oh, all right! Enjoy your physical entanglements. Far be it from me to consider the impact your philandering might have on the crew."

"Look, Quin—" I started.

"Nope. Not necessary! If Fera wants to engage in life's primal delicacies with the lowest common denominator, that is absolutely none of my business. Sure, in the off chance you two are capable of producing offspring, they'll be mentally handicapped to the point of—"

"Quin, enough," Fera snapped.

"Fine. I'll just say my last piece and then you won't hear about it again." Quin's tone was biting. "Yes. Life is like that sometimes. If we all got what we wanted, there'd be no point in living, now would there? Some people get everything, and some people have to watch those people get everything. It's ironic, but it's reality. Unfortunately, some of us have to live in it."

Fera ran her hands through her hair, toning down the frizz, slowly restoring herself to a business casual level of put together. "There's the last word. Or I'll hold you to the consequences of our agreement. You know I will, Quin. Now send a message to the rest of the crew. Meeting in the ready room in ten minutes."

"Right away, Fera."

Quin's next words came over the bone conduction comm embedded in my fiber-link. He spoke directly to me so that Fera couldn't overhear. "I'm not petty enough to hold this against you, Will, but listen up, because I'll only say this once."

Fera stood and ran her hands over her armor, moving toward the door. I nodded to Quin, hoping to keep the conversation private.

"I'm not so inane that I ever thought she'd come around to feeling about me the way I so desperately desired, but… don't forget that I *am* the *Phaelon*. You do anything to hurt her, and I do mean *anything*… you may find yourself the victim of an accident. And I don't mean the routine accidents you have that require Dumpy to change your sheets every night."

I opened my mouth to deny the ridiculous accusation, then decided against it.

I didn't expect to get the father-cleaning-his-shotgun treatment from Quin, but there it was. I gave it to him, partly out of pity and partly because I appreciated his looking out for Fera in his own way.

"Understood," I muttered under my breath.

"You coming, Will?" Fera asked from the doorway.

"Right behind you."

10

I EXPECTED that the meeting aboard *Phaelon* would be a happy family reunion. After all, it had been a while since we'd all been together. I know I missed our motley crew, and I figured the feeling was mutual. It turned out that other thoughts were riding high in the minds of my alien crewmates.

Sert sat with his bulging arms crossed, his natural scowl seeming permanently etched into his broad face. He said nothing as Fera and Benegal traded barbs, their argument over—what else?—the Federation rapidly devolving into a shouting match.

I adjusted my position at the slab that served as the table, trying to see an area where compromise could be had between the two. It… wasn't looking good.

Fera and Quin wanted a New Federation. Benegal wanted the United Coalition to stay in place. Lockett wanted money.

Sert just wanted to kill things.

"This is why you never should have dethawed that criminal!"

J.N. CHANEY & JASON ANSPACH

Quin snapped. "If the lizard gets his way, shifting and unpredictable factions will be left to their own devices. I'm sure nothing can go wrong. It's not like the more powerful ones will continue building up their respective militaries and strongarm the weaker factions to bow to their every whim. Why, something like that is *unheard of* in the galaxy!"

Benegal's snout twitched with a derisive snort. "Interstellar commerce will be worked out between factions with no intermediary. Any central governing body will inevitably want a cut of whatever deal is made, and that will make them susceptible to bribes. We saw exactly this type of corruption with the old Federation."

"Isn't politics always like that, though?" I asked. "You honestly think that no one in a position of power in these factions is going to look out for themselves ahead of others?"

"With less centralized hegemony," Benegal hissed, "those who would seek power for their own enrichment will be easier to throw out."

"Or kill," Sert added.

Benegal nodded his approval at this. "Each faction will set up its leaders according to its own laws and customs. They will be responsible for their own defense. Anything else—any centralized power structure—will inevitably become an Imperium, regardless of what it is called."

Fera rolled her eyes. "The Federation did not lord its power over the factions. It allowed a neutral zone for mediating disputes and offered protection to the weaker factions if one of the stronger ones stepped out of line. The Krayvox were able to fend off the Irvlan invasion because of the Federation's influence. Or have you forgotten that?"

118

Benegal crossed his arms. "And in return they levied a bully tax on us. Fifteen percent of all exports to our benevolent saviors."

Fera shook her head. "War is expensive. I should also point out that your Final Equinox faction was a faction within a faction. No one elected you to represent the Krayvox."

Benegal gave a sly smile. "They came around."

I stood up, not wanting us to have to go back over the insurgency that marked Benegal's rise to power. "Let's try and focus more on the future instead of rehashing the past. We already know where one another stand on that."

Benegal jabbed a clawed finger at Fera, then turned to address me. "Destroying the Imperium is a service to the galaxy. Installing a new one in its place means you have learned nothing! I will not be a part of what she demands."

Suddenly, the shifting guide lights lit up inside the crew room.

"Quin, what are you doing?" I asked.

"Showing Benegal the door."

The Krayvox shook his head. "Gladly… but not until the Imperium is defeated."

"I'm glad to hear you say that," I said.

"I'm not," Fera countered. "What's that supposed to mean, anyway? You'll wait until the official Imperium surrender is broadcasted and then stab us in the back when we're not looking?"

"I suggested—" Benegal began.

"That's not what he said," I interjected, placing my hand on Fera's back.

She shrugged me off, staring murder at Benegal.

"There are enough credits for Lockett to be paid for his work.

Phaelon must demand of United Coalition that they pay Lockett's handsome sum. None of this is possible without Lockett."

"Later, Lockett," I said, trying not to sound as agitated with the Drayth as I felt.

"I'd like to try a new track in this discussion," Quin said.

I tossed my hands up in surrender. "By all means."

"Ahem. Benegal raises several salient points, though the manner in which he came to his conclusion is biased and flawed. There was no grand conspiracy by the Federation to punish the Krayvox—or the Vorvak for that matter. Be that as it may, the old Federation allowed a power vacuum that gave rise to the Imperium in the first place. It is a mistake the Council will not make a second time."

"More reason to leave the Council in place and return the fleet to its respective factions," Benegal insisted. "A weak authority, serving merely in an advisory role with no military might to enforce their own interests… that is the answer."

Fera seethed. She looked like all she wanted to do was lunge across the table and strangle the Krayvox.

I stepped in just in case she was really considering it.

"Benegal, look… I get your hesitation. I really do. Now you keep making the point that names don't mean anything. That the Federation and the Imperium, and a New Federation would all just be different names for the same thing."

"Correct. It is the structure and function of an entity that determines what it truly is."

I inclined my head. We were in agreement so far. "Right. So, what if the name of this new governing body is the New Federation, but it operates exactly like the United Coalition?"

Fera glared at me. "Be realistic, Will."

"He's so cute in his primitive, low brain-power naivete," Quin quipped.

I rolled my eyes. "It's not all that far-fetched, okay? Just listen."

I took in a breath, preparing myself for a long speech.

A chime sounded from the ceiling.

"Oh, this should be good," Quin said. "It looks like Marcus Eddison is giving an address to the Council. Transmission going to all factions. All right, people, alcohol is now available at the nutrient station. Rules of the game are, every time Eddison mentions Will or the Hero of the Rebellion, you have to drink."

"Quin, we're not doing that," I griped.

"Why not?" he asked innocently. "You all will be tanked in the first two minutes, I guarantee it. Hilarity will surely ensue."

"Because we'll die from alcohol poisoning," I said. "Even Sert."

"Doubtful," the Vorvak rumbled.

"Fine, fine," Quin said. "I'll just play the feed."

A hologram appeared on the wall, projecting Marcus Eddison and a podium with his company's logo embossed on the face of it. He wore a button-up shirt and blazer, and had a contemplative look on his face.

Applause filtered in through the ceiling speaker as the audio synced with the visual feed. Marcus cleared his throat as the crowd's reception died down.

"Thank you. Ladies and gentlemen of the United Coalition of Free Worlds, I would like to open my address tonight with a message of unity. As the war with the Imperium continues to rage, we draw ever closer to the inevitable conclusion: victory!"

The crowd roared.

"We have seen our fair share of gallantry under fire. It has been

—quite remarkable, really—to see so many of you putting aside your differences, coming together to unite against the greatest threat to prosperity the galaxy has ever seen."

He paused and took a moment to search the crowd. It was a rhetorical tactic, one I'd seen him use to great effect on TV back home. The energy in the room was almost palpable; people were hanging on to his every word.

Behind him, a hologram of the AX-71 fighter appeared, rotating slowly in all its splendor. Striking a more sober tone, Eddison pivoted and wiped his hand over the image, changing it to a video stream.

It was me, piloting that ship. The footage Earl captured of me flying over the surface of Delluvia Astra, cut with clips of Colonel Stalling's ground forces. It showed the Imperium taking a beating on the ground, and ended with the air strikes on the mountainside. I flew by in my AX-71, closing out the footage with a focused look on my face.

"That counts as a mention of Will," Quin said before Fera hushed him.

"As the enemy continues to defy the will of the people," Eddison said, "there is one Will they cannot stop, and that is Will Kaufman, the Hero of the Rebellion!"

The crowd exploded with applause. I felt sick to my stomach.

Quin was impish. "Four drinks already. You're right, Will. You'd be dead."

"He's laying it on pretty thick," Fera agreed.

The exchange didn't cause us to miss any of the speech because the applause lasted so long. Unreal.

Even so, the more Eddison talked, the less comfortable I felt.

"In the face of such evil, heroes rise up to meet the challenge. Will Kaufman came to the stars by happenstance. As though fate itself conjured him up from the interstellar ether." Dramatic pause. "But I say, no greater hero has graced our galaxy in such a time of need as this. He is the symbol of our unity—of our *United Coalition*."

The crew ready room was dead silent. The air felt constricted, like everyone was holding their breath, expecting to see a tiny alien burst out of my chest or something.

"He's making too much of this," I said with disgust. "Fera's piloting alone has done more than anything I have. My biggest accomplishment is Navigating the Void, and I couldn't have done that without Quin. The way he's telling it, I'm single-handedly winning the war!"

Benegal shifted on his feet. "He speaks what the people need to hear. My distrust for him is over the weapon."

And I hadn't even told them about the spy situation yet.

"This is wise," Sert said. "Eddison's motivations are irrelevant. Will has grown from a spawnling to a warrior. He has adapted to the fires of war. For that alone, he deserves the title. And if he dies... his martyrdom will be well worth the loss."

I appreciated his sentiment, but I disagreed. Especially with the whole martyrdom part.

Eddison continued on, mentioning my name at least three more times over the next several minutes. When it became apparent that he didn't have anything new or important to say—this was just a morale speech—we began to tune him out, trusting that Quin would alert us to anything pertinent.

"Lockett has seen this hustle before. Many credits for you, Will."

I looked suspiciously at the Drayth. "What do you mean?"

"Will can get Eddison more influence on council. Humans should charge for this."

"Charge for what? I'm not even on the Council."

"You hold sway over them," Benegal said. "The Drayth may be correct."

"Guys, no." I shook my head and told them about the spy and the second set of plans. "We hardly see eye to eye on things."

"Do you still have these plans?" Sert asked.

"No. I destroyed this copy as well once I verified it was legitimate."

The Vorvak's head lowered. "A shame."

"My point is that Eddison knows I'm not one to just go along with whatever he wants. As an influence peddler, I suck."

"He does have your planet," Quin said thoughtfully. "That primitive mud ball is a pretty big bargaining chip."

"Now you're sounding like Prefect Tror, making this about Earth. And anyway, Eddison doesn't 'have' it. He just lives there and built a fleet to defend it. That doesn't give him control over it."

The words fell flat even as I said them. That fleet left my country's entire military industrial complex sorely outmatched. Even if all of Earth united against it, they wouldn't last long in a straight-up fight. Orbital bombardment was something humanity could not defend against.

"Still convinced?" Fera asked.

"A little less than I was, yeah." I waved those concerns away. "Look. All I want is to see a swift end to this war. I'm willing to work just as hard for the galaxy to have peace afterward. These conversations are good, because what all of us are thinking and saying probably matches what our representative species or factions will think. At least we can speak our minds without the risk of starting a new batch of interplanetary warfare."

"But it will come to that," Quin said. "Perhaps sooner than later. That weapon really did a number on the Imperium Fleet. Tror's been on the run ever since, and every time he tries to consolidate his forces, the United Coalition rushes in and smashes things up, leaving the enemy to scatter. His play for Astrada is one of desperation."

"It won't work," I said, nodding at Fera.

She didn't seem eager to agree. Probably thought I was being naive. More wishful thinking.

"Of course," Quin said, having a discussion with himself, "there are several worlds still under Imperium control. Even if Tror is gone, they may form a sort of rebellion on their own, perhaps biding time until more Imperium arrive to shore up their conquest."

Fera looked worried at the suggestion. "You think they'd do that?"

"Not if we build another fleet and take the fight to them," Sert said, sounding animated and excited for the first time. "*There's* your unifying cause! We can deal with the post-war easily once the Imperium systems are conquered."

"Need I remind you that the Imperium systems are so distant, we have only guesses as to how expansive—and powerful—they truly are. They found the Federation. We didn't find them."

Lockett popped his head up from the nutrient dispenser. "Drayth can build fleet sufficient to destroy their root worlds. Drayth always over-deliver, despite being underpaid. Unappreciated in the grand scheme of things."

I looked down and pinched the bridge of my nose. "I already

had this discussion with your representative, Lockett. I'm not having this fight with you, too."

Lockett tilted his head. "You will pay up. One day, Drayth decide no more tech. No more upgrades. Then... mountains of credits will flow into our coffers."

"Your species aren't donating the tech, they're just being paid on a rate schedule decided by the Imperium," Fera pointed out. "You won't stop because stopping means you don't get paid and someone else supplies the ships. And you know it."

Lockett froze as if the idea hadn't occurred to him. He waved her off, muttering profanities from his iron lung.

"There is no reasoning with a biomechanical freak," Sert said. "That part of his soul was replaced long ago."

Fera pressed a thumb to her Tab. Her eyes glossed over as she read something in her fiber-link. When lucidity returned to her, she looked at me.

"Will, I need to talk to you. Alone."

11

"I just got a message from Di."

Of all the things Fera could have said to me, that felt like the worst. My mind raced. Was Di... I dunno, causing trouble? I felt a sudden shadow of guilt despite having done nothing wrong. I went to my room alone and stayed alone. I didn't even hint that I wished it could be some other way.

"It's serious," Fera said.

The sour pit in my stomach grew slightly more acidic. "Serious how?"

"Serious enough that she wants to speak to us in person. She's on her way so we can talk it over in private."

I had to remind myself that I had nothing to worry about. I hadn't done anything.

No. This was all my imagination. It was something else. Something unrelated. Still, it would be nice to get an idea of what was going on.

I glanced up at the ceiling. "Quin is on this ship. So if this is a personal matter that needs to stay private…"

Fera shrugged. "As long as he doesn't interrupt, it won't hurt to have his assessment of the situation."

That answer made me feel better. Okay. So Di wasn't coming to try and play homewrecker. I felt bad for considering it as a potential option. That wasn't fair to her.

"That's right," Quin said in answer to Fera's words. "My opinion is quite often the most valuable one given. My physical body may be gone, but the mind of a Faris remains."

"Just trying to be sensitive to whatever is going on," I said.

"That's a nice sentiment, Will, although the spike in your heart rate tells me you're worried about something. What is it?"

"Nothing. I have no idea what she wants to talk about, but I can imagine plenty of bad things."

"Oh," Quin said, his voice lowering an octave. "I see. You did something naughty while we were gone, didn't you?"

Fera rolled her eyes. "Quin, be serious."

I felt pleased that she trusted me enough to ignore his suggestion.

"Okay," I said. "Should we wrap things up with the crew before Di gets here, then?"

"Good idea," Fera said and then moved back toward the crew ready-room door.

"Fera," I said, causing her to stop in her tracks. "No more politics. There isn't time."

"No promises," she said and then stepped back inside.

The crew evidently had finished their discussions. No one was paying one another any mind when we returned.

Benegal sat at the table, his star map spread in holographic light, slowly rotating around him. Faint hues of blue and pure white light shimmered over the scales on his face. The map, in miniature form, was held in the center of both of his eyes as he combed the map with a fixated intensity, searching out the locations of his former comrades in arms—the old Coalition.

"That was quick," he said.

"Yeah," I said, unsure what else to say. There was a chance that Fera didn't want the others to know that Di was coming.

"We're going to have to finish up our discussions," Fera said. "Di is coming and needs to talk with me privately."

"I have nothing further to say on the other matters," Benegal said. "We will continue to agree to disagree until that is no longer a viable option."

I didn't like the sound of that, but it was better than open hostility.

"She's here," Quin announced. "By the Void... I think she's drunk."

"What?" I said, standing up as though she were about to enter the room.

That took a little while longer. Quin saw her approach to the ramp—we didn't get eyes on her until she came into the crew room, halfway out of breath and laughing hysterically.

Still standing, I motioned to the table. "Uh... take a seat, Di."

She staggered toward the table, slipped on her own feet, and caught herself with her back against the bulkhead. A throaty laugh spilled out of her as she tugged at her red leather flight jacket and smoothed out her shirt. It didn't take an advanced, Foris AI to recognize she really was drunk.

A glance at my fiber-link's HUD told me the ship cycle was 1300. The middle of the day.

Di made a show of getting settled in and then leaned toward Fera. "Work hard, play hard, right?"

Di was fun, a bundle of energy, and a competent fighter pilot. But I couldn't think of any reason why she was sauced a little after lunchtime unless it was some sort of Anunnaki thing.

"We can go somewhere more private," Fera offered.

"Nononono," Di said, the words all running together. "Sorry, I just got this and wanted to fill you in before—whoa! Is that a *map*?"

Her voice bounced off the walls, sounding louder in the silence that followed.

Benegal ignored her, but it was clear to me he was put off by her behavior. He continued to manipulate the star map to zoom in close on a planet covered in dense forestry. Text appeared in the hologram next to it, denoting it as Lilian.

The Krayvox root world.

Wonder why he's looking at that?

Di looked at the map, then shifted her gaze to Fera and me. She rocked her shoulders against the bulkhead, swaying to a rhythm only she could feel. "Okay, so you all want to be sitting down for this."

She looked at us. We were already seated.

"Good," she said. "Because *trust me*, you want to be sitting down for *this!*"

She punctuated her statement with a giggle.

"What is it, Di?" I asked, feeling a mix of concern and annoyance.

I looked to Fera for an explanation, since she had been the one to say we needed to meet privately with Di to begin with. Fera gave a fractional shake of her head.

So, I watched Di.

The ace pilot rubbed a hand over her face, forcing her dimpled cheeks to straighten into a neutral expression. It looked like she was holding back another fit of laughter, but she managed to get her next few words out without cracking up.

"Rumor mill's working overtime right now. You know Morian Gray?"

I shook my head. I'd never heard of... her? It? Isn't that a book? Whatever it was, Fera knew of it. She nodded.

Di nodded back in a much more animated manner. "Well... someone just took it. Exterminated the Imperium down to the last man. It was a massacre!"

She covered her mouth. For a second, I thought she was going to be sick. When she lowered her hand, I realized she found the idea funny and was trying not to laugh.

"A massacre," she repeated, as though it were the punchline of a joke.

I looked at the room, confused. "The U-C is regrouping now. Who could even do that?"

"Atron," Benegal said without missing a beat. He hadn't been looking at Di, but he surely was listening.

I turned to look at him. "Atron's fleet has their hands full playing defense in the Ryvian Prime system."

"Who else, then?" he asked.

"It's Marcus Eddison, of course!" Di said. "Come on, you guys!"

"That's impossible," I said.

The words hadn't completely left my mouth when Fera let out a sigh. "No. It's not."

"The mystery fleet," Quin said ominously.

I looked at Fera. "What's Quin talking about?"

"A rumor we heard on Astrada," she said. "Some fleet making strikes against the Imperium. This is something they got from Tror."

Quin picked up the discussion. "At first we believed this was just an effective use of our existing fleets, but an analysis showed that to be impossible—unless the coalition was dividing the fleets into small sub fleets."

"Which didn't make sense," Fera interjected, "because the Imperium could have handled a small, divided fleet."

I looked between Fera and the holographic Quin. "And you think it's Eddison?"

"Of course it's Eddison," Di said, laughing at her own outburst.

Eddison was a business mogul. A billionaire tech tycoon and a visionary. I'm not sure he was any more of a military strategist than I was, though. He had built a fleet, but they were absorbed into the United Coalition.

"Why couldn't it be some other player we don't know about?" I asked. "It's not like the Imperium are the most popular people in the galaxy. Maybe the Drayth were secretly building—"

"It is not Drayth," Lockett said with finality.

Di took a step toward the table, put both hands on the lip of it, and leaned in close. She lowered her voice to a whisper, her expression taking on the crazed quality of a person trying to sell a conspiracy theory. "This is going to change everything."

Fera stood and put a hand on Di's shoulder, then guided her

onto one of the slab seats around the table. "Sit. We need to be sure about what we're dealing with."

12

"WHAT'S SO AMUSING?" I asked Sert.

The Vorvak couldn't seem to stop smiling. "I like complications. This means more killing, doesn't it?"

"It might," I said, feeling both unsettled and relieved at his zeal. There was no better fire team member than a Vorvak with a hankering for violence.

Panels in the ceiling blinked. One by one, they steadied out, with the exception of the panel above Sert's head. The Vorvak looked more intimidating with the intermittent cone of light splashing over him.

"What's going on?" Di asked.

Fera's frown told me it was our Fleuridian problem again.

"Damn!" Quin cursed. "You know, it's bad enough I can't reliably manifest in hologram form. Now our stowaway is tinkering with the lighting, too."

I looked to Lockett to get his opinion on what was going on.

The Drayth shrugged. "Lockett does many magic things. Can't fight pure energy, though. Jettison the pod, maybe. AI does not want to do this."

"Me? You said it wouldn't help," Quin huffed. "So why lose an otherwise perfectly good cryo chamber? Frankly, I'm at a loss for what to do about it. He's in there, like a venereal disease for which there is no topical cream I can apply to remove it."

Di found Quin's remark hysterical.

I wrinkled my nose. "There's gotta be a better analogy than that."

"Just trying to relay information in a way you're likely to grasp, Will."

Fera put her hands on the table. "This isn't what we need to talk about. Di, tell us everything you know."

Di's smile was ear to ear. It didn't fit her tone or the gravity of what she said. I chalked that up to the booze. "For a while now, really since Will showed up on the scene—the big hero thing—there have been rumors about *other* Earthborn spies posing as Anunnaki and infiltrating certain sectors of the Imperium."

"But the glow…" I began.

"Can be fixed, Will, c'mon." Di paused to throw her hands up.

"How does that tie this mystery fleet to Eddison?" Benegal asked.

"So that's where I'm going," Di says, tilting slightly as she speaks as though the room is slanted. "That fleet—it's not a new fleet—it's Imperium. Defectors."

My eyes went wide. "Are you serious?"

She shrugged, looking as though she were anything but. "That's what people with loose lips, the means to know, and a fondness of too much bourbon are telling me." She started giggling. "They *shouldn't* be telling me."

"You can say that again," Fera mumbled.

Di looked thoughtful for a moment. "The action happened at Morian Gray."

"Yes, you've said that," Quin said. He sounded annoyed by Di's drunken state. "That's a mining colony in the Centaurus Arm. It's a hell of a long way away from the real fighting."

"The entire galaxy is at war," Sert said. "Old conflicts become new. This is nothing new; however, this leads me to disbelieve that there is any special secret fleet."

Lockett at once piped up to add his support of Sert's assessment. "The fighting is spread over many systems. A coup on the edge of Imperium space is of no significance."

I shrugged. "If it was United Coalition forces doing this, I would say that this is us showing the entire galaxy that it matters."

Everyone looked at me like I had bugs crawling out of my ears.

Finally, Sert grunted a flat laugh. "Your ability to think of those who do not matter is… *interesting*, Will."

"Guess I can't help it, big guy."

Di looked bored as she mimicked plucking petals from an imaginary flower. "Your champion of Earth, Marcus Eddison—he's either been splitting off small sections of his fleet, one here, one there… or he's got spies who can mutiny and take Imperium ships straight out, and now they're out there, seizing territory from the Imperium, and they're not telling anyone about it."

"That is a problem for the Imperium, not for us," Sert said.

"Except that if Eddison's keeping this to himself," I said, "it makes me wonder what else he might be keeping a secret. Can anyone think of a valid reason to leave the Council in the dark about this? I say that acknowledging that we don't know for sure it's him. Just for argument's sake."

Lockett talked as he adjusted his iron lung. "He has ulterior motives. Carving out territory he can claim for himself."

Sert snorted. "The Drayth is a genius."

Lockett's breathing apparatus popped, but he didn't fire back with a retort.

Fera looked over her crew. "He'd hardly be the first person to be looking ahead to what comes after the war is finished. But to what end?"

"The answer to that is obvious," Quin said, winking in and out before staying invisible for the rest of the meeting. "No one goes to such great effort and expense to produce a fleet and a militia and just hands all of that over without expecting anything in return. Think about this logically. Are we *really* to believe that Marcus Eddison constructed a fleet just to protect Earth? Earth! That mudball of a backwater. Why an asteroid could vaporize every living being on that world and no one in the galaxy would care, unless Will here was visiting his primitive cousins while it happened."

"Valid point," I conceded through gritted teeth. "Fera's question is a good one despite that. What does this get Eddison? Is he posturing to monopolize the shipbuilding industry, or is this something else?"

No one seemed ready to provide an immediate answer. I watched Lockett fiddle with the convoluted tubing that connected to the fanny pack on his belt. Sert rolled his eyes and heaved a sigh. This was clearly a moot point in the Vorvak's mind. Quin's lack of holographic presence kept his thoughts on the matter out of view.

I didn't have an answer to my own question, either.

In the ensuing quiet, an option came to mind. This could be dealt with directly.

"I'll go talk to him," I said.

Fera gaped at me. "Will, you can't be serious."

"Why not?" Sert asked. "He will either validate that it is him or deny it. If it is validated, you will hear the reasoning that—for some reason—is so important to you all. If he denies it, the matter is finished."

"Unless he lies about that," Benegal said.

Sert shrugged. "If he lies, you learn something else about him. Direct action often yields the best results. Kick in the door, shoot the enemy in the face. Take his things, or break them. This is the same, just with words instead of flechettes."

"Well, I don't plan on going in there guns blazing or anything," I said. "But we've talked about the issue with the weapons openly. Why not this?"

"It's too dangerous," Fera said. "If there is something there, and Eddison thought he had it hidden, you don't know how he'll react."

Was Fera acting worried about me? Things *were* getting serious. But this was still the right move to make—the only move, really.

"Fera, I can handle this," I said.

Di gave me an emphatic nod.

Sert's grin widened on his turtle-like face, showing big square teeth. "Be prepared to kill him, if it should come to that."

"It won't come to that," I said, shaking my head.

Benegal swiped the star map off the table and gave it a squeeze to shrink it down before he stowed it in a compartment on his blue armor. "Assuming Eddison is the source of this fleet, the question is not whether the man is doing anything underhanded. It is when he will move these activities from the shadows and out into the open. We would do better to remove this factor from the equation before it becomes a greater threat. Eddison's fleet is in our possession. I see no further use for him. He should be eliminated."

I can't say that I didn't believe what I was hearing—this was Benegal speaking, after all—but I didn't agree with it one bit.

"We're not assassinating him," I said with a bit more force than I intended.

Benegal hissed as he waved a dismissive hand in my direction. "You may come to regret your hesitancy."

I popped up to my feet and locked eyes with Benegal. "There are certain lines we don't cross. It would make us too much like the Imperium if we just killed people because they did things we don't agree with. There's a better solution."

"Such as?" he challenged.

"I don't know yet, but we'll figure it out. We don't even know for sure it's him!"

"It's him," Di said and then giggled once more.

"To be clear," Benegal said, "your way of figuring it out involves directly questioning a man as to whether he is committing acts of war in direct defiance of the United Coalition's battle plan?" The lizard man shivered. "I admire your courage. I only wish you possessed the fortitude and foresight to sever this dangling thread before it becomes a much greater threat."

Sert seemed to agree on this new course of action. "One dead leader now, or many dead soldiers in his army later. I can kill him if you'd like, Will."

"Nobody's killing anybody," I said. "But this needs to be looked into. I'm going. Alone."

"Will," Fera started.

I grabbed her hands and held them.

"Fera, I'll be fine." I forced a smile. "Being the Hero of the Rebellion's got to be worth something."

She moved to kiss me, then paused, feeling all eyes in the room on the both of us. She bit her lip and patted my chest. "Be careful."

13

Marcuss Eddison was still at Base X, so Fera brought me down to Earth aboard the *Phaelon*. It's funny, when I first met Fera, I had to beg her to bring me home. Now she was doing her best to stop me from going.

"I still don't like this, Will."

"It'll be okay," I said. "Has to be done."

In truth, I was developing a sense of dread over the meeting. Eddison was an ally, but we didn't see eye to eye on everything. The disagreement over the superweapon being the chief example. What, exactly, did I suppose would happen if he was waging his own private war?

Is that even a bad thing? Sert hadn't thought so. But then, Sert also didn't see anything wrong with killing the man just in case.

Can't always put too much stock in what Sert thinks.

Fera waited with the ship while I was ushered straight to

Eddison by one of his aides. The value that comes with being a galactic poster boy. Marcus was waiting for me in his private office.

I'd never visited that room before. It was large and ornate in all the ways I expected it to be. The new car smell was sharp. A ficus stood in the corner, obviously fake, but it drew the eye as one of the only tangible decorations in the place. A hologram danced over the bare viewing wall, which displayed a live feed of a black sandy beach… it looked somewhat familiar, maybe the Puna Luu beach of Hawaii, definitely a tropical location on Earth. The ebb and flow of the tide played over a built-in sound system, lending a calm, sensible air to the space.

I thought of it as a thinking man's office. Sparsely furnished with little to distract, aside from the hologram. There were no news clippings, awards, degrees, or photos of the man's family. Instead, I saw off-white paint, dark marbled flooring, and a desk made of emerald-green panes of glass that rested on a very thin metal frame.

Hell, as rich as Eddison was, it might be made of legit emeralds for that matter.

The man himself was seated behind the desk, apparently in the middle of a conversation with General Mira'dna, who stood in miniature on his desk in holographic form. Straight out of Star Wars.

So cool.

Eddison looked up when Dontae, his assistant, led me inside and announced my presence. "Mr. Eddison, Will Kaufman, Hero of the Rebellion."

"Just Will," I said, and then stepped inside.

Eddison beamed, the cerebral air about him opening up, completely dissolving his normally analytical delivery. "But you *are* the Hero of the Rebellion! Good to see you, Will. Did you catch my speech? It went over *very* well, and that's all owing to you. You are just the thing the United Council of Free Worlds needs, Will."

"I hate to think I'm having a drone following me and recording just to make people hate me."

Eddison and the holographic General Mira'dna laughed.

"I can assure you that's not the case, Will," the general said. "But I do wonder how you are handling things in the wake of your newfound notoriety."

I hadn't expected Mira'dna to be there, but her question was a natural one and easy to answer. "I'm not crazy about it, but I understand the importance of it all. Still, I'd be lying if I said I was looking forward to the drone following me around again. The break has been nice."

Eddison nodded as though he wished for that portion of the conversation to be done with, like he was impatient to move on. "Amelie and I were just discussing—going over in great detail, actually—the plans—incipient stages, of course—for Astrada. Take a seat. I would love—we would both benefit from—it's a good time to get your perspective on things."

General Mira'dna inclined her head. "It is fortunate you chose now to join us."

Dontae brought a chair around so I could sit next to Eddison and better see the general.

"Thank you," I said to him and then settled in. "I just talked with Fera on her return trip from Astrada. It sounds like there is an opportunity for us there, but Prefect Tror won't make it easy."

Eddison smiled knowingly. "I told you as much."

I nodded. "And it looks like he's playing things out more or less the way you said, Marcus."

General Mira'dna seemed aware of what Eddison had told me about Astrada and its loyalties. "The way to keep the Imperium from making your root world a source of conflict among the Coalition is to thwart his attempts to mount a credible counterattack. Atron is doing his best to keep the Imperium from amassing what remains of its fleet, but the galaxy is vast. There are many places to hide."

"That sort of brings me to my reason for coming," I said, figuring I may as well put everything out there with Mira'dna present. "The Astradians shared with Fera the rumor of some sort of mystery fleet. Not Imperium, because Tror told them it was a threat they would have to face down together."

The general was shrewd and wise and poised, but she couldn't hide the twitch of surprise at the corner of her lips. "Oh?"

"And so I have to ask," I continued, "if the fleet that just kicked the Imperium out of the Centaurus Arm was United Coalition, and I just didn't know about it, or if it's the work of this mystery fleet. And what we're going to do about it?"

Eddison narrowed his eyes. "How did you come by this information? What is the source? Has it been properly vetted?"

I swallowed a lump in my throat. "I'd rather not say at the moment. But I take it you're familiar with the rumors and the Imperium's defeat?"

"There are a number of working parts in war," Eddison said noncommittally. "And our friend Atron isn't the only one with eyes across the galaxy."

"Did you know about this?" I asked General Mira'dna directly.

She raised a stony, marble eyebrow. "I confess I'm not sure what 'this' is? Are you suggesting that another fleet is fighting toward our purposes, Will? Whose? This is not something the Council has discussed."

Eddison raised one hand and covered his heart with the other. "I must apologize, Amelie. I kept this from the Council. This fleet is not a distinct entity, not exactly. But it is my work. I had been positioning my agents for some time in an attempt to strike at Tror directly. He grew suspicious, but without proof, only scuttled off several officers to the edge of what was formerly Federation space—Morian Gray."

Mira'dna nodded intently as she listened to the story. Here was proof that Eddison was behind the fleet, just like Di and the others had assumed, but so far things didn't sound all that nefarious. And yet it *was* in violation of what the Council expected. Mira'dna's reaction would be telling. I watched her as much as I did Eddison.

"Not all of the officers and crew were loyal, mind you," Eddison continued, "but enough were that it was decided to send part of my fleet to begin an engagement."

Mira'dna cut in. "Decided by whom?"

"By me," Eddison confessed. He looked sadly at Mira'dna. "We both know there are information leaks. I felt the risk was justified, given the leaks we both know affect the Council."

To my surprise, the general didn't take umbrage with this. "We are working to contain those," she said.

Eddison nodded. "Once my seemingly outnumbered ships arrived in the system via the FTL gates, those loyal to the Coalition inside the Imperium defected. We won several Imperium ships and destroyed the rest. I wouldn't go so far as to say we have a new fleet at our disposal, but ours is that much larger and the Imperium's that much smaller now. It's not a trick we can pull again, though. We're lucky that Tror didn't execute those he suspected. I'm sure he will next time."

"Tror is not to be underestimated," General Mira'dna counseled soberly. "He will not offer surrender on a whim,"

"The balance of power the United Coalition has right now is delicate," I said to Eddison. "What will the other planets think if they get the sense that you're building your own empire?"

He shook his head. "I understand the concern, but this is an armada, not an empire. I'll leave it to yours and General Mira'dna's discretion whether to publicize this victory. Word is out, but I'd hoped it would stay quiet. I do have other agents that could be traced if the full measure of what happens is revealed."

"What are you going to do with the captured Imperium ships?" I asked.

"Look to the future. Far from what will be New Federation territory, I mean. There will be a reckoning among the former Federation worlds. They will have to decide what that future is. I have no desire to be part of that process."

General Mira'dna looked stately, even in holographic form. It was clear to me that she was satisfied with the explanation. "I will be discussing this with the Council. Now, concerning Astrada…"

"What are you getting out of this, Marcus?" I asked.

He froze. "What, exactly, are you asking me, Will?"

"I'm asking you… why are you doing this? You manufactured a secret fleet on a remote world—my home planet—solely to overthrow the Imperium? Only to resign at war's end at the edge of the galaxy? Removed from the struggles that come afterward? Why get involved at all, then? Why not just go to wherever you're going—far away from Federation space, which is where the war is, and do… whatever it is you're planning on doing?"

"You don't trust me, do you?" he asked with a strange smile on his face.

I studied him for a moment. "You're a genius. That's undisputed. You have me held up as some big hero, even though you're the one who gave Earth its best chance of surviving this war. The rebellion was in hiding, hoping that Tror and the Imperium wouldn't find and crush them. I've sat in on enough meetings to know you're not being paid for any of this. What *do* you get out of it all?"

He pursed his lips and turned his head, looking wounded.

General Mira'dna put a hand to her chest. "Will, that seems an accusatory and uncharitable line of questioning, given all that Marcus has done for Earth and for the rebellion. His contributions to the effort to defeat the Imperium are a reality. I do not see a reason to question them. The proof is in what has already been done."

I couldn't stop myself from arching an eyebrow at her. It sounded like she was under the impression that Eddison was doing this as a sort of charity. I thought she was smarter than that.

"When the war ends," I said, "the Imperium will be gone. Something else will have to stand in its place. Old factions are already jockeying to have their way."

"The United Council of Free Worlds will become the New Federation," General Mira'dna said, as if it should be obvious.

Marcus smiled. "And I look forward to a continued friendship with the council. Not officially, of course. My success and perceived power comes with its detractors."

It hit me like a slap to the face. I felt like an idiot for not seeing it before. "You're hoping my influence will be enough to advance your ideas."

Eddison's smile could have melted butter. He beamed with elation and gave me a slow golf clap. "You are wise beyond your years, Will. Given time, I can turn your ambassadorship into something more permanent. More official. I would never twist your arm, but I would hope my track record proves my motives are purely intentioned. General Mira'dna, I'm sure, sees the value of what was accomplished. If you deem it worth your time to similarly assure anyone dealing in unfounded rumors... well, who would doubt my intentions after that?"

I smiled but found myself being the one to doubt his intentions. How could I be sure that he wasn't just using me as a proxy, a glorified mouthpiece to get his own way? Everyone had their eyes on something different once this war was finished. Why wouldn't Eddison?

"I want to win this war," I said, "but I also want to be sure we don't fracture the careful alliances we have in place. I need some time to think all this over. I'm not crazy about anything being done in the dark."

Eddison shrugged. "I am an innovator, Will, and I make no apologies for it. I see opportunities to improve things. To rebuild old designs into something completely new. Keep what worked in the original iteration, forge new pieces and merge them with the old... in the end, I produce better products than what I started with. Federation... meet United Coalition."

"From what I'm hearing," I said, "there's equal concern that the United Coalition is both too much and not enough like the Federation that preceded it."

"Of course," General Mira'dna said. "Things weren't perfect before, that is obvious. They never will be."

Eddison held up a finger. "But they could be *closer*. I have a lot of new ideas I'd like you to suggest on my behalf."

"I'll bet," I said, unable to keep the resentment from coming out. "Look, I appreciate what you've done for Earth, Marcus. And I tolerate everything that comes along with being a figurehead to inspire people to fight the Imperium. I'm not sure about political endorsements, I'll be honest."

"Will, you need to think about what comes next. It won't be easy. Of first importance is that we work together to take down the greatest threat the galaxy has ever seen. After that… you have a gift for mediation. You alone will be able to bring the differing viewpoints to the Council and see that they're implemented in a fair and equitable manner."

General Mira'dna shifted in her seat. She kept her face neutral, but her body language told me she was starting to get uncomfortable. "The Council is only too happy to hear from either of you. Your importance to this effort is not lost on any of us."

Eddison looked at me. "All I'm asking is that you at least listen to what I have to say. If it makes sense, like this war against the Imperium makes sense, you speak up. That's it."

"You saved my planet," I said. "And you may have helped save the galaxy, if we win this war. I'll always hear you out, Marcus."

His smile was genuine. "That's all I needed to know. Thank you, Will."

14

THE WAR CONTINUED. That feeling of imminent victory was still there, but a sense that it should have been over by now was starting to seep in among the Coalition. I could feel it as surely as I felt the soreness in my back from a quick campaign to boot a small Imperium detachment from an otherwise unimportant space station.

Quin's hologram manifested as a floating head with the ghostly outline of his thin, Foris body beneath it. The power draw on the *Phaelon*'s systems still hadn't been rectified; we had no real solution in mind for it.

"I can't make any promises, Will. As detestable as I find this proposal, I suppose it is for the good of the United Coalition."

I placed a hand on my chest. "Well, I definitely shouldn't be given command of my own fighter wing. I appreciate that Fleet Admiral Tanoka has given me my own ship, but I'm a far cry from Di or Fera. I'm no fighter pilot. I'm a Navigator. A Void Drifter."

Quin's ghostly body shrugged. "Are you going to tell him that?"

"I don't know." I adjusted my position on the bed in Quin's old room, trying to work some of the stiffness out of my back.

"Hey," Quin said, "on the plus side of things, at least the ship is at peace right now."

I nodded. "Yeah, but for how long?"

Fera was elsewhere, brainstorming potential solutions for the Fleuridian problem with Lockett. Sert was probably disassembling or cleaning a weapon, eager for the next mission and a chance to put all those Vorvaks he'd taken command of to use. That would need to be soon. An army of Vorvaks gets bored *very* quickly. Benegal had isolated himself in his room to spend some time deep in the throes of one of his meditation sessions.

The differences amongst the crew were starting to solidify. People were at each other's throats, tensions were high, and no one could agree on what the end result of the war's aftermath should be. The United Coalition had finally come out and said that resurrecting the Galactic Federation and slapping a new name on it was the Council's official position.

That idea had its detractors. Half of the *Phaelon*'s crew were among them. The war with the Imperium still kept tensions from boiling over, but a solution needed to be found before Tror was firmly defeated.

There was an answer somewhere, I just had yet to find it. Something that would appease both parties.

My best chance at figuring out what that solution might be was while I was still aboard the *Phaelon*. The crew was the ultimate testing ground for my thoughts and ideas. My attempts to make all the pieces click together.

But I wasn't going to be with the *Phaelon* for too much longer. Not for a while.

Duty called, and the "Hero of the Rebellion" must answer.

"It won't be the same, not having you on board," Quin griped. "I'm worried we'll start losing crew if this keeps up and you're not here to assuage everyone else's irrationality. And what then? Me, abandoned by everyone—even Fera—left to slowly be eaten up by our stowaway prisoner while the rest of you run off to your own corners of the galaxy."

"You're being dramatic," I said.

"I'm being a Foris. I'm smarter than you, Will. I see things, and understand things, on a much deeper level than you do. It will happen."

I chuckled, although the look on Quin's face told me he wasn't joking. "You know it's funny that *you* of all people are now worrying about losing crew. I seem to recall you not wanting any of us around, at one time or another."

"Well… it's not so much that I'll *miss* this collection of criminals. It's really just about my impending doom."

"Of course," I said. "Why am I not surprised."

"You know, my sacrifice was necessary to give Fera and the *Phaelon* a chance. It was noble. Brave. The very embodiment of a selfless captain and leader."

"Should I write this down?" I teased.

Quin continued unabated. "But I fear my time is running out. The Fleuridian will eventually take over all of my systems, and that means the *Phaelon* will no longer be me. The consequences should be obvious to you; the alien will become the ship, and even the

Great Algorithm cannot predict what that will mean for you and the others."

"I dunno, did Lockett ever give a good answer why we can't just jettison the pod?"

At the mention of the Drayth, Quin's amphibian eyes narrowed to half-moon slits. "That despicable little hacker has no clue what he's talking about."

I held out my arms. "Okay, problem solved. Just dump the cryo-pod next time you're in the Void."

Quin hesitated. "All right, fine. Maybe he knows a little."

I shook my head and got up from the bunk to start pacing. "The Fleuridian, it's sentient, right?"

"If you're thinking of going to the pod to try and reason with the thing, save your time for something useful."

"No, I mean it's aware the *Phaelon* is, at best, a limited source of food. Of energy."

"If not, it will figure it out once I'm dead," Quin said morosely.

"Hear me out on this, because I'm on the verge of an idea."

Quin made a face. "This ought to be good."

"It might be, if you just let me think." I continued to pace. "The Fleuridian is sort of like a hybrid, right? It's an organic being, but it's also highly technically advanced. So it needs power in the same way most organics need oxygen, right?"

"That's correct. Where are you going with this?" Quin asked, an edge of suspicion creeping into his tone.

"We pacified it temporarily with a bundle of power cells. And it took those power cells instead of drawing from the *Phaelon,* at least for a while. That suggests a choice."

Quin stared blankly at me for a moment. "I hadn't thought of it that way, but you may be onto something there."

"Yeah, we're assuming this is a mindless feeder, but what if it's not? And even if it is, once it realizes that the meal is almost finished, it will still need to eat. So I'm thinking… we lure it off the ship with a more appetizing source of power."

Quin's lips formed a straight line, and he spent a few seconds stroking his chin with his long, bony fingers.

"Well?" I prompted.

"Oh, you're serious?"

"You want your freedom back, don't you? Live forever as the *Phaelon*. So what's a power source that would make a Fleuridian's mouth water?"

"You know, Will," Quin began, "Lockett's upgrade has given you a dose of intellect, but you're really overextending yourself here."

I stowed my annoyance in a sigh. "I'm relying on you to fill in the gaps. I'm like… the idea guy. And I know this idea is sound because you're not ruthlessly mocking me over it. There's something we can use to tempt the Fleuridian out of the *Phaelon*, I'm sure of it. I just don't know what the thing is. That's where you come in, super brain."

From that point, Quin started to cooperate. "We know that natural phenomena like the Void or stars aren't what the stowaway is looking for; otherwise, it could have easily left to feed. The power it prefers is akin to what we create in a reactor."

I nodded. "So something artificial. Maybe it can't harness something as massive as a sun—like drinking from a fire hose. So we should try and confine whatever you think of to a small container."

Quin had an immediate suggestion. "If you want high power in a small container, you already have one."

"I do?"

"Honestly, Will, did you even look at the schematics of your AX-71? Eddison's design relies on three separate Stellarators that contain the plasma given off from their stable fusion reactions. Something like that would work perfectly—admittedly, this is pure conjecture—but it is reasonable to think it *could* work to contain the Fleuridian."

"Contain? I thought we were just trying to trick the thing into leaving the ship?"

"I've seized upon your plan and expanded it."

"What's a stellerator?" I mumbled. My fiber-link HUD conjured up the image of the Stellerator. It looked like the big electricity donut from the Iron Man movies. "Why doesn't the *Phaelon* have something like this?"

"We kind of missed out while spending four millennia buried under a mountain on your little mudball, Will. But this is a solution. An excellent one, in fact. The stellerator can not only feed the prisoner, but its magnetic fields can also contain the Fleuridian. In theory."

I made a show of wiping my hands free of imaginary dust. "Okay, so we just get one of these stellerators from Eddison and wrap the cryopod in magnetic fields, then dump the pod in open space. Problem solved!"

"It won't be that easy," Quin said. "You forget that I am contaminated! All of my systems on this ship are now partially infiltrated by this nasty little bugger. Getting rid of it—completely purging my systems—is far more complex."

"So, then my original plan is still in play," I said, stopping my pacing and framing my words carefully. "We need to lure it to a new home on a different ship with self-sustaining power sources that produce a much higher rate of energy, then tempt it to transfer itself over to the other ship."

"Yes. And then we could just program the ship to fly into the nearest star and wipe our hands clean of it." Quin looked thoughtful for a moment. "I'll be damned."

"What?" I asked.

"You're a dangerous thinker, Will Kaufman. Somehow, despite your unfathomably primitive ignorance, you've put together a plan that... that might actually work. I'll speak to the Drayth about it and see what we can come up with."

A wave of relief washed over me.

"Well, whatever you do, do it while there's still some down time. No telling when we'll get another break like this."

"No telling if it will work, either," Quin said. "But it's the best option I've seen so far."

LOCKETT LIKED THE PLAN. He suggested a few minor changes to the sequence of the deconstruction, integration, and buildup process that Quin had formulated. To my surprise, the Foris actually gave him the green light for it without much complaint. The Drayth estimated that it would take three and a half days to get things up and running. I knew by now better than to hold him to it, though.

Lockett dealt in estimates. Reality would be what it would be.

That was all good enough for me. I was happy to have

contributed to a solution and knew to let the actual experts handle the details. I left our resident tech gurus and the *Phaelon* to find Fera.

She was making use of the *Earthborn*'s fitness facility for a workout. Di joined us halfway through our calisthenics circuit, sober as a priest on Sunday this time… but it was clear she hadn't gone to bed that way.

"Hangover?" I asked.

She nodded, her eyes red and only half open. Her hair was mussed up like she'd just rolled out of her bunk. "Got to sweat out some of the booze."

It was a little alarming seeing her like that. We had joked about who owed who a drink plenty of times, but until that night when she smashed back four or five of those "bourbons" and came onto me, I didn't think much of it. When she showed up drunk with news about the mystery fleet, that was a surprise. Seeing her hungover… I wanted to ask if she still felt the same way about alcohol and taboos, because early drinker or not, I got the sense she had a problem.

But I kept my mouth shut.

We worked up a good sweat jumping over a holographic line in increasingly difficult gravity. It was meant just to get our heart rates going, but I was feeling like I was going to die before Fera finally called it good. Then we moved on to a mix of weights and cardio. It was part of the combat fitness program Lieutenant Fel and his men had developed, refined by some of the Tier-1 operators Eddison had plucked from Earth's finest fighting forces. Once we finished up, we had a quick pass through the refresher stations attached to the fitness area and gathered up in the officer's mess hall.

Fera and Di got along great. I'd seen a polite competitiveness over piloting skills, but it was good-natured and led to a lot of laughs as they recounted stories about close calls and missions they'd conducted over the last few months of the war. The conversation took on a heavier tone when it entered speculation on the future.

"Not much demand for fighter pilots in peacetime," Di said with a frown. "I'll probably start a shipping escort business. Piracy will never really go away."

Fera took a sip from her juice-electrolyte mix and set the bulb on the table. "Not keen on settling down anywhere?"

Di shook her head. "Space has been the only home I've had since Trasp was cratered. Besides, I need to be flying so I don't completely lose my mind."

Lieutenant Fel entered the gym, ready for a workout of his own. He saw us and came over to say hello.

"We were just talking about post-war plans," I said.

He gave a short nod. "War's not over yet."

His deep brown eyes relaxed into a thousand-yard stare for a moment, then he came back to himself and rubbed the back of his hand against his chin. His beard had recently been trimmed to hug tight to his face. "But I find myself thinking about the end from time to time. More often lately. Got a family to go back to once this is done."

I did a double take. Lieutenant Fel was one hard-nosed son of a bitch. I hadn't figured him a family man. Not that I'd ever really talked to him about anything that wasn't war, tactics, or weapons, either.

"Where's home for you?" I asked him.

"Ga'ar. Second habitable in Serapis Major."

My fiber-link gave me some details that I quickly pushed aside. "How long has it been?"

"Eight years," he said. "My sons were boys when I left. They're almost men now."

"That's got to be difficult," I said because I didn't know what else to say.

"Raised by two of the strongest women I know." I thought he was referring to his own mother and his wife, until he continued, "Haven't seen Ealy and Nari since our operation went south on Dennerbon station. For the boys, it was longer. Sent them a message when we had to go into hiding but haven't been able to get word back from them since."

"You have two wives?" I asked.

He nodded. Words formed on his lips, but he didn't give them voice.

I looked at Fera and Di, who seemed unbothered.

Of course. In a galaxy this large, I guess you got used to customs that seemed out of date on Earth.

Di gave me a look—or I thought she did. I shook my head before I could start thinking things I probably shouldn't be thinking about. Cultural relativism aside, I wouldn't ever go for being with more than one girl at a time. Seemed like a recipe for long suffering trouble.

Di shot Fel with a finger gun and made a click noise with her mouth. "We're almost there. This next wave could be it."

"Never thought we'd get this far," he said. "Never thought we'd get off Jyraxis, let alone get on the offensive like we have." Fel locked eyes with me. "You came to us at the right time, Will."

I put my arm on Fera's shoulder. "*We* came at the right time, yeah. I just hope this really is the final push."

"You're not alone in that," he agreed. "My men are getting a little impatient for that Imperium broadcast of total surrender."

"And then what?" Fera asked. "New Federation?"

She was asking which side Fel placed himself in that ongoing rift between Federation loyalists and the original Coalition types like Benegal.

Fel shrugged. "Don't much care what comes after. I'll be hanging it up and going back home no matter what. At least for a little while."

"They can take the soldier out of the fight, but they can't take the fight out of the soldier," Di said.

He nodded, the ghost of a smile hovering over the corners of his mouth.

THE DOWNTIME before I'd have to leave *Phaelon* again provided a great opportunity for Fera and me to get fully reacquainted, exactly what I'd hoped for back when I was longing for her return. It also allowed me to keep up positive relations with the crew and get to know Di and Staff Sergeant Berrios, Lieutenant Fel, and plenty of other United Coalition soldiers, pilots, and crew members.

It felt good to belong.

I was a central part of the war effort, which made me a fixation amongst the people contributing to that effort. Earl the camera drone was back to following me around whenever I traversed *Earthborn* proper, and a few times on the *Phaelon*, too. But I got more privacy than I had before, which felt wonderful.

I did my best to ignore the clout Eddison was building for me. I wasn't in this for fame or fortune. I just wanted to glance out a viewport and see my root world without feeling a shiver of foreboding go up and down my spine.

Prefect Tror still knew how important Earth was to me. He wasn't the type to sit back idly, either. He was building toward something. Working the angles Eddison's spies had reported on. Trying to make this war about Earth and about me. Trying to find a way to galvanize support for the Imperium among those worlds that could still make a difference.

That night, I couldn't sleep. There was a growing anxiety that came with this downtime. I couldn't shake the feeling that while I was waiting for my next mission, Tror was getting closer to attacking Earth. When I finally drifted off, I had nightmares of Earth being pummeled by an Imperium fleet and turned into a ghost world like Farakar.

I woke in a cold sweat, my heart hammering in my chest and my mind racing at a thousand miles an hour. I lay there, listening to my own breath, feeling my eyes grow heavy again.

A voice came from the ceiling. "Oh good, you're awake."

I groaned. "And getting more so by the second. What is it, Quin?"

The problem came rolling out in one quick, almost panicked sentence. "The Fleuridian's cryostasis pod has been drained of all its reserve power. It is now unlocked, and I am unable to interface with it to keep it closed."

"What?!" I jumped out of bed and tossed my blanket aside as I hopped down to the floor, where I snatched up my pants and pulled them on. Using an eye wave, I switched the interior lights up to fifty percent.

Only nothing happened. It was as dark as it had been.

"Wake up Fera and the crew," I told Quin. "Tell them to get dressed and grab their weapons."

I cinched my belt and holster over my cargo pants, looked at my shirt, and decided I didn't have time to pull it on. I stuffed my feet into my boots. Using the fiber-link, I opened the door and stepped into the hallway.

At least that worked, but the lights in the ship were all out.

The lights in the corridor are never out.

The hairs on the back of my neck lifted with static cling.

My fiber-link shifted to Color Night Vision mode. I slid my rail pistol from its holster and checked it. A flechette was chambered, ready to fire.

I made my way toward Fera's room and used the fiber-link to open the door.

"Fera," I whispered inside.

Something thunked from inside her room. She whispered a pain-ridden curse and put her hand on my shoulder.

I spun around in alarm, but she shushed me. "You're too easy to sneak up on, Will."

Irritation festered in my chest. "We've got bigger problems. Quin tell you?"

Fera drew her pistol and pull-checked it. "Yeah. Not sure a rail pistol is going to be of much help."

She had a point.

"Where's Lockett?" I asked.

"I asked Quin that, but now he's not responding," she said. "If I had to guess, Lockett's probably still in the room doing the modifications."

I nodded, trusting her own fiber-link to see it. "Okay, let's go find him."

I took a step toward the hold and stopped cold in my tracks.

A beam of pure light floated around the corner, hovering like a hologram of a lightning bolt. It angled itself toward me. Before I could get a bead on it through the holographic sights of my rail pistol, it launched right at me.

15

I DROPPED straight to my back so hard my head rattled against the deck.

Like the flash of an antique camera bulb, light zipped through the air. The crash of energy collided with metal in a sizzle close behind me. I could smell ozone. It smelled hot.

"Will!"

I rolled onto my side and found my feet, brought my weapon up, and sighted in on the bulkhead. A small, darkened patch of metal wreathed in a golden circle of molten metal rested on the bulkhead at eye level. Whatever that energy was, it had done minor damage to the interior of the ship.

There was nothing to shoot. I kept the rail pistol ready all the same. "I'm good. What the hell was that?"

Fera joined me in the corridor. Weapon raised, she pressed her back against mine, covering the opposite end of the corridor. "I don't know. The Fleuridian maybe? Quin?"

It took a moment before the AI answered. "You… might want to exit the ship."

"*Earthborn* needs to know about this," I said, keying the comm channel with my fiber-link.

The icon in my HUD pulsed, but nothing happened.

"Comms are currently inoperative," Quin said. "The Fleuridian is no longer on the *Phaelon*."

"I don't see how those two things are connected. Did the thing fry our comms? Where is it?"

"Yes, Will, it broke our comms. If I had to guess, he's probably going to try to access the *Earthborn*'s fusion coil."

My fiber-link info dumped that the fusion coil was the part where the energy between the two fusion reactors pooled together, creating a massive nexus of power. It was the primary source of energy diverted to all of the cruiser's primary and secondary systems. Everything from weapons to shields to the FTL drive and Void engine.

"That's a lot of power. Other than drain the batteries, can it cause any damage?"

"We need to warn them either way," Fera said. "If we can't use comms, we'll just have to go tell them in person."

I nodded in the dark and then put a hand on Fera's shoulder. "Let's go."

I led the way through the corridors, guided by the Color Night Vision of my fiber link, viewing the path forward through the crosshairs of my rail pistol. "Quin, where are the others?"

"The Vorvak was not on the ship at the time of the incident. Last known location was the starboard armory on the *Earthborn*. Benegal is—"

The Krayvox appeared at the threshold of his room, his eyes lit with a flare of green light. Each hand held a pistol, their barrels pointed at the deck. "I am here."

"Three's better than two," I muttered. "Fleuridian's on the loose. We're moving to alert *Earthborn*. Let's go."

"Following," he said, falling in behind Fera.

"We should find Lockett," she said.

"I'll search for him," Benegal said, and then disappeared before an answer could be made.

We reached the exit ramp of the ship. It was sealed up tight. I started working the controls to manually release the ramp while Fera ran a quick sweep of the cryo rooms.

Benegal returned. "The Drayth is unconscious, but alive."

"You sure?" I asked. "Lockett doesn't seem the most hearty being I've ever met."

Benegal cleared his throat, a note of irritation. "Fiber-link's medical diagnostics shows his axial pump is still spinning—that is a heart on a Drayth—and the isotope reactor that powers his cybernetics is up and running. He is not dead. Simply unconscious. I administered an epinephrine shot, but his onboard biome filtration systems are metering it into his system in small doses. The desired effect will be delayed."

With our trio present, I wrenched at the manual release lever on the door. It gave way with a clang. The ramp free fell into place on the deck of the *Earthborn*. Emergency lighting lined the bulkheads, leaving the docking bay draped in shadow. My fiber-link's enhanced vision allowed me to see through the otherwise thick shadows... where dozens of bots were engaged in hand-to-hand combat with Coalition maintenance techs.

We were all speechless.

It was a one-sided affair. The techs had the same fiber-link upgrade I did, which meant they could see in the dark, but they weren't soldiers. They defended themselves with their tools, and the blunt instruments did some damage to the bots, but flesh was no match for metal in close quarters.

The bots ranged from the mobile garbage cans like Dumpy to full-on humanoid—the ones usually used to do the heavy lifting for cargo shipping and receiving, or for some of the more dangerous repairs.

Now, they had taken on a different tack. They were bludgeoning the technicians with impunity. The humanoid ones were the most adept at this, swinging their arms like lead pipes and knocking technicians to the floor with broken bones and gouts of blood. The rolling cans just got in the way, or chased people down with spark emitters, paralyzing them with jolts of electricity.

"Take them out," I said, drawing a bead on the closest bot.

Quin spoke out as I squeezed the trigger. "I strongly advise against that!"

Too late. The *snap-thrum* of the magnetic fire system broke the air in front of me. My round spiked one of the bipedal bots in the head unit, dragging a trail of sparks as it passed clean through the metal.

The bot's head jerked back and hung at an angle. It turned on its feet and stalked toward me, mechanical arms raising to shield its torso section.

"Because *otherwise*," Quin muttered, "you'll alert every bot in the area that you are the biggest threat!"

"Take them down," Fera said.

She was right. Priority threat or not, we couldn't just let those machines murder our technicians.

I fired three more shots into my initial target's torso. A cascade of fibrous threads erupted from the back of the thing as it jerked and fell to the deck, twitching. Droplets of coolant and lubricant flecked onto the deck beneath it, forming a pool of foul-smelling liquid.

"Quin, can you hack them?" I asked, looking for another machine I could shoot without being a threat to a living being.

Benegal fired as well, cutting it close as I made a single, permanent hole in a Dumpy-style bot that had been jolting a female technician mercilessly.

"I am barely keeping up on what's happening!" the AI lamented. "The Fleuridian has locked them down with its esoteric encryption scheme! Even Lockett may not be able to do anything with it—if the Drayth ever wakes up!"

No help there. The dozens of bots working in the vicinity of the docking bay halted their attacks against the repair crews, swiveled toward us, and started at us.

"Well at least they're not attempting murder on the crew," I said.

"Quin, how did this even happen?" Fera asked.

"It appears the Fleuridian is a bit more intelligent than we gave it credit for… and once Lockett had the containment field in place, just before he went to activate it, the little bastard sort of… scattered."

Benegal dropped two more machines with a blast from each barrel. "What do you mean, scattered?"

"It sort of self-destructed, like an electromagnetic pulse," Quin explained. "All systems on the *Phaelon* and the *Earthborn* are hardened against such rudimentary electronic warfare measures, but some systems auto-shutdown to avoid damage. Those will take time to reboot. The problem isn't the temporary loss of power, though. Apparently, the diffuse energy is... I don't say this lightly, mind you... it appears to be sentient. That energy has penetrated and taken over all of the bots on the ship."

"What about Dumpy?" I asked.

"He's probably joined the mob," Quin said.

Fera took down more machines—some that looked like Dumpy—with her rail pistol. "Oh, well. Lockett will have to fix him if it comes down to it. We still need to link up with *Earthborn* and get to the bottom of this."

"I'll try and handle that," Quin said. "You three move to *Earthborn*'s coil because that's where the Fleuridian is headed, if it's not there already."

Benegal and I added our fire to hers. It was a different scenario than a typical firefight. There was no return fire coming our way, and we were able to put down the opposition with ease.

Bots dropped to the deck as sparking hulks of metal. The relieved technicians dragged their wounded toward the nearest traffic control tower. A dozen of the rolling can units similar to Dumpy came from further in the bay. We left them to be dealt with by the techs, who used arc welders to disable the nuisances now that the more formidable bipedal loader bots had been dealt with.

Fera hit the manual unlock next to the door. I grabbed the linkage and yanked the emergency release lever, venting pneumatics into the door until it slid aside enough to permit us access into the corridor.

Benegal stowed his rail pistols and drew the heavier pulse hand cannons. Fera and I swapped magazines in our weapons.

"Ready?" Fera asked. "Let's go."

"I have to warn you," Quin said, "there's at least one hundred and forty-seven server bots between you and the coil. It's going to be a challenge."

"Not if we pick up some help along the way," I said. "Try to get word to Fel or Barrios."

"Comm connections are still fried between us, but I'll keep trying."

It would have to do.

We took the corridor toward the aft section of the ship. Emergency lighting lined both sides of the passageway in thin red strips of beaded light. Bulkhead braces jutted out every ten meters, giving the space a feel like we were moving through the throat of a giant beast.

Benegal and I followed Fera. The Krayvox covered our left flank, and I covered the right. We passed dozens of doors as we followed the constant turns left and right, right and left, encountering no resistance for nearly a full minute.

The first wave of bots was waiting for us in the midsection of the ship. We cut them down in a hailstorm of flechettes and Benegal's pulse rounds, leaving twenty or thirty smoking heaps of scrap metal in our wake.

These things weren't designed for fighting, and their armor—if you wanted to even call it that—was rated to withstand falls, not flechettes. Still, they slowed us down, and that was probably the point.

The stench of burning metal was thick in the air as we stepped into engineering. No sign of help from anywhere. No other people whatsoever. Had something happened to them? Were they locked in their quarters, somehow unable to use the manual override?

Maybe they were just preoccupied with a bot fight of their own elsewhere and away from the coils. Just because we had a good idea of where the Fleuridian was headed didn't mean the *Earthborn* crew knew the same. Especially if Quin couldn't communicate with them.

The fusion coil, according to my fiber-link HUD, was a little over a hundred and fifty meters away. The corridor opened up into a two-level atrium. Humanoid bots swarmed the upper and lower levels, working feverishly to rip panels off of equipment stations. A dozen propulsion technicians were splayed across the room, bearing various signs of blunt-force trauma.

"How many bots are on this stinking ship?" Fera asked.

"Too many," said Benegal.

I cursed at the carnage. These bots had been let loose on the living that worked in engineering, and the results hadn't been pretty. Dead men and women lay battered and bloodied.

It was our fault.

We hadn't contained the Fleuridian. Had underestimated the creature. Now it was on a killing spree as it tried to gain access to the fusion coil.

At the end of the atrium, the blast door that led to the fusion section was sealed up tight. Four bots had liberated arc welders and were actively dumping gouts of plasma on the blast door at the seams. Another two dozen bots swarmed around them, beating the door with metal fists.

"Deal with them," Benegal ordered.

I took a shooter's stance, one foot slightly in front of the other, brought my left hand up to the gap between my right-handed grip, and squeezed tight, but not too tight. After a sharp inhale, I lined up the sights on my fiber-link's crosshairs with the rendered laser line that trailed out from the barrel of my rail pistol.

Smooth, steady, focused.

I didn't waste a single flechette as I double-tapped bot after bot. Twin pinholes popped in the back plates of each enemy I targeted, ending in spats of sparks through the chest plates. Plasma cutters and arc welders clattered to the floor. Deactivated machines collapsed on top of their tools, on top of each other, twitching and spewing fluids.

In seconds, the sentient machines became an inanimate heap of ruined scrap metal. The blast door in front of them was crisscrossed with scorch marks and deep gouges that wavered with heat distortion.

The grip of my pistol shook against my palm. Without taking my eyes off the scars on the door, the rapidly cooling metal returning to its bland gray hue, I dropped the spent magazine, retrieved my last spare from my belt, and slapped it into place.

"What's the story here?" I asked. "They need to make some kind of a breach for the Fleuridian to enter?"

"Containment fields work both ways," Quin said.

Fera kept her head on a swivel. Aside from the sizzling hiss of fluid evaporating in the high temperatures of the scrap pile, the room was quiet.

Pervasively quiet.

A clang sounded from behind us. I spun on my heels, weapon raised and finger on the trigger.

The torso of a bot rested on the deck. Severed fibrous nano

cords and spindles with fractured crystal fragments blinked discordantly where the legs had been severed from the remainder of the chassis.

"What the——"

A thunderous stomp shook the deck.

Sert rounded the corner, his head tucked and one of his eyes swollen shut. One of his turtle-like nares was cut, streaming a steady trickle of blood that dripped from his chin. He ran toward us full force, swinging his arms wildly. He had his shotgun held in one hand and a plasma torch in the other.

"Sert!" Fera motioned toward the entryway as Sert passed through the threshold.

Benegal and I immediately rushed to brace ourselves at opposite sides of the access corridor. Sert dropped to a knee and skidded to a halt in front of Fera, gasping for air like he'd just run a marathon.

"Kill box," the Vorvak panted.

Fera kept her firearm aimed at the opening but turned to look at the Vorvak. "Care to clarify that?"

Sert took three gasping breaths before he could get the words out. "Need to set up a kill box. Hundred... a hundred of them are coming."

16

THE MACHINES WERE on us almost as soon as Sert warned of their coming. The bots came in a tidal wave, charging down the hallway so close together their metal limbs scraped against each other, producing an ear-wrenching racket like a tile cutter going to task.

My fiber-link cut my sense of sound off almost completely. If it hadn't, I would have gone deaf from the clamor.

Benegal's hand cannons dumped raw plasma in vicious gouts that slammed fists of fire into the midsections of the bots. I fired incessantly with my rail pistol, dropping bots quickly. But to what effect? They just kept coming.

Fera added her fire to ours, resulting in a wall of plasma pulses and flechettes that the bots ran headlong into without hesitation. They clattered to the deck in droves, stacking up in piles a meter high.

My rail pistol buzzed in my palm. I was out of ammo and holstered the weapon aside with a curse.

"Will!" Sert called. "Use this."

I turned just in time to catch his shotgun.

Looking down at the weapon, I risked a glance up at him, just to make sure he intended me to fire it. A huge hand pressed to his swollen eye, the Vorvak saw my questioning glance and nodded.

Things must be bad if Sert is too hurt to keep up the fight.

I racked the breech back and forth on the weapon.

The *shick-shick* got my adrenaline flowing afresh.

Fera's fire dried up with a curse of her own.

Benegal faded back behind cover, both of his weapons belching thick fumes of black smoke.

I stepped out into the opening of the door and squeezed the trigger.

The shotgun screamed like a banshee. Light washed over my eyes, dazzling me with tantalizing streaks of bright confetti as dozens of plasma particles scattered at relativistic speed from the mouth of the monstrous shotgun.

My shoulder tensed. My bicep bulged in defiance of the weapon's kickback.

Coils of ozone wafted over my face as the weapon vented its excess heat, which felt like it could singe my eyebrows.

The shotgun's single blast swelled into a white-hot sphere of plasma that incinerated three bots at the front of the line. Two more behind it came apart, their connecting pieces dripping liquefied metal and glowing deep red at the edges.

I racked the shotgun and fired again. Again.

I pumped out six rounds in rapid succession, a tense grin spreading over my face in spite of the inherent danger. More bots rushed to fill the gaps I carved in their suicidal charge.

I fired three more blasts. The stack of bots was approaching two meters high when it began to shift and teem like an ocean wave. Clicks and clacks rattled the pile as still more of the bots—once servers and repair models, now possessed with the energy of an esoteric alien entity—scrambled over top the carcasses of their brethren.

The pile of scrap, sparks, and cybernetic fluid surged forward.

I dipped back behind the cutout, narrowly avoiding being submerged in a sea of broken machinery. The wreckage tumbled and rolled into the engineering section, covering the deck up to knee height for a full two meters into the larger atrium.

Automatic pulse cannon fire spooled up from the back end of the corridor.

I risked a glance from cover in time to see Lieutenant Fel and Staff Sergeant Berrios poised at the intersection twenty-five meters back. Lieutenant Fel had the stock of a rotary pulse cannon pressed into his shoulder, the tripod legs splayed out in front of him. Staff Sergeant Berrios was crouched beside him, monitoring the belt of ionized rounds as the weapon sucked them up and spewed deadly pulse fire from the barrel.

My fiber-link counted the remaining bots in the corridor at forty-one. The incoming fire from their backs switched their primary threat indicators on the fly. They skidded to a halt a meter away from me—the closest one could have put my lights out with its hardened limbs if it thought about it—and immediately reversed course.

The bots charged toward the weapon.

Blistering fire cut them down. I couldn't watch the massacre without exposing myself to the deluge of ionized rounds. I dipped back behind the lip of the entrance and shouted, "Cover!"

Movement in my peripheral forced me to risk a split-second glance.

Sert held up Dumpy by its head unit. Several slots in the bot's can were open. Spark emitters and pincer attachments and a miniature plasma welder were poised toward Sert's good eye, lancing out with more vigor than accuracy.

Somehow the little bot had made it all this way, working for the Fleuridian.

"Kill it!" Benegal shouted.

But Sert would not.

The big guy staggered as Dumpy tweedled a war cry in a distorted, macabre manner. Each frenzied stab of one of its implements drew closer to Sert's good eye, but the big guy made no move to break the bot. He could have crushed the thing in his bare hands like I would crumple a paper bag.

I froze in place, dumbfounded by the sight.

Why wouldn't he just smash the bot against the deck? The only person who would really care about the bot would be Lockett.

I didn't have time to think that through, but somewhere in my subconscious, I realized something about Sert in that moment. He may hate Drayth on principle—the Vorvak hated nearly everyone—but... did he actually *like* Dumpy?

The crashing of bots dropping to the deck fell silent. The whirring drone of the rotary pulse cannon's barrels spun to a stop.

Dumpy managed to run a plasma torch along Sert's under arm, causing the Vorvak to drop the bot onto the deck with a howl of pain.

Immediately, Dumpy retracted its implements and rolled toward the blast door.

Benegal stepped forward and leveled his hand cannon at the bot. He fired. A single flare of superheated plasma ejected from the barrel of his weapon and bit into Dumpy's backside. The bot warbled a high-pitched curse as its head unit spun in circles. Flames roiled out of the internal slots for a few seconds, then slowly simmered down. The bot's shrieking slid down to a low, rumbling groan.

I watched Dumpy's head unit stop spinning. The light in its panel dimmed, then clicked as it faded to black.

Lieutenant Fel and Staff Sergeant Berrios joined us in the room, along with a dozen United Coalition soldiers. They posted up at intervals along the sides of the room on Lieutenant Fel's order. Two of them bearing patches that identified them as corpsmen began moving from casualty to casualty, assessing their conditions. Lieutenant Fel shifted the visor over his eyes, releasing a stream of sweat that ran down the side of his face before he spoke.

Fel was livid. "Whatever the hell this is, you guys are responsible for it, aren't you?"

"What makes you say that?" Fera asked.

"Your bot." He indicated the warped undercarriage that had been Dumpy. "And you. Here. Why?"

I handed Sert his shotgun back. "We had a contain—"

Dumpy's frame came apart in a contained explosion. It was unlike any detonation I'd ever seen before.

Purple smoke filled with glittering diamonds billowed out from under the bot's head unit. No flames, no heat, no concussive force. It was almost like a smoke grenade had gone off. The fumes began to dissolve, then stopped, holding together in the rough shape of a translucent humanoid figure.

The head was cone-shaped, and there were no eyes inside it—just hollow gaps of darkness. Thin turquoise lines gave the image of a stick-figure made three-dimensional, wrapped in the translucent flesh of a being in its embryonic stage of development. I stared at the thing, blinking several times before I choked on the breath I'd been holding.

It was real. I couldn't tell exactly—smoke and lights and… circuitry?—whatever it was, it didn't go away no matter how many times I blinked.

It was real.

"Is that…." I breathed.

Every weapon was up and aimed at the thing—was this… was this the Fleuridian itself?

"Wait!" Fera called. She put a hand on my shoulder. I let her step past me, then realized she was stepping toward the thing.

"Fera, hold on—"

She shot me a look. "Will, relax. I know what I'm doing. We caught it once already."

Lieutenant Fel's open-mouthed gaze told me he'd never seen one of these things before. Ditto for everyone else.

"What is that thing?" one of the soldiers wondered aloud.

"Felon-501," Fera said in her command voice, "you have escaped custody. I'm going to bring you back—"

It spoke. My heart almost stopped beating when I heard the quality of its voice.

It was heavily distorted, felt as much as heard, like the rattling of a blown speaker with the bass turned up to max. It hardly sounded like words, and yet, I could understand it. Nothing about it sounded like a biological being.

"I will not be contained," it said.

I searched for a mouth in the formless face but couldn't discern one.

"A simple cryopod held you for four thousand years," Fera said, far too nonchalantly for me. She was going to provoke that thing, and after dodging a lightning bolt on the *Phaelon*, I shuddered to think what it could do in its disembodied state.

The purple smoke shifted to a brilliant red. The color of a carnation, with subtle hints of amber sliced through it.

"Labels. Shackles. Containment. All futile."

Fera shook her head. "You might be the last of your kind. You should talk to our people. See if we can work out a mutually beneficial arrangement."

"No discussions. I will not be contained."

Its cone changed position, and for a second, I thought I felt its hollow spaces looking in my direction. The darkness where the eyes were supposed to be felt like tiny black holes with a gravitational pull all their own. My blood ran cold just looking at the thing. I gained a new respect for Fera; she had to have ice in her veins to stand face-to-face with something like that and not bat an eye.

My skin felt electric. Like I had too much static build up and desperately needed to discharge it before I spontaneously combusted. I didn't know how to put my finger on it, but this alien made me feel like I needed to touch it. Like grounding myself against it would release some of the pressure on my skin.

I stepped forward before I could think it through, raising a hand toward the swirling light particles and reddish smoke.

"Will, what're you doing?" Fera snapped, stopping me with her hand.

I froze. What the hell *was* I doing?

"Leave him be," Fera said to the Fleuridian. "You've caused enough chaos already. Or so help me we'll drop you off in the gravity well of the closest star."

The incorporeal mist that was the Fleuridian seemed to consider that. The color hue of the cloud folded in on itself, turning a passive purple streaked with blue.

Quin was in our ears a moment later. "I believe the little cretin has played its hand and is at our mercy. It lacks the sufficient energy to do anything beyond what has already been done."

Fera gave a fractional nod. "You need food. To go to wherever the rest of your kind went? Is that it?"

"Provide power. One for one."

"We can arrange that," she said cautiously, "but you can't draw from our ships like you have been."

"Hold on," Fel said, his voice hot. "Do you see the number of dead—"

"Accepted," the Fleuridian said and then dissolved in a cascade of glittering diamonds. All at once, the smoke was gone as if it had never existed.

The emergency lighting went out, plunging us into total darkness until several clicks ran up and down the bulkheads as the lights came back on. The thrum of systems ramping back up to operational capacity could be felt in the deck.

"Where did it go?" Benegal asked.

I was about to ask the same when I saw a glow from Dumpy's

optics. I pointed to it just as Fera knelt down and scooped up the bot's head unit. "In here, I guess."

Lieutenant Fel approached, holding open his palm. "I need to take that. It's dangerous."

"It is," Fera said, shielding the unit with her body. "Which is exactly why I can't just hand it over. The being inside this unit—"

"Obviously isn't to be trusted," Fel interrupted. "Look around you, Astradian. Or did you miss the carnage."

"I see it well, Lieutenant," Fera said icily. "This creature is—it's unlike anything you're familiar with. Or me, or anyone, for that matter. The Federation—"

"Of course," Benegal hissed. "The Federation and their meddling. And here is the result."

An argument followed, heated and on multiple fronts. Animosity between Fera, Sert, and Benegal. Insistence that *Earthborn* security take Dumpy's head unit from Fel, backed up by Berrios and the soldiers. Fera insisting that the only thing containing the Fleuridian was the agreement she'd just struck to provide it a source of energy, another thing Fel and his team were aghast over.

Then Lockett showed up, equal parts asthmatic old man and drunken teenager. His body seemed weak, but he still managed to snatch Dumpy's head unit from Fera's arms then staggered on unsteady footing back the way he came.

With a nod from Fel, the United Coalition troops blocked the Drayth's passage.

"You all seem to be under the impression that you can do whatever you want, wherever you want," Fel said. "That is *not* the case."

Sert took offense. "I will do what I please, Anunnaki."

Berrios stepped forward. "No. Not on this ship, you won't."

That was far too close to a challenge for Berrios's own good. I stepped in.

"We'll get this figured out," I promised, unsure exactly how to do that. "This creature was captured by directive of the Federation over four thousand years ago. We knew it was drawing power from our ship but had no idea it could slip confinement this way, or the damage it would cause."

"At least forty dead," Fel reported. "And given the state of some of those technicians being beaten, that number might still grow."

My stomach twisted in knots. I shook my head in sorrow and disgust. "I'm sorry."

"Sorry isn't sufficient. There needs to be a full accounting of what happened."

"There will be," I promised. "You have my word."

I didn't expect Fel to accept that, but he did. Unhesitatingly. "Only because it's your word."

All of my crewmates had their eyes on me. It was an uncomfortable feeling. Had Fel truly bought into all that Hero of the Rebellion stuff? He acted like it.

And I... I had to use it.

"I appreciate that, Lieutenant. I also ask that you trust me when I say that our best chance at preventing another rampage such as this is to allow us to return to the *Phaelon* with the Fleuridian and put it in containment."

Fel gave me a hard stare that relented into a fractional nod. "Very well. But your ship is no longer free to dock with *Earthborn* or any other United Coalition vessel. Is that clear?"

That would be inconvenient, but I understood.

"Clear," I confirmed.

"Let's get a crew in here," Berrios said. "Clean up the mess."

Fel pointed at the head unit in Lockett's hands. "I want that off of this ship. Now."

Lockett was only too happy to shamble off.

Fera threw an arm around my shoulders. "Walk with me, Will."

"Of course." I moved toward the exit, expecting her to walk by my side, but she kept her arm around me, using me for support.

"Are you okay?" I asked.

Fera feebly pointed toward a door. "Just get me through there."

She didn't look so good.

"Fera, are you all right?"

She didn't answer.

Using an eye wave, I slid the door open and guided her inside. The door closed behind us, then Fera let go of me and dropped to her knees, panting heavily.

She vomited. Violently.

17

I WAS worried and full of questions that had to wait until Fera had finished and could gather herself. Finally, she was done emptying her stomach and sat back on her knees, breathing shaky breaths.

She looked at me, embarrassed, and wiped saliva from the corner of her mouth. "Thank you."

My eyes were wide with fear. "What's going on?"

She shook her head. "I don't know. Getting so close to that thing, I think."

"Well, c'mon. We need to get you to a doctor." I attempted to lift her up, but she wasn't helping, so I let it be.

"I'll be fine." She looked straight ahead, then a fiery light suddenly came to her eyes. "That was a Fleuridian. A real one. I wasn't sure when we reclaimed it from the black-market R and D lab four thousand years ago—it was a body in a cryopod. I presume that body is still in the cryopod on the *Phaelon*. But this... seeing one in real life, it's like...."

Words failed her.

Then... "A soul walker."

"Soul walker?"

She nodded, then got to her feet and swayed a bit. I steadied her.

"I'll be okay," she said, and then stood on her own. "Yes, soul walker. Astradians have all kinds of legends about them. Warriors that die under brutal circumstances, or innocents slain in war... on rare occasions, their spirit does not ascend into the afterlife, and they are left to wander the physical realm."

She paused to take in a shuddering breath.

"Oh. So, like ghosts?" I wondered why the translation software hardwired into my brain, or even my fiber-link, didn't just use that word to begin with.

Fera went on as if I hadn't said anything. "They primarily visit us in our dreams, offering guidance or calling on people to avenge them."

I felt my skin crawl as she talked. Not so much over what she was saying—different cultures had different beliefs, and I was fascinated by them all—it was more how she was saying it that creeped me out. There was a deep-seated conviction in her; this spirit stuff was as real to her as I was.

"Still feeling sick?" I asked.

Her eyes finally relaxed, no longer drawn in fear. She looked at me. "He could have killed me. If he did, he would have killed everyone in that room. A being of pure energy like that... you can't kill it, not with conventional weapons. He had no reason to let us live, and I had to... convince him it was in his best interest to keep us alive."

"You were just winging it?" my voice pinched with disbelief. "I thought you'd done this before. Wait. You hadn't. You said you just got him already in a pod."

She smirked. "It was the best option at the time. If someone started shooting at the thing, it would have lashed out and killed everyone."

I let out a whistle. "Good thing it didn't just do that to begin with. Maybe the thought didn't occur."

She frowned. "No, I think that was always an option. But it wanted what it wanted in a way that wouldn't require killing everyone. That's what I was thinking when I approached it, anyway—it could have killed us if it wanted to."

"Well," I said, brushing her cheek with a finger, "thanks for saving my life. Let's get back to the ship. I'm sure we're going to get an earful from General Mira'dna and the United Coalition brass over this."

Fera snorted. "They should thank me, too. This could have been a lot worse."

"You're not wrong about that."

She took a step, and I was at her side to help her. She patted my chest. "I've got it from here."

"You sure?"

"Will, I could kill you with my bare hands if I wanted to. Don't make me regret letting you see me like this."

I held up my hands. "Point taken."

Fera smiled and playfully batted my nose with her fingertip. "Come on, before Lockett gets the idea that the Fleuridian can speed him and his people to the point of Ascension... that's not going to be good for anyone."

BACK ON THE *PHAELON*, Fera got some water and rinsed her mouth out, then popped one of the hygiene stimulant pills from the refresher station. I waited for her at the entrance to the Fleuridian's cell. Inside, Lockett was using small tools to tinker with Dumpy's head unit.

The ceiling speaker popped as Quin decided now was the time for a ship-wide debrief. "You have all performed admirably. Even Will. It's not an exaggeration to say that a true Fleuridian is a force of nature. What you have done here is catch a tempest in a bottle, and that's no small thing. I have never been more proud of my crew."

"Don't get all sentimental on me, Quin," I said. "Also, I'm just gonna say it: how is what just happened in any way possibly worse than what could have happened if you just dumped the stupid thing in Void Space near the closest sun?"

"Hindsight," Fera said, and that was that.

Sert passed me on his way to the auto-med station. His right eye was swollen up and purpled like a dragon fruit. The blood from his torn nostril had clotted and looked like a deposit of lime crusted to his rough skin. I couldn't believe he'd taken such a beating from enemies without weapons.

"You okay there, big guy?"

He bristled. "What was your kill count?"

"I don't know. I never really think to keep track of it."

He paused, obviously waiting for me to ask him the same question.

"What was yours?"

"Twenty-eight."

I gave him a nod of thanks. "You kicked some serious ass, Sert. Like always."

He touched his wounded eye and winced. "Damn bots swarm like hornets that guard the bramble nests of the honey fields of Farakar."

I nodded. "We probably destroyed almost all of their automated workforce."

Sert shrugged like it didn't matter. "Bots are easily replaced."

The implication that the people we'd lost in the fight were not easily replaced hung in the air, unspoken but no less heavy.

Sert leaned his head in the cell door and shouted to Lockett, "You are not getting too familiar with that thing, are you?"

Lockett let loose a torrent of curses, along with something about the "Lightbringer."

Sert grimaced and turned toward the auto-med station. He disappeared inside without another word, leaving me to contemplate the curious moniker Lockett assigned to the Fleuridian. There were all kinds of implications contained in that word, and my inner archaeologist was curious.

"My turn, Lockett," Fera said. "I want to talk with that thing."

Benegal added himself to the growing number of crew members who were hanging around the Fleuridian's cryo cell. The blue armor panels that denoted his lineage of the Sapphire Den of Lilian, the Krayvox home world, shone brilliantly in the cascading lights given off by the shifting geometry of the bulkheads.

He'd spent a considerable amount of effort to upgrade his armor until it was how he liked it.

"This thing," Benegal hissed, "is dangerous. We must carry out our original plan and cast it into the nearest star."

"We're only doing that as a last resort," Fera said, whispering as though afraid it might hear her.

Benegal took the hint and lowered his voice as well. "It is the only way to be sure it will not attempt a second coup."

I was inclined to side with Benegal, but if Fera was right, there was no telling what might occur if we lost the thing's confidence. Assuming we had it at all.

"Let's just talk with it and see what happens for now," I said.

Benegal crossed his arms. "What, exactly, do we hope to gain from it?"

"I don't know," I admitted, stealing a glance inside the cell. "Maybe no more trying to kill us for power?"

Fera took a step inside the room, drawing a rebuke from the Drayth.

"No one enters until repairs are complete!"

Lockett was crouched at the station next to the vertical cylinder of the cryopod—or the frame of what had been the cryopod. Crystalline fragments littered the space, covered in a sheen of cryogenic gel that had yet to fully evaporate. The Drayth worked feverishly at the head unit of its former pet, Dumpy, tinkering with the internal circuitry like he was performing open-heart surgery.

Dumpy's head unit sparked. Lockett withdrew his hand, spewing a gurgled string of curses. A single mote of light floated up from the bot's sole remaining piece and hovered behind Lockett's head. It flashed, and when the brightness began to fade, lines of light in the rough shape of a humanoid being stood at the deck. I recognized the conehead and the dark pits where the eyes were supposed to be immediately.

"Lockett," I said uneasily, "I don't think the Fleuridian necessarily appreciates you tinkering with its… container."

"My property," Lockett corrected. "Dumpy belongs to Lockett."

The Fleuridian stood there. Watching? Waiting? It was impossible to discern its body or the body language amid what was just swirling fumes of purple smoke. It was almost like the being itself was censored from reality. The harder I tried to discern its physical appearance, the more it defied any kind of defined shape.

"One for one," it said in its rattling timbre.

The negotiations had begun.

"You need a power source to complete your Ascension," I guessed.

"Truth," it replied.

"You've been siphoning energy from this ship for the last four thousand years," Fera said. "How much more do you need?"

"Lockett observed it was recently increasing siphon on vital systems." The Drayth sounded in awe before the creature.

The Fleuridian remained still, despite the swirling smoke continuing to ebb and flow in vapor trails over its not-entirely-physical body, basking the compartment in alternating hues of blue and purple and gold. Static filled the air, buzzing along my skin with faint tickles of diffuse energy.

"I require a source. Ascension requires knowledge and power. I am knowledge. I require power."

Lockett shivered. "What quantity of power?"

"Three FOE," the Fleuridian replied.

Fera blanched.

Lockett's iron lung frothed quietly. He shook his head and sat on the deck, rubbing at the diamond-shaped plate in his forehead as if he'd been struck with a migraine.

The number didn't mean anything to me. I waited for my fiber-link to info dump some knowledge into my head, but the only thing that passed through my mind was a series of equations that, even with the information presented, I didn't have the capacity to parse through.

"That's a lot, right?"

Fera shook her head in disbelief. "It's more than a supernova."

"So wait," I said to the Fleuridian, "All at once, or like, you can store it?"

The Fleuridian remained stolid in its response, not moving or shifting its eyeless gaze as it spoke. "The Ascension took place many millennia ago. My kind discovered the secret of breaching this realm. Of becoming one with the higher dimensional plane. Those of us who were not yet given the rite of passage into maturity were left behind."

I felt a trickle of ice drop into my stomach.

"Those of us..." I echoed, my throat dry and scratchy. "You mean there are more of you still out there?"

"I sense three at various points in this galaxy." It turned its cone-head, as if it were thinking. "I do not know if, like me, they have found vessels that may contain them."

Fera broke out into a cold sweat. No one in the room seemed prepared for that little dose of reality or what it might mean.

No one spoke for some time, and I worried our silence might send the wrong message. So I asked the first thing that popped into my head. "So, uh, do you have a name?"

Fera shot me a look, letting me know she thought it was a dumb question. I shrugged apologetically.

The Fleuridian hesitated. "I am Uriel."

"Uriel?" I asked. "Is that a family name or… ?"

"It is my anchor to this three-dimensional prison. Freedom floats above in a higher realm. My people bask in the ecstasy of perfection in a place far removed from this one. Once I have attained the energy I require, I will join them."

"Okay, right, but this is a lot of energy. More than what you could hope to draw from *Phaelon*—this ship—or the ship you tried to uh… *confiscate*. So how do we find a source of energy like that?"

Fera stepped in, her expression hard. "You get the same deal as everyone else on this ship. You help us win this war, and we'll get you what you need afterward."

That sounded to me like an absolutely batshit insane thing to say to the nearest incarnation of a god I'd ever encountered. I looked at her out of the corner of my eye, wondering if she was bluffing, or really believed what she was saying. I mean, promising Lockett two million credits and a one-way trip to a vacation world was one thing. Delivering a supernova's worth of energy to Uriel, a being of smoke and light…

What was I missing?

I cleared my throat. "Fera?"

She gave me the look. I reluctantly held my tongue.

"One for one," it said.

"One for one," Fera agreed.

Lockett twitched. "And part of the deal, you tell Lockett secrets of the Ascension. Lockett forgives debts owed, past and present."

The Fleuridian dissolved in a smear of glittering diamonds,

leaving a thin wisp of purple smoke in its wake. The smoke floated like a feather in the wind and buried itself inside Dumpy's severed head unit.

Lockett gave a groan of lamentation.

"Do not," Fera said, leaning into her words and punctuating them with a knife hand poised between Lockett's eyes, "*do not* sell us down the estuary on this one."

It was down the river, but I chalked it up to a simple error in the translation. It was easy to forget that no one, except me, truly spoke English.

The Drayth held out its arms as if to ask, "What did I do?"

Fera wasn't having it. "You are staring down the barrel of a hefty price tag for this one, Lockett. All your calculations—your insistence that we couldn't just rid ourselves of this parasite has resulted in death, damage, and destruction. You're making terms for a clean slate? All debts paid? That's already done from the simple fact that Will and I haven't turned you over to be the scapegoat for this disaster."

Lockett shook his head. "None of you simple life-forms appreciate the possibilities technology brings. No understanding of what Fleuridian means for advancement of Drayth and all living creatures!"

That got under my skin. "There are two sides to every coin, Lockett. Try considering what everyone in the Coalition is going to think of you—and by extension *us*. What does it say that we're willing to play with their lives?"

"We are lucky not to be under guard," Benegal said from the back of the chamber. "And you would do well to consider the magnitude of trouble that Will saved all of us from by virtue of his position. Do not let your lust for the secrets of the galaxy interfere with the future of this war, or this crew, again."

Lockett spat a curse at him, then turned his attention back to his tinkering.

Quin interjected with a brush of static. "The other shoe has officially dropped, everyone. Fera, Will—your presence is requested in the war room. Immediately."

I locked eyes with Fera. "Okay. We're going to have to explain this to the brass. Which will probably include Eddison. First, if the Federation wanted this thing, why wouldn't the U-C? Second, how are we going to sell them on the idea that we have Uriel on our side, at least for the time being? Because I'll be honest, I'm not even sold that this won't bite us in the end."

"It's all one big, tough sell," Quin agreed.

"Tell them the truth," Benegal said. "What they choose to believe when presented with reality is their concern. Not ours."

18

FERA and I were permitted to leave *Phaelon*, but then Quin had to take the ship out of *Earthborn* and position it nearly a thousand kilometers from the rest of the fleet. A safety precaution, but also an inconvenience. We would probably become isolated from everyone. There was a good chance that I would be isolated from my friends because I had to imagine they would continue to want the Hero of the Rebellion front and center. That couldn't happen while I was locked up aboard *Phaelon*.

Whatever future concerns I had were cleared away when I got another look at the damage caused on the ship. Human crews were cleaning up the chaos from the bots, all of which had been deactivated as a safety precaution until they could be factory reset and fitted with some sort of kill switch. There was still blood on the decking, being cleaned up by white towels stained in an assortment of alien colors.

The people looked at me with some regard and appreciation.

Quin said word went out that *I* had been the one to stop the disaster in its tracks. That said, the same regard wasn't being extended to Fera. I could see the change from the way technicians charged with removing the hair follicles of coworkers whose heads had been bashed looked at her.

This wasn't over yet. Things could get very bad, very quick.

"Tror couldn't have asked for a bigger gift," I mumbled to Fera.

She only nodded.

We reached the meeting room and sat down beneath what had to be an intentional glare of lights. General Mira'dna, Fleet Admiral Tanoka, Captain Caldera who had command of the *Earthborn*, Colonel Stallings, and Lieutenant Fel sat across from us. They would be our interrogators.

Their expressions varied slightly, but there was a universal sour look of disappointment on all of them.

General Mira'dna expressed in no uncertain terms that she had an unpleasant task before her—explaining to the families of the tech workers that their loved ones had died in an accident. "Losing people is hard enough, but when it is something preventable… that makes it harder."

Earl floated in front of me, cataloging every moment of my discomfort. I was surprised to see the bot on hand to record this. I was also surprised that Eddison wasn't joining the conference from Earth.

That had to mean that the *Earthborn* leadership itself considered the item a closed affair. But with Uriel… it was much larger than that.

"All due respect, General," I began, "but I'm not sure this was avoidable."

Fleet Admiral Tanoka scowled. "That's the best you can come up with? Simple fate?"

"Please don't put words in my mouth, Admiral," I said. "I did not say that this was fated to happen, only that it was something more complicated than a simple accident."

Fera directed her ire straight at the Admiral with an icy edge to her tone. "No one could have predicted the Fleuridian's actions. We stopped it before irreparable harm could come to this ship. These deaths are a tragedy, but a far greater tragedy was avoided."

General Mira'dna pursed her lips. "That a being of this potential power and magnitude was in your care, and you did not deem to share that information with us, concerns me."

I shook my head. "This isn't about keeping secrets. This was a Federation contract, captured over four millennia ago, that proved more dangerous than anyone—the Federation included—thought possible."

"Nevertheless," Tanoka said, his hostility undiminished, "we know of it now. How do we destroy it?"

Admiral Tanoka glared at me. I'd never seen him so rattled before, not even during the escape from Jyraxis when he was barking orders as his fleet was getting atomized one ship at a time.

I held back a laugh—not because I thought it was funny, but because of how hopeless our situation seemed. "I'm not sure it can be destroyed, Admiral."

Colonel Stallings leaned forward, adding his voice to the discussion. "Then it needs to be removed from the presence of this fleet. Let it feast on Imperium power cores if it must. It is a proven danger, and we would be fools to ignore it."

"And we will be wise to consider all of our options," Fera said, leaning over the table. "The Fleuridian that caused all of this chaos has agreed to work with us until the war's end."

Everyone opposite Fera looked at her blankly. The news brought no relief or happiness.

Admiral Tanoka interlaced his fingers, as though attempting to calm himself before speaking. "A mythical creature from antiquity that carries a level of power that cannot be controlled seems far more a liability than it is an asset."

Fera was unfazed. "It needs levels of power far beyond anything our ships can provide. Yet it stayed with us, content to slowly—*slowly*—drain the *Phaelon* until we discovered and attempted to contain it. Only then did it jump ship and attempt to access *Earthborn*'s sealed power cores."

I stepped in, ready to carry the ball across the goal line. "Fera and I believe the creature—it calls itself Uriel—needs our help to achieve its ascension; otherwise, it would have left to find more ample sources of power long ago."

General Mira'dna tugged at her stone curls of hair. "And what would this being, this Fleuridian, provide us in our efforts?"

Colonel Stallings looked aghast. "General, you can't—"

She held up a hand. "I only wish to hear an answer to my question." Mira'dna leveled an accusing gaze at the colonel. "And for my staff to question my decisions—by all means—but not question the simple act of gathering information."

Chastened, the colonel lowered his head. "I apologize, General."

A nod from Mira'dna, and the matter was buried in the past.

She looked to us for an answer.

Fera and I exchanged a look of our own.

"We, uh, really can't say, General," I confessed. "But the Fleuridian does seem willing to work with us to end the war."

"Only to find a promise that we may be unable to keep," Mira'dna observed. "And what then?"

Fera's smile did not reach her eyes. "One problem at a time."

Mira'dna didn't smile back. "Platitudes will not help us, Captain Fera."

Admiral Tanoka took in a sharp breath and slowly let it out. "I assume," he said, nostrils flaring with barely checked rage, "this is an everything or nothing situation. If we do not agree to allow the Fleuridian to be a part of your crew, will you abandon the fight?"

Where had he gotten that idea?

Nothing like that had even crossed my mind.

I cleared my throat, drawing his eyes to mine. "You are mistaken, Admiral. We are committed to finishing what we helped begin. I will go to Astrada as planned and await only word that the mission is prepared. The Imperium has already had too much time to consolidate its forces while we reset."

Stallings and Tanoka shared a look.

"Our preparations will be complete in two days," Tanoka said. "But not to negotiate terms with the Astradians. We will bring the war to their doorstep. We have actionable intelligence that Tror's flagship and much of the remaining Imperium fleet are now gathering over Astrada."

The news hit me like a pillowcase full of dictionaries—right to the face. It hit Fera even harder.

This is exactly what her people wanted to avoid.

Admiral Tanoka continued, "We will need you to Void Drift the fleet into position. Then our combined fleet will destroy the

Imperium as a viable fighting force. Stragglers will persist in scattered pockets of resistance for a time. That can't be avoided. But by and large, when the *ONE* is destroyed, the Imperium will fall."

Fera blinked. She had gone rigid at the news and so far hadn't moved a millimeter. "Prefect Tror's vessel is the most dangerous and capable warship ever constructed. Tror is himself a navigator. How will you prevent it from simply Void Drifting away before the combined fleets can destroy it? While Tror lives—"

"The Imperium remains a threat, I know." Admiral Tanoka visibly relaxed. This was the part of the discussion he had prepared for, and he felt comfortable that his team had devised a perfect plan. "General Mira'dna, if the matter of the Fleuridian can be considered finished, or at least tabled for now?"

She gave a curt nod.

Tanoka sat back, his face going slack. I recognized the sign of someone manipulating data with their fiber-link. A moment later, the lights dimmed, and a hologram appeared above the table. The *ONE*.

I had seen it before, but the thing was still awe-inspiring. It put Eddison's cruisers to shame. Even the Imperium's *Seventy*, and the *Three Oh One*... nothing came close. I had trouble accepting that the thing floating in front of me was the scan of a real spacecraft. The ship was massive, bordering on the point of incomprehensibly big.

Something that large had to be built in hard vacuum—no planetary gravity well would allow an object of such scale to escape its clutches. It was, in its simplest form, a mountain uprooted from its base and tossed into space, hollowed out on the inside, with layers of armor vac-welded and interwoven across the outside, like a carapace of some monstrous beetle.

The concept of an aircraft carrier came to mind, but that was only part of it. Like an accretion disk surrounding a gas giant, a slice of deck the scans measured at twenty levels thick divided the top and bottom halves from each other.

The dorsal section was a raised spine large enough to be a cruiser all by itself. Sensor arrays and towers of avionics equipment ran the length from bow to stern. Bristling from both sides of the spine and canted at forty-five-degree angles was the single largest collection of armaments I'd ever seen.

Thousands of point defense cannons surrounded cutout slots for hundreds of launch bays for missiles. I could not imagine that many big guns firing at once. The logistics involved in managing the firing cycles, reloads, and cooldown periods, not to mention the havoc that must wreak in the orbital mechanics department… it must have been a nightmare.

But what fresh hell a mobile arsenal like that could dish out… I didn't have to imagine that. We'd come up against it and lost every time. Farakar had paid the ultimate price at its hands. Delta and wings of Coalition cruisers, fighters, and capital ships trying to surround that ship would get hulled at best, incinerated into molten husks of metal and bodies at worst.

Fera's assessment was sound and logical: The United Coalition could not hope to destroy a ship like that. I'm not sure our combined fleets could even stand against the thing.

"You had this meeting planned already," I asked. "Before the matter of the Fleuridian."

Mira'dna gave a thin smile. "The utmost secrecy was required."

Tanoka began his briefing. "The *ONE* has never lost a ship-to-ship engagement. Our battle strategy has been to simply avoid it and leave the moment it arrived. Its mere presence denies a Coalition victory, and so we have had to split our fleet, with Atron's forces drawing the enemy away long enough for us to make gains elsewhere now that the Imperium's numbers have subsided."

It was easy to see why. *ONE* looked more like a fortified mobile space station than a ship.

I shook my head. "Unless Eddison has built something to equal this, I'm not sure how we can hope to disable it, let alone destroy it."

Admiral Tanoka nodded sagely. "There are no other ships like this, you can be sure of that. It was built somewhere in Imperium space by technicians we do not know and of a design we could not comprehend... until now."

The holographic zoomed to what was labeled as the space mountain's propulsion section. It was as oversized and gaudy as the weapons—taking up the entire underside of the ship. Sixteen fusion drives directed focused plasma trails behind the vessel. The hologram peeled away several layers of deck to highlight four FTL drives and two Void engines.

"This is impossible," Fera mumbled. "How is something like this powered?"

I waited for the Admiral to continue, wondering the same thing.

"The Imperium has enjoyed unfettered access to advanced research and development technology during their reign. We knew the ship could somehow maneuver, Void Drift, and—oh, yes—destroy entire rebel fleets single-handedly. There is a reason the factions went underground. The answer is... they have discovered some means of harnessing energy from a higher space-time. Essentially, a conduit of sorts that pulls limitless energy from outside this dimension."

I sat back in my seat, unable to speak for a moment. "Well, I guess that's a good way to make the Fleuridian happy."

Fera's grip on my arm tightened. "You're talking about zero-point energy."

"We believe so, yes. As for the Fleuridian, our intention remains to destroy the *ONE*. Whatever promises you made are yours to worry about. This—*this*—will win the war."

"A ship this size can't respond to tactical movements," Fera said. "It can move in, engage, and retreat if it needs to, but it doesn't maneuver. You're intending to Void Drift on its backside, hit it fast and hard, and hope to break something important inside before it can Void Drift to safety."

Admiral Tanoka's face spread in a broad grin.

"If you intend to fell a giant, your best chance is to sneak up on him when he's sleeping. This is our plan. In all the history of the Imperium, no one has ever been able to get close enough to the aft of the ship. With the capability of Void Drifting Will brings to the fight, and the knowledge we have acquired thanks to those working for Marcus Edisson, we will stack up the bulk of our fleet on the backside of the *ONE*, and we will hit it with everything we have."

Fera let go of my arm and rubbed a droplet of sweat from her brow. The white lines on her face wrinkled as her cheeks pinched with deep thought. "You actually think this could work?"

General Mira'dna inclined her head. "The plan will require additional refinements, but yes, we believe it can."

Colonel Stallings rapped his knuckles on the table. "Fleet's more than capable, same as our ground forces. Whatever the mission, we'll execute. No fail."

"We don't have any interdictor ships," I said. "The risk of the

ONE escaping is very real. But... what if we make sure to tag along wherever it runs off to?"

I watched each of their expressions darken. Fera looked at me like I'd grown a second head.

Admiral Tanoka eyed me suspiciously. "What do you mean by that?"

"We don't *just* unload our arsenal on the ship," I said and then pointed to Colonel Stallings. "We board it, too."

Colonel Stallings grinned. "You crazy son of a bitch."

Admiral Tanoka gave me a grudging look of respect. "It certainly has merit, but... suppose we're successful at not only disabling the *ONE* with our surprise attack, but beginning a chain reaction that results in its destruction? Are any of us willing to order our men into such friendly fire?"

"If it means ending the war, you'll find volunteers," I said. "Count me among them. We already have the best warfighters on the battlefield, three capable fleets, and... we have the *Three Oh One*, too."

That was a turn of the screw no one had thought of, including myself until it just fell out.

General Mira'dna's stone eyes went wide. "The Krakoids. You intend to set loose a legion of Krakoids inside the *ONE*."

"Send them in *first*," I clarified, "and then, while the Imperium soldiers on board have their hands full repelling them, we'll hit the *ONE* from alternate breaching points. Each with a different task... including a strike team that will hunt down Tror."

Fera's frosty expression bloomed into a grin. "*This* could work. This could actually work."

"Still probably could use a few tweaks," I said, trying to sound modest, but I was proud of my plan.

Before anyone else could speak, a trilling tone split the air.

The hologram dissolved. A red-bordered message window appeared in its place. Whatever this incoming transmission was, it seemed highly important.

Lieutenant Fel popped up immediately and dropped a second blast door in place, further sealing the room in privacy. He remained standing by it as though expecting someone to attempt to force entry, his hand on the butt of his holstered pistol.

"I'm clearing you all for this message," Mira'dna said hastily. "However, nothing said here leaves this room. We must have total secrecy."

No one argued with her.

"Put the connection through," the general said.

The red box fell away in a cascade of pixelated motes of light. In its place, the face of an Astradian delegate filled the frame. I was shocked how similar she looked to Fera, but only at first. As she spoke and her face began to move, I realized the woman had some of Fera's direct nature, but none of her softness.

The General identified the Astradian for our benefit. "Prime Minister Elect Dora Nightshade, what is your situation?"

"General Mira'dna," she said in a harsh, guttural tone, "I am afraid we are out of time."

The tone got to me. It wasn't the pleading of someone who thought they were going to die. It was a negotiator about to say, "take it or leave it."

General Mira'dna clasped her hands together, her lips forming a thin line. "Prime Minister, you have yet to come to terms with the United Coalition. I am afraid—"

The Astradian cut her off, words almost tumbling over each other as she delivered information in a forceful, concerned manner. "I received FTL comms only just now. They are thirteen hours old. The Imperium has entered the Astradian system. Prefect Tror and his flagship are among them. Astrada *will not* become another Farakar!"

Fera shivered. I put my hand on hers and gave it a gentle squeeze.

A weight settled onto the general's shoulders. Almost imperceptibly, she turned her head toward Admiral Tanoka, who whispered, "It is not ideal, but we can do it."

Dora continued, her eyes hot with anger, but not without genuine concern—fear for her people. "Marcus Eddison told us the Imperium would come. He did not suggest that they would *attack*! You will deliver us aid—now—or we will relent of our planned alliance and join the Imperium. For good and without reservation. What is your answer?"

I was surprised to see how far things had come in the negotiations without me. The last I knew, I was supposed to go to Astrada and work things out there on another "Hero of the Rebellion" tour. But now it seemed like Eddison and the Council had done all the heavy lifting.

Only… things weren't turning out the way any of us would have hoped they did.

General Mira'dna was careful to keep her face fixed so as not to undermine the gravity of the situation. "Prime Minister. We will press forward with all due haste. Hold strong until we arrive. I suggest you enter negotiations with Tror to stave off the immediate attack. The United Coalition is coming. I promise you that."

Dora cut the connection without further response.

Mira'dna was silent for a moment, as if it might keep the impending reality at bay for eternity, if she only held back her next words. "Colonel Stallings, I leave details of the boarding operation to you."

The Colonel cleared his throat and leaned forward, his hands making white-knuckled fists. "Of course, General."

"Admiral Tanoka, the fleet is yours to command."

"Aye aye, General."

She looked at me next. "What remains rests on your shoulders, Will Kaufman. How quickly can you Navigate our fleet to the Astradian system?"

I could practically feel the fierce determination on my face. This was it. The final conflict that would keep Earth safe. "I'm ready now. Say the word, and we'll make it happen."

Admiral Tanoka locked eyes with Colonel Stallings. The old comrades shared a nod. They had fought together for so long, words didn't need to be exchanged. They knew each other's capabilities and could practically predict each other's words.

"Two hours," Captain Tanoka said.

"Two hours," I agreed, a stress knot tightening up in my neck.

The war could be over sooner than I thought.

19

"ALL HANDS TO BATTLE STATIONS. I say again, this is Captain Caldera with a real-world emergency announcement. The *Earthborn* is now at OPCON Charlie. All hands to battle stations! Prepare for Void Drift."

I rushed through the pristine corridors of the *Earthborn*, with Fera and Benegal right behind me. We noticed ample evidence of small-arms fire along the bulkheads. The United Coalition battle damage repair team ignored the carbon scoring in favor of patching holes.

I tried to put the incident out of my mind as we arrived at the *Phaelon*, which had been granted a one-time permission to dock with the Fleuridian onboard due to the crisis. I guess that's the military for you. Orders come and then new orders follow almost as quickly. I bounded up the ramp and poked my head into the auto-med to check on Sert.

He was crammed inside the vertical crystalline tube, shoulders scrunched and his face pinched with discomfort. The breathable medical gel that filled the tube discolored him a shade of purple. His wounded eye was open, the orange flesh rapidly healing to the point that the swelling was almost completely gone.

"You all right, big guy?" I asked.

Fera and Benegal moved past the door, sparing a glance in Sert's direction on their way to the bridge.

Sert manipulated the controls on the tank with his fiber-link, triggering the drain cycle. In seconds, the gel evaporated into the top of the unit and the crystalline tube telescoped into the ceiling. He stumbled out of the station, skin and armor glistening with a sheen of moisture.

"The call to war has been given," he said with a grin.

"Yeah. This is it. Tror's attacking Astrada. We're going after the *ONE*."

Sert rolled his shoulders and cracked the vertebrae in his neck.

"Then let us be on with it. I grow impatient for combat."

I led him to the bridge. Fera was already strapped into the copilot seat. Lockett was running diagnostics at the Weapons Officer station. Benegal sat in the fold-down crash couch behind Sert's science officer station.

"Will, you look rattled," Quin commented from his trademark position at the helm.

"And you look like you've cleared the bugs out of your circuits. It's good to see you back at peak operating capacity, Quin," I said, taking my seat in the pilot's chair.

Fera punched commands into her terminal. Screens shifted and moved in front of her, displaying everything from reactor readings to navigational data and comm frequencies.

"All systems green across the board. Preflight checks complete. Inertial compensator online. Stand by for launch."

The *Phaelon* shuddered as its magnetic clamp detached from the deck.

Quin's tall, thin Foris body paced along the front of the bridge. The main hologram display behind him showed the forward-facing camera feed, bordered by the sweeping bulkheads of the docking bay and the open starfield ahead of us.

"I've already keyed up the Void Drift suite on your terminal. This is going to be a bit more complicated than previous Drifts, as I'm sure you're aware. Remote access is going to allow you to send ships through separate Drift Lanes. You will have to remain in the Void long enough to direct each craft to the correct lane."

I bit my lip. This felt much more complicated than anything I'd done before. "So, the plan is to send the *Three Oh One* ahead of us, then drop the caravan right on the backside of the *ONE*. Do you have any experience with precision drops like this?"

Quin gave me a crooked smile. "You ask the right questions, Will. That's how I know you were born to do this."

"That's… not an answer, Quin."

The AI chose to ignore me. Which, I suppose, was an answer in and of itself.

"Okay," I said through a sigh. "Let's see how this goes."

Fera bumped the throttle to fifty percent. A tug of vertigo yanked at my stomach, settling me into the seat. Delluvian fibers conformed to my body, compensating for the increased pressure.

I grabbed my helmet from the slot next to my chair and pulled it on. The neck liner of my Drayth armor aligned with the slot at the base of the helmet and sealed with a gasp.

"Helmets on, everyone. We're not going to be part of the boarding team, which means we'll be part of the ship-to-ship action. If the *Phaelon* gets hulled, we'll lose atmosphere, and I don't want anyone going hypoxic and succumbing to a lack of oxygen."

"Let's just hope our Astradian pilot lives up to her self-proclaimed ace status. If we don't get shot, we shouldn't need to worry about it," Quin said.

Fera backed the throttle to idle and activated the autopilot suite, putting us into a slow coast on the straight and narrow alongside the *Earthborn*. She picked up her helmet and paused, then turned it over in her hands.

"We're about to end this war." Her voice shook with adrenaline. "We've got to give them everything we've got."

She pulled her helmet on. Behind us, Sert and Benegal did the same.

I laid out my station in typical fashion: main bridge display on my MFD's primary screen, scopes on the right-hand-side display, and the Void Drift suite on the left-hand-side display. The routine was familiar, and I let my instincts guide me as I laid out the coordinates and stacked three separate transition codes into the *Phaelon*'s main mission computer.

Twenty minutes passed with no one speaking. Earl the camera drone hovered at the top of my primary display like an old-style Earth webcam. I resisted the urge to punch it off my screen as Quin continued pacing. His hologram maintained itself without any signs of glitching.

Uriel must not have inserted itself back into the ship.

As much of an unknown as the Fleuridian was, it seemed to stay true to its word.

Twenty minutes became an hour. Tension and pre-combat jitters gripped the bridge like a breath held just a little too long. The nerves were starting to wear down to the point that we were all antsy. Chomping at the bit to just get this thing over with, once and for all.

A comm request lit up at my station. I patched it through immediately.

Fleet Admiral Tanoka appeared on my primary screen.

"*Phaelon,* this is *Earthborn.* The *Three Oh One* is in position at the head of the caravan. Tethers are in place, and the fleet is combat ready. Drift at your leisure."

"Nothing leisurely about it," I muttered.

"*Phaelon* copies. Stand by for drift," Fera said, cutting the connection. She turned to look at me, her helmet visor glaring in the overhead lighting. "If the history books record this moment, you don't want them quoting you as a sarcastic prick, Will."

I smirked. "You know, I hadn't thought about that. I'll have to come up with a catchphrase. Something like, 'Void Stalkers, assemble!' That's got a nice ring to it, doesn't it?"

"Hardly," Quin said with a shake of his head.

I sucked in a breath and steeled my nerves.

"Okay, here we go. Void Drift in five."

I finished the countdown and engaged the Void engine.

The starfield inverted.

IN MY MIND'S EYE, I stood on a thin layer of ice in the midst of a blizzard. The surface of the ice broke under my weight. I plunged into the depths, a gap between dimensions that was hollow and empty as far as the eye could see and as deep as the mind could sense.

White noise scratched across my brain, ending in a crack, the splitting open of a shell. The distinct snap gave way to a shrill whine, similar to the onset of tinnitus in the aftermath of an explosion.

Infinite space opened up before me, wrapping its pale light over the *Phaelon*, the *Three Oh One*, and the rest of the ships tethered to my ship's Void engine.

A trumpeting fanfare blared inside my skull.

The Void Song.

Pinned to my seat, every muscle tense from the transition, I let the music that was not music wash over me. It was a call from the heart of the universe itself—some perfect, holy place where evil did not exist, only pure, unadulterated light that was as abundant as dark matter in the temporal realm.

In a lilting, playful cascade of notes, the Void called to me. It was an anthem of angels, a song of music that never fully materialized into something tangible, and yet, it was somehow more real than the dimension I'd left behind. There were secrets contained in those notes, answers to questions mankind had sought since their first day under the sun as thinking, reasoning beings.

It was all there, all contained in the Void. The whited-out expanse of nothingness that stretched interminably in every direction held the key to existence. Something so marvelous... mine for the taking.

But only if I let go of my inhibitions. If I just allowed it to fill me—

"Will?" Quin prompted.

I blinked away the effects of the siren song. "We have entered the Void. STEM readings?"

"Normal. Latency is within standard parameters. You are free to Navigate."

In my peripheral awareness, I sensed the crew monitoring their specific stations, completely unaware of the tug of war between perfect bliss and total chaos. Sweat broke out on my forehead, automatically kicking in my helmet's environmental controls with a puff of aluminum-scented airflow.

The turn of the tide always managed to surprise me. Sweeping melodies became corrupted with gut-churning chugs, like didgeridoos or Mongolian throat singers.

Decay. Corruption. The angelic anthem became a torturous shriek that could have shattered glass. Bliss morphed into panic on the turn of the moment.

Was this the truth of the Void? Sinister and oppressive?

On the bridge, things carried on as usual. With no awareness of the Void or its schizophrenic song.

Lockett's iron lung gurgled. Benegal took slow, deep breaths.

My awareness shook with sudden force. It was tangential—something outside the ship, but also buried deep within me. A gut feeling that pierced me with a sense of urgency.

Cracks formed in the whiteout of the main bridge display. Dark bolts of lightning tore through the haunting emptiness of subspace, tracing paths light-years long from point to point. Liminal lines that came and went between stars at the whim of the Void. As soon as they appeared, they began to fade, flickering until the paths they traced disappeared completely.

Sert grumbled wordless complaints behind me. The occasional

chime from the sensors at our stations filtered through the sounds and sensations only I could experience.

The scopes showed all Coalition vessels had made the transition and were following the *Phaelon* like ducks in a line. It was all according to plan, but this was a different kind of Drift.

I needed two lanes, and I needed them one right after the other.

Not just any two lanes, though. They had to be exact.

Everything so exact…

"Are you all right, Will?" Quin asked.

From somewhere far away—I had no means of assessing the origin point—shadow bolts shot across the display in a cluster. At seemingly random intervals, they redirected their paths at hard right angles, creating jagged rifts in the light.

I studied them, noticing the gradient shifting lengthwise on each Drift Lane.

"I'm good," I muttered.

I placed one hand on the throttle and gripped the sidestick with the other.

Instinct guided me. I increased the *Phaelon*'s acceleration and adjusted course, taking a positive arc over our initial entry point. I didn't think—I operated completely from feel. It was like a sixth sense, tracing a sound that couldn't be heard, waiting for a feeling that I couldn't actually feel—but when the moment came, I would somehow know.

It was the same primal experience every time. The movements were familiar. The timing could be learned. Finding the right path, that was the trick. It never got easier. In some ways it felt like the first time every time.

Fera watched me out of the corner of her eye, her expression vacillating between casual awareness and concern. I inhaled a brief wave of cherry blossoms. The familiarity of her scent comforted me.

Quin clasped his hands behind his back and bent at the waist to look over the side of my station like a teacher inspecting the test I was taking.

"Very good," he said.

"Glad you approve," I mumbled.

I continued making slight adjustments to our course. Fatigue began to set in, but I wasn't keeping track of the time. It felt like an hour, but it could have been longer, before the drift lanes began to appear at a higher frequency. Each new lane resonated with a different frequency—a clash of bliss and despair.

Sweat clung to my brow. My helmet filters kicked on again, wicking away the moisture before it could drip into my eyes.

"I have seen this many times now, but I still struggle to believe it," Benegal said in a soft voice.

Sert's reply was dismissive. "Will is unique amongst his kind. He is one of those who walked before he crawled."

Fera smiled. She continued to watch me, her face resolving into something like curiosity, and maybe a hint of pride. I recognized the sentiment; it was the way I looked at her when we were alone.

I refocused on the main bridge display, watching the drift lanes come and go in jagged slashes of darkness. Somewhere in that maelstrom was the way out—the only way out for all of us.

If the plan was going to work, I needed two ways out.

I still hadn't worked through the logistics of how that was going to happen. How could I?

"Okay, so I know you never did, but has *anyone* ever attempted this before? Breaking the tether?" I asked.

Quin gave me a flat stare. "You ask this *now*? What do you think?"

"No."

"Take heart, young Will." Quin puffed his chest and stood tall and proud, like I was his prized student and he was talking me up to a crowd. "Everything you have done since sneaking onto my ship has been something you've never done before, and yet you somehow rise to the occasion. It defies the Great Algorithm and my understanding of the universe itself, but you don't seem to care for those sorts of things. You make your own way—one could say, you Navigate your own path."

"If I didn't know any better," I said, still scanning for the needed paths, "I might mistake that for a compliment, Quin."

"Merely a lesson: simply because something has never been done before is no reason to avoid trying it."

"Even when the consequences of failure are fatal," Sert said with a grimace.

Fera jabbed a finger at him. "Put a lid on the nihilism for a minute. This is serious."

A smile tugged at the corner of my mouth. I could always count on Fera to be in my corner.

"Lockett would not agree to this if chances of death exceeded quality of reward," the Drayth said, sounding whimsical.

Fera said something to him too, but I didn't hear it.

Hundreds of dark pinpricks off the starboard bow began to coalesce, pooling their masses into one giant cloud of shadow. I frowned, shifting the angle on the external camera to bring the anomaly into view.

"What…?" I asked.

"There it is again," Quin remarked off-handedly.

The whirling maelstrom of darkness inserted itself into the song of the Void like a turbine ramping up to thousands of revolutions per minute. It wasn't a whining or a grinding kind of sound; it had a grating, teeth-gnashing quality to it that made my skin crawl.

"But in all my years as a Navigator," Quin said, "I never heard of anything like this…"

"Can anything in the Void be… new?" I asked, keeping my senses attuned to the interplay of the drift lanes and their shifting tones.

"Who could ever possibly know. Whatever it is, I don't believe it's good. Observe: it is a hollow, empty space, but it seems to be gaining mass. And the noise…"

Loud didn't begin to describe it. The larger it became, as more dark stars rushed to join the teeming mass, the more the grating lifted from a metallic groan to the level of fork-in-the-garbage-disposal.

I cringed. I needed to find the exit lane, and I needed to find it quickly.

If that hollow space became much larger, my ability to sense anything in the Void was going to be overridden by that cacophony.

A puff of purple smoke appeared at the helm. Quin saw it and flinched, a shriek of surprise falling out of his open mouth. "The Fleuridian—what in the—"

The smoke resolved enough to show the bluish outline of Uriel.

His shadowed eyes looked straight at me. "You pass through the Void without the ability to see. This is a great danger."

"See?" I growled. "What are you talking about?"

My grip on the drift lanes was starting to slip. Like whales calling out to each other as they began their migration, the sounds I couldn't hear but felt keenly in tingles along my skull began to dissipate.

"The Hollow will consume you," Uriel declared. "Survival will come only with a rapid exit from this realm."

"I'm looking, I'm looking," I said through gritted teeth.

"Let Will focus!" Fera snapped.

Uriel didn't seem to take offense to being yelled at. Lockett, on the other hand...

"Do not denigrate the wisdom of the Lightbearers!" the Drayth hissed.

Uriel didn't move, but the Fleuridian did something. Something only I, and maybe Quin, could sense. A new Drift Lane rocketed over the pale expanse of light and forked off into two paths at the midpoint.

My breath caught in my chest.

It wasn't a streak of broken darkness.

It was a shimmering, beautiful gold, and unlike the shadow bolts, this lane held its presence with a firmness that should have been impossible. Uriel's voice rumbled through the bridge, deep and distorted, giving the impression it was lifting something heavy—or using a massive amount of its own energy stores.

"Take the path. End this nonsense before it ends you."

"Will?" Quin said, his voice choked off in awe and surprise.

I tapped my MFD, placing two markers at the ends of the differing forks, then put in a comm request to the *Three Oh One*.

"Captain Esmila of the *Three Oh One*. Go ahead, *Phaelon*," a crisp female voice responded.

"You're way marker bravo. Disconnect tether and make your transition."

"Acknowledged. *Three Oh One* out."

Fera went stiff. "Will, are you sure—?"

I wagged my chin at Uriel. "It didn't skip killing us earlier so it could do it now. I don't think it wants to die."

"You don't know that," Quin warned.

"Too late now," I said.

My words settled onto the bridge as if I'd told everyone to shut their mouths.

Complete silence wafted over me. It was eerie, being in the Void and suddenly not hearing the song. It felt wrong. Beyond that, it scared the hell out of me. Fleuridian or not, how did Uriel manage to manipulate the laws of physics in a realm no one really understood?

No one except him—it, whatever—that is.

I had a million questions and no time to ask them.

Advancing the throttle to eighty-five percent, I redirected the *Phaelon*'s angle of attack to put it on an intercept trajectory with the entry point of the golden Drift Lane. In seconds, the *Phaelon* and the rest of the caravan were on course, moving closer to our forced exit.

Uriel's smoke and light avatar blinked in a discordant rhythm. The shadow pockets over its eyes narrowed slightly, like it was concentrating and struggling to keep itself from completely fading away.

The *Three Oh One* hit the strip of golden light. Like a pinball being launched into play, the massive vessel zipped down the shimmering stream and raced to the edge of the portside fork. A split second later, it dissolved into nothingness.

"There's one," I said, working saliva into my dry mouth. "Here's two. Prepare for transition."

I couldn't make out any additional details of Uriel's face, but I thought I saw it nod in approval as I hit the switch to broadcast the countdown to the rest of the fleet.

The nose of the *Phaelon* pierced the boundary line of golden light.

The main bridge display sparked and flared with a fierce amber hue. It was like flying straight into the sun. At the last moment, just before the display became completely washed in the light, I heard it. In the same way that I heard the Void. No sound, just sensation, but this time, I felt a squeeze in my chest, like my heart forgot it needed to keep beating.

Come. Back.

Before I could contemplate or even process that I'd heard anything at all, the hologram at the helm of the bridge flashed with an intense, brilliant light.

I blinked once. When I opened my eyes, it was like waking from a dream.

The Void was gone. In its place, the starfield of the Astrada system waited for us.

"Power level critical." Uriel sounded... discouraged. The Fleuridian dissipated in a puff of smoke.

None of us noticed it, though. Because dead center on the

primary display was the largest, deadliest ship to ever terrorize the cosmos.

The *ONE*.

Prefect Tror was here.

The final battle of the war began.

20

As MYSTIFIED as I was over the Fleuridian—I was still trying to process exactly what had just happened in the Void—there wasn't time to dissect it. The battle and subsequent boardings were to begin immediately, but I was hit with an overwhelming suspicion that something was wrong.

I wasn't the only one.

The white lines on Fera's face accentuated her scowl. "Something's not right. Quin, give us an active pulse scan."

"You have it," he replied immediately, and so we did.

The scopes came to life, mapping the visual spectrum and rendering that data over the wireframe skins the passive sensors picked up and displayed on the scopes. All at once, it became obvious the starfield was cluttered with ships.

Sixteen billion square kilometers of space centered around one of two primary stars, an orange supergiant called Ibrahma. The smaller blue star, Ninala, watched the battle unfolding from a few light-years away, seeming cold and disinterested.

Fera had spoken reverently of both.

Situated around Ibrahma were the eight planets in Astradian space. Four were suitable for standard life-forms. Two orbited comfortably within the boundaries of the goldilocks zone. One just outside the zone on either side—too close and too far from Ibrahma —had long ago undergone extensive terraforming, with orbital mechanics manipulations that the wildest science fiction writers of Earth could only dream of. A lone FTL gate hung in a wide orbit at the far edge of Astrada Prime's gravity well.

The Astradian fleet stood between those worlds and the Imperium. The difference between vessels could be seen even on the initial scans. The Astradian ships were all sweeping lines and lighter shades of metal—elegance even at the expense of firepower, Fera had once told me—whereas the Imperium vessels were hulking dark gray and black behemoths that lingered in the territory like creeping predators in the night.

So far, though, no battle had begun. Perhaps General Mira'dna's recommendation that the Astradians stall the fight by "negotiating" proved useful.

The two flagship super cruisers of the Astradian fleet held position at the poles of the planet. Flanked in a ring around the gravity well, the rest of the fleet was spread out in a zigzagged line, waiting for orders to be issued to them. Pockets of additional ships stood guard over their respective planets.

"Okay, so is this a good sign or a bad sign?" I asked.

Fera blanched. "Maybe they negotiated a settlement to delay the attack—waiting on our arrival."

"Or maybe," Quin said, "they have simply sided with the Imperium."

Fera just stared at the display.

"Observe their positioning," Quin continued. "Do they look like they are poised to join battle? That's hardly an effective formation."

"They can't look suspicious," Fera said, but she sounded like she was trying to convince herself more than anything else.

Benegal leaned over his station so that he could talk and be heard without having to raise his voice. "Another option: they want to make sure they're on the winning side."

I winced at the words; I had been thinking the same thing myself. But... we weren't sold upriver. Not yet. "If they sided with the Imperium outright, Tror's ships would have been waiting to obliterate us on arrival."

Sert tapped a clawed finger against his armored leg. "It is decided, then."

Everyone stared, waiting for him to finish the thought.

"We must win this battle quickly, fearlessly, relentlessly, or they might throw in with the enemy. No mercy can be shown. We must be... destroyers."

I settled into my seat. "Nothing else changes. Tror committed his remaining forces to this. Let's make him pay for it."

My eyes roamed the scopes and the displays, tracking the positions of the ships.

There were so many. IFF transponders showed in red on Imperium vessels, green on the caravan of United Coalition vessels we'd brought with us, and blue on the Astradian fleet. Blue was the universal tag for neutral.

A flash of light lit off like the igniting of a flare. Almost immediately, the light began to recede, shrinking until it dissipated into darkness once again. Just before the last motes of light vanished from view, debris ejected from the epicenter of the explosion. The IFF tag wavered for a split second, then winked out.

"What the hell was that?" I asked.

"That was the situation developing," Quin said. "An emissary ship was just destroyed—Prime Minister Elect Dora Nightshade was on board."

"The Imperium opened fire?" Fera demanded.

Quin's scowl was fierce. "If my scans can be trusted—and of course they can—it appears the six missiles that destroyed that ship came from the Astradian flagship *Aurora*."

Fera cursed. "Prime Minister Whitecap must have declared martial law and then killed off his successor—the bastard! That's going to throw Astrada into instability for the next fifty years!"

Quin gave a slight shake of his head and mumbled, "No shortage of issues to work out in the New Federation there."

"There will be no New Federation," Benegal hissed.

"Guys, focus," I said. "The attack is underway. We need to be ready."

"What do we do if the Astradians open fire on us?" Sert asked. "Is our captain prepared to destroy them?"

Before anyone could answer, a fleetwide broadcast came in from the *Earthborn* in clipped tones.

"Incoming from Admiral Tanoka," Quin said.

"This is a fleetwide transmission from *Earthborn Actual*. I have just been informed that the Astradians have declared neutrality and are requesting a ceasefire. We will do what we came to do. The political ramifications of this will be dealt with after the conflict has ended and Astradian space is secured. ROEs for Astradian ships are do not fire unless fired upon."

I realized I was bouncing my knee over the ball of my foot and stopped it. I was getting antsy, poised for our part in the fighting to start. Space combat was a chaotic affair in any event, but there were so many ships at play… there was nothing to do but know and focus on your small part of the battle.

The *Three Oh One*, dropped into the starfield ahead of time by virtue of my Void Drift, was closest to Tror's ship and sending its sensor sweeps back to the rest of our fleet. The *ONE* had not been tipped off to our arrival. Its forward weapons systems were armed and ready to fire at the Astradian fleet, but it looked as though the rear batteries were still dormant.

Maybe that's why the Astradians fired on their own ship. It may not have been an act of betrayal so much as a sacrifice to prevent the Imperium from believing they'd been double-crossed and forcing the Astradians to pay the first price.

I focused on the salvos fired by the *Earthborn*.

Forward-facing plasma cannons along the hull repeatedly sent eight scintillating spheres of molten energy out at relativistic speed, bearing down on the exposed flank of the *ONE*.

Still caught off-guard by the sudden arrival of the United Coalition fleet via Void Drift, the four light cruisers surrounding Tror's ship began evasive action, slowly turning to improve their target profiles and bring more of their weapons around to face the surprise onslaught.

Plasma blasts erupted in momentary spools of dissipating energy half a klick from the *ONE*. Electromagnetic fields sparkled and popped as the devastating energy blasts tried and failed to penetrate the deflector shields. The light show gave the illusion of ocean waves rippling along the back end of the massive ship, a sudden aurora borealis that snaked along the impact sites of the incoming fire.

Benegal sniffed behind me. He watched the awe-inspiring display of raw power with his usual flat expression, but an intensity burned in his eyes.

The *Earthborn* cycled its plasma cannons, shifting to its secondary capacitor banks to give the primaries time to recharge ahead of the next salvo. The faster Imperium ships had turned, exchanging ineffective PDC fire for the forward pulse cannons, biding time while they worked firing solutions for their bigger guns. The distance between ships, in relative terms, was point blank.

"When do we board?" Sert asked, gnashing his teeth with excitement.

"Not until *Three Oh One* unloads its Krakoids," Fera said, though Sert surely hadn't forgotten—he just wanted a fight.

Staccato blasts from point defense cannons saturated the gap between firing lines. The *Phaelon*'s scopes rendered only a fraction of the pulses, but the visible spears of coherent light zippering between cruisers looked like a hailstorm delivered with gale-force winds.

Impacts raked along the hulls of Imperium and United Coalition ships alike. Nickel-iron plating dented and warped under the onslaught but maintained structural integrity. The larger ships wouldn't crack under pulse cannon fire alone.

"All Fleet One fighter wings deployed," came the word from *Earthborn*.

Delluvian snub fighters, AX-71s, and Anunnaki-built disc

fighters spewed forth from a variety of docking bays. The streams of small, maneuverable craft split off into units of three or four ships in tight formation and broke off into different vectors, some moving above and some below the ecliptic, all bearing full speed ahead toward the *ONE*.

"The real fight begins," Lockett said.

The comms flooded with transmissions as the flight leads checked in.

I heard Di give orders to her flight wing—designated Amber. The thought that so many people I'd come to care for might die within hours gripped me for a moment. I took a breath and tried to let all that go.

One problem at a time.

Imperium cruisers unsealed their docking bays. Streams of dagger fighters birthed from their roosts by the dozens, drive plumes lighting off as they accelerated to attack speed.

Fera turned to address her crew. "Enemy fighters launching. Keep your heads on swivels."

Di, all business, carried out her separate duties, instructing her own flight wing: "Targets of opportunity only. Do not break formation to chase them down. Primary objective is to get the *Three Oh One* force-docked with the Imperium flagship."

Acknowledgements washed over the frequency.

After several fleet engagements under various circumstances in the war against the Imperium, I had never seen a starfield like this one. The information overload was real. I was primarily focused on the engagement with the *ONE*, but my attention would momentarily divert to Fleet Two's secondary battle in Astrada's gravity well.

The United Coalition fleet was a mixed bag of Marcus Eddison's cruisers and the relics of Galactic Federation vessels that survived the escape from Jyraxis. The older ships cycled rail guns and photon particle accelerators, peppering the enemy line with indiscriminate fire.

Two Imperium destroyers, flanked by a pair of their bigger, bulkier cruisers, opened up with plasma cannons and rail guns. All ships were cycling their smaller pulse cannons at a near-constant rate, creating a hazardous no-man's-land of space that made it difficult for the fighters to navigate.

The Coalition officers were hand-picked by General Mira'dna herself, and if she could do one thing extremely well, it was read people. The captains coordinated their fires and shifted their ship's positions to keep their noses toward the enemy rather than catching the brunt of the incoming on their broadsides.

The initial wave of plasma bursts broke through the shields but didn't do any damage to the older Coalition ships. Eddison's disdain of shields was an oversight that cost one of the earth-made cruisers in the opening salvo. I watched with a shudder as two molten balls of superheated energy slammed into the nose of the *Caliban* and drilled clean through to the midsection. Metal pulsed with a red glow that took several seconds to cool down to its natural hue. Armor panels, equipment, and bodies flooded through the gaping maw, spiraling aimlessly in the hard vacuum.

The Imperium had dealt their punishment, but Fleet Two leaned into their weapons superiority and fired off dozens of missiles. Ten kiloton warheads slipped through the broken shields on both destroyers. Flashes of impact raked along the thick plating of the *Two-Nineteen* and *One-Ninety-Seven*. Clouds of irradiated energy and sublimated metal spiraled away from the hulls in devastating gouts of decompression.

Reports flooded in on the Fleet Two comm channel. Damage reports on Coalition vessels. Confirmation on Imperium ships that had just been put out of commission. Fighter wings harrying the cruisers and keeping them pinned down in their formation, making the larger vessels prime targets for the next round of plasma launches from the Earth-made cruisers.

"*Earthborn*, this is the *Three Oh One*." Captain Esmila sounded as though she were making a simple cargo delivery. "We have made contact with the *ONE*. I say again, the *Three Oh One* has made contact with the *ONE*. Boarding action commencing now."

"I hope the Krakoids leave some for me," Sert said. "I should be with them. The carnage will be delightful."

"Imagine if your Vorvak guard could have been mobilized," I pointed out.

"What might have been," Sert answered dreamily.

"We've got our own job to do," Fera said.

I shifted the focus on the scope to the *ONE*.

The *Three Oh One* looked like an engine nacelle tucked against the ventral side of Tror's much bigger vessel. The umbilical was in place, and through the combat optic suite, I could see Krakoids funneling through and into the *ONE* by the score. Tall and thin, the Krakoids were some of the more alien-looking beings I'd encountered in my trek across the stars, but they were solid. It took a lot of rounds to put one down, which gave me hope that they would put up enough of a distraction for the rest of the boarding team to breach and take command of the ship.

Once we seized the bridge and had Tror in custody, this war would surely end.

We were so close. Just one last piece of the puzzle that needed to be put into its slot.

The comm crackled with a new transmission. Colonel Stallings cleared his throat in a gruff manner. "Breach One is a go. Breach Two to follow in thirty seconds."

I traced the projected flight path of the small transport shuttle from the *Earthborn* to the *ONE*. I imagined a team of Navy Seals and Army Rangers kitted up in futuristic suits ready to kick in the door and deliver unbridled violence in the corridors of Tror's ship. The thought gave me a burst of adrenaline as I remembered that this was my plan. When I thought about it like that, a touch of pride and disbelief swirled in my chest.

One last move. Once those teams were on board, I had every confidence in our operators that they could get the job done, regardless of what lay waiting for them inside Tror's flagship. We were able to catch Tror by surprise; his ship hadn't been given enough advance notice to spin up its big guns in time to defend against the *Three Oh One's* boarding action, and now they were about to be swarmed with Krakoids.

The transport's drive kicked in, spreading a plume of propulsion from the drive cone that converted the sardine can of a vessel into a speeding comet bearing straight for the exposed underside of the *ONE*.

"Curious," Quin squeaked.

"What?" I asked, double-checking the scope and the forward feed on bridge hologram.

"Tror's already initiating a Void Drift."

Fera looked as confused as I felt. "Why would the *ONE* abandon the field?"

"Perhaps attack did more damage than we know," suggested Lockett.

"Quin, alert them!" I shouted. "Call back the breaching team!"

"We should be joining them!" Sert bellowed. "If we board, not even the Void can hide Tror from our wrath."

There would be no time for that.

Fera watched the displays, her face frozen in concentration.

A swirling vortex of white appeared at the nose of the *ONE*. A heartbeat later, jagged streaks of white lightning coruscated up and down the length of the massive ship, and then it was gone. Dozens of Krakoids were yanked out into the darkness of space to die quick, painful deaths in the hard vacuum before the *Three Oh One* sealed off the tube and retracted it.

The *Three Oh One* was left drifting like a dead whale in open space.

Quin cursed and wheeled around to lean over Fera's terminal. "I think it's safe to say things just got a whole lot more complicated."

The ice melted from Fera's gaze. She snapped back into full focus, rage rapidly replacing the shock from a moment before. "Quin, work the numbers and give me some trajectory options. Open a direct link to Fleet Admiral Tanoka. Tell him we're moving to pursue."

"Calculations done! He's not fleeing!" Quin rubbed his bony fingers together, his nervousness pulsating off of him in waves.

The connection opened. "Go for *Earthborn Actual*."

Quin talked fast, his pedantic side coming out without a filter.

"Admiral, bring Fleet Two to full alert, now! They are in imminent danger. I believe the *ONE* is drifting to engage Fleet Two."

Before the Admiral could reply, a shimmering sphere of liquid lightning appeared behind Fleet Two. The *ONE* emerged from the Void, trailing latent streams of subspace.

As the tatters of subspace dissipated, the light concentrated along the top of the massive vessel. The dorsal section of Tror's ship, where the weapons platforms were nestled inside stacked layers of armor, glowed like the surface of the sun.

21

THE FIRING SURFACE of the *ONE*—larger than two Astradian super cruisers put together—expended a massive payload all at once.

The surface of the ship became like a miniature supernova.

Plasma cannons fired. Missile racks expended upward of fifty ten kiloton warheads. Over a hundred pulse cannons cycled, spewing charged particles in a deluge.

Fire and fury lambasted the exposed flank of Fleet Two's capital ships.

I could do nothing but watch as the fire and energy leapt from Tror's ship in a tsunami of destruction.

The *Gibraltar* crumpled in on itself, gel-like swathes of plasma energy chewing clean through layer after layer of nickel-carbide alloy without showing any signs of stopping. Arcing lines of energy skittered along the exoskeleton, plunging deep into the superstructure like daggers of fire. A cascade of explosions walked along the broadside of the ship, producing eruptions of decompression as holes bloomed in the ruined hull.

All at once, the pooling energy dispersions reached critical mass.

The internal atmosphere rippled out of several mortal wounds on the ship's hull, and then the reactor went into cascade failure. The meltdown lasted only a few seconds before the back half gave way under the continued pounding. There was an explosion of retina-searing light. As the glare of the ship's death knell began to fade, the midship and forward sections fragmented into tattered bits of warped metal and spun weightlessly in place as sections rapidly disintegrated until the ship and the 1,200 souls aboard became nothing more than a cold, lonely cloud of debris particles.

Here, on display for all to see, was why no one dared fight when the *ONE* was in system.

The process repeated on *Valencia*. And *Gerebor*.

Benegal scoffed in disgust, his mouth pulled back into a fierce sneer.

Sert made a similar sound, but his face was one of… appreciation. He respected the raw power being shown and only wished to use it or test himself against it.

The Coalition vessels didn't go down without a fight. Sensing their imminent destruction, they went full berserker. Cold gas emissions whirled from missile launch tubes. Light trails from plasma cannons traced massive spheres of raw energy that streaked toward the *ONE*.

Hundreds of kilometers across, shock diamonds and arcing streaks of dispersed energy flared in an umbrella shape around the *ONE*. Not a single missile or even a lucky pulse round slipped through the ship's shields.

"It's indestructible." Benegal scowled.

Lockett shook his head. "No ship can take that punishment. It is impossible."

"We're seeing it in real time," Quin reminded them. "It's happening."

Fera's hands hovered over the controls, unsure of where to move. In a fleet-to-fleet engagement, a single Voidship was relegated to the sidelines. Our weapons couldn't do any significant damage to the larger ships, and our shields wouldn't hold up to the kind of punishment they could dish out.

Sert's nictitating membranes clicked with sideways blinks as he studied the display. "They should be firing additional missiles and plasma rounds. That they do not means they cannot. The weakness of the enemy is revealed. Unless they have an accelerated cooling capacity, it will be twenty minutes before the weapons have dispersed enough heat to fire such a colossal volley without risking damage to their launch tubes."

"That gives us reason to stick around," I said, using my fiber-link to shift my screens to bring up a schematic of the *ONE*. The active pulse scan in my HUD highlighted four shield generators at various sections of the *ONE's* underbelly. "But it doesn't help us stop the damn thing."

Quin paced at the helm like he was a professor trying to puzzle his way through a difficult equation. "Shield generators are the problem. I cannot fathom how they're able to absorb so much energy without breaking. Fleet Two's defensive fire would have turned a sizable portion of Astrada Prime into a field of glass. There's something at work here, some product of the Imperium's embargo on technology, that we don't understand."

A priority flag appeared on the display. I selected it with an eye wave, automatically slewing the long-range visual scanner to zoom in on the location.

Our fighters were three minutes out from firing range on the *ONE*. Comm chatter between them was filled with curses and a lust for vengeance at the losses of the ships attached to Fleet Two. Squadrons of Imperium Daggers came in from all angles, peppering the delta formation with fire from their pulse cannons.

"Green Wing, provide cover for Breach One," Di said, a bit of air in her normally calm command voice. She was as shocked as the rest of us. "Red Wing, stay with me. Amber Wing, do not break formation. This isn't over yet. We can still get Breach Two into the *ONE* if we move fast."

"Di, this is *Phaelon*," I said, finger on the comm switch.

"Go for Amber Lead," she replied.

"Shield generators are on the dorsal section of the ship."

"I see them."

"Prioritize your attack vectors there. Do not fire until you're inside the shield envelope."

"Oh, really? You think this is my first time? That's cute. Out."

I knew it was just her way of blowing off steam, but it still irritated me. I gave Fera a sort of "what's her problem?" look.

She shrugged. "Kind of pointing out the obvious there, Will."

I gave a half frown. "Point taken. Quin, what are the chances Tror will just Void Drift into a new position again?"

The AI blew out an exasperated breath. "I'm certain the Navigator aboard that ship is the best in the Imperium. Tror would accept nothing less for his personal vessel. It would follow that at least another one or two Drifts are possible, plus an emergency escape drift. Of course, that all depends on how much strain the Navigator can take before he overtaxes himself. It also assumes there is only one Navigator on board. In short, your question is impossible to answer correctly without more data."

Fera put the *Phaelon* into a spin and brought us around toward the docking bay. She passed along the hull of the United Coalition's flagship, moving so close that I could see the individual seams between panels.

"Key up your fires page," she said. "The fighters will need some cover until they start their attack run."

I settled into my seat in preparation. As the targeting reticle appeared on the main display and the pulse cannon readouts filled the side display, I began to feel myself relax. The nerves that came with just sitting and watching things unfold were subsiding. I hadn't realized how strong the pull to be in battle truly was.

It made me think of Sert. The big guy must be almost beside himself, but he held it together like a professional, all the same.

"If we can get those shields down, we can end this," I announced to the crew.

Fera gave a fractional smile. "Let's hope you're right."

She snapped the throttle forward and angled the nose of the *Phaelon* toward the *ONE*. Simulated gravity snapped me against the pilot chair. The Delluvian fibers rippled as they adjusted to my back.

I gripped the sidestick in the chair's armrest and spun the reticle in a few circles before I took a few shots at a passing formation of dagger fighters, clipping one of them right on the nose. The pulse bit clean into the fuselage. The ship fell out of the formation and flipped end over end like it had just slammed into a barricade. I lost track of the ship as a dozen more fighters passed through my viewing angle.

I put a good lead on them and fired.

The meter monitoring the capacitors darkened from a vibrant green to a sickly yellow as the rounds counter ticked up to forty before I let go of the trigger. I watched as the computer rendered a dozen of the pulse rounds. Three of the fighters caught glancing hits that altered their trajectory. A fourth took a direct hit to its propulsion section and atomized in a brilliant flash of momentary fire.

"Excellent!" Sert said, rubbing his massive, clawed hands together. "More. *More!*"

The remaining fighters passed through the debris cloud. A heartbeat later, Di and her fighter wing crossed over the starfield, integral cannons scattering rail-gun rounds in front of them.

"Nice shooting, *Phaelon,*" Di said. "Feel free to splash a few more."

"Plenty more where that came from," Fera replied calmly. She dipped the *Phaelon* below the ecliptic and spun the stick, inverting the starfield so that the bottom of Tror's ship was beneath us.

The sense of up and down constantly changed in space combat, and I found it disorienting unless I was the one doing the piloting. My stomach did a flip as vertigo came and went while the inertial compensator provided tactile feedback to Fera's maneuvers.

"Imperium delta at two one zero," Quin announced. "Lockett, adjust the angle on the deflector shields."

"Two one zero," the Drayth responded with a watery sigh.

A status reading on the *Phaelon* appeared in my side display, showing the pie-shaped cone of shields as they slid to the appropriate angle.

Reorienting the layout of the battle in my head, I slewed the pulse cannons to cover Amber Wing's flank. Two separate deltas of Imperium Daggers broke formation and scattered like snowflakes caught in a stiff breeze. I didn't let myself get distracted with the various targets; I sighted in on the ship closest to the reticle and fired off another salvo.

Tactile feedback rattled in the sidestick. The rounds counter ratcheted up as rendered pulses flashed in the scope.

I was rewarded with another direct hit as Fera barrel-rolled the *Phaelon* through the scattered fighters. My side screen flashed a momentary proximity alert as we passed within a handful of klicks of several of the ships.

"Such a show-off," I said.

A smirk seemed glued to Fera's face. "If they think they're going to intimidate me, they've got another thing coming."

Fera was in the zone, every ounce of her focus locked into the controls. She was at her best when she was flying, and by then I firmly believed she truly was the best pilot in the galaxy. Even after a 4,000-year hiatus.

Quin stood at the helm, trying to keep a level head. His constant shifting and glancing at Fera betrayed the AI's nervousness. Like the rest of us, he was taken by surprise with Tror's Void Drift maneuver.

This fact seemed to agitate him. As if it personally offended him somehow.

"Quin, you keeping an eye on the *ONE*?" I asked, firing another burst from the pulse cannons. "Any signs of another Void Drift?"

He whipped his head around. "I suspect his Navigator is catching his breath right now. That is, unless the Krakoids who boarded have somehow managed to assault the bridge. Such a probability is low, given how few were able to gain access to the ship. Regardless, we should have enough time to get our shots in on the shield generators."

"If only my Guard and I could have been sent ahead of the Krakoids," Sert groused. "Place ten Vorvaks aboard, and victory is sure."

"Keep up that attitude, Sert," I muttered, still focused on shooting. "If this goes right, you'll get the chance for at least one Vorvak to get in and do some damage."

"When I get my claws on Tror, I will pry his small Foris head from his puny shoulders!"

Quin instinctively felt for his own slender neck.

Fresh data scrolled down Fera's sidescreen, drawing a momentary glance from her. "Sixty seconds to target. Brace yourselves."

Rendered pulse rounds sailed through the emptiness of space between Coalition cruisers and Imperium destroyers. Dashes of coherent light scattered over the *Phaelon*'s deflector shield, jostling the ship with turbulence. The deck rattled under my boots as Fera fought the stick to keep the ship steady.

The shields were holding, for the moment.

A quick assessment of the scopes showed that, despite the grave loss of half of Fleet Two at the hands of Tror's flagship, the Imperium ships remained outnumbered. With *ONE* relying on its defensive capabilities while its fleet-reducing offensive weapons recovered, the scales were tipping fast in favor of the United Coalition as Eddison's cruisers and the Galactic Federation relics built to a synergistic attack and defend cycle.

But that was only good for as long as *ONE* couldn't fully fight back.

Fleet Admiral Tanoka came in over the frequency. "Breach Two is away. Fleet Three, move to center stage. Fighter wings, get those shields down. Fleet One, engage directly with the support ships surrounding the *ONE*. Clear the path for our fighters."

Acknowledgements flooded the channel.

Several wings of AX-71s sped across tens of thousands of klicks in seconds, booster modules acting like bursts of nitrous in a street race. The tiny but formidable craft came and went in streaks of light, leaving behind plasma trails in triplicate. Explosions cascaded over the Imperium ships, carpet-bombing their superstructures with blistering fire.

The *Two-Twelve* and the *Ninety-Four*, both destroyers moving to put up a defense for the *ONE*, were taken out of commission in short order. The husks of former Drayth ships that had been conscripted and converted into Imperium vessels long ago were left adrift in the solar winds of Ibrahma, venting atmosphere and debris. Coalition fighters zipped between the drifting slag and the deluge of pulse cannon fire.

Fera banked the *Phaelon* around the epicenter of the *Ninety-Four*'s debris cloud. The main bridge display passed over the carnage, showing dozens of white armored Imperium soldiers and a handful of officers in their dress uniforms flailing helplessly as they rode a geyser of oxygen particles into the vacuum.

It was easy to overlook just how advanced all of the technology was, even down to the ultra-high-definition cameras, holograms, and sensor equipment. I tried to imagine NASA getting shots of planets as clear as what the *Phaelon* could get with its scopes and just shook my head. Humanity was so far behind.

All the more reason to prevent this war from ever reaching Earth.

The fleeting thought came and went as Fera banked and adjusted the throttle input to dodge a burst of pulse fire from a passing delta of dagger fighters, muttering under her breath. She did that when she was intensely focused, like she was running through a checklist or narrating her movements. It was one of those small things about her I really liked, for no reason other than it was a personality tic of hers that radiated confidence.

Di filled our comm with a quick report. "We're through the shield envelope. Lots of fighters between us and the target."

The underbelly of the *ONE* came into view.

By virtue of scale, the ship appeared to be a rolling landscape in the main display as Fera brought us inside of 500 klicks from the surface. Deep rifts in the hull revealed a corrugated cross-section of nickel-carbide beams that served no purpose but to add layers of metal for potential weapons to have to punch through to deal any real damage to the ship itself. Notches in the construction were sealed bays where ships could dock in the lower levels. Sensor towers protruded at various angles, interspersed between beveled dome shapes circled with slotted exhaust vents. Roiling streams of heat waste billowed and dissipated close to the hull.

"It's like the frigging Death Star," I mumbled, but no one in the *Phaelon* asked for clarification. They've learned to mostly ignore my asides. The reference would be lost on them anyway. Although I sometimes wondered what Fera would think of humanity's idea of science fiction.

The targeting suite painted the domes with priority flags.

"There they are," I said, pointing out the shield generators.

Fera nodded. "That's them all right."

Falling from above like hail, Imperium Daggers swept toward the *ONE* and course-corrected at the last second to fly with their wings dangerously close to the hull of the flagship. The fighters weaved between sensor towers as they raced to intercept the Coalition fighters.

Half their number broke off from the main formation in unison. Behind the *Phaelon*, I saw an Anunnaki cruiser, tagged the *Akismet*, launch its reserve force of disc fighters. The bell-shaped craft moved with no drive plumes at all by virtue of their red mercury drives. They cut across the starfield in their odd zigzagging pattern, photon cannons belching blasts of light in measured barrages.

The fringe formations of daggers and disc fighters traded spaces at close intervals. A third of their number didn't make the pass, ending up as spreading clouds of shrapnel. The survivors spun on their axis and banked hard, pushing their craft to their maximum turn rate as they tried to turn their weapons to face each other on the next pass.

Like points of light in a vortex, Daggers and discs traded fire and took hits in a chaotic spiral. It happened so fast, I forgot we were engaged in our own game of chicken with the defensive half of the Imperium fighters.

"Light them up, Will!" Fera called. "Can't get you a better shot than this!"

I looked away from the hellacious dogfight just in time to see the discharging pulse cannons of Imperium fighters weaving through columns and spires on the *ONE*'s hull. I brought the lead delta into my crosshairs and fired, working the trigger in a steady rhythm, giving the capacitors enough time to recharge between bursts.

Fera inched the throttle forward.

Induced gravity pulled the back of my head against the headrest. I fired, shifted, and fired again.

Two, three Daggers became momentary balls of fire and expanding gas. A handful of spires lit up with heat damage from stray rounds. One of the sensor array towers snapped off at the tip, sending a section of layered nickel-carbide careening off into space.

Return fire raked across the *Phaelon*'s shield envelope, flashing in jagged arcs of rapidly dispersed energy. The side screen that displayed the shield rating dropped by nearly double digits with each hit.

"Incoming is too heavy," Lockett warned. "Shields will not last."

"Just hold it steady," Fera commanded.

Quin flinched as the shields broke with swirls of static electricity that crawled across the bridge hologram.

"What the hell are you doing back there?" he griped at Fera.

Sert muttered a curse. "My Day of Reckoning comes, and I am unable to return fire. This is disgraceful!"

"I'd like to see *you* do this," Fera retorted.

"Have a little faith, big guy," I said, watching Fera.

She was feeling the pressure, but her confidence didn't waver as she juked the *Phaelon* into evasive action and skittered the ship across the yaw axis while maintaining her approach. Rendered pulses whipped across the main bridge display. Glancing hits knocked into the hull like someone was throwing rocks at a windshield.

I winced, thinking of the rail-gun round that had torn through the ship during our escape from Jyraxis. I desperately did not want a repeat of that experience. Fera was lucky to have survived, not to mention the rest of us.

A transponder on the scopes lit up with a transmission tag for Green Lead, who sounded panicked. "There are too many of them! Split off!"

"Belay that!" Di snapped. "Maintain present course."

"They'll pick us off before—"

"Maintain current heading." Di's voice was adamant. "My order stands."

Di was right. Risky as it might be, nothing was going to phase Tror's ship as long as the deflector shields were still up—no matter how large our fleet was. The Anunnaki disc fighters were still keeping a sizable chunk of the Imperium Daggers locked in ship-to-ship combat, but that didn't give us a clean and clear path forward. There would be a cost for victory.

There always is.

The swarm of daggers swept across the approaching Coalition fighters like ancient knights jousting on the battlefield. Saturated pulse fire was exchanged at point blank. Imperium and Coalition alike, fighters disintegrated in atomized clouds that raked the hull of the *ONE* with debris trails.

Green Lead tried to bank away from the fire exchange at the same time as an Imperium fighter. Both ships collided nose to nose. The collision was a momentary fireball that resolved into confetti-like streamers of twisted metal.

The remainder of Green Wing stayed the course.

"Bombs away!" Di practically cheered.

Di dropped three searing blasts from her plasma cannons. Each of her wingmen added their fire to the bombing run before breaking off at opposing angles. The foursome of AX-71s lit off with their final booster module and rocketed away from the *ONE* like bats out of hell. In seconds, they were back behind the cover of Fleet One.

Geysers of molten metal erupted from the impact sites.

The unmistakable sound of Lieutenant Fel's voice cut through the comm traffic. "Breach Two is in place. Boarding action under way."

Adrenaline rippled under my skin. There was no going back now.

But then... there never had been.

22

FERA TRACED the path cut through by the Coalition fighters and got an up-close-and-personal visual on the damage.

"Three of the four shield generators are out!" she crowed, then tapped the comm switch. "*Earthborn*, this is *Phaelon* confirming shield generators are destroyed."

For the first time that I could recall, the entire crew of the *Phaelon* cheered. The *ONE* had seemed so invincible that I wasn't sure any of us believed we could destroy those shield nacelles.

"All ships, concentrate fire on the *ONE*," Admiral Tanoka ordered. "Prioritize the plasma cannons. Breach Two has made contact with the enemy flagship."

Fera sagged her shoulders and let out a deep breath.

The *Earthborn*, flanked by two of the older Coalition cruisers, inched forward. Her plasma cannons primed and fired. Photon cannons cycled on the older ships, launching spats of coherent light.

I watched it all playing out without a sound. Somewhere in my mind, I might have been hearing the pew pew sounds of the movies, but that was all in my head. True space combat is eerily silent. The separation between the atmospheric senses and sounds in the cockpit of your ship and the savage game of dodgeball with raw energy and missiles can be hard to reconcile if you aren't used to it.

Direct fire from the *Earthborn* and the *Akismet* streaked toward the threshold of the *ONE*'s shield envelope—and passed straight through. Impact trails bloomed across the mighty Imperium flagship's dorsal decks, washing the hull with surges of plasma and lancets of damaging heat and light.

Tror's command ship took the fire on the chin. It was too large to crumple under the onslaught, too well armored. It was also too well armed to sit there and take the punishment without offering at least some response of its own, even if it wasn't the withering, fleet-reducing fire it had shown at the beginning.

For every missile launch tube and wide-bored plasma cannon the Coalition destroyed, another fired. Even if they hadn't fully adjusted... what was left to lose? Better a last shot under stress than no shot at all.

"Evasive action!" Admiral Tanoka transmitted.

Fleet One dispersed, spreading out to minimize their target profile. Tror's answering salvo scattered across the hulls of the ships, doing damage, but not scoring a killing blow on any of the big ships.

"He's moving," Quin cautioned. "Could be to prepare for another Void Drift..."

Sixteen drive plumes lit off from the aft of Tror's ship. The driving force dragged the monster-sized ship on a lumbering path toward Ninala, the further of the two binary stars in the system.

"We can't let him get away," I said.

"Such insight, Will. I'm amazed," Quin said. "He's definitely setting up for another Void Drift."

Meanwhile *Earthborn* was trying to raise Fel's team for a sitrep on their assault. I listened pensively as static filled the comm in reply. A moment later, small-arms fire came through the channel.

Lieutenant Fel spoke in clipped tones, strain evident in his voice. "Stiff resistance on the loading deck. Imperium was ready for us. They've got our backs against the wall. Trying to find an alternate entry point."

I cursed under my breath. There would be thousands of Imperium on the *ONE*. It was large enough to be considered a station or a habitat, rather than a ship. We'd lost the element of surprise once Tror did his first Void Drift. Lieutenant Fel and his boarding team weren't going to be able to break through the Imperium soldiers without a major distraction or a few more breaching teams to serve as reinforcements.

"Fera, we need to get onboard," I said.

She nodded. "Yeah. And not just us."

"Switch to selective fire," Admiral Tanoka ordered. "Fleet Two, fall back to Astrada Prime and clean up the remaining Imperium cruisers. Take them down with extreme prejudice. We're sending a message, here and now, for any Imperium remnant that may be lingering in fringe space."

The landscape of the starfield and the brutal battle that waged across it shifted like an ocean tide. United Coalition ships now outnumbered Tror's fleet four to one, and that advantage was steadily increasing with every destroyer and light cruiser disabled or destroyed.

Fleet Three dropped dozens of its own missiles, slagging still more of the *ONE*'s offensive batteries. Data stacked and layered across my screen, estimating forty percent of the *ONE*'s offensive capability eliminated and marking the hull integrity of the enemy flagship at ninety percent.

It was one tough nut to crack, but we weren't trying to destroy the ship, just disable it. We had people on board by now. I imagined Lieutenant Fel and his teams spreading through the corridors, trading small-arms fire with Imperium soldiers. The fighting inside must be hectic.

"Connection request from *Earthborn*," Quin said. "Admiral Tanoka. Private Channel. For you, Will."

I nodded. "Put it through."

Fleet Admiral Tanoka appeared on my display, a determined look on his face.

"Will," he said.

"Admiral."

"The Imperium fleet is decimated. Two cruisers and one immobilized destroyer are all that remain, and they've already instituted a ceasefire. We're getting calls of surrender."

"Then it's finished," I said, hardly believing the words.

The past few months flashed through my mind in the span of a heartbeat.

The men and women we'd lost. The battles we'd fought and the enemies we'd killed to get to this point. It was all too much. Something in those words uncorked the bottled-up stress I'd been carrying.

Earth was safe. Against the odds, the fledgling rebellion I'd stumbled across had come together and built itself into something new. Something formidable.

In the moment, it seemed somehow anticlimactic.

Shouldn't there be a celebration? Some fanfare cascading over the comm channels, cheers and whoops and razzing back and forth?

There was only silence. A hallowed, haunting silence.

And the pursuit of the *ONE*. Tror had not yet surrendered.

"Almost, finished," Tanoka corrected. "General Mira'dna and Mr. Eddison believe you should be back on the bridge here on *Earth-born*, overseeing the final destruction of the Imperium."

All eyes looked at me. I could hear Sert stifle a groan. I don't think it was against me, just over the possibility that he might again be denied the chance to fight in this battle.

I looked over to Earl, who was perched and watching my every move. "Negative, Admiral. But I'll be sure to get you plenty of good footage for when this all ends."

Fera smiled and leaned out from her station, coming in view of my screen. "Admiral, we're moving to dock with the *ONE*."

He nodded approvingly. "I'll pass the word along."

"There is no need," General Mira'dna's voice came from off screen. She soon appeared in the window. "Captain Fera, be ready. You will be needed in the negotiations with your people that are sure to follow. The situation among the Astradians is currently… confusing."

"Understood," Fera said. "But one problem at a time. *Phaelon* out."

"Now," Sert rumbled from behind me. "Now for war and ruin. Now the final blow!"

Everything came down to this moment, and I wasn't sure how to process it. What came next?

Getting Tror, of course. But then?

Quin turned around, his expression flat. "Let's not get ahead of ourselves. We need to dock and breach first."

Sert, however, was well ahead, his warrior's mind fixed on the coming battle. "We must scour the bowels of the enemy flagship and kill Tror's soldiers down to the last man. You get us there, and I will deliver the violence personally."

I firmly believed that if we had chosen any other action, Sert would have mutinied right then and there in order to get our ship into the fight.

"Lieutenant Fel and his forces are currently holed up on the entry level deck," Quin said. "So if our plan is to relieve him…"

Open space stretched around the *Phaelon*. Fera bumped back the throttle and pulled the stick, swirling the stars across the main bridge display until we were facing the *ONE*.

The *Earthborn* and the rest of Fleet One continued to send streaks of fire into Tror's ship. Off in the distance, the remaining Imperium vessels flared with hull breaches and went dark, like lightning bugs winking out on a summer night in the fields of Indiana. I didn't know why the comparison came to mind, but watching something so surreal unfolding in real time in front of me left me grasping for some sense of normalcy.

My mind tried to parse through the carnage and the chaos. I was left with a loose feeling of despondency. So many lives had been lost in such a short time, it was unconscionable. To think this was the better outcome, that Tror could have glassed the Astradian worlds, even if they were attempting to remain neutral… the death toll could have been much higher.

Humanity is not ready for this.

The thought left a bitter taste in my mouth.

We didn't have a choice. This war might be over now, but there would be another. Perhaps sooner than anyone wants if the Federation and Independent factions were unable to reach an agreement.

One problem at a time.

"I'm starting our approach," Fera said, tapping at the controls to kick off the fine adjustment thrusters.

"*Phaelon*, this is Amber Lead," Di said. "Coming around to escort you."

Fera frowned. She double-checked her screen. "Amber Lead, we've got a clear path. Sit tight."

Di's ship cut across the main bridge display and stayed in the viewing frame, her drive plume a silvery blue tail whipping around behind her AX-71. The distance to target parameter appeared in the sidescreen, counting down from thirty thousand klicks.

We were nearing the halfway point when a swirling white light manifested at the bow of Tror's ship.

"Fera, abort!" Quin shouted.

She pulled the throttle back. The stars slowed their movement toward us as our acceleration cut down to a snail's pace. Up ahead, Amber Wing continued to move forward at a brisk clip, not backing off their throttles at all.

The white swirl became a full-on vortex, and it sent jagged streaks of lightning arcing along the massive length of the *ONE*'s hull.

I slapped the comm switch, fear breaking my radio etiquette as I shouted, "Di, back off!"

"Relax, we're almost there!" she said. "We can get some licks in before it goes."

"Di, get your fighters out of there!" Fera growled through gritted teeth.

The comm board lit up with Di's response. Whatever she intended to say, I never heard it. A brilliant flash of light consumed the *ONE* for a very long, slow second. Then, as if time itself realized it had let that moment last longer than it was supposed to, the light snapped and dissipated. All that remained was a gaping hole of darkness where a behemoth of a starship had been.

The comm board light winked out. Amber Wing's transponders disappeared from the scopes. All four of them.

I sat there, stunned.

Fera looked down and shook her head. "Waste."

Sert snorted with disgust. "Yes. A waste of a good warrior."

Lockett's iron lung made choking noises. "Perhaps the Anunnaki was again intoxicated."

My heart sank into the pit of my stomach.

"They're not dead, you scientifically stunted morons," Quin said. "They were disabled when *ONE* entered the Void. Honestly, too much of Will's human ignorance is rubbing off on all you."

"So they're alive?" I asked, hope springing forth.

"I mean... for now. Their life support is likely offline so it's just a simple waiting game."

"Well then I guess we'd better look," Fera said sarcastically.

Quin mumbled something unintelligible, but he turned toward the hologram and squinted.

"There," he said, pointing. "Easy calculation, quick result. You are welcome."

I breathed a sigh of relief. The four AX-71s spun aimlessly through open space, all systems dark. I tapped the active pulse scan and dialed in to focus on the ships. Biometric readings came through, showing all four pilots were still alive.

"They're alive. Quin, send this info over to——"

"To the Earthborn, yes, I've already done so, but thanks for the advice."

Fera massaged her temples and sighed. "Di and her wingmen aside, we still have people aboard the *ONE*. They're trapped, outnumbered, and running out of time. Tror isn't going to be accepting any surrenders."

Sert bristled. "No true warrior should ever surrender. They should kill the enemy and seize the ship."

Benegal turned to glare at the Vorvak. "Against such steep odds? Even a mighty one such as yourself would not prevail under such circumstances."

"Speak for yourself, skink," Sert huffed.

"He got away," I said. "After everything, he got away."

Quin looked at me, his amphibian eyes softening. "Will, this wasn't all for nothing. We've managed to do what the Galactic Federation failed to do. Without us, there would never have been a United Coalition. The Imperium would still be exploiting the galaxy, and there would be no chance for a peaceful resolution."

His rapid switch from sarcastic prick to budding idealist threw me. "Thanks for that, Quin, but it doesn't change the fact that we need to find the *ONE* ASAP. As long as Tror is out there, this war isn't won. We'll just have to hope that Lieutenant Fel and his fire teams can last until we find them."

"I hate to be a pessimist, Will," Quin said, "but the odds of the breach team holding out for the long term are practically nil. Why not just wish for a pet unicorn while you're at it?"

He may have been right about the odds, but I hated the idea of just leaving our people to their fate.

"*Earthborn* is hailing you again," Quin said. "Probably time to deal with the cleanup."

I shook my head. "Okay, yeah. But… everyone stay ready. The moment we find where the *ONE* winds up, we're going after them."

23

Dɪ ᴡᴀs a little rattled when we met up with her in the *Earthborn*'s medical bay. The sterilized scent of antiseptics and bio gel, though not in active use, hung heavy in the air. My eyes watered from the pungent odor as Fera and I entered her room, eager to check in on our crazy pilot friend.

She was seated on the cot in the medical bay, along with her three wingmen. A gentle hiss of pure oxygen circulated through the room, broken occasionally by the *beep* that accompanied new readings of the pilots' vitals on holographic screens above their cots. No one had suffered any permanent injuries, but their ships were rendered useless in the EMP wake left by the *ONE*'s Void Drift.

One of the doc-bots, a soccer-ball sized thing with dozens of articulating arms, poked and prodded at her.

Di flinched and swatted at the robot. "I said I'm fine!"

"Assessment complete," the bot said in a clinically detached voice. "Patient status is acceptable. Medical prognosis: lack of REM cycles. Recommend—"

Di snatched her red leather flight jacket, shoved the bot out of her way, and took a step toward the door. "Nothing a stiff drink can't cure. I'll be fine."

I stopped her with a hand on her shoulder. "Not even gonna say hello, huh?"

She tried to blow me off. "Hi."

Fera crossed her arms and blocked the door.

"Di," she said softly, "you're a damned good pilot, but what the hell were you thinking?"

Di stepped back, pulled her jacket over her flight suit, and gave me an up and down look that ended with her wrinkling her nose. "That we could make it. Like I said. And now we've got a breach team that is still on that ship, and no way to get them back. Those men are all dead."

"We're scanning for wherever Tror shows up next," I said, trying to offer her a small slice of hope. "When that happens, we'll Void Drift to his location and finish him."

Di gave me a hard look. She didn't believe me. "Yeah, well, either way, I guess the fighting's over until then."

She gave a flip of her dark hair and pushed past Fera. "'scuse me, Captain."

Fera glanced at the three remaining pilots in the room. All of them were unsure how to respond, either staring at the ceiling or offering a simple shrug in response.

I nodded at them and then left with Fera.

As we walked, she said, "Di's starting to lose it."

Almost instinctively, I tried to bring up the best. "She'll come around. Everyone's on edge right now. Tror's still out there, and that's going to be a damper on this reforming of the New Federation—or whatever this all gets labeled. Actually, coming up with a new name from now on is a good idea; otherwise, Benegal and Sert are the ones who are going to lose it."

Fera gave me a mischievous smile. "Maybe we lock the both of them in a room, and they fight about it amongst themselves."

"I wouldn't want either of them as an enemy. Sert has an army backing him now, remember? Besides, the last time he was locked by himself in *Phaelon*, we ended up on a collision course with a star."

"That didn't turn out so bad, but point taken." Fera's smile gave way to a frown. "Who would have thought that our own people would be such a problem?"

"Uh, I did," I said, raising my hand slightly. "This train has been barreling down the tracks for a while now."

We walked together, passing crew and soldiers on our way to the docking bay.

"You saw it coming and yet the Hero of the Rebellion doesn't have an answer?" Fera playfully *tsk'd* me.

"Don't you start on me. We need to focus on preventing a new war to replace the old one once we get down there for the talks." I shook my head. "There's got to be a way forward we can all agree on."

Fera gave me a sad smile. "If there is, I don't see it. Fighting the war was supposed to be the hard part."

Elimentia was a paradise world if I'd ever seen one.

Its buildings, like the Astradian fleet orbit over Astrada Prime, were works of art. No hard angles to speak of. Sweeping lines of white-washed metal fitted with cerulean blue windowpanes that caught the orange light of Ibrahma and sparkled like seas at sunrise. Exotic flora in bright reds and pale yellows sprouted from creeper vines that draped down the sides of the smaller buildings in intricate patterns.

The air was sweet, and it felt invigorating to step off the ramp of the *Phaelon* and stand on solid ground. Only Sert wore his natural armor; the rest of us were in what Quin called our "peace-keeping outfits."

A faintly humid breeze, carrying trace scents with floral notes on a fine mist that spoke of coming rain, sent Fera's hair dancing delicately. She wore a purple and white half-dress that looked absolutely divine. It was simple—elegant. Not the sort of overly complicated gown from movies. It seemed built for both form and function; it was perfect for Fera.

I looked around, taking in the sights, sounds, and smells as the breeze passed through my t-shirt and cargo pants. Earl watched me closely in my "Earth" clothes. There was a feeling that my being dressed in native, human garb would add to the momentousness of the occasion.

"So this is your root world?" I asked.

Fera paused to take in a breath of the fresh air. She sighed, a smile stretching the white lines on her face. "This is it. My village is forty klicks southwest of here."

Sert bumbled down the ramp, his wide face bobbing as he took in a few sniffs. "Here is a planet indeed untouched by war. It is… pretty."

I gave the Vorvak a look. "Pretty?"

Sert inhaled again. "Yes. Pretty."

"Lockett is not impressed," the Drayth said as he came down the ramp with Benegal. "Astrada is a boring world. No place to spend credits. No debauchery. Not very fun for a Drayth."

The super hacker with the magic fingers was carrying Dumpy's head unit—and presumably our Fleuridian as well—with him. The former head of Lockett's former bot friend was now twice its original size; it had been modified to include an isotope reactor, which protruded from the bottom of the bot's dome. This served to provide a constant level of power to feed Uriel.

Fera ignored Lockett's comment, her eyes roaming the gentle rolling hills on the horizon. I took in the landscape beside her, surprised at how much it reminded me of Kentucky bluegrass. The surface of the planet looked so lush and vibrant. It was such a contrast to the first alien world I ever saw—Farakar.

Benegal wore an ancient dress brown uniform he'd picked up at some point while I was doing Hero of the Rebellion work on my own. I noted that he had removed the pin that identified him as a member of the Final Equinox. His forked tongue probed the air a few times. He withdrew it and snorted with offense.

"The air is too moist."

A faint mist did hang on the air, but I didn't find it unpleasant at all. It was like a gentle breath, the slightest caress of the wind—the remnant of a summer rain in a tropical climate, or something like it. It carried a fleeting thought to the forefront of my mind.

This is what habitable worlds could become if they weren't bombed from orbit.

A buzz ran down my jawbone. By virtue of the bone conduction comm interface and my fiber-link, I heard Quin's voice as if he were speaking directly into my ear.

"Yes, yes, it's all very beautiful, and we love it, and let's all just melt into a puddle of feelings."

Fera frowned. "What's got you in such a bad mood?"

"Gee, I don't know, Fera. Perhaps it's the crushing reality that I spent the last embers of my life on Will's cloaca of a planet and can never again enjoy the simple beauty of a place like Astrada. Can we please just get on to business?"

"Hold your processors, Quin," I said. "We barely just stepped off the ramp." I offered Fera my arm. "Shall we?"

She looked at my arm, then met my eyes, confused. "Will, what are you doing?"

"It's the... gesture of a gentleman? You're supposed to take my arm, like this"—I grabbed her hand and put it in the right place—"and then we walk together."

She shot me a look of dismay and yanked her arm back. "I am *not* an invalid."

I laughed. "What? Fera, that's not—it's a way to show that we're... you know... together."

"People know," she assured me.

"Wait... what? How do they know?"

She pointed at Earl. "You're the Hero of the Rebellion and that thing broadcasts your every move. Our relationship has been big news on Astrada."

I turned red with embarrassment. "It has?"

"Big news," Fera repeated.

I turned around to look at the rest of the crew. "So the whole galaxy knows about my love life?"

"Who cares?" Sert said, moving past me.

"Yeah," Lockett asks.

"The mating habits of an Astradian and human are of no concern to Krayvox," Benegal hissed.

My face reddened further still.

"Talk and walk, Will!" Quin barked. "I believe in your ability to do more than just stand there and breathe, but I'll be honest: the more time that passes since the death of my body, the less I like organic life-forms. You are so slow and overly emotional! Especially you, Will. Tell your blood to go back down to where it *usually* circulates when Fera is around. At least then your red monkey face will return to its usual pale color. It is starting to make me queasy."

Fera scoffed but didn't offer a reply. I noticed the beginnings of a smile on her face and didn't know what to make of it.

We left the landing pad and crossed a street completely devoid of any vehicle traffic. A few dozen pedestrians were out and about, a good amount of them headed into the largest building a block deeper into the city. It looked like everyone walked everywhere. Maybe there was some sort of underground mass transit, but I didn't see even so much as an air car overhead.

As we neared the city center, the sounds of a celebration drifted to my ears. Pockets and droves of Astradians were gathered up in huddles, tossing flower petals in the air and singing songs at the top of their lungs. The celebration stretched up and down the street, wrapped around the city block, and carried out into the grassy fields of the surrounding area. Hordes of small, blue-skinned children pointed at the sky and danced in the streets, cheering and laughing.

The sound was beautiful. It felt like freedom, and that hit me in a different way now than it ever had before, probably because I felt like I had a role in bringing it about. I had fought for this, had witnessed good people die for this.

Had killed for it.

And a part of me wondered—though I hated the thought—how long would it last?

Freedom… was a precious thing. Gone too easily.

We threaded a path through the celebration, flower petals settling in our hair like snowflakes. I waved at the Astradians, who recognized Fera and me and welcomed the whole crew as conquering heroes.

Sert grunted out a small laugh. "Never did I imagine the day when Astradians would cheer a victorious Vorvak walking in their midst after battle."

"Probably because in your imagination, you conquered them," I pointed out.

"True, Will. True."

"Isn't this amazing?" Fera asked me. She gave my hand a squeeze.

"It is…" I admitted.

"But…" she prompted.

"I dunno. Just feels like the real heroes are still out there, stuck and fighting for their lives on the *ONE*."

I shook my head. Now was not the time to get distracted. "Sorry. Forget I said that. Yes, this is amazing. Your people are showing such hospitality and appreciation. I don't mean to overlook it."

An Astradian girl, maybe eight or nine years old if I had to guess, ran up to me and handed me a white flower with pink pollen at the base of its petals. I brought it up to my nose to smell it and recognized the scent immediately.

So it's not Japanese cherry blossom after all. It's Astradian *cherry blossom.*

"Thank you," I told the little girl and grabbed Fera by the hand.

"What're you doing?" she asked.

"Come here." I parted her black and purple hair, tucked a layer of it behind her ear, and stuck the flower into it by her brow. Before her shock could transform into a smile, I gave her a quick kiss.

The little girl giggled hysterically and covered her mouth. It was such a human gesture, I didn't even think of her as Astradian at that moment. Save for the blue skin and white lines, she was a simple girl, same as on Earth.

"Smooth," Fera said, smiling at me and then the child.

"Will you be at Windsong for the celebration tonight?" the girl asked.

"Windsong?" I asked. "Isn't that—"

Fera gave me a sidelong look. I took the hint and stopped talking.

"I'm sorry, young one, but we have business to attend to that can't wait."

I patted the girl on the shoulder and thanked her again for the flower. If there was any disappointment in the child over Fera's answer, it went away quickly. Her glacier-blue eyes went wide as Sert lumbered past. The hard-nosed Vorvak looked right over her head, scanning the crowd with a vigilance that was a bit overkill given the celebration at hand.

Benegal seemed intent on ignoring the revelry around him as though it weren't happening at all. "Nice enough place, I suppose. A bit moist for my liking, but you have a fair world for yourself here, Fera."

She stiffened when he used her name but seemed to relax at the compliment. "I haven't been back here in… since before the ice. We met with the Prime Minister and the Prime Minister Elect on their ship earlier and then had to return. It was very formal."

"That's a nice way of saying long and boring," Quin rushed to add.

I knew that Fera had been disappointed at not being able to visit her world in person, and now having seen it for myself, I understood why. It was beautiful.

The procession to what I took for a central government building seemed to stall. The revelry hadn't subsided, but we weren't moving any faster than a snail's pace.

"For the love of the Federation itself, what is *taking so long?*" Quin asked.

I shot back, "Gee, I don't know, Quin. The Astradians are free from Imperium rule for the first time in thousands of years. You think things might be a little off-kilter because of that?"

"The Foris would never condone such hooliganism. Crack a canister of ethyl acetate and toast to the end of one terrible thing and the start of a new, less terrible thing. Honestly, why Astradians complicate their lives like this, I never could understand."

"Yeah, well, understanding other species seems to be a weakness among… everyone," I mumbled.

"Except you," Fera said, giving me a pat on my shoulder.

I wasn't quite sure if she was being playful or sarcastic.

The line moved forward. We mounted a set of stone steps and walked across a carpet of plush royal purple. The reason for the delayed entry into the building became readily apparent.

People were pausing at the threshold and removing their shoes, then handing them to a bot that looked like an old-style post office mailbox from Earth. The bot was even a deep shade of blue with an open-faced cutout in the head of it. The base was embedded in the white stone beside the carpet. It accepted each pair of shoes and sent them down a chute, then chimed and displayed an ID tag above its dome.

"You're joking," I said. "You guys have Space TSA here?"

Fera knelt down, pulled her boots off, and slid them into the bot. "I don't know what that is, but this is our custom."

"Lockett needs no excuse. Clothing is a cage for the cybernetics, anyway." The Drayth pulled off his boots, which were more like slippers with hardened rubber pads on the bottoms, and dropped them in the slot. The feet he set on the ground were like prosthetics I'd seen amputees wear. Somehow, it didn't take me by surprise. I knew he took his devotion to upgrades seriously, and biomechanical peg legs were simply more proof of that fact.

Sert looked down at his feet dubiously. Like the rest of his body, they were covered in his naturally thick armor plating. "These only come off following great explosions."

They let him pass as is.

Benegal looked the most disturbed. "This is the sort of thing you tell someone before subjecting them to it."

I started pulling my boots off, feeling the line behind me getting irritated at the delay. "You mean you didn't know about this, Benegal? I thought I was the only uncultured rube on *Phaelon*."

"If it bothers you that much, stay outside," Fera said.

That did it for Benegal. He bent a knee, raised his foot, and stood perfectly balanced on one leg as he worked his boot off. Once the first hit the stone, he placed his green-scaled foot on the solid ground, clawed nails tapping at the smooth surface, and repeated the pose to pull off his other boot.

"One discourtesy does not warrant another," Benegal said, taking the last word before he stepped inside.

"Let it go," I said to Fera. "Or at least save it for later."

She compressed her lips into a thin look of frustration and then nodded. "Sometimes, I honestly can't believe these are my friends."

Friends, she said. Not crew. *Friends.*

Maybe there was hope for the galaxy after all.

24

THE PLUSH CARPET felt soothing through my socks. I took a moment to wonder at all of the different types of people here, and to wonder again that not all of them were wearing socks.

The chances of alien athlete's foot spreading seemed inevitable.

Two Astradian Honor Guard soldiers flanking the panel at the back of the room held PMCs at port arms. They looked fairly intimidating in their white and purple armor, except for their blue-skinned bare feet that rested on the carpet.

"They look ridiculous without combat boots," Sert lamented.

"I don't like the idea that security could be compromised by a stubbed toe," I said.

Sert gave a hearty laugh that instantly made me regret the quip. The big guy certainly knew how to draw attention to himself.

Fera scowled. "Someone would have to be certifiably insane to do anything stupid here. Or suicidal."

I looked pointedly at Benegal. Fera followed my gaze.

"Bet he's game planning how many he could take down if this was four thousand years ago," I said.

Benegal's reptilian eyes moved back and forth between examining his clawed fingers and looking at each member on the panel, like he was trying to decide if he could mount the dais and slaughter them before the Astradian Honor Guard could stop him.

"I bet he gets at least one before they kill him," Sert offered. "Maybe two. Now if it were *me*…"

"It's not four thousand years ago," Fera said uneasily. "No one is 'getting' anyone."

The stadium seating in the Grand Hall of the Asterism was packed to the gills with delegates, senators, Prime Ministers, Executors, and every other title of nobility and political office imaginable —not just Astradians, either. General Mira'dna had leaders from all the star systems that had thrown off the yoke of the Imperium present.

This was a big, big deal.

The dais in the center of the room held a long table formed of glass that shifted from frosted opaque to deep obsidian black and back again, depending on the intensity of the hologram displays hovering overhead. There, rolling recaps of the space battle that had just unfolded displayed, always ending with the *ONE* running off into Void space.

It had happened. The invincible Imperium and its invincible flagship had cut and run.

General Mira'dna waited near the speaking floor, which was a circular stage of white stone. It was as if the general had been carved of the same substance as the floor itself. I noted that there were no others of her kind amid the mass gathering of aliens, many of which I had never seen in person.

At the center of the speaking floor a solid black circle filled most of the stone, except where small perfect circles had been left unpainted, leaving a pattern of stars that formed a constellation I didn't recognize until my fiber-link dropped the information in my head.

Pleiades, also known as the Seven Sisters. Four hundred and forty-four light-years from Earth. One half of the Golden Gate of the Ecliptic.

I wasn't sure what to do with the information, so I let it fade away from my awareness, instead focusing on who else I recognized beside Mira'dna.

Fleet Admiral Tanoka, the newly minted General Stallings, and Captain Esmila of the *Three Oh One*. As far as I knew, the repairs to the *Three Oh One* were still underway and were projected to take the better part of two weeks. Every crystal diode on the ship had been fried by the EMP wake of the *ONE*'s initial Void Drift and needed a complete overhaul. Rescue ships had been dispatched to evacuate the crew, including the Krakoids, who were now planetside on Astrada Prime, where a refugee camp had been hastily erected between villages near the snow-capped mountains along the southern rim of the mountains nearby.

Sert was crouched in the aisle next to me. He stretched his neck, cracking several vertebrae and drawing attention from the people seated nearby. "I find this whole thing distasteful. The Galactic Federation did nothing for the galaxy as a whole before. Resurrecting a failure will not suddenly make it a success."

"Don't get political on me now, buddy," I said.

In part because I meant it. Mostly though, because Sert's

whisper came out at a normal speaking volume. I mean, in comparison to his usual booming, grating speech, it was technically a whisper. That didn't stop everyone around us from casting dirty looks in his direction.

Lockett and Benegal sat together. The two passed occasional whispers back and forth. Lockett's head bobbed, his cybernetic eyes looking like half-moons as he slowly lost the battle to stay awake. Uriel, thankfully, did not make its presence known.

The Astradian Prime Minister entered from stage right to an abundance of applause. He was flanked by two female political types dressed in ceremonial garb that reminded me of Polo shirts, so that was kind of funny. The shirts were a cream white and clung to the curvature of their torsos, but the sleeves were deep purple. The Prime Minister wore a variation of this, except his were long-sleeved; the sleeves grew wider as they went down, ending in wide circles that looked almost like wizard sleeves. Symbology that looked loosely related to Sumerian cuneiform ran up and down the sleeves in blunt white script, matching the artful lines across their foreheads and cheeks.

Interesting.

Jerub Whitecap, Prime Minister of Astrada, stopped in front of the center of the table at the speaking circle. He was a little over seven feet tall, with broad shoulders and a barrel chest that told me he either pumped iron in his off-time, or he'd served in a combat role at some point before taking political office. The white lines on his face were thicker than the typical Astradian pattern, including a large blocky one on his chin.

And his bare feet were covered in wispy white hairs.

Like a huge, blue space hobbit.

Whitecap cleared his throat as the females made stiff bows and took their seats at the side of the dais. He clasped his hands together, striking a non-threatening pose that did not match the stern expression on his face.

"The Great Hall of the Asterism is honored to be chosen as the meeting point for what will become an historic event. These talks will decide the future of the galaxy, by political writ, for the foreseeable future. Astrada thanks the United Council of Free Worlds for intervening on our behalf in the war against the Imperium." He turned ever so slightly to look at General Mira'dna. "I would like to begin this meeting by formally accepting entry into the United Council on behalf of the Astradian people."

"… who couldn't be bothered to take up the fight against the enemy themselves," Sert rumbled.

"I fought," Fera said.

"You are different," said Sert.

I rubbed a hand on her back, hoping the gesture would calm her down.

Because Sert was incapable of whispering, everyone around us heard what he said. But this time, among the crowd—especially the Delluvians—the expressions were less annoyed, like Sert was saying what they were thinking.

Back on stage, General Mira'dna gave the slightest inclination of her head at Whitecap's joining. "The United Council recognizes the Astradian Faction as the newest member of the United Council of Free Worlds. Please, Prime Minister Whitecap, take your seat on the council."

As he moved to take his seat to applause, General Mira'dna

smiled and pointed with an open hand at the remaining empty seat at the table.

"Will Kaufman, as Ambassador for Earth, your place is here."

A jolt of adrenaline ran through me. I fought hard not to grimace. That was the last place I wanted to sit. I was doing just fine blended into the crowd.

Fera nudged me with her elbow. "Go on, Hero of the Rebellion."

I gave her a final pat on the back. "Thanks."

As I mounted the dais, the lights in the ceiling dimmed. The stars of the asterism, the Pleiades, gave off columns of light that highlighted the speaking floor. I blinked as I stepped through the glare, trying to keep my bearings while hundreds of people all over the room watched my every step.

Someone shouted, "Speech!" and I froze.

That better not have been Sert.

Another voice bellowed, "Let us hear from the Hero of the Rebellion!"

Cheers ran through the crowd. Not like a stadium cheering for a rock band, but rolling pockets of cheers like at a high school prep rally. I glanced out at the crowd and saw diverse clusters of aliens clapping their hands, waving appendages, or in the case of the Delluvians, trumpeting their trunks.

I looked to General Mira'dna for rescue.

She smiled and nodded eagerly.

My heart sank into my stomach. I hadn't prepared anything. I didn't know what to say. I didn't know enough about the history of all of the different people gathered here. I could say the wrong thing and dredge up some forgotten blood feud between two factions—start a whole new war right here and now.

I raised a hand, acknowledging the applause, but the clapping didn't stop. Earl detached from its resting place behind my shoulder and floated up in a loose orbit, capturing all of the uproar with its high-definition recording.

Crazy as it seemed, Hero of the Rebellion wasn't just a title. I really *was* their hero.

Eddison accomplished what he'd meant to do. All of the PR campaigns and the footage of me during the war... this was the culmination of all that expense, time, and effort. But what had I done that was so special or worthy compared to everyone else who fought? I couldn't think of anything.

It was a manufactured moment. A politically motivated, financially secured, socially engineered outcome.

I gestured a request for the noise to die down. When it lowered a few decibels, I said, "With the Council's approval, I will speak."

The cheers crescendoed again, and a third time when Mira'dna formally gave approval for me to speak ahead of taking my place.

With sunspots dancing in my eyes from the strange lighting on the stage, I managed to lock eyes with Fera. In that moment, I remembered this was her root world. This was the home of her people, the place where she'd grown up. I really didn't want to embarrass her or disappoint her people... even though they had effectively played the middle ground by refusing to join the fight against the Imperium until all was decided.

And then there were those people who were unwilling to accept a New Federation...

I had to tread lightly.

The room became deathly quiet. So quiet I could hear the Drayths' iron lungs cycling oxygen in its rhythmic hisses.

I swallowed the lump in my throat and gravely said, "The war is over."

The crowd erupted in applause. I waited for them to quiet down again, which took almost a full minute. It gave me time to choose my next words carefully.

"All of us gathered here have sacrificed much just for me to say those words. The war... is over. And may the high price of victory make its rewards that much sweeter. May the peace and freedom the galaxy now has before it be a lasting one."

My speech was beginning to sound like a prayer.

"What the Council must now decide will determine more than the name and function of our new governing entity... it will decide whether or not we have learned our lessons from the past."

Benegal, who had been staring off into the corner, suddenly jerked his head around to look at me, his snout tilted up slightly. I wondered why, and my fiber-link supplied that it was a Krayvox sign of respect.

So it was with the other Krayvox delegates. I had given them hope... now I just needed to be sure I didn't lose the pro-Federation races.

"There is always comfort in familiarity. But it took something new and *unfamiliar* to form the United Coalition and defeat the Imperium. And though this war is over, we must remain focused on hunting down the last of the Imperium, lest they stir up old rivalries and set the galaxy on the same path that once led to their rising to power in the first place."

The crowd remained deathly silent. No one moved.

The room was holding its collective breath. I guessed that, putting aside all the Astradians, the members of the United Coalition were probably 60-40 in favor of a New Federation. But now both sides weren't sure exactly what I was getting at.

I laid the final piece in place, figuring that, worst case scenario, I wouldn't be asked to give any more speeches. Which was fine by me.

"Not all who are present are ready to resurrect the ideas of old simply because they are comfortable. But those who are here fought for freedom from the Imperium all the same. You have asked me to speak. Earth has a place on the Council. Therefore, as the Ambassador of Earth, I ask for something new. A form of galactic government that takes into account the inputs of each faction, regardless of size or resources, military strength, or technological capabilities. Something that we all build. Together."

No one reacted. The tension in the room made the air so thick, I could hardly breathe.

I turned to take my seat at the table next to General Mira'dna.

Just before I sat down, the applause started up again. I turned and saw, to my surprise, that it had been Sert who led the clapping that soon rippled to include others. I could see Astradians and Krayvox alike standing and clapping, while others of their kind sat, unsure.

My eyes found Fera and Benegal. Both wore the same expression on their faces.

Bewilderment.

That told me, more than anything else, that I'd walked the fine line and said what I needed to.

Unfortunately, the talks themselves wouldn't usher in much of anything.

Two hours of platitudes and empty promises; the way each faction kissed the backside of the others was so disingenuous, I actually stopped listening after the Irvlan started complimenting the Krayvox on their generous offer to only increasing their export taxes by fifty percent now that the war was over.

General Mira'dna called for a one-hour recess, and we—Council members only—found ourselves ushered into a side meeting room with the Astradian local government. I had to pull a few Hero of the Rebellion strings to make sure Fera and the rest of the crew were allowed to join me.

A recent brewing of *moola* filled the room with notes of cinnamon spice. General Mira'dna sipped eagerly at her cup. Tiny streamers of steam wafted from the undisturbed cups of the rest of the faction leaders.

Prime Minister Whitecap cleared his throat to address me. "That was a rousing speech, Ambassador. Seems you proved the galaxy at large is capable of swooning at honeyed words."

I didn't flinch. "I meant every syllable. It has been treated as a foregone conclusion that the Galactic Federation would carry on, as though the Imperium were a mere four-thousand-year interruption to its rule. That is a mistake."

He glared right back at me then flitted his eyes unapprovingly at Fera. "Is that so?"

Prax, representative of the Drayth Collective, adjusted the settings on his oxygen purifier, increasing the airflow to account for the diatribe he was about to unleash.

288

He jabbed a pale finger at Whitecap. "Astradians have the meeting place, but this cannot be the seat of the United Council. Tech capital of the galaxy will always be Divorak. Should maintain the council's headquarters there."

I had to resist the urge to roll my eyes. The issue that would decide between unity and brinksmanship was the form of government. Here, all the Drayth could think about was where the seat of that government's power could be.

Whitecap was only too happy to go rounds about that, though. "You Drayth were the chief supplier of warships to the Imperium! That hardly qualifies you as a neutral party."

Fera had been standing close by, her arms crossed. "I am Astradian, and I fought. And I wonder at how you sit here speaking on behalf of me and my people when Prime Minister Elect Nightshade was murdered."

Outrage came to Whitecap's face. "Serious allegations against your own kind, Miss. Murdered! You know nothing of what you speak."

Primus Heptali, leader of one of the Anunnaki collectives, scoffed. "This matter must be addressed. Captain Fera saw what *every* ship in the fleet saw—it was an Astradian super cruiser that fired on Nightshade's transport vessel. Not the Imperium."

Grumblings circled the table. The local Astradians were displeased, but the rest of the Council was unified in their concern over Whitecap's legitimacy.

I found myself wondering why they had allowed him to join at all. My vote would have been no, if I had been asked. The answer was likely… "politics."

"If I may"—General Mira'dna held up a hand to stave off further argument—"disputes within factions can be handled by the factions themselves. The Council will function best simply as an impartial arbiter when called upon. No doubt your own people will have questions when a full accounting of the battle is provided."

"Nightshade's sacrifice was just that!" Whitecap shouted. "She ordered that she be fired upon to belay Tror's suspicion that Astrada had joined the Coalition. We all know what the *ONE* is capable of. Our entire fleet would have been destroyed before you arrived. We had no choice. My people will understand that."

Maybe the guy was lying, maybe not. I was glad it wasn't up to me to decide.

"As I said," Mira'dna began, nodding her head in acknowledgement of the Prime Minister's explanation, "that is for Astrada to decide. What *is* of dire consequence to this council, Jerub, is your lack of military action during the battle."

The Whitecap's accent lines on his face shifted as he put on a wolfish grin. He'd been expecting this, and he had a rousing defense already prepared to meet it. He looked around at the delegates. "I do not see a faction that joined this Coalition while the *ONE* orbited their planet. I see several who waited for Tror to leave their system before throwing in. Astrada would have fought had our situation been that of the Drayth or Delluvians. It was not. We faced the dilemma of the Vorvak. We could not risk the Imperium turning their weapons on the surface of our worlds."

Fera pushed back. "The Imperium is an Anunnaki collection, but they have many Astradians serving in the old Federation space. You honestly believe they would have fired on their own root world?"

"I believe Tror's will to be one of iron. The Foris is not the type to come unprepared. It would have been done. Surely. Root world or no. You may judge my decision-making after the fact. You will not—any of you—lead me to doubt or apologize for what was done."

Whitecap gestured toward Sert. "Ask the Vorvak here what *he* would have done if provided the opportunity to save his Farakar before it was destroyed."

Even I knew that Whitecap had just miscalculated. I could have mouthed Sert's answer in real time as the big guy said it.

"I… would have fought."

Whitecap blanched.

I couldn't help but feel a little satisfaction at the turnabout. Fera, I could tell, was no fan of her leader. She looked like she wanted to see Whitecap in front of a firing squad.

But it was clear to me that the man was a survivor who would use that silver tongue of his to talk his way out of any real trouble. And… the reality of things was that the United Coalition, and the galaxy, needed Astrada to be among its ranks. Whitecap held power. Tror was still out there somewhere. We couldn't drive Astrada back to the Imperium as soon as we left Astradian space.

General Mira'dna shook her head, her expression firm and a little sad around the eyes. She saw right through the man, but she couldn't welcome the Astradians into the new alliance and then interfere with their sovereignty by demanding they elect a new leader.

"The New Federation will not intervene with the sovereign actions of each individual faction." She gave me a nod of acknowledgement. "That mistake, we must learn from first and foremost.

Secondarily, what we build here will come with its detractors. What do you propose we do to alleviate any misgivings some of the lesser factions hold against the larger ones?"

Benegal leaned forward in his seat, his eyes narrowed to slits.

Sinegar, the Krayvox delegate, let out a low hiss. "Any Federation will inevitably suffer an inclination toward corruption. I speak for more than Krayvox when I say this. There are many who wish to remain without shackles of some greater entity. What is ours, is ours. If you wish to partake of it, you will pay on our terms. This is the only means we will accept."

Sert crossed his arms and shifted his shell armor against the wall. "The Vorvak are ungovernable by any but Vorvak. You tried your political games under the name Galactic Federation. You exploited us, ignored us, and left us to fend for ourselves against the Imperium. Farakar is a desolate wasteland because of it. We will never bend the knee to any. The Krayvox speaks truth. Many will revolt if you attempt to step into the void left by the Imperium and simply raise a banner by another name."

"Wise words, Sert," General Mira'dna said evenly. "And yours are heard as well, Sinegar."

Benegal snorted. "Forgive me, but that is the response of a leader who does not know the will of the people over which it seeks to govern. These are not empty promises or the dark dreams of a madman. This is cold, objective reality staring you in the face."

He made a fist and slowly released it.

Sert nodded his large head. "There will be much pain and suffering if the Federation is reborn."

Benegal looked to Sinegar, who blinked in a way that must have been giving assent for the lesser den to speak further.

"Indeed," Benegal said, "the only path to peace is a simple non-interference treaty. All factions are to be left to their own devices. No meddling from another."

"Impossible," Prime Minister Whitecap said derisively.

Benegal shrugged. "Then peace is a dream, and you will wake to the reality of war in short order."

Several of the other faction leaders flinched.

"You dare to threaten us, Krayvox?" Whitecap said. "Here in the Hall of the Asterism?"

I could see how tense Fera was that, despite her dislike of Whitecap, she was still solidly on his side when it came down to an inter-species fight with the Krayvox.

This was going nowhere fast, so I spoke up again. "We're getting ahead of ourselves. Prime Minister Whitecap, the Imperium, prior to pointing its fleet at you, had come to talk. What did Tror want?"

General Mira'dna, grateful to get clear of the brewing spat, latched onto this. "You said you would inform the council after the resolution of the battle. That is done. What is your answer, Prime Minister?"

Whitecap smoothed out his expression, lips drawing into a straight line. The question made him uncomfortable, which told me that he had something to hide. In the room with every faction's delegate staring at him, his wiggle room was limited.

It felt like the first nibbles on a fishing line. All I had to do was hook him, and maybe then I could reel in the rest of the situation.

"What were you discussing?" I pressed.

Whitecap shifted in his seat. "They… Prefect Tror did make an offer to us." He hastily threw up his hands to wave it off. "Less an offer as than a veiled threat. We never seriously considered it."

"Unless it was forced on you," Fera said as if she didn't believe him. "As your non-participation in battle had been."

Caught blue-handed, Whitecap smirked, but his reply was cut off by Prax.

"Prax will tell you of this offer. It was surely the same the Imperium made to the Drayth. Prefect Tror knew he was on his last line of defense. After millennia of iron-fisted rule, he sought to loosen the chains with which he bound us under his control. Even talked of allowing a limited Federation under supervision of the Imperium if we were to realign ourselves with him."

Whitecap looked at Prax as if he didn't believe that the *Drayth* had been offered the same terms as Astrada.

"Is it so?" Mira'dna asked.

The Prime Minister gave a fractional nod. "That is exactly the offer he made to us, yes."

General Mira'dna let out a sigh. She looked at each of the representatives in turn before speaking. "Are we so fragile in our alliance that we must fear each faction succumbing to the wiles of a warlord who arrives with a fleet and makes threats against our worlds? To the Krayvox, Vorvak, and others... *this* is why we seek a united government, a New Federation. If even the greater factions amongst us can be manipulated through the destructive power of an enemy like the Imperium, how can we avoid a repeat of Imperium rule without a unified, standing military force that can guarantee the protection of all?"

Benegal seethed. Sert shook his head, a savage smile darkening his face.

The door to the room opened with a pneumatic puff. General

Stallings poked his head into the room, locked eyes with Fleet Admiral Tanoka.

"Apologies for the delay, but we have a priority message from the Foris Collective. Will, you're needed. Admiral, you, too."

I looked at General Mira'dna. She gave me a weary nod.

"Fera, come on."

I could think of only one thing this could be.

25

"WE'RE GOING BACK to the *Earthborn*," General Stallings said as he led us through the Hall of the Asterism, marching like a man on a mission. "This demands immediate attention."

"Anything's better than those peace talks," I said.

Admiral Tanoka shook his head. "Leave the politics to the politicians. I'll back-brief General Mira'dna."

Stallings filled us in on the rest in gruff whispers as we retrieved our boots from the mailbox-style storage bot, then navigated through the crowd outside. By the time we were on board the *Phaelon*, the adrenaline was flowing freely through my veins.

As I suspected, the *ONE* had been sighted exiting Void space in a far-flung system on the fringe of space. Apparently, Tror's intent was to rendezvous with one of the few remaining contingents of the Imperium fleet. The remnant had yet to mobilize, but once they did, they'd Void Drift in and Tror would complete his escape with a small Imperium fleet.

Perhaps all he intended to do was run back to the Imperium home worlds—a trip that took years even while using the Void. But maybe not.

Whatever the case, a lasting peace could be established with the destruction of Tror and the *ONE*.

We had to race against the clock.

"Tror had all the galaxy to choose from," Quin mused after being filled in on what Stallings had told us. "Why would he choose a fringe corner of the galaxy?"

No one had an answer until a message came through from Marcus Eddison, directly to me. I watched the message through my fiber-link and decided everyone else needed to see it, too.

It was news I couldn't keep to myself.

We reconvened on the bridge of the *Earthborn*. General Stallings dismissed everyone but his deck officer, Captain Caldera, whom he ordered to key up the message playback window. Quin beamed my personal message from Eddison onto the main display for everyone to see.

Stallings kept giving Lockett suspicious glances. The Drayth had Uriel's container held under his arm like a football. After what happened the last time the Fleuridian had escaped, I didn't blame the General for being suspicious. So far, the powerful creature hadn't made any moves toward its own purposes.

The display flashed.

Eddison's face was covered in a huge grin. "Will Kaufman, word has reached me of your victory in Astradian space. Let me be the first to formally congratulate you on your triumph over the Imperium. I am contacting you for more than the acknowledgement of the United Coalition's success, however."

Eddison paused to run his thumb and forefinger over the sides of his mouth, as if trying to keep the grin on his face from spreading wider. As if he were trying not to laugh. Like he was holding something back.

He didn't hold it back for long. Dropping his hand, he leaned forward, his face filling up the entire hologram, and when he spoke, it was in a hushed, conspiratorial tone that even on the second viewing raised the hairs on the back of my neck.

"You know as well as I do that this war isn't truly over until Tror is out of the picture. Fortunately for us, I have an agent aboard the *ONE*."

I looked to Stallings to gauge the General's reaction. The man's mouth fell wide open.

Ever the showman, Eddison paused, waiting for his words to land.

Fera took in a sharp breath, her eyes locked on the hologram.

"Of course he does," Benegal sneered. "This man is just like Atron; he has his tentacles in everything."

Sert grunted in agreement. "Spies are cowards. They deserve a quick and painful death, nothing more."

"Quiet!" Quin said, his voice tingling along my jawbone.

Eddison cleared his throat.

"My agent—a Foris by the name of Riva—has informed me that Tror's Void Drifter was injured in the assault. According to her report, the Navigator's Void Drift capability has been degraded to the point of uselessness. They aimed to leave the galaxy proper but have ended up adrift. As soon as my people caught wind of this, they immediately engaged the scraps of the Imperium fleet in the area and have effectively stalled them from Drifting to his aid. Tror's only option is to limp his way out by using FTL gates. If you pursue him now, you should be able to catch him before he escapes the galactic border.

"I leave this in your capable hands, Ambassador of Earth and Hero of the Rebellion. I have full confidence you will bring this war to a swift end, and that Prefect Tror will suffer the consequences of his ruthless imperialism."

Eddison signed off, leaving the logo of the United Coalition in the center of the screen.

I looked to Fera. "I thought Tror was a Navigator. Why wouldn't he just Void Drift if his was injured?"

She could only shrug. "Maybe he lied. I don't know, Will."

Stallings cleared his throat. "Lieutenant Fel and his team were still on board the *ONE*. I wish Eddison's spy might have reported on *that*."

"Since he did not," Sert rumbled, "assume they are dead and any attack will be without their aid."

I pointed at Stallings. "You knew when you pulled us out of the meeting that we were going for Tror. Are your people ready?"

Stallings gave a curt nod. "Of course. Lieutenant Berrios and his men are ready for boarding action."

I raised a brow. Promotions had been doled out across the board, it seemed. Berrios had been a staff sergeant, the last I knew of it.

Admiral Tanoka said, "Our ships have remained on standby. We can leave as soon as a Void Drift can be arranged."

"Good," I said, wheels turning in my head. "Let's get back to the *Phaelon*. Quin, check the integrity of the Void tether."

"Already done. The tether is secure," he said, dissolving his hologram. His next words came through the bone conduction comm of my fiber-link. "I agree this is the proper course of action, Will, but it is not without risk."

"Nothing worth doing ever is, Quin."

THE COLD AIR aboard the *Phaelon* was all too familiar.

Sweat. Tension. Astradian cherry blossoms.

Sert disappeared inside the armory. Benegal hurried to follow him.

I went with Fera into her room, where our armor awaited us.

We stripped out of our civilian clothes and pulled on the under suits, then helped each other into our armor. I slid the shoulder plates into place and locked them over her back, and I was surprised to see her flinch when the armor snapped into place.

"You okay?"

She nodded, but her face told a different story. She was uneasy, and I wanted to know why.

"What? What is it?"

She shook her head. "Eddison's a problem, Will. I don't know... I don't trust him."

I brushed a hand across her cheek. She rested her head against it, as if she were tired and needed a nap.

"If he's a problem, he's not the one we're taking on now. Tror is. This could never be over until that Imperium bastard was captured or killed, and we have our opportunity. Whatever Eddison ultimately wants, we know Tror and the Imperium aren't a part of that."

She wrapped her arms around me. I held her.

The embrace felt like home. It made never going back home to Indiana seem like a small sacrifice.

"We can do this," she said.

"You don't sound very confident."

"I am if you are."

I pulled away from the hug and looked into her icy blue eyes. "With you by my side? Always."

I kissed her. It was a tender moment that I wanted to last forever.

But that couldn't happen.

Fera sighed as we parted.

We made our way to the bridge of the *Phaelon* and took our seats. Lockett was the next to arrive. I was shocked to see Uriel in his disembodied cloud of light particles floating along beside him. The energy field given off by Uriel sent static rippling along my skin.

They were in conversation.

The distorted buzzing of the Fleuridian's speech echoed off the bulkheads. "The secrets of my people are not for sale, cybernetic being. This will not be discussed again."

Lockett pouted his way to his station and set the bot's head unit on the console.

Fera shot the Drayth a look. "Lockett, I thought I told you to leave the Fleuridian alone."

Lockett only bubbled quietly in his sorrow.

Uriel's hollow dark spots shifted toward Fera. Motes of light flared, sizzled, and faded within and around the manifested being in an endless reaction.

"It has entered my awareness that there is a power source on this vessel you pursue that may be suitable for my purposes. It is a Fleuridian conduit, restored to full functionality by this Imperium. What is your intent with this device?"

Quin's hologram spun around with an expression of disbelief on his face. "Who told you about the Quantum Gate Sequencer?"

"What are we talking about?" I demanded.

Quin made a gesture like he was brushing dust off his shoulder. "Right. I forget that you're human sometimes. Eddison's transmission contained more than just a message, Will. His Foris spy provided a further detailed schematic of the *ONE.*"

I looked to Uriel. "And you can read what comes in on my fiberlink?"

"What is contained in all of your minds is no secret."

That was disturbing to hear.

Quin continued, full of pride. "Of course, only a Foris could have gotten their hands on the schematics in the first place and actually understood what they were looking at."

"So why didn't that Foris spy send them to us sooner? Maybe Tror wouldn't have gotten away."

"The answer should be obvious," Benegal said as he entered the bridge. "Eddison had the plans but withheld them until he decided it was in his best interest to share."

Fera cursed. Sert bellowed a sarcastic laugh.

I squeezed my hand into a fist until my knuckles went white. My desire to punch Eddison in the face burned in me like a furnace. "I'm going to straighten him out the next time I see him. We could have made a better breach and board plan if we had those ahead of time."

Uriel floated toward Quin's hologram, hovering half a meter above the deck. The cloud of light particles flickered, shifting between hues of red and blue, alternating between opaque and translucent.

Quin took a step back and leaned away from it.

"This conduit draws power from higher space-time. It can be dialed in to provide the three FOE required for me to complete my journey to the higher realm. Our agreement binds you to acquire it for me, though the cybernetic being has also offered."

Quin glared at Lockett. The Drayth shrugged.

"Lockett only makes offer. No deal was made."

Fera reached over the back of her chair and grabbed Lockett by his breathing tubes. She pulled him up until he was standing on the balls of his feet, gurgling in pain as she constricted the oxygen flow by pinching the convoluted tubing in her clenched fists.

"I gave you an order not to do that! You don't have anything to offer Uriel that won't cost the rest of us!"

Sert leaned forward and ran his bumpy tongue over his large teeth, no doubt hoping to see the Drayth experience a little corporal punishment.

"Let us watch the cyborg squirm his way out of this one," he rumbled eagerly.

Lockett tried to talk, but all he managed was a choked gasp.

"Fera, let him go," I said. "It's better we find out about this now than when we're already on board the *ONE*."

She growled in frustration and released her grip. Lockett slammed down into his chair, chest heaving as he tried to catch his breath.

"Seriously uncool, Lockett," I said.

Uriel floated close to Lockett, his cone-shaped crystal-faceted head panning back and forth between Fera and the Drayth. "The agreement was my assistance in exchange for Ascendancy. This is what is required. It must be done."

Fera looked at Uriel, the barest hint of hesitancy on her face. "That is still the deal, Uriel. We'll get you your energy beam or whatever it is you need. But whatever this one asks"—she smacked Lockett on the head—"is *not* part of the deal."

"His is a species of schemers and con artists," Sert added helpfully.

Uriel's cloud darkened a few shades.

"Okay, well this isn't all bad, really. Uriel said he would help us defeat the Imperium, and if this power supply thing on the *ONE* is the real deal, this... Quin?"

"Feh. The human mind. Quantum Gate Sequencer."

I nodded. "Right. We make the Quantum Gate Sequencer a secondary objective. Board the ship, find Tror, then give Uriel access to the Sequencer. It's not that big of a deal."

Fera feinted another slap. Lockett flinched and coiled up in his chair like a scared child.

"I won't forget this, Drayth," she promised.

He peeked out from behind his hands. "Lockett makes no apologies."

Uriel was fixated on his power source and eventual ascendancy. The inner strife of the crew was all but meaningless to the Fleuridian. "I will conserve my energy for the impending action. Once I gain access to the conduit, I will achieve Ascension. The deal will be complete."

Like the flip of a light switch, the Fleuridian dissolved.

Lockett cursed. "So much data. So much information. Answers to all questions in the Lightbearer, and you would cast it off into the ether."

"Didn't sound like he was willing to hand any of that over to you, Lockett," I said. "Nice try, though."

"If you're so set on your galaxy-wide upgrade, figure out your own Ascension," Fera said through gritted teeth. "We have a war to finish. People that need our help. Can you focus on that, or should we leave you here?"

"Lockett will go. No debate."

Fera caught my gaze.

I nodded.

"Quin, power up the Void engine," Fera ordered. "Once the *Earthborn* is ready, let us know."

"Of course," he said, eyeing the captain warily.

"Well," I said, "this ought to be interesting."

26

I slapped the controls.

The Void Drift suite populated on the main screen. I put in a connection request directly to General Mira'dna's wrist tab. She answered after a few moments, seeming rattled.

"Will, what is it?"

"General, we just received a message from Marcus Eddison. He has a spy on the *ONE* that's telling him Tror's ship has lost Void Drift capability."

She frowned. "I saw the report from the Foris Collective but not —did he send you this message directly?"

I nodded. "He did, ma'am. I shared it with General Stallings and Admiral Tanoka. We are preparing to Void Drift."

She smiled and shook her head. "Marcus hasn't changed in five thousand years. Forever the long game."

Quin gaped at the general, his large dark eyes bugging. "General, please tell me you don't mean to brush this aside as a simple quirk? He's had an agent embedded in the enemy flagship this whole time and has only just now let the rest of us in on that fact! That's tantamount to treason by the omission of relevant facts! According to Federation Code—"

The General silenced him with a raised hand.

"You rush too quickly to judgment, Quintar. Do not forget that there currently is *no* Federation. The proceedings have yet to truly begin, and when they do, it will be a lengthy process at best. I have little doubt the outcome will trend toward that direction, but there is a very long series of discussions that need to take place before that is decided in an official capacity."

Fera stepped in before Quin could reply. "General, this doesn't feel right."

Mira'dna smiled. There was a gravity to her expression, like she felt guilty that she would be staying behind. She forced herself to pause for a sip of *moola* before she spoke again. "I agree. But we haven't time for a discussion. Your plan to leave is shrewd. Do so immediately."

I felt a little guilty at how quickly the decision had been made, mostly for Fera's sake. I trusted her intuition, but if the situation was reversed and I were stuck in a shipboard gunfight with the Imperium, I would hope the United Coalition would kick down the gates of Hell itself to come to my aid.

Quin stood ramrod straight and gave a nod of farewell.

"We'll be in touch," he said, dissolving the connection. "Idiots! All of them—how can they not see that this is a disaster waiting to happen?"

"That's paranoia talking," I countered. "We get in there, and it's stiff fighting to the bridge. So what? We go in expecting that. We bring Lieutenant Berrios and his team from the *Earthborn* to even the numbers a little bit, and we do the damned thing."

Quin looked like he wanted to argue, but he decided against it.

Sert was spoiling for a fight. He leaned back and cracked his neck. "Stiff fighting it is. After Tror is a corpse, the real fun begins."

His comment lingered in the air, tinged with foreboding. I couldn't believe, as big and intimidating as he was, no one at the Council meeting had thought to ask the only Vorvak in attendance what he and his people were planning on in the aftermath. That was a major point that needed handling before it turned into an outright purge of the Vorvak remnant.

And Benegal seemed on pretty good terms with Sert. What would the galaxy do if the Krayvox and the Vorvak formed an alliance? I made a mental note to talk with both of them and feel that situation out.

Old habits don't die hard… they don't die at all, I thought.

Benegal put his scaly hands behind his head and raised his snout, as if he were settling in for a nap. "This new entity we have fought to secure will never know true security as long as the Imperium threat looms beyond the galactic rim. Killing Tror is a requirement."

I felt something shift in the air around Fera. A distance appeared in her eyes, like she was caught up in a stream of moving pictures in her head. Guessing at the future, or thinking deeply about something.

She spoke, sounding distracted, or just tired. "This is a mistake."

I searched her gaze for a clue as to why she thought that but came up empty.

"It's the right thing to do," I insisted. "It's what we have to do."

Fera sighed and looked me straight in the eyes. "I know, Will. But sometimes, the right thing at the wrong time is just as bad."

"We're not going to get another shot at this," I reminded her. "This isn't the right or wrong time—it's the only time."

Quin announced that the *Earthborn* had signaled they were ready to deploy. "Might as well get this over with. But let me say this much to you, Will. If I'd have listened to Fera the last time she had a feeling like this, I'd probably still be alive."

I looked around at the crew and thought, *and then none of us would be together*.

It strengthened my resolve.

"Let's get going. Prepare to Void Drift."

***

THE SONG WASHED over me like I was sitting front row stage right at the orchestra.

Without warning, the intensity of the music increased tenfold.

"Breakaway Fleet has entered the Void. Tether integrity is holding." Quin paced with the soundless footsteps expected of a hologram. He moved in and out of my field of view, the whiteout of the Void highlighting the orange tinge of his skin. His head probes waggled slightly with each step, and I noticed he never took his eyes off me, not even when Uriel's cloud of smoke and light materialized on the bridge unannounced.

Yes, Uriel was there; I didn't feel the static crackling within the cloud of its sometimes-here-sometimes-there avatar, but I did hear it speak in a disembodied, echoing tone.

"Your sensitivity is perplexing."

"Oh, yeah?" I asked, my voice echoing like it was underwater.

Or like it was someone else speaking my thoughts.

"You do not simply receive the inputs of the Void. You also transmit your own outputs."

"That is… unusual?"

"Very. That is the mark of my people's influence on the Void itself."

Quin stopped pacing. "Don't lose focus, Will."

I took in a sharp breath and held it. The melody of the entry lane cascaded somewhere in my headspace. I felt like I was chasing it with my awareness, running a metal detector over the sands of a beach, hoping to feel a rattle or hear a beep.

Only I was searching for a single flake of iron on a beachhead made up of individual sand grains that defied calculation. It was an impossible task, and yet… like the surety of high tide at noon, I knew I would find it. It was only a matter of focus and discernment.

Then finally, action.

"What does that mean, Uriel?" I asked absentmindedly.

The Fleuridian didn't respond. My focus remained on locating the melody I'd lost as I sifted the streaks of black lightning that forked across the endless white expanse of subspace.

"STEM core operable with no significant latency," Quin reported.

I gripped the throttle and the sidestick. Fera's eyes bored into me, not with hesitancy or jealousy but something gentler. Concern, and maybe a bit of awe. I liked it when she looked at me that way. Little such moments served as reminders that the impossible was real; the beautiful Astradian was into me with the same intensity I was into her.

Memories of her flooded me as I sank deeper into the folds of the song, plunging into the metaphysical depths of strings and woodwinds serenading the stars themselves with a private display of reverence known only to Navigators.

A cluster of shadow bolts streaked across the hologram, cracking the whiteout into two halves. Mere moments later, the streaks faded back into the white as if they had never been, leaving only trace notes of their existence.

In perfect contrast to the haunting beauty of the Void, darkness coalesced in the distance. Inverse stars began to collect themselves together, forming the anomaly. Amidst huge swathes of unbroken light, a new kind of storm was brewing.

It was a void within the Void.

"The Hollow," Uriel said, its body of living smoke leaning forward.

The Fleuridian's empty eyes of shadow were not unlike the inverse stars displayed on the bridge hologram's forward feed. A tug of force compelled me toward Uriel—all at once I felt torn between watching the creature and giving myself over to the Voidsong.

"What is it?" I asked. "What's the Hollow?"

"The chaos and tumult of this realm defied the understanding of my people for many generations. Unlocking its secrets cost us much."

A shiver ran down my spine. I could sense Lockett at the edge of his seat, hanging on every word uttered by the mystical being of smoke and light hovering at my shoulder.

The Hollow started as a single point, one lone dark star light-years away. As more stars began to meld with the mass, the teeming shadow swelled and vacillated like a fusion reaction, growing and rotating like the birth of a new star.

It grew. Expanded.

I couldn't shake the feeling it was aware.

Aware of me, specifically.

It was a nebula of darkness.

My palms began to sweat. If my sense of time was accurate—always hard to know while in the Void—I hadn't gone this long without locating the exit lane before. I resisted the urge to check the mission timer and prove myself right. Quin would have said something. Besides, panicking wouldn't do anything but guarantee that I'd lose focus.

I continued talking to Uriel, believing it would help me remain calm. Distract me from the mounting fear I felt.

"Your people figured it out? The song?"

Uriel made a sound like the opening of an old vault door. "The message is in the movement. Can you not hear the movement?"

What the hell does that mean? I wondered.

"I don't hear anything, not really. It's more like… a feeling. A sensation. There are certainly no words. No message."

"Will," Quin said softly. "I need you to focus on the Drift Lanes. The Hollow is expanding exponentially the longer we remain in Void space. Find the exit lane and get us out of here."

The skin at the back of my neck tightened.

Come. Back.

I remembered the words I'd heard on my last exit from the Void. I'd written them off as pure imagination, but… could it be possible that they came from the Void itself? What did it mean? Was that the calling of the siren song, the malevolent force of raw power that enticed with melodious promises of paradise, only to devour the unwary Navigator that fell into its clutches?

I didn't know, and now wasn't the time to find out.

"You will know it one day." The confidence in Uriel's words set me ill at ease.

Suppose I didn't want to?

Fera leaned back in her station to look around Uriel's avatar of dancing lights. "Will, you still okay?"

"I'm good," I lied.

The Fleuridian was creeping me out. I hadn't felt the exit lane present itself, nor even the faintest indicator that it was still out there somewhere, lingering in the ether, waiting to reveal itself. It felt like being adrift at sea in a fog—nowhere to go, and even if land was a few feet away, I couldn't see it through the obstruction wrapped around me.

The Hollow was like an inverse lighthouse. Rather than signaling with an oscillating beam of light, it spread darkness and malevolence.

"Hear it," Uriel said.

"I don't hear anything, and I need to focus!" I snapped, waving a hand dismissively. "Give me some space. You're crowding me."

Uriel didn't move.

Quin considered the alien being for a long moment before he said, "Will, make your exit. The Lane should have presented itself by now."

"Well it hasn't, Quin."

Uriel leaned closer to my station, scattering light particles in front of my face. None of them touched me. It took every fiber of self-control I possessed—and a good deal of my concentration—not to flinch away from the being. Static skittered along my cheek and under my chin. My hair felt itchy with electric charge. I was convinced that if I touched the frame of my station, I'd send a spark into the equipment and start a fire.

"It is there, but you must go deeper. Hear it," Uriel insisted.

Peace became war.

The oasis of ambiance was usurped by the fanfare of hell itself.

Drift Lanes dragged across the Void like wound channels, unleashing shrieks of pain and suffering so stark, their soundless vibrations grated in my inner ear.

I could let go. I could slip away right now, and no one would ever know.

"Will?" Fera asked, reaching out to put a hand on my arm. Her voice was full of concern.

I flinched away before she could touch me.

"Do not leap," Uriel instructed. "Fall."

"Don't listen to him, Will," Quin warned, his voice high and agitated.

My heartbeat became audible. Time stretched, slowing to a painful slow motion that was somehow simultaneous with reality moving at normal speed.

"What—?" I mumbled.

"Will! Stop this! You'll get us all killed, you ape-faced, rock-chewing, bipedal smooth brain!"

Quin's words sounded odd. Like I was hearing two of him speak —one slow, one normal speed. The vibrations of his voice were tangible, like droplets of water pattering across my face.

The floodgates broke open inside my mind. Panic assailed me, and I began to drown. It wasn't a conscious decision. It just happened.

My chest tightened and loosened of its own accord as my body tried to force breath into my lungs. No oxygen made it in, and a dark ring of hypoxia locked over my view, steadily filling my sight until I was left with a pinhole of the Void on the main hologram display.

My face must have gone a shade paler because Quin placed his hands on my terminal and leaned in close, his amphibian eyes perfect circles of concern. "Will! Don't listen to it. I don't know what it's doing, but you know better. Don't give in to the song. It will ruin you! It will destroy all of us!"

Springy flutes intermixed with the slamming crescendos of war drums. The laughter of innocent children was drowned out by the death rattles of millions of men on battlefields from time immemorial.

Uriel's laugh rattled the bulkheads with its deep, distorted timbre. "You have already achieved equilibrium. Reach out and *know*."

The guillotine of understanding dropped, severing the fear and removing it completely from my awareness. I lost my sense of hearing. Quin, Fera, even Uriel... I was deaf to everything... except the Voidsong.

The sound waves generated by their speech touched me as physical things, but they did not enter my awareness. Their syllables were packets of information encoded with a cipher I had suddenly lost the ability to decode.

I struggled for breath. A band of pressure tightened across the top of my head.

My heart slammed in my chest, keeping in time with the racing of the war drums of new Drift Lanes—a thousand new paths between stars forming every second. The chaos was too much; my sensitivity was so heightened, I felt like I could detect every individual particle of each lane, like looking down at a map and being able to read the names of the individual cities and towns at a glance.

A single jagged bolt of pure darkness slithered through the expanse between stars. It was one of a million, seemingly no different from the rest of the lightning storm, and yet, there was no sound. No signature melody.

But there was a word.

TROR.

I came back to full awareness, convulsing in my chair.

Fera had already unstrapped and was moving to work me out of my restraints. Quin was shouting at Uriel, who stood defiantly in its position, not moving or even acknowledging the Foris hologram.

"He has attained. This is the first step of Ascendancy."

I was going to vomit. I was going to pass out. The very next heartbeat was going to be my last.

I reached over Fera's shoulder and tapped the hologram on my primary display. A waymarker materialized under my finger.

"There," I gasped.

Fera shook me and looked at the display. "Are you all right?"

"Go," I wheezed. "Now."

She hesitated, but only for a second. Fera was a pilot, and that fact reasserted itself, overriding her fear at my condition. She hopped back into her station and assumed the controls.

Quin called my name again and again. "Will? Will… Will!"

I drew ragged breaths, hungrily stealing sips of oxygen. Blood thundered in my head. Darkness swam in my vision. Digging deep, I fought my body's insistent urge to quit consciousness. The Delluvian fibers adjusted their position against my convulsions, reforming each time my back and neck pressed into the seat.

"We're almost there," Fera said, bumping the throttle.

My eyes sailed lazily around the bridge, unfocused. I had gone too far, but I had not gone beyond the point of no return.

As I slowly came around, my heart rate slowed to normal. My breathing returned to its typical cadence. Sweat ran down my forehead and the back of my neck. The climate control settings on the bridge, coupled with my Drayth armor, kept everything at a comfortable temperature. Despite that, my body shivered like I was standing in a blizzard in nothing but a t-shirt and shorts.

I recovered enough to catch both barrels from Quin.

"What the hell were you thinking?" the AI demanded.

My focus was back in place, but I felt drained. A hike that took everything from you, an illness that sapped all of your energy—that practically sucked out your will to even live.

The scopes showed the Coalition Breakaway Fleet lined up behind us at standard intervals, caravan style. Fera guided the *Phaelon* toward the waymarker I'd left in the display. It was the ultimate trust exercise; for now, the waymarker hung in the open space of the Void, with no Drift Lanes in the immediate area of the spot I'd indicated.

Quin frowned. He'd noticed it, too.

"Will, are you sure—?"

"Prepare to deactivate the Void engine," I said. "I'm sure."

"There's no Drift Lane here, Will! I can't in good conscience—"

I did it for him. I hit the switch, unsure why I was so confident but knowing with iron-clad certainty the danger would be greater if we weren't ready for transition when we arrived at the waymarker.

The countdown started from five and worked its way to zero.

Before Quin could argue, the *Phaelon* made contact with the waymarker.

The Drift Lane I recognized as Tror aboard the *ONE* knifed through the *Phaelon*—not truly him, more like a hologram. Our passing through his position in Void space.

The hologram was hit with a sonic storm of darkness. Static shadow billowed over the viewport, stealing away any trace scraps of the pale light of the Void. The countdown hit zero. A low rumble passed through the deck beneath my boots—the Void engine deactivating.

All at once, the starfield materialized before us. We were immediately in attack position against the *ONE*. A perfect placement.

Sweat dripped from my brow and flecked onto my terminal.

Quin muttered a curse of disbelief. "How did you do that?"

My body relaxed. Fast-twitch muscles pulsed in my legs and shoulders.

I stared at the twinkling lights of millions of stars, marveling at their majesty as if seeing them for the first time.

"Success," Uriel declared.

I turned to look at the Fleuridian. It vanished like smoke in the wind, leaving trace light particles.

27

"Okay let's do this," I said, standing wearily.

Quin crossed his arms. "Absolutely not. We may need you to Drift out of here. You need a rest cycle—probably three, by my estimation. That's a minimum. Looking at you, I'd say you need five or six REM cycles before you're back up to full operating capability."

I was fatigued, that was true. Lieutenant Fel and his team, if they were still alive, needed help *now*. All that they could get.

"I'm good," I said.

Fera looked askance. "Will, this isn't going to be easy. We need you in peak condition."

"He is capable," Sert disagreed. "Will is a warrior, same as the rest of us. He will rise to the occasion. Your warriors, if they still fight in the belly of the beast, need reinforcements."

"Can we get comms with Lieutenant Fel?" Benegal asked. "Is there any way to know if they're still alive?"

Lockett shook his head. "Imperium tech is too advanced. Even better than Drayth cybergenic communications. Need physical connection with the *ONE*, and even then… magic might be limited."

The starfield showed two planets—one daffodil yellow gas giant composed mainly of hydrogen and helium, the other a rusty red and lavender ice giant with huge quantities of ammonia and methane. My fiber-link filled in the gaps in context that the raw telemetry data did not provide.

Ignotius and Agnostus, the two largest celestial gas stations in Foris-controlled space. The Foris Collective often makes the thirteen light-year trip in a single day via the primary FTL gate in the Meridionalis system, where their root world orbits its binary star pair.

I let the information dissolve before it could give me a history lesson I didn't need at the moment.

Quin inhaled a deep breath, as if he were so close to his ancestral home, he could smell it.

"Even the stardust seems brighter here in the civilized sector of space," he said. "A fitting place for the final stand of the Imperium."

Fera plotted a course for the *ONE*'s ventral section, according to the plan. "If we're doing this, I need an active pulse."

"You have it," Quin replied mechanically.

I dialed in the visual scopes and panned the feed over the firing surface of the space-station-sized ship. The bland icon rendered into ultra-high definition as the scanners painted the information into an accurate visual representation of the ship.

Huge gouges were carved out of the *ONE*'s dorsal panels. Launch tubes were fused shut or had been ripped completely away from their berths. Reinforced nickel-carbide panels were misshapen and scored with blackened scorch marks. The ship registered thirty percent combat capability on the scanner. It had taken a tremendous beating, and yet somehow its hull integrity reading proclaimed seventy-five percent.

I put in a connection request to the *Earthborn*. Fleet Admiral Tanoka answered immediately.

"Will, is everything all right? I'm not an expert on Void Drifting, but that seemed... chaotic, from our perspective."

I felt irritable but resisted the urge to lash out. What did he know about Void Drifting. About the song. The song...

Come. Back.

I shook my head clear. "Are your breaching teams ready, Admiral?"

He blinked. "Yes, they are. You brought us in nice and close."

"I did. The time is now, Admiral."

"Very well. Breakaway Fleet is surrounding the *ONE*. Breaching teams Alpha and Bravo will be dispatched momentarily."

Alpha Team would be led by Lieutenant Berrios, Bravo Team by an Astradian Major named Adenka, who'd volunteered to lead a small force of his people in this last combat action of the war. It felt like a showy act of demonstrating loyalty, but Admiral Tanoka did not leave any room for argument. He was firm that the United Coalition had to give the Astradians the opportunity to save face after their sandbagging the space battle in their territory.

Fera put a hand on my arm. "Will, you don't have to prove anything to me. Sit this one out."

I gripped her hand and gave it a gentle squeeze. "I'm going to the armory."

I unstrapped from my station and mounted the bridge. Sert gave me a pat on the back.

"War awaits. Let us finish this!"

"That's right," I said, not knowing what else to say.

A chime sounded from the bridge. An odd register that I hadn't heard before. I stopped and turned my head.

Quin looked up at me, his thin lips curling into a smile. "Priority message from the *ONE*. I think it's for you, Will."

28

EDDISON'S SPY aboard Tror's ship was a Foris female named Riva.

There wasn't anything obvious about her that differentiated her from a male, though. Her skin-and-bone frame was topped with an elongated head, the trademark probes atop them a bit longer than Quin's. The pigmentation of her alien skin held vestiges of a pale blue that seemed faded with the passage of time. All Foris gave off the fragile, intellectual vibe, but she seemed spry despite the obvious signs of age embedded in her features.

When she talked, there was a tinny rattle, like she was speaking from the bottom of her throat.

"*Phaelon.* I detected your arrival in the system." She paused, casting furtive glances over both shoulders, then lowered her voice to a whisper. "I am on rotation at the third deck sensor station. Our mutual friend gave me the go-ahead to bring you aboard. Your first two breaching teams have their hands full at opposing midship sections, which should give your survivors holed up in the life-support banks a much-needed reprieve."

I breathed a sigh of relief. Lieutenant Fel's team hadn't been killed down to the last man. That meant we could link up with them, establish communications, and finish this. If they had secured part of the flagship and were holding one of the more important shipboard systems hostage, all the better.

Quin's interest was piqued. "They're alive. How?"

"Trapped. They have life support. Prefect Tror was content to starve them out. He is a patient man."

My blood boiled at the thought of Fel and his men being left to die of hunger and thirst. It seemed like classic Tror, though. Why waste men and energy when time would do the killing for you? After all, Tror had lived thousands of years. What was another couple of weeks?

"Are we clear to approach?" Fera asked.

"Proceed to the coordinate pin attached to this message," the spy said, "and I will see to it that the cipher and magnetic locks are disengaged."

"Nice for something to go our way for once," Benegal said with a sigh.

In the background of the feed, an Imperium officer barked a command. Several white armored soldiers ran from one side of the frame to the other, SMGs held at low ready. Riva rolled her eyes and rested her thin cheek against the palm of her hand.

"You should know that the situation on board grows more dire by the moment. Unlike your Coalition fighters, Krakoids cannot be starved out. Many still roam the corridors, killing those they come across indiscriminately—crew or soldier, no difference to them."

"Okay," I said, "we've got our path inside. Breakaway Fleet is going to keep other ships in the area off of us. Everyone load up, and we'll rendezvous with Eddison's spy at the airlock she's indicated."

Benegal turned his snout up at me. "ROEs?"

It was a question that ought to have gone to Captain Fera, but since the two weren't exactly getting along, I answered without having to think about it. "Valid targets are Imperium soldiers and officers. Secondary targets are any crew that display violent intentions. Lieutenant Berrios is leading the initial breach team that will serve as a distraction while we rendezvous with Eddison's contact. She will escort us into the life-support bank, where we link up with Lieutenant Fel."

Sert slammed a massive fist into a catcher's mitt-sized palm. "And then we mount our final assault on the bridge. The War Torch burns brightly once again."

"Let's go to the armory," I said, offering a quick prayer that I'd have the stamina I needed when the time came.

Fera took over from there. "I want everyone set up in the hold except for Will and myself, in case we need to do an emergency Drift for whatever reason. Once we're docked and Eddison's contact opens the airlock, we'll follow her instructions on what she thinks is the best means of gaining access to the bridge."

"Understood," Benegal said.

In unison, everyone except Lockett unstrapped from their stations.

I shot the Drayth a stern look. "You're coming with us, Lockett. We need to establish comms with Lieutenant Fel's team, and that means a hardpoint connection. You said so yourself."

Lockett looked over each of his shoulders, as if searching for who I could possibly be talking to, because it surely wasn't him. A beat later, he shook his head. "Lockett does snooping and repairs. Hacking and encryption. No shooting."

I tossed him my rail pistol. "Today, you might just change your mind."

He caught the weapon—mostly to prevent it from smacking him in the face—and scowled. "This is unorthodox."

"But necessary," Quin said sagely, "as I'm projecting at least two full battalions of Imperium soldiers aboard the *ONE*. That's about twelve hundred soldiers."

Lockett's cybernetic eyes dimmed to tiny blue pinpricks. "Too many."

"Hardly enough to break a sweat," Sert said, lumbering off the bridge and into the corridor. "But it's a start!"

The Drayth made one final attempt to be left behind. "What of the Lightbearer? Someone will need to watch it."

He patted the bot-dome and isotope reactor contraption at his station.

I shrugged. "Strap it to your back and bring it with you. Uriel wants the drive anyway, so let's bring him. Hey—" I called to Dumpy's former head unit. "If you feel like coming out of there and killing every Imperium soldier before we arrive, go right ahead."

There was no reply. Would have been too easy.

I followed Sert and exited the bridge with a knot forming in my gut. The cascading pattern of geometric shapes pulsed along the bulkhead, lighting the path. I entered the armory and paused, feeling the beginning stages of adrenaline tickling under my skin.

The weapons racks were stacked to the gills with spoils of war, pilfered from the Imperium over the course of the last few months. There was a surplus of weapons, magazines, armor kits, spare helmets, racks of grenades in incendiary, stun pulse, and fragmentation varieties, as well as a pair of MD-300 light machine guns and a fully functioning rotary pulse cannon.

Sert went for the ATM-G anti-tank launcher.

Fera arched a brow. "A little overkill, maybe?"

The Vorvak double-checked that the integral trigger lock was set to SAFE, then popped the seal on the chamber and loaded an H-E round. He slapped the chamber cover closed and grabbed a bandolier with three more H-E rounds clipped onto it, then he hooked a second bandolier and held it out to me.

"We face an enemy force of significant numbers. Without weapons superiority, this would be a suicide mission. Besides… it's a big ship; it can handle it."

I slid a bandolier over my Drayth armor and moved to assist Fera with her loadout. She pulled her preferred rifle, an Astradian PMC, from the rack and checked it over. The P-90 style weapon looked good in her hands, like she was born to use it. I passed her six battery packs in pairs.

The clicks and clacks of weapons and equipment filled the space. No one spoke.

Fera slid the battery packs into the battle belt at her waist, which expanded to accommodate them, and grabbed a loop-and-hook bandolier of nitrate cartridges. She slid back the breech on the launcher mounted under the barrel of the PMC and loaded a single cartridge into it, then racked it shut.

Benegal scooped up his four pistols—two pulse, two flechette-firing rail pistols—and tucked them into the holsters under his arms, then filled the loops in his belt with larger caliber flechette magazines for the MD-14 he preferred. I gave him a nod as I moved past him to the rack of KR-44 rifles.

I took one from the rack and pulled back the charging handle to inspect the chamber. The weapon emitted a slight odor of fresh lubricant. Satisfied the weapon was clean, I loaded up with flechette magazines, which were retention-clipped together for quick changes. The fighting was going to be close quarters, and ammunition was going to run out fast. The ability to rapidly swap to a fresh magazine would be useful.

I stowed my KR-44 on the magnetic slot at the back of my armor and felt my biceps bulge as I lifted one of the MD-300s from the weapons rack. I popped the chamber open and liberated a link of the large-caliber flechettes from the bucket beneath the weapon, slid the leading three rounds into the chamber, and slapped it shut. Next, I grabbed three spare belt links of ammo and draped them over my shoulders.

Sert hefted the rotary pulse cannon, or RPC, like it was little more than a duffel bag. He swung the four-foot-long barrels around toward the exit and nodded at the rack he'd taken the weapon from. "Drayth, you will carry the extra ammunition."

Lockett poked his head from behind Benegal. The way he crouched and eyed the Vorvak, he looked like a petulant child. "Lockett will do no such thing. Not suited for manual labor. Vorvak are beasts of burden, capable of carrying their own loads."

"Lockett…" I began.

He waggled his fingers at me. "How will there be establishing a comms connection if the magic is weighed down?"

I picked up six belts of linked ionized rounds and draped them over his shoulders.

"Like this."

Fera snickered.

Lockett shook his head but resigned himself to the role of pack mule. I saw my rail pistol poking out of his waistband, grabbed a replacement for myself from the rack, and tucked it into the holster on my belt.

"Everybody ready?" I asked.

"I was spawned ready," Sert said.

Benegal gave me a curt nod.

Fera's smile was all determination. There was a layer of revenge in it. She knew Tror from before the war. Before the Imperium rose to its full power. Whatever happened prior to that four-thousand-year cryo-sleep, she was finally going to get her chance to do something about it.

"Will, update for you," Quin said.

"Let's hear it."

"Breakaway Fleet has placed itself between the nearest FTL gate and the *ONE*, but that's not all. We have word from our spy that the Imperium remnant in this sector will be arriving shortly."

I pulled on my helmet and sealed it. The tactical map appeared on my HUD, mirroring the scopes of the *Phaelon*. I saw the starfield with the signals Quin indicated from the FTL gate. Breakaway Fleet's signatures formed a semi-circle between the gate and the *ONE*.

"Form up on the airlock," I said. "Time's wasting."

29

THE STATUS LIGHT by the airlock flipped from yellow to green.

"Unsealing the hatch now," Quin said.

Coiling fumes of oxygen encircled the seal and wafted over us. The door irised open, giving way to a maintenance bay aboard the *ONE*. The space inside was a thin darkness broken up by a dizzying amount of status lights on switchboards, servers, and crystal focusing chambers, as well as more than a few holographic displays.

Standing in the center of the room was our Foris friend. She had her head bowed slightly, a billowy white uniform that could have been called a robe if it had sleeves over her very thin frame. The vulcanized rubber appearance of her armor was familiar to me—I'd seen Atron wearing a similar kit. I wondered if that was Imperium tech, or if Eddison had devised it and she wore the armor under her smock-thing to keep it hidden from her counterparts.

"You have arrived," she said.

Something about her delivery and her appraising stare

reminded me of a stuffy librarian. By virtue of my profession, I was one of the last few people on Earth whose job still included visiting brick and mortar libraries and skimming through old books for research purposes, so I knew the type pretty well.

Her eyes bugged when she saw Sert step out from the airlock, and it wasn't just because he was a Vorvak. He had a new helmet—one I assumed he'd taken as a trophy from his recent conquests on Farakar. Two horns knifed up at the sides, curved like elephant tusks. It reminded me of an ancient Viking helmet from Earth—although the popular image isn't historically accurate; there's no evidence Vikings ever wore such helmets. But I digress.

Sert's helmet made him look like a demon from the seventh circle of Hell.

If that fearsome image wasn't intimidating enough, Riva also had to take in the fact that our resident one-being wrecking crew was carrying an anti-tank rocket launcher on his back and an RPC he swung around like a battering ram as he walked.

I chinned the external speaker in my helmet. "You're alone?"

She looked left and right, demonstrating the emptiness of the room around her. "It seems that way, does it not?"

"Foris," Fera said over a private comm channel. Then, out loud. "That's not an answer. Are you alone?"

Quin broke into the channel, rushing to her defense. "She's offering us help and putting herself in great personal danger. Keep that in mind."

"We're ready," I said. "Let's move."

Riva turned and walked deeper into the room, waving a delicate hand for us to follow her.

I switched to the squad channel. "Stay alert."

The rest of the crew fell in step behind me, forming up in pairs as we exited the maintenance bay and passed through a vestibule of gunmetal gray bulkheads. I tightened my grip on the MD-300, finger poised over the safety selector switch. The linked flechettes tinkled against the housing of the weapon as I walked, sounding ominous in the otherwise quiet space.

The odds were as much in our favor as we could hope for, but that didn't mean it was an open and shut case. Our Foris spy might have been able to sneak to rendezvous with us without detection, but our group was *much* more conspicuous. It would only take one look and an alarm would be triggered. I looked up in the corners of our isolated walkway, searching.

"I assume you spoofed or disabled security cameras?" I asked the spy.

"Of course."

"Is there a terminal we can plug our Drayth into? If we can establish comms with the breaching team that's holed up in the life-support node, it will make reaching the bridge easier."

"Our first stop," Riva said. "The communications matrices are bifurcated for redundancy. The comm matrix you are concerned with is through the docking bay and secured with a double-walled hull, in a vacuum-sealed chamber."

"Awfully secure for shipboard communications equipment," Fera muttered.

Riva was quick with an answer. "The wormhole generators are located on this level. They require cryogenic coolant to prevent overheating when emitting the level of power they need to send rapid burst transmissions."

Fera shook her head. "They can generate wormholes?"

Riva didn't slow her pace as she explained, "Only a few nanoparticles wide. Just enough to send and receive instantaneous transmissions across the stars. It is dangerous, unstable, and requires massive power loads. Hence, the cryogenic coolant."

Quin marveled over the frequency. "The technology on this ship is a treasure trove! It is no wonder the rest of the galaxy could never mount a meaningful attack on the Imperium. Their monopolization of technological progress guaranteed Tror would always be hundreds of years ahead of any faction he did not trust. Could you imagine if Eddison had this capability? He would have been able to communicate with Atron much more efficiently."

"We certainly wouldn't have had to trek across the stars to dig him out of his hole," I muttered.

"Pity," Benegal said in a tone that conveyed he didn't think it was a pity at all.

I knew the two Krayvox from opposing clans had a hard-coded dislike for each other, but after they'd bled together in combat, there had been a shift in their relationship that transcended those tribal lines.

Benegal double-checked the chamber on his MD-14 with rote precision. It was impossible to see through the flat expression and the overriding calm he kept about himself. It bordered on a complete disconnect from the outside world.

It gave me pause, wondering if Benegal had more loyalty to his Krayvox friend than he did to the crew of the *Phaelon*. Then again, his loyalty was more to himself than it was to anyone else, and I couldn't pry his true motivations out of him no matter how hard I tried. I knew he would be a liability if the New Federation was formed, but aside from that… I also knew he had our backs, at least for this mission.

Riva paused at a dead end. If there was an access node or some means of interfacing with the bulkhead, my fiber-link didn't detect it.

She placed her hand on the bulkhead and raised her chin, as if she were inspecting the ceiling. I saw a glaze form over her amphibian eyes as she consulted her fiber-link.

The bulkhead rippled like a waterfall. As the thick material partially faded into a cascading mist, I could see what lay beyond.

Imperium Dagger ships rested at slots in the floor, linkages holding them to the deck in case of a loss of artificial gravity. Swarms of Imperium soldiers in their white armor and helmets moved between servicing carts, maintenance terminals, and tool cribs. Dumpy lookalike bots skittered between ships and narrowly avoided being kicked by the crew as they raced from ship to ship, disconnecting fuel servicing lines and unlatching the deck clamps.

A yellow and black catwalk ran across the upper third of the bulkheads and wrapped around the three sides of the bay. The fourth was a force-field protected opening that led to the starfield. Situated at the inboard bulkhead was a traffic control tower with several panes of crystalline that allowed an unblemished view of the activity on the deck.

Two officers in Imperium dress whites stood at parade rest, heads on swivels as they watched their people prepping the daggers for launch. We waited for a few moments, watching plumes of venting oxygen and excess heat emissions billowing from vents on the fighter ships as the pilots ran through their preflight checks.

A large holographic strip of light along the spaceside deck illuminated blue.

Drive plumes fired off one by one. Vibrations thrummed and rattled along the deck, shaking the bulkheads with propulsion blasts as the Daggers rode the fusion fire into the deep dark of space. I counted twenty-four of them, and then I counted my blessings that we weren't going to have to worry about them cooking us with their pulse cannons at point blank range.

Lockett leaned forward to examine the bulkhead. His eyes changed shape and color, moving from blue spheres to green triangles, then back again just as quickly. He grunted—probably with grudging respect—and stepped back to adjust the straps on the backpack he'd rigged to carry Uriel's reactor.

"Hard light," the Drayth muttered in his frothy tone.

"Hard light?" I parroted.

His iron lung popped derisively. "Imperium has accessed discarded Lightbearer technology. This should have been shared with the Drayth. Drayth built ships. Imperium greed—they kept it for themselves."

My fiber-link ran a few images through my mind, but I didn't need a detailed breakdown of particle physics, so I let them fade away before they could distract me.

Quin interjected. "Hard to stay on top making all your discoveries open-source, isn't it?"

Riva came back to herself, the fog lifting from her eyes as she disengaged from her own fiber-link. She pursed her lips.

"Nowhere on board is totally safe. Prefect Tror expected to be boarded. Patrols roam every deck. Beyond this door"—she rubbed the semi-solid bulkhead, causing the script and the tiled trapezoids to ripple like the surface of a small puddle—"they will be waiting for you."

"What, you're not coming with us?" I asked.

Sert shifted uncomfortably.

Riva narrowed her eyes. "I will guide you, but I am no warrior. My service to the Imperium has been as a sensor operator, and before that, a long-range scanner technician. Can you guarantee my safety?"

"Sure," I said, not wanting to separate from what could be a major source of intel on the ship. "Just stay behind the big guy, here."

Fera shook her head but kept her comments to herself as Riva rubbed her palm in a circle over the bulkhead. Lines of light traced under her palm, forming a glowing spiral. The bulkhead disappeared like a waterfall suddenly drying up, leaving an opening three meters wide. She turned her shoulders to make herself small enough for us to slip past her.

"There are no guarantees in combat," Benegal scoffed. "Surely a spy understands the risks."

"We can't walk through all that Imperium traffic without being noticed," Fera pointed out. "This is the only way forward?"

"Yes," Riva said. "The only way."

I don't know exactly what I was expecting. Maybe that we could sneak throughout the ship until we linked up with Fel and his men.

Eventually, there would need to be a fight.

It was just sooner than later.

"Okay. Let's hit them hard enough that they can't hit us back."

Sert shifted the MD-300's carry handle to his left hand and shrugged to bring the rocket launcher up to his shoulder. His gnarled scutes wrapped around the pistol grip, and a single claw flicked the integral safety to OFF before coming to rest on the trigger.

"Walk in my shadow, Foris, and witness the swift death of my enemies."

Air pressure swooned. The rocket launcher belched flame and conical spirals of smoke. Sparks scattered through the opening and danced along the deck at my boots.

The H-E round careened into a servicing cart and exploded with an audible thunderclap. Two technicians and one lone Imperium soldier who stood too close were bathed in scorching plumes of ignited oxygen. Concussive force rippled along the deck, knocking the victims caught in the blast radius to their backs. They made no move to get up as the intense heat chewed through armor and seals, gnashing at the flesh beneath.

Flames and shrapnel radiated from the impact site.

All at once, Imperium soldiers halted their patrols in their tracks. Several soldiers glanced at the sudden destruction in the center of the docking bay, then brought their weapons to bear.

Sert popped the latch on the rocket launcher, expending a thick cloud of black smoke from the vents. He held his left hand out toward me, palm up.

I ripped an explosive from my bandolier and passed it to him.

Benegal and Fera rushed into the docking bay.

"Tower first, door controls second!" Fera said over the comm.

The alarms began to sound, but I was only dimly aware of them. My focus was on our target: the access door across the length of the docking bay, which was firmly sealed shut.

Four hundred meters covered with Imperium fire teams was a lot of room to clear, and we needed to do it quick.

As if reading my mind, Quin broke into the frequency, sounding uneasy. "Until Lockett gets us a hardpoint connection, I'm grasping at needles here, Will."

"Straws," I said, pressing the MD-300 into my shoulder.

"What?"

"You're grasping at straws," I said, drawing a bead on an Imperium soldier standing out in the open. I pulled the trigger and launched a single flechette dead center in his visor. His helmet snapped back, trailing blood and crystalline shards.

"You are such an ass!" Quin groused. "You understand that the translation just had you say 'needles' to me, right? Honestly, your caveman brain... no one but you is speaking human!"

Fera cut in, her breathing heavy as she talked while she was on the move. "Will, if you don't have anything nice to say... save it for another time!"

"Yeah, my bad." I pivoted and sent back-to-back three-second bursts along the catwalk up high, dropping two soldiers that were trying to put rounds into Fera. The flechette bandolier snaked up into the chamber as the weapon hungrily chewed through the rounds.

One soldier fell over the railing and hit with a bone-rattling crunch on the deck. The second staggered backward until Benegal's MD-14 barked and pinned his helmet to the bulkhead. The soldier struck the bulkhead, twitching as his nerves fired off erratically in a death throe.

Quin sighed. "A conservative estimate is three minutes until enemy reinforcements arrive. You're going to want to be out of any compartments they can vent before that time."

Incoming fire converged on the opening we were crowding. I waved for Riva and Lockett to move up.

"Stay together, and stay close!"

They both nodded.

Sert loaded the ATM-G and slapped the latch closed. He fired a second rocket.

The blowback of sparks and heat simmered into thin streamers of smoke behind him. When it cleared, the bulkhead we'd come through was perfectly solid; whatever hard light tech was in play, the door was now a wall.

We weren't going back, but I'd be lying if I said I was perfectly fine with seeing the escape route close shut.

The threat detection suite came online in my HUD, painting upward of fifty Imperium soldiers at various points around the docking bay. Broken up into fire teams of three or four apiece, the separated units moved from cover point to cover point, alternating fire to saturate our position with constant streams of incoming.

Sert's rocket slammed into the deck half a meter in front of the lead fire team. Armored soldiers fragmented in a geyser of flame and liquefied metal. Helmets and DK-5 submachine guns joined the spreading cloud of shrapnel and scattered. The carnage spread over a five-meter radius, blocking the path of a group of maintenance techs that were trying to escape.

Sert transitioned to his heavy weapon and ran through his first ammo belt in seconds, halting the Imperium advance in its tracks as they succumbed to the withering deluge of high-volume fire.

Without the tripod, Sert was firing the weapon from the hip. What he lacked in accuracy, he more than made up for with saturation of fire. And honestly, he was pretty damned accurate with that thing.

The ranks of the forward charge were cut in half.

The surviving half didn't stop to check on their fallen comrades. Knowing their SMGs would be devastating at close range and too far out of cover to change their mind, they surged forward, firing as they ran.

A wild spray of incoming synthetic rounds smacked into the deck at my feet and the bulkhead above me. The Imperium's submachine guns weren't designed to peg targets at range, and desperation didn't change that fact. Working the four hundred meters of distance in the docking bay that had become our battle-field, Benegal and Fera swung wide to the flanks while Sert posted up behind a row of shipping-container-style storage bins—the lockers where the Imperium kept spare parts for their fighters—and flipped the chamber open on his MD-300.

Two Imperium fire teams, smarter than their counterparts who rushed through the middle of the open bay, concentrated their fire on Sert's position. Sparks and spall chipped away at the thick plating on the lockers, unable to penetrate. Sert spun to put his shell armor between him and the incoming, grimacing as he fumbled with the chamber and settled his second and final ammo belt into the weapon's feed and latched it shut.

"Drayth! My weapon requires ammunition. Feed the beast!" he roared.

I slapped Lockett on the back. "You're up. Go!"

Weighed down with ionized belts and the container housing the

Fleuridian, Lockett staggered forward like a medieval prisoner carrying a stockade around his neck.

I shouldered my light machine gun and moved into the space between storage racks as the targeting reticle appeared in my HUD. It was slightly larger and showed a distance-measuring ticker off to the side—a bit different than what I was used to with standard rifles. I wondered at the delay in the targeting suite powering up but didn't have time to think through if it was a hardware problem or if it required my conscious thought to conjure it up. The augmented weapon system of the Drayth armor immediately interfaced with my fiber-link and drew a thin beam that followed the barrel of the MD-300.

I lined up the laser and the reticle over the enemy and squeezed the trigger.

My breathing was steady, concentrated, but magnified in the confines of my helmet. Adrenaline sparked under my skin as the familiar feel of combat against the Imperium settled over me.

I wasn't the new gun on the squad anymore.

The rapid fire rail gun snapped and rattled with the thrum of opposing magnets energizing with every pull of the trigger. I sent ferromagnetic rounds into the enemy with steady, concentrated bursts as fast as I could line up a shot. Armor sparked. Visors shattered. The soldiers fell one at a time, but I didn't keep a running count. I fired and pivoted, working single targets as they broke cover, suppressing entire fire teams before they could advance.

The tinkling of the ammo belt against the weapon went silent. In no time at all, the pistol grip shook insistently against my palm.

After pointing the barrel of the MD-300 toward the ceiling, I grabbed Riva's hand and yanked her along with me to a refuse pallet, where I popped open the empty chamber and pulled one of the ammo belts from my armor. I took a second longer than I needed to just to ensure I fed the belt into the chamber correctly, then slapped the chamber closed. It took three full seconds, and then I was back on target, laying down heavy bursts of covering fire for Lockett.

The Drayth was a prime target for the Imperium as he bumbled his way across twenty meters of open deck, iron lung sounding like a hacksaw sliding back and forth.

Sert worked the RPC like a pro. The monster of a weapon shrieked as it stacked high volume pulses into the Imperium advance with savage snaps and eruptions of raw energy. Pulse rounds punched into the enemy with a hailstorm of blistering fire that chewed through the deck, knocking equipment loose from the stowage racks. Bulkheads and terminal housings bloomed with superheated wounds of glowing metal as Sert swept the barrels side to side. Enemy soldiers caught in the deluge were knocked onto their backs, thin trails of smoke wafting up from mortal wounds.

Benegal selected targets of opportunity and hammered them back into cover with concentrated single shots of accurate fire.

Soldiers died on their feet. Arterial spray trailed from direct hits. The Imperium soldiers outnumbered us, but they weren't equipped to deal with our tactics.

Fera moved toward the control tower, leapfrogging between terminals and equipment pallets. Each time, she paused for a few heartbeats between sprints to send a three-round burst of pulses before she fully committed to the sprint to her next vantage point.

Shoulders rocking, armor sparking, I ran through a hailstorm of synthetic coated rounds. Miraculously, I cleared the brunt of the fire without sustaining a lethal hit and slid into one of the tracts beside a berth that had recently been vacated by a dagger fighter ship. A heartbeat later, I shifted my fire to the base of the control tower.

The belt ammo wriggled and shrank way too fast. I covered the base of the tower with enough flechettes to change the appearance of the face of the structure, and then the pistol grip rattled, in desperate need of a reload.

"Changing," Fera said as she crouched beside the entrance. She held up a fist and popped open the breech on her PMC, then tossed a spent charge pack and shoved a fresh one inside.

Not willing to sacrifice the time for a reload, I dropped the MD-300 and the last belt of ammo I'd brought for it, then transitioned to my KR-44 rifle. The reticle changed in my HUD to compensate, presenting me with a more precise scope than the rough estimate of the MD-300's targeting reticle.

Six Imperium soldiers funneled out of the base of the tower, unaware of Fera tucked behind the entrance. They opened up with their SMGs, firing at Sert with wild sprays. Errant streaks of rounds radiated in a haphazard spray that served no meaningful effect.

Benegal's MD-14 rang out like multiple hammer blows driving a nail.

Two, then three of the soldiers caught rounds in the faceplates. As they hit the deck, the soldiers behind them stepped over the bodies of their fallen comrades, continuing their defensive rush with rapid trigger pulls that sent five-round bursts our way.

Fera finished her reload and fired on them from behind, putting five-round bursts into their backs.

"Clear!" she called. "Moving into the tower."

"Benegal, go!" I called.

"Moving," he replied.

I put down suppressing fire to cover his move, sighting in on targets of opportunity and dropping them with careful, precision headshots. Even taking my time to make every shot count, the magazine went dry, and I had to transition to the spare I'd rigged to sit side-by-side with it. My jungle-style magazine made the reload more of a momentary bump than a true drop-and-swap, taking the reload time from about three seconds to only a fraction of a second.

I continued putting rounds in the soldiers between Benegal and Fera, keeping them free of the enemy fire.

Fera slipped inside the tower, pulse rounds flashing with gouts of coherent light as she cleared the room. Benegal hopped up onto the raised platform and followed her inside.

"Behind," he said.

"Two on the stairwell," Fera said, her transmission garbled as she worked her PMC.

Benegal's weapon crack-cracked.

On the threat detection suite in my HUD, red highlights winked out. Fera and Benegal put them down at point blank as they mounted the stairwell shoulder to shoulder.

Riva crouched close behind me.

"You good?" I asked, sparing a glance at her.

The firefight continued to rage with unchecked fury, drowning out her reply.

I gave her a quick once-over to check for wounds. She had her hands on the top of her head, covering the probes with her long, thin fingers. I didn't see any blood or perforations in her clothing.

I turned my attention back to the tower.

With three pulls of the trigger, I knocked out one of the crystalline panels at the upper level. Broken shards tinkled into the control room. A few jagged pieces slipped out of the track and fell to the deck below, forcing the Imperium deck officers to crouch with their hands shielding their heads.

Fera stormed up the stairs, PMC blasting pulse rounds as she cleared the stairwell.

Two more bursts put the officers down.

"Tower is clear," she said. "Will, move up!"

Sert's comm signature flashed in my HUD. "Reinforcements inbound."

I whipped my head around so fast the vertebrae in my neck creaked.

Even the best tactics couldn't overcome numbers once they reached a certain threshold. What I saw at the door on the far side of the docking bay exceeded that threshold and then some.

The door we were fighting toward irised open. A platoon of Imperium rushed into the bay, SMGs up. Right on their heels, two heavy weapons squads with their own MD-300s, two RPCs, and another thirty soldiers apiece poured into the fray. The rotary cannons went up at each side of the door, barrels already starting to spin.

"Cover!" I shouted.

In the span of a single heartbeat, the scales tipped firmly in the favor of the enemy.

30

"SERT! FADE BACK!" Fera shouted.

The MD-300's rotary barrels spun with a shrill whine. Twin streams of searing fire launched from our target and zippered across the deck, walking damage in sparks and spall toward Sert's position, jostling the lockers against their weld points in the deck and forcing him to drag his own heavy weapon back into cover.

Refuel receptacles and hoses dented, cracked, and severed at their connection points on the deck, spilling pungent fumes and splashes of clear fluid everywhere.

Lockett dropped the ammo belts and fell flat on his back. The air he had just vacated ignited with angry spats of sizzling energy. Metal warped and belched liquefied slag. Thick clouds of black smoke rolled across the deck like a malevolent fog, broken only by lines of torsion as flechettes and pulses pierced the din.

Sert glowered at Lockett, a snarl on his face. "I require reload, abomination!"

Lockett gasped and rolled to the side, fumbling with the belt ammo. He managed to get his squirrely fingers wrapped around the links and handed it to the Vorvak while his other hand shielded the diamond-shaped plate in his head as if he anticipated a slap.

Sert took the ammo and fed it into the chamber on his weapon, then passed the rocket launcher to the Drayth. "This one, too."

Lockett muttered a curse, his fingers working at the tube to pry open the receiver. Encumbered by his backpack rig that carried the Fleuridian inside, he moved slowly and deliberately. The rest of the interaction was lost to the billowing smoke as trails of aerospace-grade fuel ignited, tracing lines of fire across the deck between berths.

My HUD automatically switched to photon-collecting view, filling the darkness with silhouettes of Sert and Lockett—and the four-man Imperium fire team creeping up on their flank.

"Sert, watch your spaceside flank!" I said into the comm.

"Eyes on target," Benegal replied.

The lead Imperium soldier opened up with his SMG on mag dump. A swathe of synthetic coated rounds snapped out of the weapon in a chaotic funnel.

Lockett slapped the receiver closed on the ATM-G and turned to see a scattered blur of orange-hued energy swarming toward him. He didn't have time to react as the rounds slammed into his chest. Candle lights of flame sprouted along his armor.

The Drayth's comm indicator flashed in my HUD, followed by a whoosh of air squeezing out of his iron lung. Lockett hit the deck, his backpack rig scraping and sparking. The rocket launcher dropped onto his chest with a clang. Flames licked at the weapon like serpentine tongues flapping.

Sert roared with unbridled rage.

The Imperium soldier dropped to a knee to execute a mag change while two of his counterparts stepped in front of him and followed up his barrage with controlled bursts of their own. Through the fire and the smoke, a second fire team was moving in on the opposite flank.

Riva shifted against my back.

I patted her on the shoulder. "Stay here."

I stepped out of cover, rifle up, reticle sweeping over the second fire team as I squeezed the trigger, going as much for suppression as I was for accuracy.

Flechettes raked over the enemy in dances of sparks and jets of aerosolized blood as some of my rounds cut through the weak points of the enemy armor. I put them down before they could bring their weapons to bear on Sert and Lockett.

Rapid booms split the air as Benegal went to work with his MD-14. Flechettes lanced into the two soldiers, cratering their visors in a one-two clash of broken crystalline. Their heads snapped back violently. Weapons dropped.

Benegal drilled the third before he could finish his reload.

I pivoted and put the fourth down with a headshot.

Both sides of Sert and Lockett's position were covered with Imperium corpses. A third fire team had crept up to replace the downed one on the spaceside flank.

Sert dropped his empty weapons and bellowed a war cry that shook the air in nearly the same decibel range as a jet engine. He tucked his chin and surged forward in a trademark Vorvak bull rush.

The Imperium soldiers stopped in their tracks, boots sliding along the deck. One of them brought his SMG to bear, unaware that his three comrades were turning to run the other way.

Sert collided with the lead soldier before a shot could be fired on target. Errant rounds went wide as the thick, armored Vorvak skull contacted graphene-woven armor with lung-crushing force. The impact was like a crack of granite splitting under a sledgehammer.

The soldier went airborne, sailing back three meters before he hit the deck, his lower half bent at an angle that made me cringe.

"No escape!" Sert roared, charging after the three fleeing enemies.

"Sert, let them go!" I shouted into my helmet comm. "We need to move forward!"

He didn't listen. But then, he was Sert, and battlefield carnage was to Vorvak what baseball was to Americans.

Swinging out both huge arms, he swiped two of the soldiers by their waists and slammed them together with a savage crunch. Their helmets smacked into each other and flew away, neck seals snapped and frayed. The faces of the Anunnaki were slackened, their eyes showing only white sclera as they rolled up into the backs of their heads. Their weapons clattered to the deck.

Sert dropped both soldiers like toys he was done playing with and wrapped his clawed hands over one of the SMGs, then mag dumped it into the back of the last fleeing soldier.

"Are you done?" I shouted in disbelief at what I'd just witnessed. "Check Lockett. Make sure he's not dead!"

Sert rapped the side of his horned helmet, as if shaking some of the bloodlust out of his head, and turned to run back to the fallen Drayth.

Fera was in my ear. "Will, clear the path to the door. We need that terminal!"

Yeah, if Lockett's still alive to do something about it, I thought.

I didn't need to say out loud that we were screwed without Lockett. Everyone knew that if he was dead or incapacitated, things would go from bad to worse.

Sert grabbed Lockett with one hand and lifted him off the deck, using the back of his other hand to swat at the flames on his chest.

The Drayth's head lolled to the side, one of his breathing tubes disconnected and swaying limply by his feet. White smoke floated away from his chest. At a glance, it looked like he was dead.

Sert grabbed the convoluted breathing tube and reattached it to the triangular apparatus connected to Lockett's face and rotated it to seal it. "Lockett. Awake."

He shook the Drayth like a rag doll, then looked back at me. "Will, move! They will surround us if we don't push through."

Insistent wails of SMG fire drew my attention toward the door.

A dozen more of the enemy were running fast between points of cover, firing at us to cover their movement. Both RPCs were being actively reloaded, giving us a few seconds before they were primed to cut down anything not hunkered down behind solid cover.

Sert was right. I had to let him worry about Lockett. We still had to clear our way to the terminal vault.

"Overwatch on the tower, cover me!" I said, changing direction and heading for the door. I leaped over a line of fire half a meter tall, relying on my armor to shield me from the flames that my HUD measured at 370 degrees Celsius.

"Covering," Benegal said.

Incoming SMG fire gnashed at the deck. Two rounds punched into my chest plate. A third notched into the armor of my left thigh, but I didn't slow down. The woven cords of my armor prevented the rounds from penetrating into my flesh, for now.

I cleared the smoke and flames and slid on my side, armor scraping across two meters of open deck as light trails streaked orange, danger close to my visor. I came to a stop behind the relative safety of a reinforced liquid oxygen servicing tank, my lungs stretched from the burst of speed that carried me through the enemy fire.

"I'm coming to you, Will," Fera said.

I took a few seconds to suck in an adrenaline-laced breath and swap my depleted jungle-style magazine for a second one, then exited cover, rifle first. The hairs on the back of my neck raised with static cling as my danger sense pegged. I faded back immediately before I fully committed to the rush.

The air exploded with savage pulses of coherent light.

Slag trails spattered across the deck so close my HUD blared a TEMP warning, highlighting my leg panels as they neared the critical heat threshold. Sweat dripped down my back.

"That was close," I gasped.

"Will!"

"I'm all right, Fera. Benegal, where's my suppressing fire?"

"Enemy working both heavies at the door," the lizard man hissed.

"Yeah, no kidding! I got a little cooked, but I'm okay. Keep their heads *down*!"

"Working," he replied.

Gritting my teeth, I snatched a grenade from my belt, hooked the pin on the charging handle of my KR-44, and separated it from the shell.

After a two-count, I shouted, "Frag out!" and tossed the grenade up and over the liquid oxygen tank. I followed the arc as it descended toward the door. My HUD wiped away the visual on the tank, showing me a clear view of the two rotary cannon emplacements and the ten or more Imperium holed up at our target exit.

The grenade hit the deck and bounced between the two heavy guns.

Not bad for left-handed.

The explosion shook the deck and rattled my knees.

Concussive force burst forth in a shockwave. Both heavies smacked into the frame of the opening and hit the deck. One of the weapons separated from its tripod and collided with the helmet of the soldier actively firing it. Two of the soldiers closest to the detonation were caught in a blizzard of shrapnel that eviscerated them in a confetti mess of torn flesh and sheared armor. The assistant gunners that had just finished feeding spare belt ammo into the heavy weapons lost both legs and rag-dolled against the bulkheads.

"The Drayth is awake," Sert reported.

Lockett coughed over the frequency, then gasped a weak response. "And deep-fried."

"Shake it off, short circuit! We need you!" Fera snapped.

"He will be ready," Sert promised.

"Lightbearer vessel is intact as well," Lockett added, sounding weak.

I felt a slap on the shoulder and turned to see Fera tucked into cover beside me, her PMC held tight to her chest, her face a grim mask of determination.

"Nice throw. Let's go."

We rolled our backs along the tank and came out on opposite sides with our weapons up.

Sert bellowed, "Hold position! I've got something more for them."

A plume of sparks and smoke erupted from the ATM-G. Sert sent an H-E round dead-center of the target exit. The detonation unleashed a crescendo of creaking metal and screams of pain as Imperium helmets were blown apart from the armor as the enemy was consumed in the blast.

The opening filled with a wall of fire.

Imperium soldiers stumbled out of it, dripping flames, white armor panels blackening and flaking as they writhed and collapsed to the deck. The flames died down, revealing shriveled husks of armor and the ruined rotary cannons of the heavy weapons. The corridor beyond appeared empty, but I knew it wasn't going to stay that way for long.

In the wake of the blast, a heavy quiet descended on the docking bay, broken only by the occasional bark of Benegal's marksman rifle as he tagged stragglers that tried to shift positions.

"That's one way to clear it," Fera said, waving her PMC's barrel toward the carnage. "Glad I told you to bring that thing, Sert."

"Told *me*? I—" The joke dawned on Sert. He let out a deep, booming laugh.

"Docking bay is cleared," Benegal said.

I chinned my helmet's external speaker and shouted, "Riva, get up here!"

She slipped out from behind a storage rack and moved hastily toward me.

Reassembled, Fera told the team, "Form up. Move to the objective. Let's go!"

Riva stayed a few paces behind as Fera and I moved side by side toward the door, scanning each side of the corridor for any sign of Imperium.

"Keep moving," Fera said, slowing down to let me take point. "Lockett, what's your status?"

"Lockett would prefer death."

"Keep it together, magic man. We're almost there," I said.

The crackling of active flames faded into the background as I advanced further down the corridor. The tactical map in my HUD showed only the friendly signatures of my comrades behind me and no enemy nearby, but without a hardline connection to the systems of the *ONE*, I didn't trust it.

My instincts were proven correct as I approached a dead-end intersection and turned back to look at Riva.

She indicated a left turn.

I took one step around the corner and withdrew immediately.

"What is it?" Fera asked.

"Imperium. Lots of them."

Riva shivered. "The terminal banks are at the end of the hall. If you want communications with your other teams, that's the only means of getting it."

Fera nodded. "We knew this wasn't going to be easy."

Benegal checked our six down the scope of his marksman rifle, then turned and asked, "What's the play?"

Sert shouldered past us, Lockett limping along behind him. "Clean house! No Imperium walks off this ship on two legs!"

The Vorvak hefted his MD-300 as he rounded the corner. The barrels spun and whined as they ramped up to firing speed.

"He's going to get himself killed," I said.

"I believe that is always a Vorvak's goal," Benegal hissed.

Fera patted my shoulder. "It could be worse. He could be on *their* side."

31

IT WAS close quarters combat all the way to the vault. Most of the war had been fought in ship-to-ship space combat as we chased around the scraps of the Imperium Fleet. The ground engagements stalled our forward momentum, and we avoided them as much as possible, but they could never be avoided entirely. Boarding Imperium ships or space habitats were necessary.

Because of that, I thought I knew what to expect.

Elbun Gal had been the worst of the fighting, but this was fast approaching that level of desperation.

I shook off the ghosts of the past and put one boot in front of the other, placing flechettes on target and swapping magazines like a war machine. Incoming rounds skirted the bulkheads, punched into my Drayth armor, and came much too close to my visor on more than one occasion. I moved in spite of it all, focused on the rhythm of the battle, guided by the fervent hope that my actions would keep the comrades left and right of me safe.

Sert lumbered forward like a monster from ancient myth, his huge shoulders swaying with each step. He held the MD-300 against his hip, spraying three-second bursts of blistering pulse rounds in steady sweeps that painted every surface of the corridor with scorched streaks of blackened heat damage.

An entire platoon of Imperium soldiers—probably a QRF diverted from dealing with one of the other breaching teams on this deck of the *ONE*—were cut down in droves, but still more appeared through the walls like phantoms. The hard light technology throughout the ship made it difficult to detect where the doors actually were, which ultimately led to us getting flanked.

At the end of the corridor, covered by a dozen Imperium soldiers, the obsidian-dark blast doors of the vault stood locked.

Riva and Lockett's only cover was the armor of our fire team as we rushed through the onslaught of synthetic coated rounds. Direct hits sparked against Fera and Benegal's armor. I staggered through a three-round burst that bit into my chest plate, hitting hard enough to squeeze a rush of air out of my lungs. In the absence of hardened structures to cover behind, our only option was to keep up a high rate of fire to suppress the enemy.

The air was thick with flechettes and pulse rounds. We were running the gauntlet, and our armor wouldn't hold forever—the Imperium played the numbers to their advantage.

Sert's heavy weapon sucked up the belt ammo and went dry. He dropped the useless bulk of the rotary cannon, white smoke wafting from the still-spinning barrels, and transitioned to his plasma shotgun. He continued his steady march forward, ignoring the incoming that lanced into his chest and arms and pinged off his helmet like fists of fire. An abdominal panel under his barrel chest dented and knocked loose, exposing the thin EVA liner beneath. He didn't seem to notice as he dumped gouts of scalding energy into the teeth of the enemy.

We approached the door, stepping over the bodies of the dead we left in our wake.

"Contact to the rear," Benegal said with a calm insistence.

Six red threat signatures slipped through the wall, sealing off any chance of a retreat. It was the last thing on my mind, but losing the option was a blow to morale. It felt like the noose was being tightened around our necks, and the light at the end of the tunnel was slowly fading to black.

"We can't go back. Push!" Fera growled, working her PMC.

She sent barrages of pulses in controlled bursts that knocked the enemy back on their heels. After seamlessly transitioning to her barrel-mounted launcher, each pull of the secondary trigger ignited a nitrate cartridge, expending concentrated incendiary rounds that punched fist-sized holes clean through Imperium armor.

I stepped up my rate of fire, scattering flechettes over the Imperium in a hailstorm of fury. Return fire lanced into the woven cords of my Drayth armor, in front of me and from behind. My HUD flashed with a temperature warning, highlighting my chest and the backs of my shoulders, my thigh plates and knee covers… pretty much everything was beginning to lose structural integrity.

I fired off my last three-round burst and quick-changed to the second half of my jungle-style magazine setup, losing only a split second of fire in the process.

Two flashes of orange light flared in my vision.

The first hit the crown of my helmet.

The second slammed into the left side of my visor.

Crystalline shattered. Searing hot pain knifed across my face.

Instinct squeezed my eyes shut and pulled a yelp of shock out of me.

I dropped to a knee, hearing Fera scream my name in the comm and through her external helmet speakers at the same time. With my helmet open to the environment and my breathing sawing the air with existential panic, I smelled ozone and scorched flesh and fresh blood mixed with my own sweat.

Someone stepped in front of me—the insistent *crack-crack* of the MD-14 told me it was Benegal—and shielded me from the steady stream of SMG fire pouring in from our target thirty meters ahead. We were committed, and the enemy had us boxed in at both ends of the corridor.

The intense heat and cutting pain across the left side of my face swelled in rhythm to my racing pulse.

Sound rushed over me, amplified through the opening in my helmet visor. Each blast of Sert's shotgun thundered in my head, rattling my teeth. The magnetic snap-thrum of Benegal's MD-14 marked the cycling of flechettes as fast as he could pull the trigger. The *thunk* of Imperium soldiers collapsing intermingled with the zing and ping of SMG rounds smacking into us with unfettered abandon.

I drew in a ragged breath, wiping my forehead and eyelids with a gauntleted hand. Bright red rivulets of blood were caught in the weave of the armored glove.

"Forward!" Sert bellowed between concussive bursts of his shotgun. "Until the dawn of the Day of Reckoning!"

Blinking furiously through hot, irritated tears, my panic dissolved in a surge of survival instinct.

"Wi—*argh!*" Fera tried to call my name but flinched as a barrage of rounds smacked into her chest plate, dropping her to a knee. She refocused with a blur of motion, then slid open the breech and fed a nitrate cartridge into it. The instant the breech was closed, she pulled the secondary trigger, unleashing a spark-ridden trail of fire from the secondary barrel of the weapon.

The blast caught an Imperium soldier in the stomach. The stopping power of the incendiary round laid him out on the deck, where two reinforcement soldiers stepped over each arm, SMGs up.

It felt like the end... but I couldn't accept that.

Even if it was, I was determined to face it head on.

I clenched my gut, still blinking through tears, wondering if any microscopic shards of crystalline had embedded in my eyes.

The right-hand bulkhead cracked. I blinked again. Dark red drops of blood dangled from my brow like stalactites on the roof of a cave. I stared at the wall, opening and closing my eyes furiously.

The crack wasn't a trick of the light. A heartbeat later, the crack swelled and began to spread.

Imperium soldiers, too many to count, formed up in a sort of phalanx position of two firing lines; the forward soldiers dropped to a knee and braced their elbows on their knees, SMG stocks in their shoulders, barrels aimed right at us. Behind them, a second line stood tall, their weapons up to their visors as they sighted in for accuracy.

The cracked wall erupted in a spray of shimmering crystal and multicolored fractals of light.

I thought I was dreaming, but the more I blinked, the more real the spectacle became. A rockslide poured into the corridor. Boulders stacked over two meters high and thicker than Sert knocked against the bulkheads, sliding across each other with ear-wrenching scratches and crackles.

The boulders poured over the Imperium soldiers in a sea of churning rock.

I stood there, one hand pressed to my left eye, wondering if the round that destroyed my visor hadn't actually pierced my skull and this was all some strange fever dream as I took in my last breath.

Sert planted his feet and raised his shotgun, then threw out his left hand to stop Fera from advancing. "Krakoids! Permit them to finish this but stay clear."

I decided I must be in a bad way. *Sert showing restraint? I* have *to be dreaming.*

The Krakoids looked like small mountain peaks with arms, legs, and craggy, pointed heads. The face of the mountains sported shrubbery in the form of pale frills of wilted tubers in varying colors. There were no recognizable facial features—nothing that could have been called eyes, a mouth, or even a face.

The skeletal reeds that made up their bodies were covered in thick bundles of rock with jagged edges. The plant aliens swung their appendages like bullwhips, snapping the air.

I got a front-row seat to the Krakoid show. It came to a rapid, violent end for the enemy.

The Imperium formation opened fire all at once.

Synthetic coated rounds raked across the Krakoids, peppering them with tiny streamers of flame and coils of smoke. The impacts sounded like light bulbs blowing their filaments.

White armored soldiers crumpled under the swinging limbs of rock. The plant-hybrid life-forms stomped and smashed and broke the enemy against every surface of the corridor.

One Krakoid rammed the end of its arm-like rocks straight into the faceplate of an Imperium soldier. The blow made a *crack* like a boulder cleaving in two as the soldier was forcibly embedded up to his shoulders in the bulkhead. His legs twitched half a meter above the deck. When the Krakoid wrenched its arm back, emulsified fluid spilled out of the hole and trailed down the white chest plate.

In seconds, the corridor went silent.

Twelve of the small mountain creatures stood covered in blood and the fading embers of direct hits from point-blank SMG fire. They stood like golems—inanimate drones awaiting a command from their controller.

Riva peered from behind Lockett, her Foris eyes wide and dark.

"Will, you're still bleeding," Fera said, moving to stand beside me, concern on her face.

She touched a finger to the side of my helmet.

I grabbed her hand and pulled it away. "I'll be fine."

A new Krakoid crouched through the ruined opening in the bulkhead, face tubers puffing in the act of respiration. Tiny yellow and green spores ejected from the flowery features, scintillating in the light of the corridor.

The creature didn't look any different than the other twelve, but the way it moved while the rest of them faced it, as if awaiting a command, told me this was a Root, and the rest were Stems.

The Root Krakoid took one step toward me, then pivoted on its feet—growths of dark metamorphic rock, rather than boots or actual feet—and inclined the peak of its head toward Sert.

Sert made the visor of his horned helmet translucent, his orange eyes staring straight at the shrubbery beneath the cone-shaped peak of the creature's head. "You fight on behalf of your liberators, the United Coalition. So do we."

The Root Krakoid froze.

Sert pointed at the vault door behind the cluster of Stem Krakoids. "We require access beyond that door. Then, we will fight to the bridge."

The lack of movement coming from the thing made me uneasy. I finished rubbing my eye, deciding if there were crystalline pieces in it, they weren't going to cause me any trouble for now, and took a step forward.

Rock grinded against itself as the Root Krakoid turned to acknowledge me.

Standing less than two meters from it, I got an up-close view of the thing. It made my head hurt, trying to puzzle out how something that was essentially a sentient tree that sprouted rocks possessed the intellectual capacity to reason at such a high level.

The body itself was striated rock in shades of dusty sandstone to full-on jet black. The lighter sections were porous, the darker sections smooth and almost polished. Supporting the different types of stone was a thin, reed-like skeletal structure that reminded me vaguely of bamboo shoots, even down to notches of dark rings along the length of the reed.

"Thank you," I said. "You saved us. What is your name?"

"Krakoids do not speak. They have write-only linguistics," Lockett wheezed.

"What does that mean?" I asked.

"It means we wait for him to form a response," Benegal said, like it should be obvious. "But time is a factor… We should blow the door and let the Drayth begin to establish communications."

Sert held up a colossal mitt. "We will need the strength of the Rock Warriors. Let us see what they have to say."

Lockett pushed his way past me and offered his small, frail hand toward the Krakoid. As if in response—and for all I knew, that's exactly what it was—the Root Krakoid... sneezed.

I didn't know what else to call it when the facial tubers swelled and flattened, spewing a dense globule of viscous fluid that smacked onto Lockett's open hand. Lockett's fingers wiggled slightly, as if he were testing the weight of the sputum.

Before my eyes, a thin squiggle sprouted inside the jelly-like liquid, which began to congeal. The sprout grew until it broke the surface of the sputum and offshoots branched out from the central stem, swelling into bulbs at the ends. With a flourish of color, the bulbs bloomed and fanned the air, transforming into a small flower on the Drayth's palm.

It was more intricate than a chrysanthemum. The petals swooned and rippled as if caressed by a breeze, resolving into the shape of a star lily, but with hundreds of individual petals in varying lengths. Lockett brushed his fingers over the flower, his cybernetic eyes pulsing steadily. The plant quivered.

Lockett seemed to know how to interpret this most peculiar form of communication. "The Krakoids accept no master. The time of their servitude is at an end. They seek an understanding."

Fera looked around for more trouble, then refocused on the Krakoid Root. "What do they want?"

Lockett tickled the flower. Some of the petals wrapped around his fingers and stretched to brush against the back of his hand. "They demand safe passage to rejoin the Maternal Root on Zenith. They will fight for this only."

"They want to go back home?" Fera asked, astonished. "That's it?"

"We can do that," I said, nodding toward the vault door. "But we still need to get inside."

"Enough talk," Benegal said. "Hack the door, Lockett."

The Drayth shrugged. "Faster for the plants to batter it down. I will tell them we will return them."

The flower containing the message of the Root Krakoid wilted. The color drained from the petals. All at once, the petals detached from the stem and floated to the deck. Lockett shook his hand and dropped the organic material at his boots with a wet slap.

He rubbed the grime off his hand on the back of Sert's shell armor and covered his action by adjusting the backpack rig as he came to stand beside the door.

Sert seemed not to notice.

Lockett raised a hand, pointed a fist at the reinforced doors, and bumped them. The metal made a dull ringing sound as his armored glove tapped the unyielding surface two, three times. "This one."

The Root Krakoid huffed a plume of glittering spores.

The Stem Krakoids turned in unison toward the door and raised their rock-covered limbs over their heads. Like wind-up toys being let loose, they began to pummel the vault door with a deafening clamor. The cacophony of stone striking metal made my head ring.

Metal groaned under the savage strikes. Chips of igneous rock broke away from the Krakoids, but they didn't stop. The frame warped and cracked, allowing the heavy door to droop inward. Two of the Krakoids near the center of the door paused to set their bases, like martial artists bracing for a kick. Together, they reared back and punched the door dead center.

The door ripped clean out of its track and bent around the impact site like it was cheap aluminum. The screech of rending metal ended in a rattling *wham*. Flakes of diamond and crystal whirled through the open air.

The detritus cleared, and the room beyond was revealed.

Fumes of coolant moved like mist between rows of server-like equipment. Crystal boards in deep blues were stacked atop each other and organized in a grid. Waiting at the end of the room only a few meters back was an orb-shaped device with a bank of receptacles beneath it.

Riva's relieved sigh was audible. "We have arrived at the terminal."

I patted Lockett on the back. "Get plugged in. Let's see what the situation is with the rest of our people."

Lockett bumbled over to the terminal, unspooling the hardline from the base of his helmet. He paused before inserting it into the terminal and turned his cybernetic eyes toward me. "Cover. Lockett does not need his ass shot off while he works the magic."

Sert moved to stand behind the Drayth and spun his shell armor toward him, angling his plasma shotgun at the vault door.

"Surprised you haven't upgraded it away already," Sert rumbled, and then moved into position to guard the Drayth.

32

THE RESPITE DIDN'T last long. Lockett interfaced with the terminal, muttering frothy syllables through his iron lung as he worked to hack the encryption through his fiber-link. Data streamed over his cybernetic eyes and passed in vertical lines of light, symbols, numbers, and a myriad assortment of colors.

The Krakoids stood around us, still as statues. Only their facial tubers occasionally flitted or leaked floating particles that smelled faintly like petrichor.

Fera leaned close to me, her visor going transparent as she inspected the wound near my eye. She stowed her PMC on the magnet attached to her armor's back panel and produced a small vial from a slot on the side of her armor. "Here."

She twisted the top, causing a small needle-like protrusion to extend from the top of the vial. It dripped clear liquid as she held it toward my face.

"I'll be fine," I insisted and took a step back. "We need to keep after things."

She locked eyes with me, her face gentle but insistent. "Will, the bleeding hasn't stopped yet. Hold still."

My fiber-link scanned the substance in the bottle and told me it was a combination analgesic/antiseptic. Something like a mixture of Novocain and isopropyl alcohol, I guessed.

I didn't need a fiber-link to know that Fera wouldn't quit until she'd taken care of me, so I stopped resisting. She grabbed the chin of my helmet and turned my head to the side, then rested the edge of her palm on the crown of my helmet and slowly guided the needle down.

"Might feel a little prick," she said.

It felt like a slight poke, until she gave the can a gentle squeeze. Acid burn raced into the injection site. It felt like my eyebrow was on fire, and the flames were moving into my eye and cheekbone.

"Getting shot was less painful," I muttered.

She withdrew the needle and twisted the vial. The used needle tip popped off and rolled across the deck. Fera tucked the vial back into the slot on her armor and pressed a hand against my chest.

"You can take it," she said coyly. "You're the Hero of the Rebellion."

I wiped at the wound. A clear liquid mixed with blood transferred to the back of my gauntlet, but not much.

I blinked a few times as the pain began to numb over.

Lockett twitched at his terminal. "Encryption is like nothing Lockett has ever seen. Difficult. Smart. Certainly not of Imperium design. Stolen technology, no doubt."

"Stolen from who?" Benegal asked, a slight challenge in his

voice. "Are the Drayth not the preeminent technologists in the galaxy?"

"Drayth design, yes, but this is"—he paused to shake his head—"something more."

He went back to work for only a few seconds more and then bounced on his knees. "Got it!"

A deep, electronic warble played through the frequency, sounding like feedback from Hell itself. All of us cringed at the unpleasant sound, but Sert took it personally.

"We have comms?" I asked, moving toward Lockett.

"Should," was the Drayth's one-word answer.

"Lieutenant Fel?" I tried. "Lieutenant Berrios? Major…."

I looked at Fera. She shrugged.

"Adenka," Benegal supplied.

"Major Adenka. Any Coalition forces that copy this transmission, respond immediately."

Static filled the frequency. I searched Fera and Benegal's expressions and realized we were all thinking the same thing—the rest hadn't been as lucky as we had. Our strike team had taken down a decent force of Imperium soldiers to get this far, and that was a mere drop in the bucket compared to what was still roaming and patrolling the ship.

The others didn't have a spy serving as a personal escort, either.

"Will? Is that you?"

Relief flooded my chest, and I couldn't hold back my smile. The voice was weak, but it was familiar. "Lieutenant Fel—it's good to hear you. How are you holding up?"

"Alive. For now. What's left of us. We're down to five men, including myself." He paused for a beat, either to gather his strength, or to work his way through the horrors he'd witnessed since being trapped on the ship. I felt for him.

"Well, we're going to see about getting you out of there and then hit the bridge," I said.

Fel got down to business. "The Imperium don't know how dangerous… how dangerous we still are. We brought sixteen kilos of breaching charges. Used two on the airlock, and another two to get where we are now. Stroke of luck, it turned out. Thought we were going into a janitor's closet, but it's actually one of the main oxygen recycling stations. I've got the remainder of our charges linked to a deadman's switch and rigged up on the vestibule containing the oxygen scrubbers."

A glint was in Benegal's eyes. "And there is the *true* reason Tror sought to starve them out instead of breach and kill."

Fera smiled and shook her head. "You're one tenacious bastard, Fel, I'll give you that."

"We didn't know they were going to Drift. Once it happened… options were limited."

"You made the right call," I said and then paused to look at Riva, but I didn't want to announce her presence over the frequency in case it was being monitored by the enemy. "Sit tight, Lieutenant. We'll link up with you momentarily."

Lieutenant Berrios stepped into the conversation, slightly out of breath. The background filled with small-arms fire exchange that made it difficult to hear him. "Will, it's Berrios. Breach Team Bravo… resistance three decks below… send them to the bridge. Standing by for advisement."

Fera pressed her hand to the side of her helmet. "Breach Team Bravo, this is Captain Fera. Say again. What is your status?"

Static rushed across the frequency for the next few seconds, then resolved. Berrios must have fallen back to cover because this time his voice came through loud and clear. "...encountered two Imperium patrols, and they've called for reinforcements. We're pinned down in the galley three decks below our point of entry. We can hold position or peel off a strike force and send them to the bridge."

"Berrios, it's Will. I copy. Hold position. We're preparing to hit the bridge as well. Will advise."

"Roger that," he said.

Fera turned to Lockett. "Hey! How many Imperium are on this ship, and where are they concentrated?"

"Lockett just finished comms. Wait for magic fingers to work all the way, Astradian."

Quin entered the conversation. "It seems obvious to me that there are quite a few more than we anticipated. I don't want to be the one to say it, but since someone has to, I will: we're screwed."

"Don't be so pessimistic, Quin," I said.

"Lockett is in!"

In the span of a second, Quin must have processed whatever Lockett had gained access to.

"We've officially crossed the line from pessimism to realism, Will. Ship-wide biometric scanners are ours to observe. Check your tactical map."

The visor of my helmet was a ruined mess, so I wasn't going to be able to check the HUD there. I unsealed the neck piece, yanked the helmet off, and tossed it. The fiber-link pulled the HUD up into the far edge of my field of vision, showing me the tactical map. As I focused on it, it became more solid.

By then the mood had already shifted as the others in the crew saw what Quin was talking about ahead of me. Hisses of disgust and grunts of resolve sounded among the crew.

The map was a cross-section of five decks of the *ONE*. Threat signatures appeared on each deck, too many to count. A large portion of them were stationed at the three entrances to the upper-most deck—the one that contained the bridge. I thought about how we'd almost died just getting to the terminal banks.

Imagine fighting our way through a force three times the size.

Success seemed highly unlikely. Especially if we tried to take things head-on.

Dozens of additional signatures moved like tiny bugs in a terrar-ium, shifting from the forward section of the ship toward the aft in droves.

"What's that?" I asked.

"It's a clearing pattern," Benegal said. "They are moving room to room, deck by deck; they will purge every last invader from their vessel."

"The Imperium certainly knows where you are," Quin said. "So whatever you do next, do it before you can be cornered."

"We know where they are now, too," I said. "Their advantage is numbers, and that can't be fixed."

"Oh, I can think of a way to fix it," Sert said, racking his shotgun for emphasis.

But even our resident Vorvak would be overwhelmed by the Imperium teeming aboard the *ONE*. We needed to consolidate, or at the very least coordinate our attacks so that at least one breaching team had a chance to get on the bridge.

"Any sign of Major Adenka?" I asked.

Quin's reply was solemn. "You see the yellow indicator on deck four?"

"The airlock? Yeah, I see it."

"It's a *blown* airlock, forcibly separated from the hull of the *ONE* during its pressurization cycle. That is to say, prematurely. It is likely the Imperium caught them on approach and detonated the airlock during the pressurization cycle with Breach Team Alpha's vessel. Adenka and his entire team—if they made it on board at all—didn't stay long. Those are confirmed KIAs. I'll spare you the visual scan."

My gut churned. Nearly a hundred Astradians, gone in an instant.

A tinny pop sounded in the frequency. Lockett flinched, which told me it wasn't something he did.

A throaty rasp entered the frequency. "Coming aboard was a foolish error, Coalition Forces."

Prefect Tror.

"You waged war well to this point. Destroyed more of my ships and soldiers than I care to admit. It would seem that your success deluded you into believing you were invulnerable. The *ONE* is hardly defeated, and your pitiful blockade will be destroyed soon enough. Here are the terms for your surrender: I require that the so called 'Hero of the Rebellion' and the crew of *Phaelon* remain my prisoners. They will stand public trial for insurrection. All other boarders will be allowed to return to their ships and leave."

The voice hadn't changed since the last time I'd heard it. It was the creaking of an old door. Tired and malevolent and disdainful.

Fera snatched her PMC from her mag holster and adjusted the safety selector. She shook her head at me, which meant *do not respond*.

I didn't have it in me to remain silent. When I heard him speak, I thought of the commands he'd given throughout the war. The actions of the Imperium firing on civilian-occupied worlds. The cities he'd glassed, the indiscriminate destruction he'd wreaked on a dozen worlds.

I thought of Farakar. And Minastra, the crown jewel of the late Galactic Federation. The Imperium had swiftly decapitated the old order by transforming the capital of interstellar trade into a smoking husk.

Fera saw it on my face. She made a slashing motion over her throat, warning me, but I didn't heed her. Injustice filled me with blind rage. Exploitation of the innocent and defenseless was the quickest way for me to lose touch with my rational side.

"Take your deal and shove it up your ass," I said.

Benegal brought his MD-14 to his shoulder as if expecting Imperium soldiers to start charging through the walls at any second. Sert inched back, closer to Lockett.

"Thank you for that," Tror rasped. "Your location was… hidden from us. There is no doubt a spy in our midst, one that will be dealt with in the most torturous way imaginable. My soldiers will be coming for you shortly."

All eyes glared at me. I gave a sheepish shrug of my shoulders. "Guy's still an ass."

"Will, are you trying to get us killed *faster?*" Quin hissed. "Honestly, Fera was using non-verbal communication. Most of the time a primitive like you can pick up on at least *that* much."

Quin cleared his throat and affected a business-like tone. "Prefect Tror, it has been some time since last we spoke."

Tror made a raspy, wheezing sound that was probably supposed to be a laugh. It sounded like he was trying to catch his breath after suffering an acute allergic reaction.

"Quintar, my old Navigator. The rumors are true, then. You survived the purge orders after all. I wish I could say I had high hopes for you, but here at the end, I'd rather us not make liars of one another."

"Yes, well, I suppose it's true what they say about us Foris, then, isn't it?"

Tror responded, his voice carrying the tune of rote memorization. "Even the Great Algorithm cannot predict all variables. It is so."

Benegal lowered his rifle and turned his helmet toward me. "Will, we need to move. Staying here is inviting an attack."

I nodded as Tror started speaking.

"My offer is final, and it stands for the next sixty seconds. The Coalition has won major victories—I am in no position to win back what has been lost. I am also no longer the greatest threat you face. The next war will be waged against one another, the same as it was before the Federation—and then the Imperium—brought order."

"We're not surrendering," I said, using my rifle to motion toward the exit. "After everything Tror did, he needs to face justice."

Riva followed me, staying a few steps behind. "I should go. If Tror discovers—"

Sert put a big hand on her slender Foris shoulders. "If we die, it will be as one, spy. Lead the way."

"Quin," I said, "keep up comms with Berrios and the others. Make sure they know we're moving and not out of the fight."

Lockett unplugged from the terminal and bumbled along, taking two steps for every one of Sert's. "Others have likely surrendered. Lockett would… if Lockett could."

"No," I said with a quick shake of my head. "That's not who they are."

I locked eyes with Fera. She gave me a hard, cold stare. I'd really stepped in it, letting my emotions get the better of me.

"Sorry," I said quickly. "Guess Quin is right about me being overly emotional."

"If you got my crew killed by mouthing off," Fera said, "I'll never forgive you."

I swallowed, feeling like a fool. Why couldn't I have just kept my mouth shut?

For reasons unknown, but greatly appreciated, Quin didn't pile on or gloat. He stayed focused on business. "I have Lieutenants Fel and Berrios linked up. Both are ready to assault the bridge."

I stopped at the entrance to the corridor and looked at the Root Krakoid that stood guard in the corridor.

"Okay, I've got an idea…"

33

I FINISHED GOING over the plan, resisting the urge to sneeze. The Krakoids pollen emissions, or whatever it was they exhaled, tingled in my sinuses. As far as I knew, I wasn't allergic to anything, but the longer I was in the presence of the rock-covered plants, the more the itching in my forehead intensified. The majority of the rock warriors stomped off to provide Lieutenant Fel relief. They left two of their number to escort us to the bridge.

"Divide and conquer," Benegal said. "I agree. It is our best chance for success."

"Those chances will alter as time and circumstances change," Quin warned. "The Breakaway Fleet has effectively cut off the *ONE* from the local FTL gates. Imperium reinforcements will alter the battlefield. And we should not rule out the possibility of Tror taking desperate measures—he has very little to lose and would likely never allow *ONE* to fall into enemy hands."

"You mean he might blow the ship up?" I asked.

"Sounds like Tror," Fera said. "If he can't win—no one else can, either."

I pulled my last magazine from my belt and slid it into my KR-44. The grip rattled against my palm as it locked the high-capacity magazine into place. I stretched my face, working some of the numb stiffness out of my left cheek. After that, I would have to rely on battlefield pickups to stay in the fight.

"At this point," Quin said, "any further delays only give the enemy more time to get their defenses in place or to isolate and destroy our various elements. You should make all possible haste to the bridge."

I gave a quick nod. "All right, let's go."

Fera opened the breech on her PMC and fed nitrate cartridges into it. She slid the breech closed and waved her left hand. "Riva, lead the way. At the first sign of trouble, get behind us."

The Foris spy moved ahead, flanked by Stem Krakoids that traveled with clobbering steps. Each slam of the rock-like appendages on the deck left tiny deposits of sediment and soil like footprints.

Just like aboard *Phaelon,* the air in the corridor was cool despite the shipboard environment controls. It carried the faint smell of stagnant water, though I wasn't sure why. Maybe a side effect of the coolant used to keep the massive amount of systems from overheating, or to provide water flow to the living quarters.

Moving toward the front of the ship, we followed Riva for the next two minutes without encountering a single Imperium soldier. She moved slow and steady, her narrow face pivoting left and right, amphibian eyes forming suspicious slits. I wasn't sure if the Krakoids gave her pause, or if she was expecting to encounter Imperium patrols at every turn. I kept her at a distance of a pace and a half ahead of me, just far enough I could reach out and yank her back if we ran into an enemy patrol.

Evidence of combat on this deck was plentiful: spent magazines abandoned at random, carbon scoring on the bulkheads, discarded SMGs at intersections, sheared armor panels left where they had been shot off, and flechettes everywhere.

"The bodies must have already been collected," Benegal mused aloud. "A curious decision."

It did seem strange, but I wrote it off as unimportant. "Maybe bots."

We took a left turn, then a right. The tactical map in my fiber-link's HUD zoomed in to our respective deck, three levels below the bridge. Lieutenant Fel and his team were holed up one deck below and at the outermost portside of the ship. Lieutenant Berrios had split his team into two elements and was actively fighting his way up the access corridors toward the bridge.

That left us to flank the bulk of the enemy position on the command deck.

Once the Krakoids cleared a path through locked doors to get Lieutenant Fel's team to the rendezvous point at the bridge, all elements for our final assault would be accounted for and in place.

It wasn't perfect, but it was the best we could do.

The corridor came to a seemingly dead end. Riva moved to interface with the hard light technology and wiped her hand over it in slow circles. In the distance was the sound of weapons fire.

"We should be purging the ship of every last Imperium," Sert grumbled, clearly wanting to run toward the action. "Leaving a single one alive is a potential enemy later."

"I agree," Benegal said, "but not right now. Taking the bridge is the better option. Rest assured, though, after all this, the Krayvox will eliminate any Imperium stragglers in our territory."

"Guys," I said as our spy hesitated at the door, waiting for someone to nod for her to continue, "I want to talk about something that needs saying. Why do you think the various rebel factions never succeeded against the Imperium over the last four thousand years?"

Benegal snorted. "Because they are incompetent."

"And weak," Sert agreed.

I shook my head. "Because they didn't have unity of effort. They shared a common enemy, but they went about fighting it in exactly the every-faction-for-themselves kind of approach I keep hearing from this crew."

I paused to look each of them in the eyes. Their expressions told me my face must look like hell. I ignored the tingling numbness around my left eye and laid my point home as Riva finished making an opening in the wall.

"We're different. All of us are different. But we've learned something the United Coalition still hasn't. Those differences can be used for the advantage of the greater good—but only so long as we work for common prosperity. Not each for his own special interest."

I let my words marinate in a pregnant pause. Not too long, because time was fleeting. But I was thinking about what would come next. We couldn't be anything but a united crew in the fight that came.

"*Phaelon* is the prototype for the perfect system. We've proved it time and again. Once this is over, we need to get the factions on board with that. Our track record speaks for itself."

No one argued. Little cues from my friends and comrades told me I was on the right track. Fera's smile. A subtle nod from Sert as he examined his shotgun. Lockett refraining from a scoff or a shake of his head.

The only one that didn't seem convinced was Benegal. He stared at me with his cold, dark eyes, his expression completely unreadable.

"We should be going," Riva urged.

Benegal raised his MD-14. "Let's move."

I stifled a sigh. If the *Phaelon*'s crew was going to go their own separate ways after this, Benegal would likely lead the charge. I still didn't know what the Krayvox wanted, but there had to be some way to get him to compromise. If I could figure out Benegal, I felt the rest of the galaxy would fall into order as well.

For now, we moved. I kept my KR-44 up, finger on the trigger guard as I flowed into the corridor. A pair of Imperium fire teams stalked the far end of the corridor, their backs to us. A total of twelve soldiers moving in clusters of three.

"Take them out," I said.

Simultaneously, we opened fire on their exposed backs.

Lockett and Riva ducked behind us, the thin Foris woman covering her ears and squeezing her eyes shut.

We cut the enemy down before they could return fire. There was no ceremony, no discussion, and no delays. We pressed forward, leaving the corpses behind us, everyone checking over the status of their weapons and armor as we moved closer to the bridge.

Comm transmissions played over the shared frequency.

"Four tangos down, more incoming. Can't hold out much longer," Lieutenant Fel said, his voice scratchy with fatigue.

"We're en route to your position. Hold the line!" Lieutenant Berrios responded.

That was a change in plan. The Krakoids were supposed to relieve Fel. Evidently, something in the fighting had prompted Berrios to select another option. In the end, it was Berrios, and not me, who was the expert. I didn't comment.

To do so would have been tantamount to admitting that the Hero of the Rebellion stuff had well and truly gone to my head.

Benegal picked up his pace. "We need to move faster."

"Double-time," Sert said, turning his lumbering gait into a pounding charge.

I stepped up to a jog, leaving Fera just behind me as I glanced at the tactical map and then back to the corridor ahead. We made a right turn and entered an atrium of sorts. It was a common area used for staging of equipment, or massing soldiers for briefings, or maybe even for roll calls and shift changes. My fiber-link HUD measured it at a hundred and twenty meters long by half that length wide and tall.

At four positions along the crystal-faceted walls, distortions wavered like heat lines on the horizon in a desert. I pulled Riva back, came to a halt, and raised a fist. The team stopped and brought their weapons up, then spread out into a line beside me.

"They're coming," I said. "Be ready to put out maximum firepower. Riva, any chance you can stop them from opening the doors?"

She shook her head. "Maybe one."

"Lockett?" I asked.

The Drayth also shook his head. "Mostly read-only access. Stealing comm capability was difficult enough."

Sert smiled as he aimed down the invisible sights of his shotgun. "Nothing left but the killing now. Eventually, it is always so."

Fera brushed her shoulder against me. "Eyes still good?"

I nodded my head and blinked, thankful that some of the upset over my speaking to Tror was fading. "I can see. I'm good for now."

"We're almost there," she muttered.

Quin's face appeared in the upper corner of my HUD. "Will, good news. Lieutenant Berrios's men have increased the likelihood of Fel's team getting out alive substantially."

"Good to know," I said, waiting for him to get to the point.

"Those human fighters don't quit, and they don't go down easy. They're stacking Imperium bodies like they're going out of style. Truly a marvel to witness on the shipboard camera systems. You're a human, why don't you fight as—"

"The *point*, Quin," I hissed.

"Right. Krakoids have breached the berth immediately preceding Lieutenant Fel's position. The Imperium is being routed on that deck and have pulled more troops to assist. Good news for you, because just fifty Imperium soldiers are pushing on your location presently."

"Fifty?" I asked.

"Fifty-one, actually. You may want to seek cover and try to fight from a position of strength, if you can. Unless you sense another tantrum coming on and wish to yell at them about truth and justice and feelings. Your call, caveman."

"Sert, cover that door." I indicated the closest one on the left.

"Benegal, that one." I nodded toward the opposite door on the right.

Fera, apparently reading my mind, moved to the forward door on the left side. I stepped up to the one opposite hers, steadied my weapon against my shoulder, and waited.

Lockett and Riva moved to the dead end up ahead, where Riva started working on turning the wall into a door. The two Stem Krakoids stood motionless, facial tubers wilting and swelling rhythmically.

"You two," I said, and then pointed to Lockett and Riva. "Guard them. We need them to get us to the bridge."

The Krakoids moved to stand behind them, their rocky bulks shifting like rockslides.

The doors dissolved all at once.

Imperium soldiers streamed through them, SMGs firing on mag dump. Behind the initial burst of bodies and synthetic coated rounds, RPCs lit off with tantalizing flashes of raw energy.

Fera and I both side-stepped the threshold of our doors, letting the opposing gouts of RPC rounds chew lines of fire across the deck. Columns of fire spewed up, carving depressions of slagged metal in a tract between the doors.

Fera alternated between nitrate cartridge rounds and bursts of pulse fire from her PMC. Imperium soldiers hit the deck.

I worked my KR-44, spiking flechettes into armor and visors, dropping the enemy one at a time. They continued their blind charge, stumbling over the bodies of their fallen comrades, spraying their SMGs in a frenzy.

The Krakoids weren't good at following orders.

Resounding thumps rocked along the deck as they charged for the closest enemy they could see—the soldiers pouring out of the doors Fera and I were actively trying to suppress.

The moving rock faces caught huge salvos of pulse blasts from the RPCs. Rock chipped and flaked away. The Krakoids slammed their jagged rock edges into the soldiers, crushing them against bulkheads and splintering armor under wicked blows of blunt kinetic force.

The doors were only two meters wide, and that left the Imperium with little room for cover or maneuvering. They ran forward like bots, heedless of their own sacrifice as they died on their feet.

Sert put them down with repeated blasts of his shotgun.

Benegal made short work of his enemy fire teams with a rapid series of headshots. Even the RPC in his column went silent as he tagged both the operator and the assistant gunner with flechettes right between the eyes.

I dumped the last of my magazine into the corridor.

Fera paused to reload her PMC.

The room, once empty, was now filled with the wreckage of Imperium soldiers that had met a chaotic, violent end. It was over as quickly as it had begun; it all felt a lot like murder.

Riva finished with the door, stepped to the side, and waved for us to move forward. We flowed as one unit to the new opening, which led into a corridor that turned to the left and to the right. The Krakoids turned and withdrew to their assigned positions. One of them held flames along its chest but seemed not to notice.

"The bridge," she said.

I could hardly believe it. That was it? That was all we'd been put up against?

Tror could have put two hundred men in this position. Instead, he chose fifty, and they'd done what they could to help us kill them all by rushing headlong into our hasty ambush.

Something didn't quite sit right, but we couldn't burn up time giving it a good think. The bridge door was right there… waiting.

"Sert!" I called.

"Moving," he responded in his rumbling basso.

Before any of us could stack up in an attempt to breach the doors, they opened of their own accord.

A thundercrack split the air.

Two volleys of RPC pulses rocketed into us.

The Krakoids caught the full brunt of it. One of them disintegrated into a pile of smoking rubble, proving that, tough as the creatures were, they weren't invulnerable. The surviving Krakoid charged through the maelstrom, only to collapse in like fashion as the rate of fire intensified.

"Cover!" I shouted.

We formed up along both edges of the blast doors until the fire ceased.

"Damn," Fera muttered. "Might have to wait for the others. No way to maneuver out of this."

I keyed the comm. "Lieutenant Berrios, we're at the bridge and pinned. What's your ETA."

"I've got Lieutenant Fel and his men. We're moving up to your position now."

"Faster the better, Lieutenant," I said and then cast my eyes toward the bridge doors. "I think both sides have the other where they want them."

34

"STAND DOWN, ALL OF YOU," Tror rasped from within the bridge. His voice was carried over comm speakers and seemed to float along the corridors where we covered.

"How 'bout you come out!" I shouted back. "Talk this over face-to-face."

A loose light panel in the ceiling flickered, sparked, and gave way. The formed crystal panel hit the deck and bounced, too thick to shatter but too damaged to maintain its shape. It splintered into a handful of pieces with a dull cascade of blunted edges tapping along the deck.

Sert pressed his shell armor against the side of the entrance, feeding cartridges into his shotgun. On the other side of the door, I dropped my KR-44 to the deck and drew my rail pistol.

"Lockett is working further into the systems," Quin reported. "The longer you can stall for Berrios and the others to arrive, the better this final push may go."

Evidence of Lockett's work came when Quin's voice then sounded throughout the same shipboard PA system Tror had used. "You had a good run, Prefect, but it's well past time to admit defeat. You have two options before you. Only one option before you doesn't involve a quite painful death at the hands of a Vorvak—surrender."

Tror made a hacking sound, like he was clearing phlegm from his throat—his ancient laugh.

Fera slid her back along the bulkhead and bumped her shoulder against me. "I'll be honest, Tror!—I hope you *don't* surrender."

Silence.

The ruined husk of a Krakoid lay just inside the entrance to the bridge. Sert made eye contact with me. "Let me go inside. I will kill him, even if I must die in the process."

"No dice, big guy," I said. "We'll get more out of him alive."

Sert nodded sagely. "Only shots below the belt. Can do."

That wasn't exactly what I had in mind, but Quin's counsel for us to build up our chances might work both ways. The longer we delayed, the sooner Imperium help could arrive.

"Interesting," Quin said. "They're attempting to close the bridge doors again, but Lockett is fighting the attempt off. I think they intended to kill a few of us in an opening bout and then seal back up."

"We should move," Fera said. "No more waiting."

"Give the count," Sert said, barely controlling his passion for the impending fight.

I held up my fist and uncurled three fingers. Despite the grim circumstances that led up to this point, I couldn't help but feel a surge of pride that he was deferring to my lead to commence the fight. It was only a few months ago that he had personally trained me, a clueless fish out of water, overwhelmed by a galaxy beyond the scope of my understanding.

I pumped my fist, stowing one finger at a time, tension gnawing at my gut. When I threw out a knife hand, Benegal tossed a pair of grenades inside the open bridge door.

Sert pressed his shotgun into his shoulder and went in at the first explosion, veering to the left. I followed, moving through the smoke to the right. Benegal and Fera were right behind me and took the inside lanes, one to each side.

The bridge was a grotesquely opulent design that immediately presented a problem for us. It was orders of magnitude larger than any ship control center I'd ever been on. Stairs at either end of the room connected to a boardwalk style viewing deck above, where half a dozen officers were poised at the railing with pulse pistols trained on us. Behind them, a floor to ceiling hologram showed the FTL gate in the distance, with the *Earthborn* floating in front of it.

The bridge was designed to repel an armed ingress. The terminals were bucket-style, sweeping half-eggshells that offered plenty of cover. The captain's chair was situated on the viewing deck and was more a capsule than it was a chair. Encased in crystalline, veins of exotic metal were woven into the structure, creating an eye-catching work of art with its strange patterns that also served the functional purpose of being fortified against small-arms fire.

Beneath the chair was a transparent cylinder, not unlike the box I'd first encountered on the *Phaelon* that contained Quin's organic brain matter. Suspended inside was a beam of light, broken at both ends. It looked like a pulse round frozen in time, a living snapshot of pure red energy that quivered, as if waiting for a chance to escape whatever containment field held it in place.

Stringed instruments began to play from somewhere far off in the distance. It was a song from another dimension. The siren song of bliss concealing eternal damnation in the space between notes.

The song of the Void.

I thought it at the same time Quin said it.

"The Quantum Gate Sequencer. Tror's going to attempt a blind Void Drift!"

I didn't see the ancient Foris Prefect, but I imagined he was safely tucked inside the captain's chair, preparing to execute a Drift with coordinates set to anywhere-but-here. It was a desperate maneuver and would likely lead to the entire ship being destroyed, but at this point, he didn't have anything to lose. The fact that I could hear the Voidsong told me he had already started the transition process.

But I couldn't stop it until I dealt with defenses that were already rising back up from the floor after our booming entrance.

Below the viewing deck, Imperium officers opened fire, their limited experience showing as they chased us with flechettes. Their accuracy suffered further with each boom of Sert's shotgun.

The electric whine of pulse rounds reverberated off the bulkheads of the confined space. Sparks cascaded along every surface. Coherent light whizzed by danger close, millimeters from my face. I put the reticle and beam of my fiber-link enhanced targeting system to work, double-tapping the trigger each time I lined up a target.

The initial deluge of fire diminished by half in the first few seconds, taking some of the heat off us as we moved deeper into the bridge.

Plasma from Sert's shotgun punched the nearest officer's head clean off in a gout of flame and evaporating fluids. The body collapsed with a wet thud. Flechettes knifed into unarmored faces, necks, and shoulders.

Behind me, the insistent wail of Fera's PMC firing on burst mode was intermingled with the steady drum beat of Benegal's MD-14 relentlessly hammering high-caliber rounds into the enemy on the viewing deck. Officers were knocked back, or fell over the railing, their dress whites shredded with fire and pin-holed with bleeding entry/exit wounds.

If this was the best defense Tror had left, then no wonder he was desperate enough to Drift his way out of here blindly.

I fired off the last round of my rail pistol, spiking an officer between the eyes. I moved further to the right bulkhead, making myself small against the back of the nearest terminal as I thumbed the mag release while simultaneously pulling a fresh one from my belt. The spent mag bounced off my boot as I locked the replacement into place.

I was about to call in my firing lane clear when a flicker of light drew my eye to the right-hand bulkhead near the back of the bridge.

Tror had yet to initiate the Drift, but we were running out of time.

I made a move for the stairs when a second shimmer flared and flickered at the opposite bulkhead. At the same time, both distortions expanded to three meters across. The light winked out, revealing an opening in the bulkhead on each side of the bridge.

Imperium soldiers poured onto the bridge from the sides, SMGs firing on Fera and Benegal.

"A trap!" Quin screeched.

"We see them," Fera said, pivoting her fire toward surging fire teams on her side. She moved her left hand to the secondary barrel and pumped incendiary rounds at a frenetic pace.

Incoming fire raked over us.

Sert caught the brunt of it, but he shouldered his way forward like he was running through heavy rain, losing curled segments of his armor that burned and flaked away from his body.

Benegal kicked off two rounds that caught the lead soldier on my side of the room, then dropped his rifle and transitioned to his two pulse pistols. Moving steadily forward, he lit off rounds as fast as he could squeeze the triggers, spraying the enemy with scattered shots.

I slipped around the right side of the terminal and rotated my shoulders so that my back was against the bulkhead, then pushed forward.

The distance between us and the enemy dissolved in seconds.

Fire exchange at point blank became hand to hand as our fire teams met Imperium soldiers on the dais beneath the viewing deck. Four Imperium backed steadily away from Sert, SMGs firing on mag dump. At such close range, they couldn't miss. The big guy's chest and shoulders sprouted columns of sparking flames. Rivulets of blood spurted where flechettes found the narrow spaces in between armor.

The Vorvak transformed from competent soldier to enraged berserker caught in the depths of primal bloodlust.

Sert cycloned forward like a demon with wings of fire trailing behind him, external helmet speakers rattling with a war cry. He batted aside the Imperium with overhand slams of his huge, clawed fists and followed up with vicious backhands that hit with bone-crushing force. It was raw power unleashed with no filter, a savage act of violence played on repeat.

Imperium knees buckled. Helmets dented.

Soldiers crumpled into broken heaps in front of him, but this wasn't a routine engagement. This was the final fight on the Imperium flagship, and they knew it. The option to run was off the table. Soldiers who might have otherwise fled dug their heels in, set their stances, and issued blasts of synthetic-coated rounds in one vicious mag dump after the next.

Sert twitched with each blow. The sporadic bursts bit into his armor, taking scraps of panels with them. Each successive gout of rounds chewed deeper, burning closer to his rough turtle skin, one direct hit away from finding a vital area.

I leveled my rail pistol and fired, fired, fired.

Suit liners frayed and trailed in tatters from weak points in the armor. Gouts of blood traced fractured pieces of helmet visor and pattered across the deck, then dripped down terminal stations. I kept up my firestorm, one trigger pull, one flechette at a time, knowing my magazine was going to run dry at any second.

The butt of an SMG knocked into my left shoulder. I hadn't seen the Imperium trooper before he'd gotten so close. I staggered half a step back and tucked the elbow of my firing hand to bring the barrel of the weapon between me and my assailant.

Two flechettes zipped into the throat of my enemy. The soldier's hand flew to his neck. I raised my knee and snapped the heel of my boot forward to kick him off-balance and out of the way. He staggered and fell, blood spilling between his gloved fingers.

I knew now that the troopers were seeking to surround and overpower—to take me alive. The Imperium soldier I'd just killed could have shot me just as easily as he battered me; that he didn't meant either incompetence or following orders. More would come.

I broke for the stairwell, feeling that I had to get to Tror.

Fera dropped her empty rifle and switched to her rail pistol. She called my name and then picked off several chasing Imperium on my heels.

Without warning—at least no warning I ever heard—columns of fire erupted at the railing, consuming any Imperium officer that didn't take cover. The start and stop wail of an MD-300 spewing automatic pulse fire throbbed in the air like a repeated bass drop. Huge swathes of heat damage billowed at the exotic armored surface of the captain's chair, staining the angled fractals a sickly yellow.

Every inhale came with the stomach-churning flavors of ozone and blood.

Lieutenant Fel and his men arrived. They still had some fight left in them after all that had happened.

I listened for Fel or Berrios on the comm but heard someone else altogether.

A deep, distorted voice said, "Move in."

Uriel. And he was speaking to the Drayth that held his vessel.

"Lockett will not move in. Too much shooting!"

"Move in," Uriel repeated. "I demand it."

"Stay put, Drayth!" Sert growled between discharges of his shotgun. "Don't listen to the demonic pixie, it will get you killed!"

Benegal's pulse pistols belched plumes of black smoke until they went dry. He transitioned to his rail pistols and fired flechettes in a hailstorm, even as a concentrated burst of incoming fire bit into his thigh panel and ripped the armor clean off. A chunk of flesh went with it; his dark blood flowed.

The Krayvox grunted and staggered, his aim faltering—but only for a second. He was back on target a moment later as though nothing had happened, his Zen-like focus restored.

A second barrage came in from the overhead railing. Synthetic coated rounds slapped into Benegal's left shoulder and ignited, chewing through the damaged panels and clawing at the exposed flesh beneath.

Adrenaline flared in my chest. An Imperium soldier moved in for the kill, slapping a fresh magazine into his SMG, barrel trained on Benegal. I hesitated. Tror was a priority but Benegal…

My crewmate lost his grip on his weapons and dropped to the deck, swatting at the new wounds. Other men might have screamed; Benegal remained stoic—but the spasms wracking his body told me some of the rounds had penetrated his chest and were still burning.

Quin was focused on a bigger problem. "I'm detecting transition signatures! The crazy bastard Tror is Navigating without prep. I'll be fine, but if any of you were planning on surviving this… someone has to stop him!"

I felt imminent death clamping down on me like a vise. Every second had counted, and now we were nearly out of them.

My fingers shook with adrenaline sickness as I switched to my final magazine. Before I could bring the weapon to bear, two soldiers rushed me and might have tackled me had I not turned and fired on them.

They fell at my feet. I charged past them, aware the incessant weapons fire of Fel and Berrios was evening the odds for us. My mind narrowed until I was serving a single, Vorvak-like creed: if I would die… Tror would die first.

My boots hit the stairwell. In my peripheral, I saw Fera reach the top, right by my side.

An Imperium officer rushed her, trying to shove his pulse pistol in her face where he couldn't miss.

She threw her forearm out in a defensive block. The pulse pistol went wide and discharged into the ceiling. Fera brought the butt of her own rail pistol down into the man's neck so hard I thought I heard the vertebrae snap.

We were taking the stairs two at a time. My breath fumed with every push off the balls of my feet. Pulse rounds chittered between my boots and zinged into the railing with trials of sparks. Some of them struck true and bit into my armor.

A persistent sting was in my left calf, threatening to make me hobble.

A new stab of pain pierced into my right side. Fire chewed at my ribs, but it didn't stop there. Kinetic force hit me again with a one-two blow that knocked me off my feet. I bashed my forehead against the stairs and slipped down three full steps before I caught the lip of a single stair with the tips of my boots.

I tried to breathe. My ribs stretched and creaked. The wound above my eye opened and began bleeding again.

The pain prevented me from sucking in a full breath.

Lieutenant Fel's command came out in clipped tones. "Now or never, people. Forward!"

The intensity of the firefight reached a fever pitch.

The incoming continued to spark along the parts of my armor that were still intact, jostling me against the stairs. I guess they no longer wanted me alive—or maybe they just didn't care. Maybe all that was left in this war was to kill everyone and everything until you were the last man standing.

My vision started to tunnel—I couldn't catch my breath.

Stars danced in front of my eyes. I used my left hand to force myself to my feet and hobbled up the next few steps, blinking furiously. I found the viewing deck, dropped to my stomach, and rolled end over end twice before the pain flared with enough intensity to force me to stop.

Tightening my core to stop the roll on my belly sent fresh pain in a snarling blaze from my armpit to my hip. Nerve endings pinched and gnashed, pulsing in rhythm with my racing heart.

Like the rising of the sun over the horizon on a new day, light spilled in from the main bridge display.

The Void sang in force, drowning out all other sounds in my head. The beginnings of an entry lane melody were starting up, unformed but nearly there. An intricate piece of sheet music ready on the stage as the musicians took their positions.

Quin's voice quivered as he said, "Void Transition in five...."

An intense flare of light speared the bridge, so bright I had to cover my eyes to stop it from stabbing at my retinas.

All gunfire ceased at once.

Static cling snaked along the back of my neck and arms.

A series of thuds sounded from various points around the deck —some near, some further away. Someone shouted in pain. The voice was filtered by a helmet speaker, and unfamiliar, which marked it as Imperium.

I parted my fingers. The light was still there, but it didn't hurt. It was like a 300 lumen flashlight shining directly in my face.

Drawing ragged breaths, I peeled my eyes open, just a hair.

My breath caught in my chest.

Lockett was crouched in the center of the bridge, shielding the top of his head with his stubby hands.

The isotope reactor rig attached to his back was a blazing mushroom cloud of pure energy. It was like a nuclear detonation three meters tall, and without the fire. Electricity cackled and flittered. Jagged red bolts snaked through the space, but these weren't simple discharges. These were not the flashing kind of natural phenomena observed in storm clouds.

It was like peering *inside* a storm cloud.

I recognized this kind of lightning bolt because I'd been attacked by one just like it on the *Phaelon*.

"Uriel?" I gasped.

The mushroom cloud of pure energy began to spin like a celestial body rotating about its axis. As if responding to a shifting wind, the angles and positions of the lightning bolts began to change. The whole shape of the lightning storm shifted subtly with the movement. Like a table puzzle composed of rings with a sphere in the center, the bolts seemed caught in rings of some unseen force, moving at the command of one person.

Or one Fleuridian.

The bolts swiped like scythes. Light trails followed them, blurring like glow sticks shaking in the dark.

Imperium soldiers caught in the path of travel froze like statues.

Then they fell apart. It was without ceremony—no blood, no outcry of pain or suffering. Where one man stood, the lightning energy passed through, leaving him in pieces.

Death in the style of *Raiders of the Lost Ark*.

And yet none of the beams passed through the United Coalition soldiers.

Secondary chain reactions arced in coiled tails of light, crackling until they dissipated after two or three points of contact.

All at once, the light disappeared.

Quin continued his countdown, unabated. "Three..."

If Tror executed the Drift, I felt it was only to destroy us and the ship.

I could think of but one thing to be done, but I didn't know if it would work.

If it didn't, we would be dead either way.

I recalled Quin's words from his Void Drifter logs: *Focus to discern. Courage to act.*

Lockett jumped as I rolled off the viewing deck and slammed on the bridge level right next to him. Without speaking, I grabbed Dumpy's head unit and wrenched it free from the isotope reactor.

Lockett sputtered profanities.

"Uriel, go!" I shouted, tossing the head unit. "The ship will be destroyed!"

"One..." Quin announced in sorrow.

The bot's head unit rotated end over end, painfully slow despite how hard I'd thrown it. The beveled edge of the metal contacted the containment shield—

Then bounced off and pinwheeled wildly away. A hairline crack formed in the crystalline surface. I hadn't mustered enough force to break through.

With trembling hands, I opened fire on the unit, aiming for the crack. Hoping to widen it.

Hoping that—somehow—it would all work.

Dumpy's head unit puffed with purple smoke and streamers of faint blue and red light. Uriel's avatar manifested next to the Quantum Resonator, its billowy fingers probing curiously at the tiny crack.

The Fleuridian looked back at me. Swirling darkness in the eye sockets somehow grew darker. I thought I saw it nod. Then it raised its fist and punched a hole in the Resonator's capsule and grabbed the beam of energy inside.

"I strongly advise *everyone* to brace yourselves!" Quin cried.

35

DARKNESS FELL OVER THE BRIDGE.

I thought I was dead. Then I realized I was thinking.

You can't think when you're dead... right?

I could also sense my body—I could feel the deck under my hands and knees.

A faint spark of red light appeared up ahead. It was in the approximate area where the Quantum Resonator had been.

"You feel it," Uriel trundled. "Send me home."

"What?" I said, though maybe I just thought the word.

Uriel heard me all the same. "Stretch out and feel it. The path is there. You must call it."

Something felt strange in my head. Like I was hearing something without really hearing it. Because I was. It was a memory. Not an insertion of data from my fiber-link, but like....

The dream of a memory that never existed but was as real and true as anything. And then, comprehension slipped in place before my eyes. I was witness to a memory that had not yet happened.

It was a future memory.

The Drift Lane I needed… I would one day remember—even as I remembered now—that it was there. In the opposite direction we now traveled.

Through the realm of subspace known as the Void, an infinite number of Drift Lanes ebbed and flowed, connecting every point of matter to another point of matter in a true lattice of quantum mechanics that defied my understanding.

But I didn't have to understand it to recognize the pattern. Just as one doesn't need to be a painter to recognize a canvas.

I leaned into the future memory. A buzzing sensation started in my lips.

Then it came out. A sound that wasn't a sound. Something… ethereal.

Otherworldly.

It was like lip syncing a familiar tune. A song I had never heard before but had always existed somewhere deep inside myself.

The song of angels and demons that serenaded and condemned the beings of light and dark whose names and likenesses I would never know… in this hidden part of myself, I heard them.

And they heard me.

A golden bolt of lightning appeared out there in the Void—so far away the distance had to be an abstract number—but it did not stay there.

It went from there to here in a zeptosecond.

Pure energy broke through a higher plane of space-time and struck the red ember in front of me.

The bolt pierced through Uriel's body.

The Fleuridian dissolved, but not in its usual manner.

There were no flakes or pixie dust. It was a solid outline of perfect golden light.

Pure energy.

And then it was gone and all that remained was darkness unbroken.

My eyes were open. I'd never shut them, but I hadn't seen through them until that moment.

I came back to my awareness shaking, sweating, nearly hyper-ventilating.

I fell over onto my back, my arms splayed to the sides.

The pain returned. My body felt... too small to be me.

"Will!" Fera cried.

My eyes roamed the ceiling panels, searching for her. Lights flickered intermittently. Darkness floated over my vision.

Two distinct sources of pain vied for my attention. The one in my side, and a new pain in my throat.

With the pain came awareness. Clarity.

Riva was straddling me, one hand squeezing my throat.

In the other, she held a knife—my fiber-link told me it was a Foris knife, though I'd never seen one before this moment.

What an odd thing to think about before dying.

A hollow split lengthwise down the center of the blade separated the two cutting edges. Ten centimeters of perfect molecular edges, perfect for one strike.

An assassin's blade poised to deliver the killing blow.

Riva's narrow face stretched in an open-mouthed scream. "For the true Prema-General of the Imperium!"

I instinctively tried to raise my hand to fend off the blow, but my mind wasn't working right. My body wouldn't respond.

I could have punched the skin-and-bones alien off of me otherwise. Weak as I was, I would have probably distended her stomach. Broken some ribs, at least.

But all I could do was shove my hand toward the tip of the strange knife and catch it. The blade's twin cutting edges pierced through the back of my hand down to the hilt. With the last of my strength, I locked my elbow, changing the weapon's path from my throat.

Riva's face distorted in a sneer and then a concussive boom robbed me of my hearing and the Foris of her upper torso.

Oxygen suddenly came rushing back.

"Gah!" I choked, watching a streamer of blood drip from my hand as I looked through shocked eyes at the impaling blade.

I expected to see Sert's form tower over me.

Instead, I saw Tror, holding a wicked hand cannon in his grip, the barrel still smoking from the liquid nitrogen round it had just fired. "You are welcome."

I blinked. Fatigue set in, and I went limp, staring up at the ceiling.

"Wh-wha—" I attempted but couldn't summon the strength for a single word at that moment.

Tror's face was no less sinister for having saved my life. "The sheer tenacity of that Anunnaki can never truly be underestimated. Eddison always did have his spies embedded everywhere. I cannot imagine what is in him that inspires such loyalty. But perhaps you can, Will Kaufman."

Sert racked his shotgun. I lolled my eyes toward the Vorvak and wished I hadn't.

His armor was in pieces. Exposed flesh was mottled with blood blisters, some of which had broken open and oozed foul yellow fluid. His helmet was off, showing the contempt on his face as he raised the weapon and trained it on Tror.

Fera, one arm wrapped around the railing and panting like she'd been holding her breath the whole time, called out to him, weak but insistent.

"Sert," she managed. "No…"

She could see what they all saw—Tror had my life in his hands. I wanted to tell them to finish it. Let me die. But I still couldn't summon the breath or strength to speak.

The Vorvak lowered the weapon without protest and used it as a makeshift cane to hold his massive frame upright.

Benegal was still alive. He rolled to his knees, one arm pressed into his shoulder. Blood poured from his nose and mouth. Trace elements of gray smoke clung to him. His helmet visor had broken at some point during the fighting.

Tror looked from Sert and the *Phaelon*'s crew back down to me. "You will, one day, look back on all of this as a continual series of mistakes. And the last—one mistake too many, human."

I tried to respond but managed only a gurgle. My throat raged in pain.

"The vaunted Hero of the Rebellion is nothing but a child. A simple, naive child. You were the perfect victim, playing unwittingly into the hands of the Anunnaki scum who calls himself Marcus Eddison."

My body wanted to lie down and die, but I couldn't let it. I forced myself up to my knees, reached out for a nearby terminal station, and hauled myself to my feet. I needed the terminal to remain standing as blood rushed to my head.

"Eddison... he was Imperium. Before"—I took in a shuddering breath, every word torture—"before you destroyed his home planet. He told us."

Tror paused and opened his palm with a flourish. It was such an odd gesture, I didn't know what to make of it until he spoke again. "That is true. Partially true."

The Prefect kept a space of two meters between us. The sight of his tall, fragile body filled me with disgust. The wrinkles on his pale face clashed with the darkened coloring of his skin. I couldn't believe it was really him. After everything that had happened in the war, and the fight here on the bridge... all of this was to capture this decrepit alien geezer?

It felt... anticlimactic, in a way.

"The full truth," Tror scoffed, "you will learn that soon enough. An Anunnaki of his ilk will not stay hidden forever. He may be Eddison now, but he was, in his time with the Imperium, known by another name."

Tror coughed. Licked his lips. Stared right into my eyes.

"He was a personal political rival for quite some time. Possessed with an equal thirst for power and ambition, he overstepped his birthright. His actions were shamefully self-motivated, and he did not possess the intellect to so much as cover his tracks."

Tror's smile was sad, like a disappointed parent.

"He was dismissed in shame for his failure. Vowed revenge on me and the Imperium itself. But a fleet is required for such things. Or several."

"What the hell are you talking about, Tror?" Fera demanded, using the railing of the viewing deck to pull herself to her feet. "Because when you first showed up, your only rivals were the Foris trying to keep the Imperium from gobbling up all the Navigators."

Tror didn't take his eyes off me as he responded to her question. "I'm speaking to the Hero of the Rebellion, not a Federation lapdog. Will... Hero of the Rebellion... the man who let Eddison pull all the strings that needed pulling so that he could regain his former power. And for what? That little mud ball you call a root world? Do you honestly think that if the Imperium wanted Earth, we wouldn't have already taken it?"

Tror's words chilled me to the bone. Worse, I got the sense that he was telling us the truth.

I cringed at the pain in my side. "You're... you mean... Eddison orchestrated this whole thing? From the beginning?"

Tror gave one slow nod. "The Federation was always meant to fall. Eddison thought he would be Prefect. He was not—I was. Since then, he sought to grow his own power under a different banner. To retake that which he believes was stolen from him."

Ice water dropped into my gut.

This whole time, I thought I was fighting against the Imperium.... When I was really just fighting for another version of it.

At that moment, I could reject what I was hearing. Insist that I was right for no other reason than because it was the course I had taken and thinking anything contrary was too unpleasant.

But that's not how an archaeologist's mind works. At least not a good one. When confronted with evidence, you evaluate. And—if necessary—you change according to the facts.

I looked down at Riva's headless corpse. Then realized that her knife was still in my hand. With a grunt, I removed it and tossed it next to its owner's body.

She had meant to kill me.

Eddison was more dangerous than I thought. We all had our suspicions about him… but not like this.

"You killed her to save me," I said, nodding at Riva's dead body. "Why?"

Tror shrugged. "I imagine you'd rather know why Eddison's spy would use her dagger for you and not me… Understand, Hero, that you have served your purpose. Your savior of Earth sought to discard you. It is the way of the Imperium."

"You didn't answer my question."

Tror stooped down beside Riva's corpse. He scooped up the knife and examined it, turning it over in his hand.

"Eddison wants you dead. For that fact alone, I wish you to live. I loathe that Anunnaki to the point that it defies language. I despise him as much as I value the Imperium for the order and balance it once brought to the galaxy."

His amphibian eyes quivered with emotion.

"I saw what so few have seen. The banner of the Umbraic Curtain flown above the capitals of a thousand worlds across the spiral arms. Strength through unity."

"Prove it then," I said, and then wiped excess blood and saliva from the corner of my mouth. "If he's a threat to the galaxy, come to the United Coalition and tell us how to stop him."

Fera stiffened like she'd been slapped.

Tror dismissed the idea with a wave of his hand. He turned to stand, still studying the Foris knife that had nearly killed me. "I am not like him. I have a code of honor that is unimpeachable. I will die before I betray my beloved Imperium."

He reversed the blade and plunged it into his stomach. The two-tanged weapon slid easily through the thin flesh of his body and didn't stop until the hilt contacted his sternum. The wrinkles around his eyes grew darker. His face remained a resolute mask, as if it had been carved from marble.

"Always... honor," he managed before coughing a trickle of blood.

I shook my head in disgust.

Tror rotated his wrist, giving the knife a savage twist. The narrow wound ripped into a gaping hole, spilling dark blood over his fingers. It pattered onto his boots and stained the deck.

Then he did the most unnerving thing he could have done: he smiled.

Blood stained his teeth, pooling over his tongue and dripping down his chin. His body started to convulse irregularly, as if he was fighting off a sudden chill in the air.

"It will be a long and bloody new w—war," Tror gasped. "Against an enemy m—more... more vile and bloodthirsty than you r—r—realize."

I stood, transfixed by his parting words. I didn't want them to be true.

Tror fell to his knees, sagging his shoulders and bowing his head. He wrenched the knife out of his stomach and tossed it at my feet. A thin trail of blood traced the path from the mortal wound to the strange blade in front of me.

A weak, raspy, frothy sound came from his lips, bringing bubbles of saliva and blood forward. With great effort, he raised his head to look at me with eyes half open.

Lucidity faded from his eyes as they fluttered closed.

"*Sagda.*"

Tror, Prefect of the Imperium, died on his knees. Killed by his own hand.

With full bridge access, Lockett and Quin broke the final layer of encryption on the *ONE*'s internal security measures. The remaining 1,200 Imperium soldiers and sixty officers, along with a crew of nearly 2,000 maintenance technicians, surrendered once the *Earthborn* was able to communicate directly with the ship.

That led to the crippled Imperium Flagship being swarmed with the *Earthborn*'s entire complement of United Coalition soldiers.

Lieutenant Berrios headed up the roundup of the prisoners and escorted them to the *Seven Oh Seven*, a captured Imperium ship that was actively being converted into a POW transport vessel.

Fleet Admiral Tanoka boarded the vessel once the all-clear was given. He entered the bridge, flanked by a guard detail of United Coalition soldiers and a full staff of combat medics. Before he so much as offered a word of greeting to us, he dispatched his team of medics to assess Tror's body. In seconds, they declared him medically deceased. A minute later, they picked up the corpse and stored it in a hermetically sealed pod for transport back to the *Earthborn*.

"The Coalition thanks you for your contribution to the war effort," the Admiral said with stiff formality, speaking to us while medics tended to our wounds. "The crew of the *Phaelon* were instrumental in defeating the Imperium, even down to this last battle. You have killed the enemy's general. Severed the head clean off the snake. It is admirable, to say the least, and we are in your debt."

I shook my head. "You've been spending too much time with General Mira'dna. You're starting to sound just like her."

Tanoka smiled. "I'll take that as a compliment."

"I'm leaving, now," Sert announced.

I wasn't sure what was in the minds of my friends, but I felt the need to stay with them. "I'll come with you."

Admiral Tanoka shot out a hand and pressed it lightly against my shoulder. "Not too far, I trust? We will still need to Drift back with the rest of the fleet. And after that... the New Federation will need an experienced Navigator to train up the future Void Drifters. Without that, it will be centuries before enough Navigators are available to meet the shipping demands of an interstellar government."

Benegal, bleeding through the patches administered to his body, hissed at the Admiral's words. New Federation. Here we go...

I studied Tanoka's face, trying to decide if I thought he was being straight up with me, or concealing some other reason why the United Coalition wanted me close. I couldn't decide, so I opted to believe it was both; Admiral Tanoka was a decent Anunnaki, with morals and values, but he also had a job to do.

Part of that job, it seemed, included keeping me in the pocket of the new government, and I wasn't convinced it was solely for my sensitivity to the Void. There would be plenty enough stranded Foris Navigators who could do that job, now that the *ONE* was ours and the Imperium was soundly defeated.

My mind shifted from unknown to unknown.

Eddison had manufactured his own personal fleet to defend Earth. What would it take for him to turn those ships around, point the weapons at Washington DC or London or Shanghai?

"Tell you what, Admiral," I said, motioning for Sert to wait up for me. "I've spent way too much time running from one end of the galaxy to the other. Let's hold off making any more plans until I've had some time to visit the root world we just saved."

He grinned. "I can get behind that."

I left him standing there, overseeing his medics while they checked each and every corpse for signs of life.

Fera joined me and rested her head on my shoulder, not saying a word. We couldn't reach Sert before another person stood in our path.

Lieutenant Fel held out his hand. Fera and I both accepted it and shook in turn. Fel's eyes were hidden behind the helmet visor he always wore, and he made no attempt to take it off. I wondered about that; why did he keep his eyes hidden from everyone?

"We couldn't have done it without you," I said, feeling sober and solemn seeing him and his three surviving soldiers standing behind him.

"And we couldn't have done it unless you came back for us." Fel looked at his boots and then back up. "It'll make for one hell of a story to tell my ladies. And the boys."

"A story I'll never forget. Thank you."

He shrugged. "It's the job."

I pressed my other hand against his shoulder and gave it a squeeze.

One of the medics who had been shooting bio gel into the cracks of Benegal's armor came and pulled Fera aside. He whispered something to her. She nodded and the medic hurried off.

"Everything okay with Benegal?" I asked, fearing the report had been bad news.

"He'll be fine," she replied flippantly. "He's a Krayvox. They have the fastest healing rate of any species in the galaxy."

She put a hand on my warped chest plate. The woven cords that had once been enmeshed so tightly were now frayed, cut, and broken. "You, on the other hand, need to get looked at before you go running after Sert."

"Which I plan to do with the auto-med station as soon as we get back to the *Phaelon*. I don't want to stick around here any longer than I have to. I'm done with this fight. Done with this war."

My fiber-link popped with an incoming transmission. Quin's face appeared in my HUD, his eyes wide and his mouth hanging open in shock.

"Will Kaufman, you look like hell. Which, in your case, is an improvement."

"What can I say, Fera just doesn't go for the pretty boys like you, Quin." I cracked a cheap smile.

Quin sobered. "I've got the auto-med suite keyed up and waiting for you. We have a lot to talk about once you return, but I'll grant you the respect of getting patched up before we work out our next move."

Our next move. The words carried more weight than they

should have, and it cut me deep. It felt like a confirmation that we'd made the biggest mistake we could have made, and yet....

It was going to be a lot of work, but it was work that needed doing. Eddison's motivations for starting this war had to come to light. The galaxy—this supposed New Federation—needed to know what they were buying into and who was hiding the trump card up his sleeve.

Maybe Tror had been lying, spreading one last bit of chaos in the galaxy before killing himself. Denying all those who had suffered under his rule a chance to see him face justice directly.

But I didn't think so.

Eddison's mystery fleet was probably even now scouring the fringes of the galactic rim, seizing systems that had no capability to call for aid once they were attacked.

He wasn't liberating them. He was wiping the slate clean.

Purging the last remaining pieces of the old Imperium as he sought to raise a new one in its place. Only this time, he planned to disguise it under a different name.

"Lockett thinks we should take technology from this ship on the way out the door." He gestured up and around with his hands. "Bring to a Drayth lab. Reverse engineer, then sell. Rich overnight!"

Fera shook her head. "There are more moving pieces on the board now than there were before the war. Everyone's out for themselves, and if what Tror said is true, Eddison plans to exploit that for all it's worth."

Benegal limped his way over to us, his seething rage only tamped by the devastating injury. "The job is done. The Imperium is ended." He paused to glance at Admiral Tanoka. When he returned his slitted pupils over to me, his nostrils flared. "This iteration of it, anyway."

"Benegal, we can figure all that out when—"

"No," he said, standing tall. His shoulder rose with sharp inhale. "The moment has arrived where we must part ways, Will Kaufman."

I suspected this would happen, but hearing him say it stung. I hadn't been able to penetrate the walls he put up around himself, but the lizard man was a competent tactician and a vicious warfighter, and he had earned my respect. I knew ordering him to stick around wasn't going to do any good, but the thought of letting him loose on the galaxy without us to watch his movements felt... risky.

Fera, I knew, didn't like it either. After all, she had risked her life to bring Benegal to face the consequences for his actions the first time around. She didn't give voice to her concerns.

"Where will you go?" I asked.

Benegal considered the question for a few beats, tracing the sealed bio gel with a clawed finger. His typically calm demeanor seemed frayed, held together by something temporary, much like his damaged armor. "You ask me that for the sake of your new government. To keep an eye on a potential threat."

"I ask you that as a friend," I said. "In case I ever want to reminisce about old times."

Benegal stared at me for a long moment, then smiled, revealing his needle-sharp teeth. "The Krayvox were taken advantage of by the Imperium, and by the Galactic Federation before that. My Coalition, my Final Equinox, was the first opportunity for us to give voice to our plight for freedom. I do not speak for Atron, but I surmise that we will watch, and we will wait."

"You did more than give voice before," Fera said uneasily, verbally walking on eggshells. "Has *anything* changed for you in that regard?"

Benegal kept very still. He looked at Fera, then locked eyes with me.

"You are the change. I know the power of one. I was that power, long ago. I see the same fire in you, Will. If anyone can find a solution, it will be you. You will have my ear when you need it… until you are no longer worthy of such." He stood tall, wincing as his armor creaked. "Until then… we will watch, and we will wait."

Benegal walked past us and disappeared down the corridor.

Fera's eyes watched the criminal who had caused her so much trouble walk away freely. Every muscle in her body was tense.

"He's right, you know," she said.

"About what?" I asked.

"You've got a lot of people looking to you now, Will."

I let out a long sigh in answer. "Yeah. Guess Quin's right—we're going to have to figure out what our next move is, and we're going to need to do it quickly. The galaxy's in flux, and it could go one of a million different ways."

Fera smiled. "We'll figure it out together."

"One problem at a time, right?"

Her smile broadened. "Simple as."

The moving pieces locked into place in my head. I needed to find out the motives of Eddison and his private fleet. I needed to keep the peace between the United Council of Free Planets and the United Coalition.

Somehow, I needed to keep the crew together, too.

Benegal had always felt like something of an outsider. But to lose Sert and Lockett... I didn't want that. I wasn't going to stop them from taking some time off to sort out their personal lives, but I was convinced our team on the *Phaelon* would need to be at the tip of the spear to face whatever came next.

But, somehow, the specter of responsibility settled on my shoulders, bearing down on me like a sudden increase in gravity. My knees wanted to buckle under the weight. If I made the wrong decision... or if I couldn't get a diverse galaxy to find common ground with each other... the consequences would be disastrous.

There's so much that could go wrong....

But in all the dire uncertainty was also an opportunity to get things right.

I looked Fera in the eyes. "The war *is* over, isn't it?"

She looked back at me. "It's supposed to be."

"Yeah, I know... but, I want to hear it. The war is over, isn't it?"

"For now," she said, "the war is over."

EPILOGUE

In a dark sector of space nestled between the Perseus and Orion Arms of the galaxy, a lone star provided its last vestiges of dying light to the thirteen planets in its orbit. The system was known as Rubicon, and it served as the dividing line between one iteration of intelligent life and the next.

The historical context had long been mythologized, canonized, and elevated into legend among the citizens of the Imperium.

It started as an idea. The seed of an idea.

And that seed had germinated. Grown. Spread.

It evolved into an ideology, stretching its branches and bearing new fruit, complete with thistles and thorns to defend each new offshoot. Left unchecked for millennia, the maturation of the ideology became a part of the interstellar infrastructure.

Over time, stars were born. Given more time, stars died.

The cosmos continued to expand without ceasing.

Within that equilibrium of birth and destruction, the first breath of life came to the Imperium. Contingents did not form alliances; they took the Oath and were conscripted, one after the next. The snare of power trapped them all, and the Imperium reigned uncontested under the banner of the Umbraic Curtain.

The breakaway civilization became a self-sustaining entity. Then, it expanded beyond its borders. To the Sagittarius Arm, to the Scutum-Centaurus Arm, and to the many vestiges between.

It was not until the mighty Imperium of the Umbraic Banner entered the Orion Arm of the galaxy that their momentum stalled. This was no barren wasteland, no sector of farmers or simple gatherers of resources.

The Orion Arm was mired in war.

And from the day of emergence, so too was the Imperium.

As star maps were redrawn and territories contested endlessly, the seat of power in that famed birthplace of the greatest empire the galaxy had ever known did not move.

It was first established on Piradium, the sixth planet from the primary star, and it remained always in that place.

Prema-Generals issued dictates, orders, tactical direction, and ultimate control of the many expansionist arms of the Imperium from the Arrow Cathedra in the Grand Archaeum of the Senate.

It was here, in the oxygen-rich atmospheres of Piradium, that the Anunnaki who had taken up the appearance of a human disembarked his ship and set foot on his adopted root world. He was not alone, but he did not consider his entourage, nor did he consider for more than a passing moment the Navigator responsible for bringing him here. The older Anunnaki was his prized possession at the moment; he had once been a captain in the Imperium Fleet. An obsidian prosthetic boot machine-fitted to his right knee had replaced the damage done by a demented Vorvak and his clubgun.

The man put his Navigator out of his mind.

His thoughts were in the past, but also, in the future.

The present existed only as a bridge between the mistakes of the past and the promises of the future.

And of that bridge, he was the sole architect.

The galaxy did not know this. One day, they would be made to know.

The rough edges of slate rock pebbles crinkled under his boots. Black sand beaches stretched across the isthmus of earth and clay and volcanic rock that had formed this place long ago. The wan sunlight illuminated the monochromatic landscape of black sand and the white-capped tide, painting the Grand Archaeum with a high-contrast that drew the eye. The image, were it a painting, would have been declared a chiaroscuro in the language of Earth, the world he held in the palm of his hand.

It would be a small matter to formally conquer it.

One day, he would do that. A simple step among many yet to come.

Everything in order.

Strength in Unity, so saith the Imperium.

He was that strength.

As the cerulean seas broke against the black sand beach head, he spared one solitary moment to savor the scent. To watch as the hundred-meter flag of the Umbraic Curtain stretched and rolled in the whisper of wind that swept over the seas, carrying the preeminent mist of a coming storm.

The dark clouds had not yet reached the horizon, but they would.

The tiny crackles of mist floating in the wind made a promise that would be fulfilled before the last ray of daylight withdrew its touch from the Grand Archaeum.

A smile turned up the corners of his mouth.

Memories kindled under the surface of his mind, like embers wafting slowly away from a fire.

Marcus Eddison, they called him now. A new name, because of those who knew him before. Eddison did not come to this place bearing the shame of a man in hiding.

That man—the old man—had left in disgrace. The parting of an outcast.

Now, he returned as conqueror.

By and large, one and all, they would bend the knee.

If not out of reverence and respect, then out of fear.

Because he had achieved the impossible.

The destiny of the Imperium would soon be fulfilled, and that only because of what he had achieved. They had once declared him a detriment to the Umbraic Curtain. The day they cast him out, banished him, fated him to an obscure and lonely death.

They knew not what they did.

Despite everything, Eddison achieved what no Prema-General had been able to do.

Uniquely, he returned to stake claim on what was rightfully his.

The members of his entourage sauntered into place, the six large and imposing warriors that comprised his honor guard smelling the air, not out of curiosity but with suspicion. These were the galaxy's premier warriors; they could sniff out malicious intent at great distance. The ways of war guided them in all facets of their lives, and that made his deal with them a mutually beneficial one.

"Prepared for violence at your direction, Emp—"

Marcus silenced him with a raised hand. "Not yet, Gurk. They will bestow the title upon me. It shall not be spoken on this world until it falls from the lips of the Anunnaki Imperium. Have the remainder of the contingent ready at my command."

"As you say, sire."

Marcus gave the brute an approving nod.

He walked the beach head, every crunch of the slate rocks conjuring up a different memory of time spent here long ago. The battle plans, the counting of casualties after a campaign, the savoring of victory and the consternation of loss, the machinations of allies and enemies of the floor of the Grand Archaeum.

And the unquestioned authority of the Prema-General who held the Arrow Cathedra, only to stare down upon him with bitter contempt.

Eddison moved with his honor guard close beside him.

The grinding of rock under his boots became echoing claps of immaculate pale marble. The streets were a mosaic of black and white, an alternating pattern that formed the symbol of the Umbraic Curtain. The symbol of chaos and order, with a lone crimson dot in the center.

He crossed the red line of polished stone that encircled the Grand Archaeum and mounted the sleek black stairs.

Four Imperium soldiers garbed in their white armor, faces hidden behind helmets with thin black visors, adjusted their weapons from the ceremonial position of port arms and brought them to bear on him.

Eddison did not halt. Nor did he take offense at the aggression displayed by the guards. They did their duty, but they also stood in the way.

"Remove them," he said.

The six members of his honor guard drew their clubguns and fired.

A deafening roar sounded like lightning striking the ground.

Six blazing plumes of plasma energy punched holes of fire through the chests of the guards. In unison, they dropped to the grandiose marble promenade, smoke rising from the holes in their chests. They lay frozen with the stillness of sudden death.

The tranquility of the Grand Archaeum's natural ambiance resumed as if nothing had happened.

Eddison entered the open-air chamber of the Grand Archaeum.

Senate was in session.

The Prema-General stood in front of the Arrow Cathedra on the dais in the center of the room. He appeared tall and articulate in his flowing red robes. His poised expression soured as he made eye contact with Marcus Eddison, a man he once knew by another name entirely. His hands slowly lowered to his sides.

Suddenly, the Prema-General had lost the ability to speak.

One thousand Anunnaki seated in the stadium-style wrap-around shifted their attention from the Prema-General to Eddison. A dozen guards abandoned their posts to close in on him, weapons raised, fingers on triggers.

Eddison's confidence—not to mention his fierce honor guard—gave them pause.

Like the crash of the tide on the beach head outside, gasps

rolled through the crowd as they recognized the prodigal, returned with beasts led into the very heart of the Imperium.

Eddison allowed himself a small smile. The stage was set. Expectations had been subverted.

All that was left was the final flourish.

He strode past the guards, who stood slack and impotent, bringing his entourage with him. The Imperium soldiers lowered their weapons but kept their visors trained on his back.

The Prema-General worked saliva back into his mouth. He would speak now or never again.

"What is the meaning of this? Who is this rogue villain that dares enter the Grand Archaeum by means of violence, and with the lowest scum of the galaxy as your protectors? You disgrace the Imperium with your militant wiles!"

Eddison mounted the dais. "Do not be coy. You know me, man."

The Prema-General stiffened. "The Arrow Cathedra recognizes only the stain of disgrace upon you. Your endless campaigns were met with harrowing defeats that undermined all that we sought to build. Yours was a legacy of failure. Were it allowed to continue, the Umbraic Curtain would have surely fallen."

He raised a hand toward Eddison and turned to address the senate.

"Gaze upon the outcast this hallowed body exiled from our midst long ago to wander foreign stars in squalor and shame! Shall we suffer his pale attempt to seize power for himself at the expense of us all?"

No one moved. No one breathed.

Eddison cleared his throat.

"Your Prefect is dead. Tror was not the military mastermind you believed him to be." He made a sweeping gesture, drawing the eyes of the senators to himself. "All of your aspirations placed on the shoulders of a *Foris* whose ambition exceeded his capability. Tror—the name of a fool who was killed in shame and misery. But, for the Imperium, I have corrected his errors. Even now, much of the Coalition Arm of the galaxy is in smoldering ruins, conquered by an army of *my* devising! I alone saw the means of victory, and I alone bring you the opportunity to complete our conquest once and for all."

Eddison paused, letting his revelations marinate among the Senators.

"I was banished—not for the benefit of the Imperium, which I have fought only to strengthen even through the same of exile—but for the hubris of this man." He pointed at the Prema-General. "My securing of a Coalition and my conquest of all but a handful of worlds in that territory… is the only thing that prevented the outmatched and out-generaled Tror from stopping a campaign that would have struck in the very heart of the Imperium itself!"

Whispers rippled through the senators. Eddison sensed a subtle shift in the room, like a sudden spike in temperature, or a door slowly creaking open. He knew full well the Imperium considered Tror to be unstoppable. His military prowess was considered a divine gift, the concentrated favor of the Imperium's manifest destiny imbued into a single tactical mind.

And now, with this revelation, they knew they were wrong.

The Prema-General's lips curled in a sneer. "You were exiled. The law demands your removal… and execution."

Eddison raised his hand and slowly turned, surveying the Senate. "Am I to die? Then let me die! Let me die before an

Imperium beset by cowards such as this squanders all unto its final ruin!"

Boot stomps echoed from the open door. A rolling thunder cascaded along the vaulted ceiling of the Grand Archaeum as his praetorian guard—more warriors of the same race as the honor guard—marched into the senate chambers, clubguns held tight across their chests. The shell armor he'd manufactured for them—improving on their own native technology—was an obsidian black, machined to perfection.

A hundred and twenty Vorvak, marching under the banner of the Umbra Torch, formed a circle around the dais, their large orange eyes facing outward to the senators.

The senators stared in awe at the might and power of the praetorian guard.

The Prema-General's eyes grew wide. His face paled.

"See how I might take this world! See how I might flaunt the laws and defy my execution." Eddison pulled a dagger from his belt and tossed it at the feet of the Premera-General. He bore his breast. "But I will not. I serve the Imperium. Slay me and remain a slave to your own power. Or… shall we forge a new future and grasp all that our forefathers bent us toward. In Strength… Unity!"

A cry rose up from the Senate. A single voice. "Strength in unity!"

Another voice. "Strength in unity!"

A chorus, a raucous chant.

Then, the moment Eddison had been waiting for… it happened. The old leader of the Imperium called him by his true name, sealing the change in status from exile to conqueror with a simple phrase.

"Vincere, your strength will be our unity."

The Prema-General dropped to his knees. He reached under the sleeve of his robe, removed a ring from his index finger, and offered it with unblemished reverence.

Eddison—Vincere—the Anunnaki who had left in disgrace returned a conqueror.

He accepted the restoration of his name and slid the ring onto his own index finger. The black diamond was the size of a human eye and contained within it a fiber of hard light that vacillated between the extremes of the red spectrum.

A symbol of status that carried with it the limitless power of command.

Vincere had been his name once, and it was his name again.

The cheers began as a slow rumble from various pockets of the senate body. It built on itself as more voices joined in, increasing their reverence with each recitation. What began as an excited acknowledgement of ceremony escalated into a religious climax of deference.

"Vincere!" they chanted. "Vincere!"

The Vorvak guard slammed their feet in unison to the chants.

"Vin-cere! Vin-cere! Vin-cere!"

The fires of vengeance and power burned within Eddison. He looked regally upon the Senate, the well-practiced mannerisms of an unassuming tech mogul gone and replaced with high-born nobility.

The chanting chorus reached its crescendo, making the declaration permanent.

"Behold Vincere, Emperor Imperium, Lord of Stars!"

END BOOK THREE

Amazon won't always tell you about the next release. To stay updated on this series, be sure to sign up for our spam-free email list at jnchaney.com.

Will will return in Void Drifter 4, available on Amazon.

CONNECT WITH J.N. CHANEY

Don't miss out on these exclusive perks:

- Instant access to free short stories from series like *The Messenger*, *Starcaster*, and more.
- Receive email updates for new releases and other news.
- Get notified when we run special deals on books and audiobooks.

So, what are you waiting for? Enter your email address at the link below to stay in the loop.

https://www.jnchaney.com/void-drifter-subscribe

ABOUT THE AUTHORS

J. N. Chaney is a USA Today Bestselling author and has a Master's of Fine Arts in Creative Writing. He fancies himself quite the Super Mario Bros. fan. When he isn't writing or gaming, you can find him online at **jnchaney.com**.

He migrates often, but was last seen in Las Vegas, NV. Any sightings should be reported, as they are rare.

JASON ANSPACH (1979-) is the award-winning, Associated Press Best-selling author of Galaxy's Edge, Wayward Galaxy, and Forgotten Ruin. He is an American author raised in a military family (Go Army!) known for pulse-pounding military science fiction and adventurous space operas that deftly blend action, suspense, and comedy.

Together with his wife, their seven (not a typo) children, and a border collie named Charlotte, Jason resides in Puyallup, Washington. He remains undefeated at arm wrestling against his entire family.

Made in United States
Troutdale, OR
12/22/2024